JUNGEE

A warrior's journey

Priya Sharma Shaikh

Copyright © 2019 Priya Sharma Shaikh

All rights reserved

This book captures some interesting events / episodes that happened half a century ago and more. It is possible that not all the descriptions are exactly as they happened by chronological or descriptive sequence, some names may have been missed and others included in error - the book merely captures the essence and the spirit of a person's lifetime, and not necessarily the exact details. A lot is learnt from hearsay. Any such omissions or commissions are not deliberate and may kindly be read as such. The effort is not a 'breaking news' of a recent event but of things that happened over a time span of many decades. Kindly bear with the author. Read it as literary fiction if you may but note that the hero of this saga - Commodore (Retd.) Inderjit Sharma, AVSM, VrC, Indian Navy, is real and alive as on date.

No part of this book may be reproduced, or stored in a retrieval system, or transmitted in any form or by any means, electronic, mechanical, photocopying, recording, or otherwise, without express written permission of the publisher.

Cover designer: Manasi Gut Jain
Illustrator: Nicola Gut Jain
Editor: Raunaq Shaikh

This book is dedicated to

PAPA and MAMA,
who taught me the importance of presence and unconditional
love

AND

My ever so perfect English teacher, at Cathedral and John
Connon School,
FLORENCE HALLEGUA

CONTENTS

Title Page	1
Copyright	2
Dedication	3
Foreword	7
Prologue	9
BOOK 1: THE PEACOCK	15
Chapter 1: The Chill at Delhi Station	16
Chapter 2: Okara to Tandlianwala	24
Chapter 3: Does Bharat really win the bet?	59
Chapter 4: Hit and miss	92
Chapter 5: A home away from home	105
Chapter 6: Making a choice	151
Chapter 7: Head over heart	161
BOOK 2: THE LION	178
Chapter 8: North to south	179
Chapter 9: Touch down at training base	185
Chapter 10: A leap of faith	206
Chapter 11: A commitment for seven lifetimes	223
Chapter 12: Love blossoms in Bombay	251
Chapter 13: Taking command	301

Chapter 14: Unprecedented realisations and validations   351

Chapter 15: Gearing up in a new horizon   372

Chapter 16: To fight or not to fight, that is the question   409

BOOK 3: THE COW   468

Chapter 17: Radio City Hall, here we come!   469

Author's Note   483

FOREWORD

I am privileged and humbled to be writing a foreword to this classic on the life story of a brave man, even though our bond is really one of friendship.

IJ has been a giant of a human being, his cool, calm and unruffled ways notwithstanding. He has had the distinction of decimating the might and pride of the Pakistan Navy, a fitting reward for him, on the night of 4th December 1971, after having been mercilessly driven away from his home in Tandlianwala.

Though the Lion in him with its significant mane has roared loud and clear, IJ has displayed his softer side as well, regaling us with his romantic rendition of 'Chaudhvi Ka Chand' and several other hit songs of the 60s and 70s. Many times, we have stalked the Colaba Causeway in then, Bombay, searching for and ogling the dolled up 'Polar Bears'. We seemed to have been always in love!

Wanting to help me add a few inches to my sad height, he used to greet me with a 'long neck' – clasping my neck in the crook of his elbow and jerking upwards. I may not have added inches, but I sure learnt to stand tall.

To his credit, IJ, almost throughout his career at sea has always been specifically 'selected' for the next assignment and not just moved to a vacant slot. He has been time and again, 'wanted' by his selectors. Indeed, from very humble beginnings, IJ has stood taller and more prominent than the brightest of us in our batch.

Compassion and caring and single mindedness of purpose, one can learn only from him. To me personally, IJ is sheer warmth as a friend, a source of joy and inspiration and an example to emulate.

Having spent the best part of our lives in the Navy together, one has been aware of his impressive 'timeline', at least since 1959, but the saga has been put into such vivid perspective, which only an imaginative and involved writer can do. I cannot help but admire Inderjit's first born – Priya for the superb manner in which she has made the reader 'live' every bit of the captivating book from start to finish.

My congratulations to IJ, Rekha his 'Lioness' wife and of course to the author Priya.

Happy reading!

Davy Das
(Rear Admiral S. K. Das)

PROLOGUE

04 December 1971

The salty spray of the Arabian Sea's rough waters lashed the ship's port side, moistening the young sailor's face as he emerged from the hatch onto the deck. He had decided to take the Captain's advice and wear a pullover. The wind was chilly, and it blew against his face, making his short crop of hair stand straight. He hurried along the wet deck, wiping his face and body. His heart felt a rush of emotions.

He and the boys had done the preparatory work on the four missiles. It had been a consuming process, but he was sure the checks were thorough. They were ready to follow the orders for action.

He was a handsome young man hailing from North India, having started his career with humble beginnings. He had left his home and family swearing to serve his country and joined the Navy as a sailor at 17. Fear was not in his nature, and neither was pride.

It was the final countdown to action. This was the moment that he and the rest of the ship's company had waited for. The Captain was right about them being the best men and that they would prove their mettle in this moment of trial.

He looked fondly at the pullover that was knitted by his new bride. He had called her from the sailor's mess before setting sail from Bombay a few days ago. She had sounded as excited as ever to hear his voice, while he had tried to control his tone and reactions, conscious of his men around him at the reception desk of the mess.

He had flirted with her playfully in a monosyllabic code that sounded like gibberish to the clerk on duty. And then he had unabashedly blown her soft kisses on the phone. Tickled by his embarrassed romantic overtures, she had laughed at the other end of the connection. He adored her unbridled laughter and would do anything to hear it again. He missed her, he had said. And she had instantly responded calling him a liar, saying that if he did miss her, he wouldn't have left her behind. Gibberish had ensued again. He had closed his eyes and reminded her of their last union together. The visions had flashed in front of his eyes, and his cheeks had blushed with embarrassment. And then he had become silent. Following his cue, so had she, both of them breathing together in a cadence that they were so familiar with, soaking in the beauty of their love for each other.

He had opened his eyes to find the clerk glaring at him. His expression pointedly said he had to stop talking. The sailor had straightened up and turned away from the desk, pulling the wire to a maximum stretch. Knowing that he had to hang up, he had said in a steady tone that he would be back by her side soon. She had protested and he had said he loved her and then he had hung up. He didn't know that she had sat there holding onto the black receiver, with an amused smile as a tear escaped her eye to make a blot on her turquoise dupatta.

He headed to the storm corridor, manoeuvring his way past the crew members. They were all moving to their action stations. His team was in position next to their respective missile hangar doors, awaiting his orders to commence the missile's final preparation.

...

Inside the bridge, the burly ExO shifted around the chart desk. He watched the target's position on the scanner like a hawk and reviewed his plotted position on the chart. He padded across to poke his head into the radar room, giving the operator a thumbs up.

He returned to his charts and looked at the figure of his Captain. Over the past two years, he had grown to like and admire him so much. His square frame was sitting up straight as he stared ahead into the night. It wasn't easy being in his chair. He had the weight of the mission at hand on his shoulders, which could pivot the course of history. His decisions would impact the ship, her men, their families, the Navy, and India.

INS Nirghat was about 70 miles off the coast of Karachi, in the Arabian Sea. The ship had sighted a target. And the Captain had given the order to radio ahead a few minutes ago, for permission from K-25 to engage it. The ExO wondered when they would get a response. His headset beeped, and he instinctively put his hands on his muffs to listen.

It was a message from K-25 - Engage target on your port bow.

"Sir, we have permission to engage the target," blurted the ExO to the Captain, holding his breath.

The Captain nodded, "Noted. Complete the final checks on the missiles and get ready for launch."

"Aye Sir," said the ExO and called out the necessary orders to the ship's company.

The crew sprang into action, slamming doors and hatches. The range of the target was now at 18 nautical miles.

The Captain turned to the petty-officer. "Alter the ship's heading towards the battle course."

Within a few minutes, the ship shut down all her air passages and the operation room got shrouded into darkness. A lone red light gave the room the surreal effect of a disco. The Captain and his crew were ready for their dance with destiny.

The range of the target was down to 16 miles. The Captain altered to a parallel course to allow for the completion of pre-launch checks. The green signal came in from all the teams, one by one. And the Captain once again got Nirghat to approach the battle course.

"Standby number 1," stated the Captain in a steady tone.

"Number 1 standby," reported the Gunnery Officer.

"Launch number 1," ordered the Captain, and pressed the green button to launch the missile.

The red lamp blinked, indicating readiness in all respect.

The next few moments were the most uneasy ones in their lives. They held their breaths waiting for the missile to launch.

Nothing happened.

The ship continued to slice through the dark ocean towards her target. The Captain knew that the missile had to launch now, or it would be too late. In the red gloom of the operations room, cold sweat beaded the foreheads of all the men.

Everything depended on the missile taking off now, for all the 30 men that had made the vessel their second home.

Another few pensive moments passed. The men in the operations room looked at each other and then at the Captain. His look was of wonder - what had gone wrong? With every passing moment, the furrows on his forehead deepened. The nervous energy on board peaked as grown men fidgeted, bit their nails, and blinked their worry-filled eyes.

Still, nothing happened.

The ship was already on the auto steer and was closing rapidly on her target. The Captain clenched his fists, scanning all the indicators, assessing their readings. He mumbled to himself, "Something is wrong. She seems unsteady," and then in a blink; he shouted out, "Check the radar room."

The ExO darted with unusual speed and stuck his head in the radar room. His mouth fell open in shock.

– – –

PRIYA SHARMA SHAIKH

BOOK 1: THE PEACOCK

His was a world of fantasy. He lived in the dreamland where Kartikeya, the supreme Commander-in-chief, sat astride him. The jewel tones of blue, lime green, and earthy brown coloured patterns, on his fanned-out train of feathers shimmered in the bright sunlight as he danced with aplomb in the wild.

He sat on tree trunks. He pranced in the grass, stepped over dancing streams of water, and flew above the roofs of hamlets. He watched the children play, and the colourful kites fly high in the clear blue sky.

He was fearless, for he had with him the son of Lord Shiva.

CHAPTER 1: THE CHILL AT DELHI STATION

January 1954: A hurdle before the journey commences

It was a misty winter night in Delhi. The PA system on the railway station crackled to a start. "Your attention please, ladies and gentlemen! The Madras Express, scheduled to leave at 10 pm this evening, is facing technical problems. The train will leave at 6 am."

The platform broke into a collective sigh of despair. The travellers that had expected to board the train grumbled. The grumble rose to louder chattering and arguments. People shared similar incidents that they had found themselves in with much anguish. Situations they had been in that they could not do much about. The noise soon dropped back to a resigned grumble. Most people who had lined up their baggage and themselves along the platform's length started to rustle around in varied measures. They gathered their belongings, regrouped, and finally left the station to find a warmer place to retire from the cold night.

A few men lingered on, murmuring and jibing about this and that, and moved with their bags to the only open eatery on the station. It was a battered hole-in-the-wall tuck shop, situated near the main entrance. It had a crooked and worn out black signboard atop it, that read - *Banna Tea Stol*. A single zero watt bulb hung from a loose wire on its back wall, and a lantern hooked onto a nail on its front gave it a dim look. A string of dead marigolds were hung across the faded red and white hand-painted lettering. Remnants of a few burnt-out incense sticks poked out of the frame of the board. A small black leather-covered Murphy transistor sat holding place-of-pride, on a lopsided pink and cyan crocheted napkin, atop a small shelf at the back wall. It was playing the news in Hindi.

The brewing tea's aroma had worked like a charm to attract the men to the stall. They covered up in their jackets and shawls, with arms crossed in a self-hug. Their palms stuck deep into their armpits or pockets. The night chill bit into their bones. They edged closer to each other to warm themselves around the dancing yellow flame of the small stove in the stall.

A short middle-aged man named Banna, with a distinctive toothy grin and animated eyes, stood behind the counter. The look on his face was in variance to the tired and grim faces that stood around his shop. He wore a multi-coloured sweater that covered his protruding belly. His small, round ruddy face peeked out of the folds of the maroon muffler wrapped around his head and neck. The news was wrapping up, as Banna pressed a few ginger pieces with the side of his knife and added them to his cauldron, with a clump of mint and a dash of black pepper.

He stirred his formulation with a flourish, in quick concentric circles, and poured a few piping hot drops onto the thick of his palm to taste, and clicked his tongue to his palette a couple of times. Seeing him look pleased, his guests licked their dried lips and urged him to be quick.

"Oye Chotu, take out ten *kulhars*," said Banna and then turned to his eager customers, "And gentlemen, my fresh ginger tea will give warmth to your hands and soul, in a minute."

Chotu, a boy not more than eight, was sitting in a squat on the floor while his head bobbed in sleep. On hearing his name, he jolted awake. He mechanically reached out to the cane basket, from which he produced ten clay cups, to serve the brew.

"Two cups of tea bhaisaab," said a muffled voice from behind a brown hand-knit monkey cap, while handing ten paise to Banna. The opening of the cap revealed bleary tired eyes.

"Stranded in the cold, huh?" said Banna.

"It's only a few hours," shrugged the monkey-cap lad, glancing at the slouched Chotu.

"I like your positive attitude. One has to play the cards that life throws at you. Here is your tea to keep you warm," smiled Banna placing two *kulhars* on the counter.

"Play, we must, because there is no other way," said the muffled voice.

"Now that is intelligence! Did you hear that Chotu?" said Banna nudging the sleepy boy, who opened his eyes, "My son!"

The monkey-capped lad acknowledged Banna by nodding and blinked at Chotu. He pulled out of the motley crowd and walked away—the warmth of the kulhars on his cold palms felt good.

Childhood. What great joy it holds, he thought. But it has its challenges too. And some children have it tougher. Starting life in a daze. Unsure and drifting like dried leaves in the strong winds of time. Not knowing where their destiny could take them. Hurtling down paths, as people stepped on them, crushing their voices and their very being. Is their suffering fair? Who was to blame? Where is the justice? So many questions. So few answers. A deep sigh made him exhale a bigger cloud of white, which merged into the mist that enveloped the platform as he kept walking.

. . .

"Namaste Daroga Saheb, the train is late again!" called out Banna to the burly policeman sauntering along the platform, "Please come and have tea at our *stol Darogaji*."

The policeman's 'good name' was Inspector Parminder Singh. People called him Darogaji. He was a man an average person would call huge. And huge he was, in every sense of the word - tall and broad-chested, with a well-twirled heavy moustache and a thick beard. His turban and uniform were stiff with starch. And the overcoat thrown over his shoulders framed his body like a dramatic cloak. When he walked, the iron in the soles of his shoes made an authoritative sound.

He held a long silver coloured torch in his left hand and a thick wooden baton in his right. He strode, not unlike a lord. He'd tap his baton on hard surfaces of the platform, now and then. He believed it warned onlookers that he would use it if the need arose. He revelled in the respect he got from the common people. In comparison to his imposing persona, his face was jovial. And he had laugh lines and dimples that shone despite his facial hair.

"Ahem! No thank you," he said, moving his baton to the crooning of the foot-tapping song playing on the transistor *'Ajab Teri Duniya Ho Mere Rama'* by Mohd. Rafi from the film *Do Bigha Zameen.*

"Such a cold night sahib. A hot cup of tea will help cut it."

Parminder waved his hand at the tea seller and made a funny face at Chotu, making the boy laugh. He hummed the song and swung his baton like a music conductor as he walked away. The satire in the lyrics questioned *Rama*, the incarnation of *Lord Vishnu*, the Hindu deity of creation, about his world's anomalies.

*'O Rama, your world is strange, religion is sold and traded by
your people.
Troubled are those with empty pockets, having to sell their souls.
It will indeed be your world only when we can all win,
Without having to sell our souls to earn our bread...'*

Parminder had walked some distance from the stall. Mid-
strut, his torchlight stopped on a figure stretched across one of
the benches. A dark green and black checked woollen *shawl*,
fraying at its ends, was draped over it. A battered tin trunk
stood alongside the bench. A limp hand was around its handle.
Parminder poked the figure with his baton. It moved with a
start. A bleary-eyed head appeared from one end of the shawl.
It was the monkey-capped boy from the tea stall. Parminder's
eyes widened as a Sikh boy's head appeared at the other end of
the shawl. The boys jumped up to their feet. Their warm cover
slipped, to reveal their slim frames. Their hands instinctively
embraced their chests to ward off the beast-like chill. They
had a puzzled expression, and they blinked their eyes and
looked around, trying to get their bearings as they sized the
imposing figure in front of them. Parminder held up his torch
to get a better look at their faces. The boys folded their hands
in apology. Shivering like culprits, they waited to hear their
verdict.

The Sikh boy whispered to his friend, "Are we in trouble?"

"I don't know," whispered back the monkey-capped boy.

Parminder looked at the monkey-capped boy's clothing.
He wore a crumpled pair of white cotton pyjamas and a white
shirt. His feet had worn out brown canvas shoes. A maroon
coloured, full-sleeved, v-neck hand-knit sweater made him
look heavier than he was.

"Take off your cap," barked Parminder.

The boy pulled off the cap as instructed, to reveal a handsome wheat complexioned face. His bushy eyebrows met above his straight chiselled nose, shadowing his deep black, almond-shaped eyes. His cheeks stretched from his small but well-formed lips up to his high cheekbones. His wide eyes and natural well-formed pout gave him the endearing innocence of a teenager. Yet, his stubble, tousled thick black hair, and crumpled clothing made him look unkempt and questionable. His Sikh companion, who was of similar age, was humbly clothed too. He looked as much in a mess. The little facial hair and his plait lying over his narrow shoulders gave him the appearance of a young woman.

"Namaste Darogaji. Is there something wrong? Please forgive us. We are new to Delhi," stammered the monkey-capped boy quivering with cold. "It is freezing, and we have a train early tomorrow morning, so we thought it best to sleep here for the night."

Parminder looked at them turn by turn, narrowing his eyes and lips to slits, trying to weigh what they were sputtering. He threw his hands in the air and sat on the bench and threw back his head and laughed aloud. The boys shifted in their places and smiled unsurely. Parminder caught his breath and poked the monkey-capped boy in the stomach with his baton and then touched his face.

"Well! Look who it is. A film hero! Your face does look good, and the acting is good too. So, you are going to join the films, in Bombay, huh?" His expression was comical. He imitated Dev Anand's stereotypical loose-limbed gesture with his hands, and giggled again. Realising that his audience was not amused, he cleared his throat. "Harrumph!"

The money-capped boy looked embarrassed. "You are right and wrong, Darogaji. I indeed want to go to Bombay, but you are wrong about me wanting to be an actor. I'm going to be the hero of my own life."

"You are naughty and a liar, too. So, before you become a big star, it gives me great pleasure to receive your contribution to the government."

"What do you mean, Darogaji?" stammered the Sikh boy, moving closer to Parminder.

"I'm giving a ticket for the Hero and you!" he chuckled.

"Film ticket?" said the money-capped boy with a puzzled expression, "But I ... we don't want to see a film, Darogaji."

"It's not a film ticket, you twit. It is a fine you have to pay for assuming government property as your personal space. This bench is for sitting. Not sleeping."

"Sorry, Darogaji, we will leave. Please don't fine us as we don't have any money to spare," pleaded the money-capped boy.

"You are a big man, Sir, and we are like your children. Please forgive us if we have wronged," said the Sikh boy, joining the pleading.

Parminder's amused expression turned to rage, "Silence! Do you take me for a fool? You two have been up to mischief. And now you are hiding here on the station, thinking that nobody will catch you. And you have the gall to lie to Inspector Parminder. But you are not going to escape my clutches! If you don't have the money, you will come to the police station with me."

The boys shivered, desperately trying to find words that failed to reach their lips.

"You have run away from home to become heroes in Bombay. Rascals!"

"No, Darogaji. We have not run away. You have misunderstood..." said the money-capped boy.

"Didn't I say silence?" interrupted Parminder, striking his baton with a loud twang on the bench, making them jump with fright. They swallowed hard and nodded dolefully, as Parminder brandished his baton in the air, threatening to strike him. Tears pricked his eyes, and he blinked hard to fight them back. He stepped back and sat down on his haunches, biting his upper lip in exasperation.

I will not cry. Why is it that when I have taken the courage to take control of my life, destiny flips me on my head and jeers at me? I promised I will make something of my life. And I will. I will overcome every obstacle. I am a fighter, a winner, and I will thrive and not let anyone crush me. Not anymore! I jeer right back at you, destiny. You can't scare me anymore.

He put his arm around his trembling friend and looked up at Parminder, who had put down his baton, and flipped open his receipt book. The inspector paused his pen and looked at the monkey-capped boy.

"What is your name?" said Parminder, as the whistle of an approaching train rang in the background.

– – –

CHAPTER 2: OKARA TO TANDLIANWALA

1912 – 1946: Going back to the roots

A few decades before, in 1912, Jaikishen Das Sharma awoke in a cold sweat in a small dark room. He was six. His small hands reached out to make sure his older sister Draupadi was beside him. Her warm body and deep breathing reassured him.

He let out a long, stifled sigh. It had been the same nightmare again. He had expected it, as it came every night and frightened him each time. It had started after that fatal night. Their parents had met with an accident, and they had become orphans overnight. He looked up at the starry night, wondering which of the stars was his mother and father. A small sniffle escaped him. His sister turned in her sleep and draped her arm over him. Jaikishen's eyes fluttered, grew heavy, and finally closed.

Their *Chacha,* Melaram, and *Chachi,* Ratandeyi, had arrived to perform the last rites and took the grieving orphans to live with them, in their ancestral home in Okara, Lyallpur, situated in northwest India. They cared for them as they did for their daughters, Vidya and Kunti.

Melaram was a tall man with fair skin, a thick, well-groomed moustache. He had the demeanour of a lion that ruled his brood with pride. He was big-hearted and never hesitated to display his affection to the people he loved.

Ratandeyi was a beauty, but she was tough as nails. She kept a strict cleanliness regime in her home. And she never let anyone or anything get out of line. Their home was large, and so it was easy to accommodate the new arrivals. Jaikishen and his sister were happy to have a roof over their heads. Most of all, they revelled in the adulation they received from their cousins. Jaikishen grew to love and respect Melaram and trusted him completely for all decisions. For example, Jaikishen was a good student, but his education came to a grinding halt after moving to Okara. He missed studying. But he never said a word of complaint. Instead, he taught himself from borrowed textbooks. As time passed, he did become adept in Mathematics and Urdu.

Melaram supplemented his ancestral farmland income by working with the Indian Railways. He worked in the goods office, as a night guard for the godowns. When Jaikishen was old enough, he too joined Melaram to work there. He was glad to assist him on the inward and outward flow of goods between the Railways and traders. He felt pleased that he could be of service to his beloved uncle. People thought of Jaikishen as responsible, honest, and pleasant natured. He was a valuable asset to the goods office. Jaikishen was happy to be his uncle's pride.

At 18, Jaikishen's fair skin, light eyes, and tough physique drew the attention of many a visitor to their home. Melaram was aware of his nephew's eligibility. One morning, as soon as Jaikishen returned from milking the cows, he asked him to get dressed and took him to Pandit Daulat Ram Mishra's home.

"He is a very wealthy man, son. A shrewd freedom fighter too. He has unchallenged clout in the neighbourhood. He has taken to violence on several occasions. People speculate things about him in hushed tones. They say he had killed and buried two of his detractors in his backyard."

Jaikishen listened and turned to look at the imposing man

in question. He wore elaborate clothing. He had rugged features and a well-curled moustache that sat with pride on his stiff upper lip. His steely eyes could never fail to intimidate a stranger.

That morning they were here to see his daughter, Geeta, for marriage. It was a mini *swayamvar*, of sorts. Like Jaikishen, other suitors waited for the proceedings to begin. Jaikishen saw Geeta from the corner of his eye. She sat on a low stool at the end of the courtyard. She was petite, with wheatish skin and a thick black plait that snaked over her shoulder and ended in her lap. She kept her head bowed, staring into her lap, twiddling with the red ribbon at the end of her plait. Her bent head obstructed the view of her face. Jaikishen was left with only his imagination to rely on what the bride looked like. She wore a turquoise blue *salwar kameez* and a pink *Phulkari dupatta*. Devoid of any jewellery or props, Geeta was the picture of simplicity and modesty, in Jaikishen's eyes.

Daulat Ram surveyed the suitors with his steel eyes as they ate the served breakfast. He had done his homework and had already made his decision.

"My daughter Geeta is illiterate, but she reads the text in the scriptures. She is a devout believer of Lord Krishna. She spends hours singing songs in praise of the lord," said Daulat Ram with pride. "I am happy to choose Jaikishen Das Sharma as the husband of my daughter. She will be a good wife to you, son," he said in a steady assertive tone.

The other suitors rose and made an abrupt exit. Daulat Ram proceeded to place a one rupee coin as *shagun* in Jaikishen's palm. The coin shimmered in the morning light, and young Jaikishen looked towards his uncle for guidance. Melaram's nodding head was a signal of his validation.

"Congratulations on your engagement, son."

Jaikishen got up and touched Daulat Ram's feet. The steel eyes showed a flicker of emotion as he picked up his prospective son-in-law and hugged him. The family gathering broke into joyful exclamations. Jaikishen looked towards Geeta, who, by now had, buried her face even deeper into her dupatta.

Daulat Ram organised a simple wedding ceremony. Jaikishen and Geeta got married according to Hindu rites, with immediate family members in attendance.

. . .

Geeta came from a wealthy home, but she tried her best to settle into the humble abode.

She was obedient and respectful and veiled herself from Melaram and all other men. Housework was new to her. She was slow, and the work was a lot, but she put in her best under Ratandeyi's strict supervision.

"Move your hands faster, girl. You still have to cook. Lunch is within an hour," snapped Ratandeyi, shaking her head in frustration.

"Last few clothes left, Chachiji. I will get done in a few minutes," said Geeta in a meek voice. She beat the *thappi* as hard as she could on the pile of clothes, wincing each time the impact hurt her blistered hands.

"And for God's sake, please don't burn the *rotis*," scowled Ratandeyi, fanning herself.

"Why do you have to be so nasty? She is young and not used to housework," protested Melaram on his way out for work.

"What do you mean nasty? What do you expect? Her father has pampered her. And I am to deal with her idiocy and train her with patience, huh?" she fumed at her husband. "And on top of that, you have the gall to tell me how to manage my home! Do I interfere in your work matters? No, I don't. That is because I know it is not my business to do so. Running this house is my business, and I will run it my way," she snapped. Melaram stepped out into the street without another word.

Geeta teared up, knowing that nobody could save her from her mother-in-law's tyranny. She feared the task of making rotis the most. They never turned out to be round, and they always got burnt or she burned herself. Despite all the taunts and the body aches induced by the rigid regimen, Geeta didn't say a word to Jaikishen.

One morning, Jaikishen saw Geeta sniffling into her dupatta in the shadows of their room.

"What happened?"

"Nothing."

"Then, why are you crying?"

"My eye is hurting."

"Wash it with water, and it should get better."

"Washing won't help. It has broken," she stammered.

"What do you mean it has broken?"

She wept even more bitter tears.
"Show me your eye."

"No"

"Why not? I'm your husband, Geeta."

"I know. But there's something you don't know."

"And what could that be?"

"I injured my eye as a child, and the doctor had replaced it with a glass eye," she blurted out. "It has broken today," she wept.

"Oh, my God! Now I know why you never looked up at any of us. You have been worrying we will find out about your glass eye. You are my wife, Geeta. I cannot have you suffer a damaged eye. Let's go to the hospital right away."

The Doctor declared that nothing could salvage the damage. Geeta feared the family would condemn her for her blind eye.

"Listen to this update about your beloved daughter-in-law. She is a *kaani*," jibed Ratandeyi at her husband when he got home that evening.

Melaram fumed. Daulat Ram had made a fool of him and his family by hiding Geeta's defect from them.

"I will teach him a lesson," shouted Melaram. "Come on, son; we're going to his house right away."

For the first time, Jaikishen stood still; his head bowed low.

"Chachaji, I ... Chachaji, it was an accident many years ago. It could well have happened to Geeta even after our marriage," his voice trembled.

"Are you a dimwit or a saint? Can't you see he has cheated you?"

"Chachaji, what would I have done if I were in her father's place? This question has come to my mind, again and again, since morning. As a father, he thought for the good of his daughter. He has all the money in the world. And yet he had no option but to marry his daughter to a man with no education and the personal status of his servants." Jaikishen put his palms together and looked at his uncle with tears in his eyes. "Geeta has already been through enough. I don't have a problem with her eye being blind, Chachaji. Please forgive me. I request that we put this matter to rest without ruffling any feathers."

"But ...," started Melaram and stopped, as Jaikishen had already turned away and walked into his room.

"Will you still defend her?" hissed Ratandeyi at Melaram, who left in a huff.

Geeta overheard the exchange of words. Her heart was full of emotion when Jaikishen entered their room. He hung up his shawl and jacket on the peg as usual and turned to look at his wife's sobbing figure in the dim light of the lantern. He walked up to her and placed something on her lap. It was a pair of dark glasses. She looked down at them and then up at him.

"This is for you to wear so that you don't have to feel conscious of your eye ever again."

She continued to cry, looking at the object in her hand.

He sat next to her on their bed and lifted her veil to reveal her tear-stained face and wiped her cheeks dry. "You will make things worse if you cry so much. Let us put this behind us, Geeta."

Geeta stopped crying, feeling shy at her husband's proximity. "How can I wear this," she protested. "People will make fun of me."

"I don't believe these goggles are funny, so why would they make fun of you? Besides, what others think of you, is that your problem or theirs?" asked Jaikishen smiling at her.

"Theirs," said Geeta and fiddled with the glasses in her hands.

"Correct answer. So wear the glasses without being conscious. And don't worry about Chachiji's words. She has had her circumstances, and that is why she is the way she is. You do your duties with love because you are your best when you are loving, is that possible?"

"But ... I am not used to so much housework. My hands are peeling and burning, and my body aches all the time," she sniffed.

"You're a homemaker now, Geeta. There is no escaping the work and responsibility that comes with that title. And your husband is an illiterate man struggling to make a living." He took a deep breath and looked away. "Geeta, ever since I was a little boy, this is the only family I've had. And today, for the first time, I spoke up to them. I did so because I felt responsible for you as my wife. I did not want to blow this out of proportion. See, my hands are still trembling. But I had to do it for you. I want you to know that I do not have a problem with you having a blind eye." Geeta looked at him in disbelief.

"Our bodies are nothing but dust, and we will be back to dust again someday. So why have pride in how we look. I am not perfect either, but my family has loved and looked after me since I was a little boy."

"But they didn't even put you through school. What good is such an upbringing?"

"They gave us shelter and food and a family that I could love," said Jaikishen.

"In the beginning, I did pine for school, but then I learnt to value what I had instead. And I studied by myself. But what is the point in looking at the past, Geeta? I'd rather live in the present and cherish all the riches I have – parents, sisters, a wife, a home that I can call my own, and a decent meal at the end of the day. I could not ask for more."

"This is not your home. This small room is all you have."

"My sister and I would have been living on the streets, Geeta, if they hadn't taken us in. We had nowhere to go when our parents died. We are indebted to them."

"I understand now. What about the fact that I have to slog all day without a moment's rest. Won't you ever say something to Chachiji?"

"Geeta, I can't do that, and I won't in the future either. I will not disrespect her. All I can say is, embrace the tasks as yours to keep for life. It is a privilege to be of service to others. Your Krishna says that, doesn't he? Do your karma with joy, as that is the only thing you can do. You will soon get used to it, and you can always depend on me for help. On that happy note, let's call it a night. Get your rest. It has been a long day," Jaikishen yawned. He stretched out on the bed and closed his eyes. Within seconds he was fast asleep.

Geeta looked at the sleeping figure of her husband in the flickering light. She felt a surge of mixed feelings. Disturbed, that he was content to live in the shadow of his uncle and aunt. Sad about his acknowledgment of his social status and that she didn't know how to help him improve his status or make him feel better about himself. And immense love, knowing now what it took for him to defend her. He'd dared to speak up for her when she needed it most. *He's right. I will have to be stronger and embrace my life as my very own with love. Pitaji chose well for me.* She turned off the lantern to plunge the room into darkness and lay beside her husband.

The next morning, after her bath, she fiddled with her new goggles for a while, and then put them on. She stared at herself in the small mirror for a while and decided she liked them. To her amusement, she saw Ratandeyi's mouth fall open, looking at her walk past the courtyard, with her goggled head held high.

Jaikishen's prediction had been right. Geeta did adapt to the workload and her shaded view of the world. She felt relieved that she had nothing to hide anymore. Time strengthened her bond with Jaikishen, and soon they got blessed with a son named Brijmohan, who they nicknamed Brij. The Melarams had their first son too, who they named Sansarchand. Two years after their firstborn, Jaikishen and Geeta had a daughter, named Soma. The Melarams also had another son, Dwarkanath. Two years after that, the Melarams had one more daughter, called Santosh. With the headcount increasing by the year, Geeta's responsibilities increased. More mouths to feed, beds to make, and clothes to wash. Her chores were endless, making her days go by in a tizzy. Something began to change in Geeta steadily. Her time with Krishna came down to the quick lighting of a *diya* and a murmured prayer at dawn and dusk. Snapping became second nature to her, children being her easiest targets. Jaikishen got the brunt of her whip-like tongue too.

She damned him for putting her through the gruelling life she led. She hissed in loud enough undertones that he wasn't man enough to move into a separate home. "A slave and a child-producing machine! That is what you have got home under the pretext of marriage," she bickered.

Jaikishen said nothing and did nothing to assuage her. He noticed she had less and less time for herself. The dreamy, meek girl had metamorphosed into a negative perturbed woman. Every evening, he returned to an irritable atmosphere, in which Geeta never failed to vent about her day's angst. And he listened without comment or any commiseration. His silence drove Geeta more bitter towards him with each day. He turned his attention to Brij and Soma, ensuring that they joined school and studied well. Their already strained relationship got struck with tragedy. Within two years, they had two more sons, who died in strangely similar accidents - They fell to their death, from the same window. Why? Because Geeta was too busy to watch over them.

Geeta felt weighed down by grief, guilt, and anger and Jaikishen stood by her, strong and comforting. The tragedy also drew the couple together. Geeta conceived her fifth child. This time she decided to make some changes so they would never have to face such darkness again. She took obsessive care of her health and made a conscious effort to make time for Krishna.

. . .

It was a hot and clammy morning on 06 August 1936, when Geeta went into labour. As she struggled with her pains, sweating and groaning, the skies darkened. Lightning flashed across the sky. Thunder rumbled the skies as they opened to a heavy downpour cleansing the courtyard and everything beyond. An hour into the storm, the *Dai Ma* helped Geeta give birth.

"It is a boy," she announced, placing the swaddled baby in Jaikishen's arms.

"We will name him Gopal Das," said Jaikishen, giving the baby a tight squeeze.

Brij and Soma had strict instructions to look after Gopal, and Geeta watched over him like a hawk, never letting him out of her sight. A few weeks later, Ratandeyi also gave birth to a son - Tirlokinath, who was younger but by relationship, he was Gopal's uncle!

. . .

The kohl smudged at the corners of Gopal's closed eyes was the only blemish on his otherwise clear face and a *kala teeka*. His plump cheeks had a natural blush, as he slept in the warmth of his father's arms. It was the 41st day after Gopal's birth, and following tradition, Jaikishen and Geeta took him to the temple.

They offered prayers to Lord Krishna and went to meet the

head priest Pandit Sukhdev.

Sukhdev was an elderly *Brahmin* and a *brahmachari.* He had earned undisputed respect over the two decades he had spent in the village of Okara. People in the village addressed him as *Panditji.* They went to him for advice on all their matters of worry, joy, beginnings, and ends. Panditji was sitting under a huge banyan tree, surrounded by a few locals. They were in the midst of an animated discussion about the costumes for the upcoming *rasleela.* When the villagers left, Jaikishen rose and put Gopal into the holy man's lap.

"Namaste Panditji. As you are aware, we lost our last two children. We seek your blessings for our son's long life."

Gopal, by now awake, blinked and gurgled and waved his hands and legs. Panditji held him and placed his hand on the little head.

"Such a beautiful child you are, little one! My blessings that you live long, healthy, and happy."

"He is the blessing of Krishanji to us, Panditji."

"Indeed, he is a blessing. What have you named him?"

"Gopal."

"Ah! The very name of Lord Krishna himself. Your son is going to have a very adventurous life."

Jaikishen and Geeta were paranoid after the recent loss of their two children. They exchanged worried glances.

"What do you mean, Panditji? What kind of adventure?" asked Geeta.

"Don't worry so much – life itself is an adventure, and your son will be the perfect exemplar of it. *Jai Shri Krishna.*"

. . .

Gopal's nickname was *Koogh*. His mischievous ways soon made him the centre of everyone's attention at home and in the *mohalla*. One day, two-year-old Koogh walked alongside Jaikishen, who was carrying two bags full of groceries. Koogh pointed to the sky and started groaning and tugging at his father's kurta. He then tried to climb his legs. He wanted to sit on his father's shoulders and wave at people as they passed by.

"Pitaji lap! The sun is shining owww... my feet are burning Pitaji, please."

Jaikishen looked down at his son, amused. "Kooghey, you *badmaash*! The people in the mohalla are right when they say that you are a naughty boy."

Seeing Koogh scowl, Jaikishen added, "That is not the sun; it is the moon. There is no sun at night! And I can't carry you as my hands have bags. My aunt is coming from Mathura to see you tomorrow. You must be nice and touch her feet. Now walk alongside me quietly. Your mother says I spoil you by carrying you all the time. So, no more lap for you. You have to learn to carry your weight and look at the world from your height."

. . .

Many seasons passed, and one afternoon, when Koogh was four, he sneaked out of the house while Geeta was busy. There was a massive open drain behind Melaram's house. All the children were instructed not to go close to it. Not too far away was a banyan tree with wooden planks strung up as swings. Koogh's curiosity got the better of him, and he ventured close to the drain. Mucky water flowed through it. Girls from the mohalla chattered at the swings while a group of boys on the other side of the gutter flew kites.

Koogh stood at the edge of the drain, not paying heed to his grandfather's warning. He called out to the boys, wanting to cross the drain, but they ignored his frantic calls. So, he backed up a bit and ran at full speed towards the drain, taking a flying leap off the edge. But his tiny body wasn't able to jump far enough, and he flailed in mid-air, missing the other side by a few inches. He fell straight into the gushing water. He flapped his limbs desperately. He managed to get his head above water for a few seconds and sank again. He struggled and choked against the force of the water, trying to move to the edge.

Luckily for Koogh, Pinky, a teenaged girl from the neighbourhood saw his unsuccessful jump. She screamed when she realised what had happened. She ran along the drain to get ahead of him, jumped in, grabbed him by his shirt, and pulled hard towards the edge. She hauled his small but heavy body with all her strength and rolled him to safety. Koogh lay lifeless on the ground, soaked to the bone.

"Oh my God, Is he dead?" Pinky saw his heaving chest and realised he was unconscious and not dead. She turned him over again and pumped his stomach. A little water came out, but Koogh remained unresponsive. Panicking, she slapped him several times.

"Koogh, Koogh, Koogh! You, silly fool, look at what you have done. Open your eyes. Wake up, please. Please don't die, Koogh," she cried, shaking him, feeling helpless, but Koogh's body lay lifeless in her arms. "Bauji! Kamla! Somebody help me!" she shouted.

Nobody heard her cries. She turned him on his side, and it was then that his thin chest heaved and jerked him into consciousness. He spluttered out more of the greyish black water and began to cry, clinging on to Pinky. He looked like a dirty little rat. Pinky felt relief, picked him up, ran to the local hand-pump around the corner, and put him under it

She pumped hard till all the muck that had got stuck to him

got washed away. She then carried him to the nearby clinic where Dr. Sunder stared at the unlikely duo.

"Koogh, Pinky, what happened to both of you?"

"This silly fool jumped into the gutter, Doctor uncle. He would have died if I wasn't there to save him. I am to go to a wedding and look at how my clothes have got ruined. I'm going to get a hiding from my mother thanks to this fool."

"So, you have been out creating trouble again, huh, Koogh? Your *Babaji* is going to be very angry!" he said, shaking his index finger down at him.

Koogh looked dismayed at the thought of getting a scolding for what he had done. He looked up at Pinky and then at Dr. Sunder and started bawling.

"Now what happened, Koogh?"

"I have already almost died, and now I'm going to get a scolding from Babaji, too," he squeaked.

"You are such a baby, and still, you are so naughty. Why did you jump into the gutter?" Pinky's relief was turning to anger now.

"I wanted to fly a kite like the boys."

"Look at your size, and you want to fly a kite! Do you know you could have died?"

"I know. I won't do it again. Please don't tell Babaji."

The Doctor watched this exchange with a smile. "Do you promise not to get into trouble again?"

Koogh nodded with a contrite expression on his impish face. He made haste to add with folded hands, "But please don't tell Babaji." Dr. Sunder and Pinky laughed aloud. Nobody could resist the little prankster, and so his secret was kept, and

Koogh too never again dared to jump the drain.

. . .

A few months later, Melaram decided to move the whole family to Tandlianwala, a town built by the British in Punjab's north-western region. It was a haven due to its modern layout, good infrastructure, and large natural spaces around the residential dwellings for children to play in. Its biggest draw was the huge grain market, which presented a better opportunity for Jaikishen and his skills. Melaram rented a house in Lakkad Mandi. Geeta and Jaikishen gave birth to one more daughter. They named her Tripta and nicknamed her Bhollo.

"Son, it is time that you have a home of your own. I will help you settle to start with."

Jaikishen felt dismayed. "Chachaji, I want to be close to you to be able to look after you in your old age. Besides, how will I manage? I have never done it before."

Melaram smiled. "It is time for you to learn to manage your own family and home. And don't worry, we will get you a home close by, so you can come and see us when you wish."

It was Ratandeyi's turn to feel dismayed. This change meant that the housework would become her responsibility once again. That was not acceptable to her after so many years of having it easy. She argued with her husband, but to no avail. Melaram stuck to his plan. Jaikishen and Geeta settled on renting a shared space, in a neighbouring mohalla - Ward No.6, which was a little over a furlong away from Melaram's home.

. . .

Koogh felt excited to move to a new home and went with Jaikishen and Brij to do a recce of the mohalla. Like the rest of the roads in Tandlianwala, the Ward 6 lane was wide and at a perfect right angle to the main road. It was a gated community with 20 two-storeyed homes. In its vicinity was a set of temples, a gurudwara, and a masjid. There were separate schools for boys, girls, and toddlers, a hospital, a police station, and a telephone exchange. Adjoining the lane was the formidable grain and wood markets. Not too far off was the railway station.

Their new home was a two-story structure. The owner was a steel trader called Chothuram. The main door of the house opened into the *deodi*. To the immediate left was a hand pump for people to freshen up. And to the right was the *baithak* for guests. At the deep centre of the deodi was a door that opened into the lane behind them. Due to a lack of natural light from the two windows overlooking the lane, the room was generally dull.

Beyond the hand pump was a steep staircase that had foot-high stone steps. The steps led up to a large landing. Here Chothuram had stored his excess wares, which were steel rods and plates piled up to the roof. A narrow pathway along Chothuram's laid out wares led to a stairway, which led to the next level.

This level had all the living spaces. Chothuram's son, Santram, lived on this level's immediate right with his wife Kanta, and their sons - Kulbhushan, Subhash, and Kailash. Above their space was a terrace, overlooking the central lane of the ward. Access to the terrace was by a narrow stairway at the immediate right of the landing. On the terrace was a set of charpoys and clotheslines. The far-left and immediate left corners of the landing had a room each. These rooms measured 50 square feet. Outside, each room was a small open kitchen.

At the immediate left of the landing was a staircase led to an open landing, on which were the toilets. These were for use by the women and children of the house. The toilet consisted of two cemented blocks about one foot in height. These were set one foot apart from each other. Users would sit on their haunches with one leg on each block and relieve themselves in the centre. It was necessary to carry a small mug of water along to clean up after the job. Liquid refuse drained into the narrow open gutter lining the boundary of the ward. The next user was subject to the discomfort of using the same space, adding to the pile of excreta and stench.

The refuse that remained got scooped by the local sweeper woman into a basket, which got finally dumped into a common pit. The men never relieved themselves inside the house. They went out into the fields surrounding the area.

Jaikishen and Geeta occupied the room on the immediate left of the landing. Geeta got about setting up her little house with zeal using help from Jaikishen, Brij, and Soma. Koogh helped too, but only after he'd had his fill of poking around the new neighbourhood.

. . .

One day, Koogh helped Jaikishen bring home a bag of vegetables and handed them over to Geeta. He peeped out of the only window at the back of their room and waved to the milkman below.

"Kooghey," smiled Jaikishen. "Do you like your new house?"

"Yes. It is small. And it is big. I like the terrace most. And I've found loads of hiding places in the ward. I like the canal too. Bhushan says that children swim there in the summers. And there is the banyan tree in the wood market. I am going to climb it soon."

"I'm glad you like it. And how do you like the school and teachers?"

"School is okay. One teacher likes me. But my classmates

PRIYA SHARMA SHAIKH

make fun of him."

Jaikishen frowned. "And do you join in with them?"

"Sometimes." Koogh shrugged, looking out of the window. "Because I don't want to feel left out, Pitaji."

"Is that how you want to make friends - following a crowd that is being mean to someone?" Koogh turned around to look at his father, puzzled. "Kooghey, it is wise to step out of friend circles that make you choose the wrong path, even if it means that you are to stand alone. So how do you think you'd rather make friends in school?"

"There are a few boys that I want to befriend, but none of them talks to me, Pitaji. Every day I eat my tiffin alone."

Jaikishen reached out to tousle his son's head. "Respect and love take time to build, son. Have patience. Do your work well and give them time to get to know you. And when it happens, they will love you."

"Oh yes!" said Koogh with a cheeky smile.

. . .

Every evening after dinner, Jaikishen visited Melaram's home, a 7-minute walk.

He would discuss the day's events and massage his uncle's legs and feet. Koogh would tag along. He listened with a keen interest in their discussions on work, politics, society, and the world. He found their discussions fascinating.

"Pitaji, I like how you press *Babaji's* legs every day," said Koogh, one evening on their way back home.

"It is because I love and respect him and your *Dadima* with all my heart. They are my parents, son. And whatever I am is because of them. They are my foundation. When you become a big man, Kooghey, you too should stay connected with your roots. Your humility and care for your roots will take you far."

"I know why," said Koogh dancing on the road in front of his father. "Because strong roots make the tree stronger," said Koogh jumping up and down ahead of his father.

"That's right. Your village and your family are your roots. They teach you your values that make you grow stronger and higher."

"I like Babaji. Even I press his feet sometimes."

"Yes, I see that. It is good to care for others, son."

"But I like Toshi Bua the most. She always gives me treats and plays with me."

"Yes, Santosh is good. I'm glad you collect so much love and affection."

Koogh was silent for a while. Then he asked, in a lower voice, "Pitaji, am I a slave, of the *angrez*?"

"You've been listening to our conversations this evening. The angrez have ruled us Hindustanis for more than 200 years, son, and their word is final on most things. But we are not slaves anymore, and yet we are not free," sighed Jaikishen. "They do rule our country. They did some good things, but they did a lot of bad things too, that have left several scars."

"But this is our country Pitaji. Why did we allow them to stay and do things here? I don't think Pabbi would like it if Santram Tauji told her how to run our house?"

"Good point. But, if Santram Tauji knows something better than your Pabbi, then she would be wise to listen and learn from him. Don't you think?" he said. "I believe there is no harm in learning from others. That is how progress happens. And that is what we did with the angrez too. We tried to learn as they taught us their ways."

"But did we ask for their help?"

"Maybe or not."

As an afterthought, he added, "But, we made the mistake of indulging them with our trust, hospitality, and large-heartedness. In the process, we became sitting ducks for them. And before we realised it, it was too late. It is too complex for a child like you to understand," said Jaikishen, his voice trailing off.

"But Babaji said it is never too late and that it is always the right time to start anew."

"Yes, that is true."

"Pitaji, what was he saying about the independence struggle?"

"You're asking questions beyond your age, Kooghey. Let's focus on you being a child for now. Come on; I will race you to the house."

With a deep sigh, Jaikishen watched his son charge ahead of him, and as he ran behind him, letting him win, his thoughts ran too. *There will never be an independent India. Being a slave to a regime is what I, too, have always hated. Thus, I did not want to marry and have children that would become the British workforce. But I didn't dare to speak up to Chachaji then, and marriage to Geeta became my destiny.*

. . .

Jaikishen got a job at the railway station. He earned small commissions from the traders he serviced. The money was enough to afford the family's expenses. They couldn't afford the luxury, but he felt wholly empowered for the first time in his life. Geeta was happy too. She had more control over her life, and she was able to pray to her Krishna again. The new home saw their seventh child's birth, a son named Charanjit, and nicknamed Ghonni. Happiness abounded Jaikishen's family.

Koogh got busy too. His days were packed with school and playing with his three new friends. The first was his landlord's son Bhushan, who was a brilliant student. Then there was Bhollu, the naughty plump Sikh who loved food. The last one was Vaid, who was older and a member of the Rashtriya Swayamsevak Sangh. He attended their physical drills and occasionally dragged the rest of them too.

The four of them played rowdy contests with marbles before and after school and soon became known as the neighbourhood's pranksters. Koogh got into trouble every other day, facing the fury of other despairing mothers. But neither the house rules nor the yelling and punishment made him mend his ways. The foursome planned new pranks, played for hours, swam in the canal, and flew kites in the fields. When Koogh was with his friends, time as if flew – He decided that he loved Tandlianwala.

The older boys in the neighbourhood had regular kite-flying contests. Koogh and his gang always managed to position themselves around them. They would gape in awe, cheering at their tricks and technique. "Flying kites is an art. The string is dipped in glue and then brushed with powdered glass. So this is not a toy. It's like a weapon," said Bunty.

Bunty was a tall handsome well-built teenage boy, who was quite the favourite of the mohalla. He had a fondness for Koogh and his friends and often taught them tricks of flying.

"Flying kites is all very well, but if you can cut the string of someone else's kite, then you are a real winner," said Bunty.

Koogh keenly listened as Bunty gloated. He'd do errands for him, in the hope of getting lessons on kite flying. Each time a kite started its fall to the ground, Koogh and his gang raced each other in the tall fields of wheat and corn to retrieve it. They helped repair the kite and waited until one of the bhaiyas taught them how to string and give the kite flight. He got sores on his little hands with the severe rolling and tugging of the glass tempered strings. But he didn't mind one bit as it was the best time of his day.

"Oye, Koogh! Why haven't you gone home the whole day?" said Gumma, an older boy from Ward 6.

"Can't you see I'm flying kites?"

"You're not flying a kite," he laughed, "You're holding one, you fool!"

"Don't be jealous - Bunty *paaji* is going to teach me," he said, dancing on his toes.

"Ha-ha,... you wish!" he jeered. "Your mother asked me to tell you that she has made *halva* for you. And hey, why would I be jealous – and that too, of you? You silly baby," he said, lifting his hand to whack him.

Koogh dodged and stuck his tongue at him. Then, he thought again. If there was anything that he loved more than kite flying, it was sweets. He huddled his friends and tempted them to join him for the treat.

"Let's go," said Bhollu, licking his lips.

They headed towards Koogh's house. Their mended colourful kites flailed in the wind behind them, past the fields, the railway station, the community well, the Lakkad Mandi, and finally down the Ward 6 pathway.

Koogh's house was a good 10-minute run from the fields. They were breathless when they reached. However, his friends made an abrupt halt, yelped, and turned to make a reverse sprint. Outside Koogh's home stood Geeta with a *thappi* in her hand. She shouted out at them as they scooted. Koogh turned to make a run for it too, but Geeta was quick. She chased after him and grabbed him by the collar, picking him up around his waist. He shrieked and yelled, but she kept walking.

"You rascal - you're going to get the spanking of your life for going missing yet again. You think I have nothing else to do but wait on your lordship. My foot!"

"Pabbi, I'm sorry, please let me go." He looked around for support, looking with a piteous expression at everyone. "Bhaisaab, Soma Bhenji! Help me," he wailed, as Geeta rushed past them into the deodi with Koogh dangling against her waist.

"Pabbi, please let him go," pleaded Soma.

Brij looked on, amused at the commotion caused by his little brother.

"Paaji, Paaji," screamed little Bhollo, running after her mother.

Geeta ignored all the protests and carried Koogh up the stairs to the first landing. And then she turned on them. "Shut up all you scoundrels! Unless you all also want a spanking!"

Geeta took him to the attic between the two stairways and put him down. She slapped him on his cheek and twisted his ear hard until he shrieked and pulled away. She then caught hold of him again and pushed him inside the attic and bolted the door shut.

"Pabbi, please forgive me. I am hungry and thirsty," wailed Koogh banging on the door.

"You can stay hungry in there until the evening. And don't you bang on the door anymore unless you want one more slap." She turned to look at the rest of her children. "And none of you dare open the door or talk to him," she spat.

PRIYA SHARMA SHAIKH

Koogh called out to his mother several times and offered profuse apologies, but he got no response. He rubbed his smarting ear and kicked a few pieces of the furniture in the attic in frustration. He finally resigned to his punishment and sat down in the hot and musty room. Sweat trickled down his face and body, making him very uncomfortable. He felt hungry too. He felt sorry for himself, and tears slipped out of his eyes onto his cheeks. *Why is Pabbi so mean to me? All I was doing was having some fun with my friends. She has broken my kite too. I hate it when she does things like that.* He wiped his face on his sleeve. Then, he noticed a small window in the corner of the room behind the furniture. He scrambled towards it and pushed the window open, peering outside. The landing was 12 feet below. It was desolate.

"There is no way I am going to spend the afternoon locked up here," he said with a grin and hauled himself onto the window's sill to let himself hang out and make a deft landing. He looked around cautiously and then slunk out of the house.

An hour later, after spending a restless afternoon, Geeta began to wonder about the silence from the attic. She went to let him out and was in shock to find that the room was in a state of disarray, and there was no sign of Koogh. She shouted out for him and looked under all the stuff lying in the attic. He was missing without a trace. She suspected the other children had let him out and called out to them. None of them would dare to defy her strict order, she knew. They shook their mute heads, looking at each other, wondering who would have had the courage to let Koogh out.

"Was it you, Soma?" Geeta's eyes bore into each child.

"No, Pabbi. I swear I didn't."

"Then, where is he? Brij?"

"How would I know, Pabbi? I have been studying next to

JUNGEE

you all afternoon. Are you sure you locked the door?" he giggled.

"Wipe that giggle off your face right now and find him."

"Koogh?" said Soma running down to the deodi while Brij searched the terrace.

"Paaji?" called out little Bhollo, waddling around the landing, calling out to him in the attic.

Geeta, too went downstairs to look for him. Just then, the front door opened, and Jaikishen walked in. Koogh was hanging onto his back, with a defiant expression on his face. Geeta put her hand to her mouth in shock. On seeing Geeta's glare, Koogh hid his face behind his father's head.

After slinking out of the house, he had waited at the gate for Jaikishen's return. As soon as he saw him approach their lane, he had run up to him and narrated the whole day's events. Jaikishen had laughed and carried him piggyback the rest of the way home.

"Oh, Krishna!" Geeta shouted. "What sort of a boy is he turning out to be? I tell you he will be the end of me! How did you get out of the attic, you rogue? I am tired of his antics." She tried to reach for his ear again, but he dodged her, so instead, she slapped his buttocks.

"That's enough! Don't raise your hand at him. How could you lock him up for so long? He is a mere child. Children play and be naughty. Playing doesn't warrant a punishment," he said and proceeded to freshen up at the hand pump.

"But he ..."

"I've said my piece, and let's close the subject. Now can I have something to eat please? I'm famished," said Jaikishen, climbing the stairs to go up to their landing.

Koogh stayed close to his father during dinner and there-after accompanied him to Melaram's home. He went straight to look for his favourite Toshi Bua. When reprimanded by Geeta, he would complain to her, looking for her generous sympathy. She always had time for Koogh - listened to his tales, taught him, cracked jokes with him, laughed at his mimicry, and shared secret treats with him too. But, she too was not spared when it came to his pranks. He had once run after her with an angry hen in his hands. They had brought the whole house down with her screaming and his cackling laughter. She was the best in his eyes, and for her too, he could do no wrong.

Like always, that evening, he talked to her about what happened. She listened and then told him a story, weaving into it the reason for his mother's anger. "She only wants the best for you, Kooghey. She loves you and worries about your safety and health. Will you say sorry to her?"

"I'll do it tomorrow."

Koogh slept on the terrace with Jaikishen that night. As they lay on the charpoy together, he looked up at the twinkling stars in the sky. Jaikishen told him a story of adventure and travel, where animals talked like people. Koogh listened to his father's deep voice, snuggled close into his warmth. He visualised the characters as the story unfolded and smiled in wonder, saying 'then' each time Jaikishen paused until the story was complete.

"Pitaji, you are the best," he mumbled finally and slipped into his dreamland. Jaikishen lay there, listening to Koogh's gentle breathing. Geeta and her temper came to his mind. *How time has changed the frail and quiet girl, I married.*

. . .

Koogh didn't like to pray at the family shrine like the others in the family. He did love accompanying Geeta when she visited the temple. He would sit cross-legged by her side and imitate her chanting, much to her annoyance. He also enjoyed her stories about Krishna. His pranks with the *gawalas* and *gopikas* of Gokul and the grand battle of the Mahabharata. One afternoon after lunch, Geeta herded her young ones for a nap, while Brij and Soma studied.

"But Pabbi, I don't want to sleep in the afternoon. Can I please go kite flying with my friends instead?"

"No! Off to sleep. Look how Ghonni and Bhollo are sleeping."

"But they are babies."

"And are you a big man? Shut your eyes!"

"Okay, tell me the story of Krishna's birth," shrugged Koogh, lying down next to her.

"But I told you that story two days ago," she said, pulling a sheet over herself and him.

"Please, once more, or I'll not sleep," said Koogh with a pout.

Geeta rolled her eyes and then smiled at her son's dramatic expression. She put her hand on his head to push his hair back and wiped the sweat from his brow and lips with her sari and smiled. She breathed deeply thinking of the joy of being his mother, and hugged him tightly. He snuggled with her and looked up at her patiently waiting for her to star.

"Once upon a time, the land of Mathura had a wicked King called Kamsa. People in his kingdom feared him. He had a sister called Devaki, who he loved dearly. He got her married to his dear friend Vasudeva. An ascetic prophesied that their

PRIYA SHARMA SHAIKH

child would be the cause of his death. Kamsa was furious. He locked up his sister and her husband in his dungeons. And just to be precautious, one after the other, he killed seven of their children. When their eighth child was to be born, he tightened the security and waited for its birth.

Koogh held his breath, waiting for the part he knew so well.

"It was a dark and stormy night. The sky thundered with dark clouds. Rain poured from the skies like never before. And Devaki gave birth to a boy, who was none other than the avatar of Lord Vishnu himself. Vasudev and Devaki hugged their son weeping bitter tears. They worried that the gates would soon open, and Kamsa would walk in and kill him too. But then, miracles started happening. Their chains and the gates of the dungeon fell open, and the security guards plunged into a deep slumber. Devaki urged Vasudeva to seize the opportunity and escape with their son. She swaddled her child in a soft sari and bid him a tearful goodbye."

Koogh sat up and listened with excitement in his eyes.

"The anxious Vasudev stepped into the pouring rain with his baby in his arms. He protected him as much as he could from the howling winds and the downpour. He knew that if he had to escape from Mathura, he would have to cross the raging waters of the Yamuna River. He placed the baby in a wicker basket and made a canopy of leaves over him. He then stepped into the Yamuna. She rose higher. Vasudeva lifted the basket above his head to save his child from the water's fury, but the Yamuna rose all the more."

"The river wished to touch the feet of the baby, because he was God," blurted Koogh.

"Yes, that is right. Then another miracle happened," said Geeta, with a smile.

"I know. The baby put his leg out from the basket," said

Koogh waving his right leg.

"Yes," laughed Geeta while Brij and Soma exchanged looks of amusement.

"This is the best part," said Koogh, rolling onto his stomach and cupping his chin.

"And the moment the river touched his feet, she ebbed. And then, magically, she parted, allowing the surprised Vasudev to walk through, to the banks of Gokul. *Om Naarayanaaya Vidmahe Vasudevaaya Dheemahi Thanno Viṣhṇu Prachodayath.* Vasudev took his son to the home of Nanda and left his baby by the side of his sleeping wife, Yashoda. The next morning, when Yashoda awoke, she was beside herself with joy as she set eyes on the gurgling baby next to her. She loved him instantly and named him ..." All the children shouted out, "Krishna!"

"Yes. Krishna grew up in Gokul as her son, along with, Balarama and Subhadra."
"As a young boy, he was a *gowala* who played the flute. Cows followed him wherever he went. And of course, he was very naughty."

"Like me."

"Like you, indeed. Krishna would climb up to *matkas* hanging from the kitchen ceiling to steal fresh butter. He played pranks all day on the govalas and gopikas. They all complained to Yashoda, and she scolded and punished him. But her heart would melt when Krishna looked at her with his twinkling eyes and adorable smile."

"Krishna is like me, Pabbi," announced Koogh, grinning to himself and sitting up.

"And how is that?" asked Geeta, trying to pull him down and cover him, patting him to sleep.

"Because I too was born on a rainy night, and I have an older brother and sister, and I am naughty like him. I am Krishna. Krishna is me," said Koogh.

"Yes, Krishna resides in us! You are my Gopala, and that is why I had named you Gopal. But if you truly are Krishna, you must be strong and brave, and protect the Dharma and the weak that seek your protection like him. But for now, shut your eyes. Let's get some sleep," she said, turning over. As soon as she shut her eyes, Koogh jumped up and dashed out to the door.

"Koogh! You rogue! Come back right now!" screamed Geeta, sitting up.

"I'm Krishna, and I am naughty, and I'm going to fly kites. You can punish me later," he said, doing a jig at the doorway before running off, as Brij and Soma rolled with laughter.

Geeta's threatening calls to him were a waste as Koogh was on his way, running to the fields. He felt great to imagine himself as Krishna. After flying kites to his heart's content, he sat by the brook. He knew Geeta would be angry if he tarried any longer.

But then I will give her a sweet smile like Krishna, and she will forgive me. He deliberated and rolled in the sun. He snuck his foot into the water like Krishna did in the Yamuna and looked to see if the water did any tricks. The brook hurtled down its path, singing its song and dancing on to its destination.

Why wasn't there any reaction like in the story of Krishna? Pabbi said that Krishna is in us. If he is, then the water must react to my foot too. He dipped his foot in again and again. Nothing extraordinary happened. *Well, I bet Krishna can't fly kites as well as me. And at least he got punished by his mother for all his pranks. Like I will get punished.* He smirked to himself and ambled his way back home.

. . .

Time passed. Koogh's friendship with his gang grew stronger, and their mischief even more daring. They often competed in games of imagined gallantry. One such contest was the test of who had the toughest knee. The test result was to measure how many times and how hard they could bang their knees against the solid metal of the hand pump. Each of them hit the pump with their knee turn by turn, as hard as they could. When Koogh's turn came, he hit his knee so hard that he fell back, screaming, with excruciating pain. The Doctor announced that the damage was permanent - Koogh would limp all his life.

"What have you done, Koogh?" wept Geeta holding her worry strewn forehead.

"We were having a bravery competition, Pabbi," said Koogh looking doleful. His tears had left dried streams on his cheeks.

"Putting yourself in danger without thinking through the consequences is not bravery. It is foolishness, Kooghey," said Jaikishen.

"But Krishna fought so many battles and dangerous ogres. Mine was only a knee hitting competition, Pitaji."

"Krishna is God. His battles were always to preserve *Dharma*. He was an intelligent warrior Kooghey, while you are a mere boy. He grieves and celebrates with us. He rewards us when we do the right thing and punishes us when we do wrong. What you have done is not valiant by any standards, son. It is stupid and wrong. And for that, we are all getting punished."

Koogh looked dismal. "Pitaji, won't Krishna make my knee okay?"

"You can be sure of that, son," said Jaikishen with a smile.

But in his heart, he was worried. The treatment provided by the hospital had shown no results. Jaikishen took Koogh to a variety of local healers too. But all attempts of healing remained fruitless.

...

One winter morning, Jaikishen was basking in the autumn sun at their doorstep. He poured over the Urdu daily *Milaap,* while Koogh sat next to him, chewing on a peeled turnip.

Their neighbour, called Bharat Sharma, stopped by. He was a well-read man and well placed at the Imperial Bank. He had a fondness for Jaikishen and his family. He sat next to Koogh and looked down at him through his dark-rimmed spectacles.

"Turnip has Vitamin C. It is very good for your health, Koogh."

"Namaste, Tauji," said Koogh looking at the half-eaten turnip with new eyes.

"Namaste, puttar. Jaikishen, what do you think of the uprising?"

"The newspaper says it's growing, Paaji."

"Yes. And the skeletons are finally coming out of the closet —thousands of Indian soldiers that went for the Second World War, young recruits that never returned home. The Raj is upset with all the noise Bose has created with the Indian National Army. So many of his soldiers have been arrested and tried for following his fascist ideology."

"So many ideologies! It's a joke, I tell you. Gandhiji is leading the non-violence dialogue, Bose is riding his horses to fight, and Jinnah talks of a separate state for Muslims. We are cooking a big *khichdi* and that too, with a variety of cooks. Mark my words, the British are not going to leave India. They benefit from our divided views."

"I bet 10 Rupees that we will have our independence within a few years."

"And I bet that we won't," said Jaikishen emphatically.

"What do you think, Tauji, will the British leave India?" asked Koogh, joining the conversation.

"Yes, they will, my son, and very soon," said Bharat.

"No such thing, Kooghey," said Jaikishen. "The Raj will remain, and I'm going to win this bet. They benefit so much from being here. Cheap fabric, grain, and most of all, cheap workforce, to build their infrastructure and fight their wars all over the world."

"No, brother. The heat is on in political circles. Freedom fighters have gained traction, and the Queen hears their voices in London. The British will soon have no option but to leave."

"Bah to all these attempts!"

"There is no point in arguing, my dear friend. Only time will tell us what will happen.

And the bet stands. How is your leg now, son?"

"It is the same, Tauji."

Jaikishen's face fell. "God is trying our strength, Paaji. We have lost hope."

"Never lose hope, because hope will keep you alive!"

"What good is hope, Paaji? Just believing in it is not enough."

"Of course, hope needs mindful action to support it." Bharat got up and prepared to leave. "This may sound odd, but I have heard of a *mazhabi Sikh* that lives a few streets away behind Lakkad Mandi. He is a cobbler by profession, but they say that he also practices alternate medicine. Take Koogh there - maybe a miracle is waiting to happen."

. . .

Jaikishen decided to consult the Sikh and arrived with the wiry 8-year-old Koogh at his shop. The brawny, deeply tanned, salt and pepper haired Bishan Singh dressed in a *lungi* and kurta gave them a pleasant greeting. A shawl strewn across his broad shoulders made him look overbearing to little Koogh. He listened to Jaikishen and held Koogh's injured leg in his huge but gentle hands. He applied heated mustard oil to it and then held it above a mild fire massaging it in slow and firm circles.

"What do you think, Singh sahib?" asked Jaikishen.

"All will be well when the time is right. Bring him back to me for the next ten days."

And lo and behold, at the end of the 10-day consultation, Koogh's leg felt better. And within a month, he could run around as before.

— — —

CHAPTER 3: DOES BHARAT REALLY WIN THE BET?

15 August 1947: The harsh reality of divide and rule

News about the country's independence from the British Raj had been gaining strength. Each day India woke up to a clearer vision of an independent nation. The topic was the centre of heated debate in all sections of society. Koogh overheard a lot more conversations about Bapu, Bose, ahimsa, satyagraha, swaraj from elders. And he heard of a vociferous apprehension about the future of the nation. It was imminent by now that the British would leave India's reins in the hands of her very own leaders. How will the leaders of India manage the vast subcontinent that is an epitome of plurality?

Amid this unique political backdrop, Jaikishen's family experienced change too. The handsome looking and by now well-built Brij got a job at the Imperial Bank of India, which took him to Lahore.

"It is time you get him married," said Ratandeyi. "My brother's daughter, Sharda, will make the perfect bride for him."

"Brij is lucky, Chachiji. She is a lovely girl, indeed. She has all the right values, and she is sure to blend in well with our family," said Geeta. She exchanged a happy, hopeful glance with her husband.

"I will go and meet Sharda's parents tomorrow itself to finalise plans for the wedding," said Jaikishen.

"But what if bhaisaab doesn't want to get married now?" asked Koogh looking anxious.

"It's none of his business to decide who and when he marries. We know what is best for him. And you stop eavesdropping on adult conversations," said Geeta.

In early 1947, Brij married Sharda. At the end of the wedding ceremonies, Koogh watched his brother and new *bhabi* from a distance.

Sharda wept relentless tears at the *Bidaai.* Koogh tried to console her, but she would not stop crying. He couldn't believe that she was going to come home with them forever.

"Why are you crying? Please don't cry, Bhabi. I will look after her for you," said Koogh with tears in his eyes, reassuring Sharda's father.

He sat next to Sharda on the train and peered into her veil.

"Why are you still crying, Bhabi? Has someone troubled you? Tell me, and I will put them in their place," he whispered.

Sharda looked down at his innocent face and smiled through her tears. The very next day, her brother arrived at their doorstep to take her back home for the customary *Gauna.*

"*Tauji*, I have reached here with great difficulty. Our train was stopped for several hours by revolutionary miscreants."

"Oh God! We should avoid Sharda's Gauna ceremony under the circumstances," said Jaikishen looking worried.

"Yes, please don't take her away. She just got here," protested Koogh.

"Beta, I am taking her for one day, and I will bring her back tomorrow. But you are right, Tauji; if you feel that she should stay back, I don't have a problem at all. I have met my sister, and I can go back and share your rightful concern. I'm sure my parents will understand."

"What nonsense! Governments will come and go. We can't break tradition because of this political tomfoolery. It's a matter of a day's separation. She can be back tomorrow. Stop overreacting, as always," said Geeta, standing her ground.

"Geeta, you are obstinate. The whole country is rioting. The talk in the town is that things will worsen, so why jeopardise her safety. And why separate the newly-weds?" said Jaikishen in a terse tone.

"I don't care about what you think or what you have heard. People talk nonsense, and you are the first to fall prey to loose talk. You have no business involving yourself in matters related to the home. Your turf is outside these four walls. Do not interfere with my decisions," interrupted Geeta with aggression.

Jaikishen threw up his hands, feeling infuriated, and said, "Well, that's that then." He turned to Sharda's brother. "Please take care of her. She is our daughter now and very dear to my son and us," said Jaikishen with a heavy heart and folded hands.

Much to Koogh and everyone else's disappointment, Sharda returned to Ludhiana with her brother. The unrest grew. As expected, Jaikishen received a telegram from Sharda's father - She will remain in Ludhiana until things settle, it said. The excitement of the wedding came to a hard stop, and the forlorn Brij left behind a tearful Koogh and the rest of his family and resumed work in Lahore.

...

"Kooghey, wake up son, it is time for school, come on and have your bath," coaxed Geeta. She moved her palm over her son's sleeping face. She pushed the thick clump of hair off his forehead and looked at him fondly. *How beautiful is my son, oh, Krishna. I love him so much. I wish he didn't give me such grief and bring out the worst in me on most days.*

The new school year was commencing that morning, and Koogh would be in the fifth grade. His reluctant eyelids blinked and then opened wide with excitement.

"Pabbi, I am going to my new class today. New teachers. New books." he said and jumped up on his charpoy, almost falling off in excitement. "And ... and I will wear my new shorts and shirt!"

"Yes. Well, come on then, you don't want to be late on your first day!" said Geeta steadying him.

"I won't be late, Pabbi. Vaid and Bhollu are meeting Bhushan and me at the gate," said Koogh dancing around the landing with joy.

"Ah, my *badmaash* is awake. You better have a proper bath. And don't forget to pray," said Jaikishen at the doorway of the landing. He walked up to Geeta with a canister of fresh milk and sat to read the newspaper.

"Yes, Pitaji. Do you have any more instructions before I bathe?" said Koogh poking his head out of the landing door.

"No," laughed Jaikishen.

Koogh decided to bathe at the hand pump. He stripped to his underwear and filled the bucket. He poured a *gadvi* of the cold groundwater on himself and giggled as it splashed against his body. He hurriedly lathered himself with the tiny piece of Lifebuoy soap tucked into a nook in the wall and gave himself a thorough scrub. Once done, he wrapped himself in a towel and jigged up to the second landing.

His reason for the celebration was not unfounded. The school had no prescribed uniform. The only directive was that they wear clean clothes. And on days of physical drill, they were to wear khaki shorts and white shirts. His usual school clothes were Brij's hand-me-downs, which were either faded or mended. He had outgrown most of them, and some were too big for him. Geeta had no option but to dig into the fist-sized bundle she hid in the wheat canister's depths. The evening before, she took him to the market and bought him a new set of shorts and a shirt. He hugged them with glee before slipping them on. *Thank God Pabbi agreed to buy me new clothes.*

"How do I look?" grinned Koogh, moving his hands and legs.

"Very nice, although they are too big. You should have bought a size smaller Geeta," said Jaikishen looking up from the newspaper.

"All you can do is find fault. Have you seen how fast he is growing?" snapped Geeta.

Jaikishen sighed and winked at his son and resumed reading. Koogh looked into the small fading hand mirror, moving it from up to down to view himself. *Pitaji was right.*

He tucked his shirt in deep into his shorts. He then slipped on his old tattered belt to tighten the shorts at the waist and looked at himself again. *A lot better. So what if they are big, at least they are new and mine.*

He rushed to their shrine with folded hands. Krishna seemed to have a bigger smile for him that morning. He bowed his head, took some *prasad,* and sat for breakfast. The cumin *parantha* and a tall glass of sweetened hot milk got gobbled as Bhushan headed towards the stairway. While still munching his last mouthful, he touched his parent's feet and grabbed his heavier than usual sling bag. It had a slate, a few textbooks, a notebook, and an old battered stationery box in which was a sharpened pencil, two pieces of chalk, and an old rubber. Geeta had placed a copper tiffin box in it too. His eyes lit up when he opened it a crack – she had packed his favourite *Suji halwa and puri. What a first day!*

He met his friends at the gate, who exchanged quick smiles. "New clothes," sniggered Vaid, "but they are my size, yaar!"

"Vaid you give him your old clothes and take these new ones," added Bhushan.

"Get lost! You are all jealous," said Koogh stomping ahead.

"They're joking, yaar," said Bhollu catching up with him, "I like your new clothes. We losers are all wearing the same old ones."

Koogh smiled and looked back at Vaid and Bhushan, who smiled back and slapped him on his back, and they scampered off, chattering to school.

. . .

Jaikishen had murmured a silent prayer after Koogh left. "The news has not been good lately," mumbled Jaikishen.

"You're talking to yourself again," said Geeta, her brow crowded.

"I'm saying, that India has finally got her independence from the two-century long British regime. Freedom fighters, politicians, the rich, the poor, all are celebrating. And yet the goings-on are not good. We have agreed to pay too heavy a price. Despite resistance, the divide and rule policy has played out. And the dreamt idealism is gone with the wind as the dark shadows of partition shroud our country."

"What do you mean?"

"Pakistan is now a reality, Geeta. A separate entity, with Jinnah as her Premier. And Tandlianwala is now a part of this new entity. The news every day gets worse as new fires of rage get set ablaze. The mother state India, is grieving the birth of her offspring, which is spewing latent fury. We have inadvertently given shape to a new form of hatred that is breaking loose in every direction. Embers of massacres are smouldering everywhere."

"Such exaggerated news, none of which is affecting us. So, why have this discussion?"

He sighed and left the landing as she was not able to understand or chose not to understand. He knew his fears were well-founded. Daily the headlines screamed of the seething ferocity of imprudent wrongdoers. Believers in Ram and Allah were at loggerheads. Overnight, their co-existence for generations bore no relevance. They swore and spilled blood at each other on both sides of the newly formed border. Millions became outcasts in their own homes. Ashes of a partition that they had not asked for clouded their vision. Scarred for life in more ways than one, they tried to seek clarity at any cost to resurrect their lives.

Bhatia, their neighbour, called out to Jaikishen as he walked out of the house. He sat listening to the morning news on the radio, along with Santram and Bharat.

The newsreader was talking in his practiced placid tone. '... and rioting is spreading like wildfire'.

The men broke into sighs and speculation of the devastation. They sat, shaking their heads with expressions of dismay. The debate that ensued yet again was whether they should leave for the newly formed India or stay on in Pakistan.

PRIYA SHARMA SHAIKH

Jaikishen stared at nothing in particular as they talked animatedly around him. Not so long ago, he had been of the view that the British would never leave India.

. . .

Koogh liked school. Despite his prankster reputation, he did well in his studies. His class teacher was Mr. Ram Charan Gopinath. A middle-aged man with a portly structure. He sported a unique bushy moustache, akin to that of a walrus, that camouflaged his thin pursed lips. A circular bald patch shined on the back of his head. He was a learnt man and well respected amongst his peers. Every morning, he arrived at school on his bicycle, wearing black trousers, a tucked-in white shirt, black sandals, and a black bag on his carrier. He taught English, Maths, and History and had immense patience with weaker students. But he had an intolerance for tardiness and brats. He had thrown student's notebooks in the bin if work was shoddy or incomplete. And he had hit truant students on their knuckles with his wooden ruler if they dared to repeat their misbehaviour.

But that was not all. They also had to pledge in writing, 'I will finish my work on time' a 1000 times. And the ultimate straw that broke the brattiest camel's back was to get the Principal and a parent to sign the pledge. This harrowing experience ensured that no student dared to repeat a mistake. It also set an example for the rest of the class to fall in line. A silent rebellion got built against him in which he got referred to as Gopi *Daku* or GD - he was the same teacher that Koogh had spoken of to Jaikishen at the start of him joining the school. As usual, Gopinath entered the class at 8 am and placed his bag on the head table. The first session of the 5th grade was an introduction to a new subject!

"Good morning, children," he said aloud, prompting them to repeat after him.

The children looked at each other, wondering what he had said. Some giggled, and a few tried to imitate him in murmurs. He then explained to them in Urdu that they would learn the English language from that day on.

"Good morning," repeated Gopinath, this time with a dramatic wave of his hand.

"Goo mornin," chorused the whole class in an uncertain tone.

"Good mor_ning," said Gopinath once again, pronouncing the syllables with emphasis.

"Good morning," chorused the children. This time they were louder and in unison. Gopinath smiled.

"Very good. Take out your slates and let us start learning the alphabet - A B C D ..." he said, writing on the blackboard. "Copy these letters on your slates, and I will come around to see how you fare."

Gopinath smiled as he watched Koogh write the letters on his slate.

"This is what I call neat work," he said to the rest of the class, "A new language and writing so well. He is good at Urdu, Math, and Art too. Keep it up, son!"

Koogh looked embarrassed but felt good. He liked the sound of English. Pronunciation of its words fascinated him, and he spent a lot of time learning to speak and write English.

But, he found it challenging. He felt baffled that two completely different words sounded the same. *To* and *two*, *son* and *sun!* And that words that ought to have similar pronunciation didn't: COW and SOW; TO and GO! He was fascinated to know that he was a B for BOY and that his favourite T for TOY, was K for KITE. And that when he did something right, Gopinath said, "Good boy."

PRIYA SHARMA SHAIKH

. . .

Geeta gave two paise to Koogh every day. He spent one paisa on a plate of yellow rice and dal, on the way back from school, at the grain market. He saved the remaining one paisa and soon collected over 50 paise in an old tin box. He hid the box in a secret spot on the terrace. It was behind a loose brick in the wall. In it were also 20 emerald green marbles and his favourite *Lattoo*.

Eight weeks into the school term, Koogh awoke to Bhollo, tickling him. He groaned and covered up, but she tickled him again. He pulled off the covers and opened his eyes a slit. She had bathed and dressed up in a red salwar kameez.

"Wake up, Paaji," she prodded, "I have to tie a *Rakhi* for you before school."

Koogh turned away from her onto his side. She tickled his nostrils with her dupatta.

He grabbed her hand and rolled over with her. "Let me sleep, Bhollo, and you sleep too."

"No, Paaji, get up."

"Has Pabbi made any sweets?" he said, beginning to awake at the thought.

"Yes, suji halva and Pitaji bought some *barfi* too."

"And puris?" said Koogh, with his eyes still shut.

"Yes. Which Rakhi do you want? You can choose first."

Koogh's smiled at the thought of the delicious treats that awaited him, and his eyes fluttered open. He liked the festival of Rakhi. Brothers got treats and loads of respect. At the same time, the sisters got a promise of love and protection. But annoyingly, the symbol of the promise was in the form of money to the sisters!

Bhollo dangled three shiny Rakhis from her hand. Each of them had several baubles held together with gold strings. He did a quick survey and chose the biggest and shiniest for himself.

"But I won't give you any money."

"You have to give me money. I want to buy some *chiji*."

"Pabbi will give you money for your chiji."

"No, I want your money... please."

"I don't have any money," he snapped aloud.

"Yes, you do."

"Go away, miss-know-it-all!"

"It's on the terrace, behind the brick, in the tin box ... your money and marbles too."

Koogh sat up with a start and looked at her with his eyes and mouth wide open. His heart pounded as he jumped off the charpoy and ran up to the terrace. He counted his coins and marbles. Everything was intact. He heard footsteps scampering up the steps. He put the box away as Bhollo appeared at the doorway.

"Bhollo, you sneak – you have been spying on me! Go away! I don't want your Rakhi."

"But Paaji, I haven't taken anything, and it's not my fault, I know."

He took out his box and started walking off the terrace.

"Paaji listen to me. The other day when you thought you were alone on the terrace, looking at your box, I was behind the charpoys hiding from Soma Bhenji. We were playing hide and seek. When you left the terrace, I checked the box and saw your treasure!"

"Have you told anyone?"

"No. And I won't tell. So, will you give me money when I tie you Rakhi?" she bobbed her head to an angle with a cheeky smile.

Koogh rolled his eyes, realising he had to comply, fearing she would tell the others about his treasure.

"Okay, I will give you five paisa. And now I will have to give Soma Bhenji too. So much of my savings will be gone! Urr-rgghh!"

Shortly after, Koogh, Brij and Ghonni, got dressed. They sat on a mat laid out on the floor in the courtyard. Soma held a copper plate laden with barfi, halva and puris, fruit, sugar crystals, and peeled cardamom. It also had some red powder, a pinch of rice grains, and a lamp made of wheat flour and *ghee*. Geeta lit the lamp.

Soma wet the ring finger of her right hand before dipping it into the red powder. She then created a *tikka* on each of her brothers' foreheads and pressed a few rice grains onto it. She did *aarti* of her brothers and finally tied a *Rakhi* on their right wrist. It ended with her feeding them a piece of barfi. Bhollo repeated the process ditto.

To Geeta and Jaikishen's amusement, Koogh awkwardly gave five paise to each of his sisters. Brij elbowed him with a quizzical look.

"What? I saved it from my daily allowance."

"Well, that is nice of you, Kooghey. Keep your money with you, big man," said Jaikishen.

Koogh looked puzzled.

JUNGEE

"I put money aside for you all to give your sisters. Promise to be good caring brothers to them if and when the need arises," said Geeta.

"Yes, Pabbi," they all replied in varied tones.

"Good, and here is the ten paise that I had kept aside for you all to give both of them."

Koogh joyfully accepted the proposition. He caught Bhollo's eye and made a face at her. And before leaving for school, he changed his hiding spot on the terrace.

. . .

One day when Jaikishen returned from a trip to Mathura, he brought back gifts for his children. He placed three figurines in Koogh's hands. They glistened in his tiny hands – a Lion, a Cow, and a Peacock.

"What are these, Pitaji? They look so shiny. Like royal emblems."

"Emblems, huh? Interesting. So, what do you think these emblems represent?"

"I don't know. The Peacock is colourful. And it dances with his feathers in the rain. The Lion is the king of the jungle and the leader of his pack. And the Cow cares for us by giving us milk and ploughing our fields."

"Very nice. Okay, so let me have a go at your emblems. The carefree Peacock has a child-like innocence. It represents your childhood, a phase in which you will enjoy games, music, dance in the rain, and show off all your colours to the world. You will have no fear. The Peacock is also the ride of the son of Lord Shiva and Goddess Parvati - Lord Kartikeyan. He had a dream of being the brave Commander-in-chief someday. It is great to have dreams as a child. Imagine that the world is yours, and you will bring forth the rare jewel within you when the time is right. What do you think of that, my Kooghey?"

"I don't understand, Pitaji," said Koogh, as he turned over the Peacock figurine in his hands and gave Jaikishen a puzzled expression.

"It means that you can achieve anything you want in this world. All you need to do is dare to dream. To be anything you wish to. Very much like Kartikeyan." said Jaikishen.

"I also want to be a Comder-in-chief when I grow up," said Koogh, jumping up with excitement.

Jaikishen laughed. "You can be Commander-in-chief if you want and work hard for it."

"What about the Lion? I like him – he looks like a king."

Jaikishen smiled and tousled his son's hair. "The Lion is the Commander of his life. The Lion is Narasimha, the unsurmountable Vishnu-incarnate. He represents your youth.

You will have courage, wisdom, and energy to face adventure. You will take risks, break boundaries, and explore things that excite you. You will seek clarity and make your place in the world."

"That sounds like a lot of work, Pitaji."

"Yes. You will have responsibility of so many people when you are the Commander."
Koogh looked bemused.

"And as you craft your world, you will learn many life lessons. Life will test you and toughen you, which will make you the man you were born to be."

"Wow! And the Cow?"

"This beautiful Cow, along with the little calf, represents the phase of maturity and sacrifice. It will bring within you the gentleness to nurture your family and society like Nandi, the vehicle of Lord Shiva. He is the epitome of patience, which is a precious virtue."

"I like them all, and I am going to make stories about them."

"You are the hero of your life, son, and you have these three roles to play at different life stages. And if you do so with presence, you will feel complete, and you would have lived an incredible life."

"Presence?"

"Presence is when you are in a harmonious flow inside and out. And when you are present, you bring your best self to that moment. Like when you fly kites, you focus on just that, or when you sketch, you focus on just that create such beautiful art. You will understand more as you grow, Kooghey. Now run along."

Koogh looked up at his father, trying to assimilate all that he had said. He didn't understand everything, but he decided that his figurines or *avatars*, were his unique treasure. He imagined each of them to have special powers. He mumbled dialogues on their behalf, playing make-believe games with them on the terrace, and kept them in his treasure box. It was only his most trusted friends who made their acquaintance.

"Welcome to my 'game of life', played by four people. Three players and one commander-in-chief," he announced, with élan.

"The game involves a race of my three glorious avatars – The Peacock, Lion, and the Cow. They will line up at the head of the bed. Each player will roll the dice. The highest gainer will have the privilege to choose his or her avatar to race first. All the avatars will get lined up, and at the count of 3, the race will begin. Each participant will tap the bed in front of his avatar to move it forward. Since the head of the bed is higher, when you tap the bed with your fingers, your avatar will move ahead towards the centre of the bed," he said with aplomb.

His friends looked intrigued. "If your avatar falls, you go back and start over. The winner is one who reaches the finish line first. Are the rules clear?"

"They are made of brass," said Vaid, looking intently at the toys in his hands, "The rules are clear, brother, but won't you play?"

"I will be the Commander-in-chief of the race," he smirked with a glint in his eyes.

The moment the race began, the Peacock toppled over due to the weight of his feathers. Meanwhile, the Cow and the Lion leaped forward. It required skill to ensure that the animals moved forward without toppling over. The players concentrated hard to win, while onlookers indulged in cheering the avatar of their choice. The end of the race had a nail-biting excitement. And post the race, arguments and fights broke out about who had cheated.

The Lion won most races, but sometimes so did the Cow and the Peacock.

. . .

A few weeks later, during the first lesson of the day, the school gong rang. Gopinath paused his chalk mid-fraction to check his wristwatch. He looked puzzled. It was an odd time for the bell to ring. It was also not the regular single clang at the end of each class. It was the kind of ring one heard at the end of a school day.

The children's murmur became an excited chatter about going home early.

"Sir, can we go home?"

"No! Sit down, and be quiet. Let me check what the matter is."

Gopinath and the other teachers quickly assembled in the Principal's office, as instructed. Their town was on high alert. The rioting had spread across neighbouring towns, and there were expectations that it would be in Tandlianwala next. The school would have to get shut early. Gopinath returned to his classroom in a state of panic. When he announced that the school was closing early, the children broke into a joyous uproar and got up to leave. Gopinath raised his hands, indicating that they sit down.

The children grumbled and went back to their seats, sensing something was amiss. Gopinath took off his spectacles and wiped his sweaty face with his handkerchief. He looked at his students, taking in the anxious look on their young faces.

"Children, I had so much more to teach you, but unfortunately, our journey is coming to a close, and this is the last time I will say something to you," he said to his puzzled students.

"As adults, we shield you from the bitter truths of the world. Our country India is no more what it used to be. We have gained independence from the British, but we stand divided into two beings. India and a new country called Pakistan. And we are all going to be in great pain because of this religious divide. But, a bigger divide has also emerged - of 'good' and 'bad' people. The bad are inflicting wounds on the property and people resulting in fright and flight. I know that you all fear me and that you call me names. Gopi Daku, right? I know it is because of my strictness."

Koogh squirmed and looked around at his classmates.

"Children, the dangers that will encounter you in the

days to come, will be a lot more horrifying than smarting knuckles. I want each of you to be alert and watch out for the bad people. Be brave young men, and use your intelligence to fight to protect your families and yourself. I pray that someday we meet again. God bless you. Go home now."

The children's faces looked pale as they tried to fathom what he had said. They filed out of the classroom in a murmurous wave. Gopinath put his hand on Koogh's shoulder and took him aside.

"Son, remember what I am going to say to you, all your life."

"Yes, Sir," said Koogh, noticing his favourite teacher's eyes for the first time.

"You are a very bright child, made for great things. I don't know what lies ahead for you, but if you survive this madness, challenge the limitations that people might set for you. Always believe in yourself even though the tide may seem against you – for it is so, only to make you stronger. Be safe, son, and God bless!"

"Thank you, Sir!" said Koogh and bent to touch his feet.

Gopinath picked him up and put a trembling hand on his little head. Koogh bid him goodbye and made a run for the front gate. He turned to look back at Gopinath. He was walking towards the cycle stand. *The last time, did he say? It means I won't see him again.*

...

Bhushan, Vaid, and Bhollu were waiting for him outside school.

"Let's go home," he said as he reached them, wiping his brow and cheeks.

"Why are you crying?" exclaimed Bhollu jumping off the

school wall.

"Bhollu said that in class you said we'd play marbles. And then you disappeared with GD. What the hell did he say to you?" asked Vaid.

"Stop calling him GD!" snapped Koogh.

"Oh! So touchy!" said Vaid.

"The rise of the ideal child!" said Bhushan, mocking him by pointing his chin up.

"Stop it! He just wished me luck. Let's go home."

"But we have the day off. Let's get a rice plate and play a few rounds," said Bhollu.

Koogh was reluctant, but seeing his friends' eager faces, he agreed. They stopped at the grain market and gobbled their usual yellow rice.

Koogh followed the others to the banyan tree to play marbles, but his mind was restless, and he lost several rounds. His partner, Bhollu, sulked. They all got into an argument, and Koogh said that the only reason he lost was that Vaid had cheated. After a heated word squabble, Koogh pushed the unsuspecting Vaid to the floor. He then kicked Bhushan in the shin, making him hop about in pain. Bhollu rolled with laughter, jeering at them, while Koogh gathered his lost marbles and schoolbag and ran homeward. The boys chased him to his doorstep, gasping for breath. Good old Bhollu jumped in as the mediator, and they finally parted with a promise to play on Koogh's terrace later.

The moment Koogh and Bhushan stepped into their home, they knew something was not right. The usually vacant baithak was teeming with people. Family elders and a few neighbours were in the midst of a heated discussion about the

PRIYA SHARMA SHAIKH

conditions of unrest and looming danger. Koogh washed up at the hand pump and stood next to Jaikishen, nervously measuring the gravity of the situation.

"... butchered children, women, and men. Nobody is getting spared! Our town is next. We should leave brothers. This country is now for Muslims. We Hindus have no place here. We must leave for India," said Jaikishen looking peeved at the crowd that seemed to have deaf ears.

Most men shook their heads, remained non-committal, or insisted that it was unwise to move. They should lie low and stay put in Tandlianwala itself, they said. The only one who was sure that he was going was Santram. He had already arranged tongas and was leaving for Jadanwala, the refugee camp that afternoon. Koogh and Bhushan exchanged open-mouthed glances as the elders dispersed.

"I'm sorry I fought with Vaid and you," said Koogh and gave him a handful of marbles.

"I'll see you in India," said Bhushan and rushed up the stairs with his parents.

Koogh watched his father's distraught face. He had not been able to convince his neighbours to leave. Jaikishen sat pondering over what to do next and made a flash decision. He grabbed a stick and ushered his family to follow him to Melaram's home. Geeta put Ghonni on her hip and grumbled all the way, dragging Bhollo along. Soma and Koogh kept pace with Jaikishen. Koogh noticed his father's determined look.

...

The atmosphere of Melaram's home frightened Koogh the moment they stepped in. An unbelievable number of people had assembled in the courtyard, and Melaram was addressing them in an anxious tone. His audience consisted of several known and unknown faces from the railway office. Their respective families were there too. Some of the men held sticks and crude indigenous firearms. Hostility was written all over their faces.

"Thank God you are finally here, son," exclaimed Melaram.

The crowd talked out of turn with heated urgency and made aggressive gesticulations. Elders and women looked forlorn as their men debated their future. A chill ran down Koogh's spine. He reached for the side of Jaikishen's kurta and stayed close to him.

"Have you heard the news today, Jaikishen?" said Kairon.

"Yes, I did. And that is why I have come in the middle of the day, Chachaji. I've been in a similar discussion at my place too."

"I say, how can the government not do anything about what is happening? How can I be expected to vacate my ancestral home? This is our India, and it will always be our country," said Kairon.

"What India are you talking about, Kairon Saab? Wake up! We are now in Pakistan," said an exasperated Jaikishen. He banged his stick to the floor, "For God's sake, stop living in a fool's paradise of ideal India."

"Bah to this partition and government! I, too, disagree with the decision to move. We have built our homes with our sweat and blood. How can we abandon things and be expected to flee? Who will compensate us for all our immovable assets?" exclaimed Bhatia in an angry tone.

"I agree. Who is the government to change our status for us?" said Bhatia's perky wife, Pinky.

"My family and I have decided to stay back," said Mishra, banging the butt of his gun on the floor. "We are not scared of anyone. We are the lions of this land. Anybody dare threaten me! We have organised guns and ammunition too. We will fight back!"

"And you plan to fight an aggressive armed mob with this single gun, Mishra? You have little sons and a daughter too. Are you willing to put their lives at risk to protect your assets? Don't you see you are fighting a losing battle?" said Jaikishen, letting his impatience rise in his voice.

"Yes. Yes. Yes. And I will protect them fiercely till my end," screamed Mishra.

"And what happens to them when your end comes?"

Mishra looked away as tears sprung from his eyes. His little daughter hugged his legs and started crying aloud at seeing her father's tears.

"I agree with Bhatiaji and Mishraji. How can we be expected to go? Utter nonsense! At this moment, we cannot be weak. There is might in unity - if we all unite, nobody can harm us," asserted Geeta, finding her voice, even as Ratandeyi and the other women looked on.

"Where will we go? What is the guarantee that we won't get killed on the way? And when we get there, where will we stay?"

"Geeta, we don't need your hysteria at this hour. I request you and everyone else here to please listen to me even though I don't have all the answers. All I know is that we can't stay here because we are sure to die if we do stay on. The horrors of the neighbouring towns are written in blood – We are in grave danger! And we can't sit around debating and waiting for things to happen. We have to get into action and claim our destiny. Somebody has to make a decision and take responsibility - I am putting myself in charge. I take the responsibility of leaving with my family and whoever else that decides to accompany me."

"As regards where we will stay in India, your guess is as good as mine. My instinct says that God is setting us on a path. Something good is sure to come of it. If we Hindus are leaving our homes behind, so will many Muslims that lived in India. I'm sure the government will provide a housing solution. They will have to do something to provide for the migration of lakhs of people," said Jaikishen.

"Geeta Bhabi, he is right. I know it is a tough decision to make, but we Hindus have to vacate or get killed," said Goel, pushing back his hair in exasperation.

"Yes. We can't get mercy from an angry mob," shouted Jaikishen. "Come on, my brothers, let us not delay this decision."

Koogh sensed the fear in each of their voices. Bhollo started crying and hugged Geeta. Koogh rushed to take her aside near the cattle hold.

"Look, Bhollo, that calf is playing with his mother. See Tirloki Chacha trying to catch its tail," said Koogh, wiping her tears while keeping an eye on the adults.

"You still haven't answered my question - how do you know we will be safe leaving from here? What if we get attacked on the way?" asked Geeta.

"We will be under Army protection. That is where we have to show our unity as we will be in thousands. If we all stay together, nobody will dare attack us. I have found out that under the Army's protection, tonight, we will reach the refugee camp at Jadanwala.

From there, we will all leave for India," said Jaikishen looking pointedly at Geeta and then at the crowd around him with a steady gaze. There was an unsettling quiet among them as the weight of the decision landed upon them.

Koogh saw Geeta wiping her tears with her dupatta as she walked into the kitchen. Two other women from the neighbourhood were making rotis with her. They were cooking for all the people that had taken refuge in Melaram's home. They spoke over each other, worrying about the safety of their families - How would they manage the cooking? - How would they stay out in the open? - What would they eat? - What should they take with them? - And what should they leave behind? As Geeta served her children lunch, Koogh said, "Pabbi, don't worry, we will all be fine. I will look after you and everyone."

She nodded, looking at the innocent faces of her four children. Tears rolled down her goggled cheeks.

After lunch, Jaikishen left Geeta, Soma, Ghonni, and Bhollo at Melaram's home. He and Koogh went to inform the Army of their intent to join the camp at Jadanwala. They then went to Ward 6 to gather a few belongings for their journey to India.

. . .

By the time Jaikishen and Koogh reached their home, all the other houses in Ward 6 were empty. Jaikishen took out the only holdall they possessed and spread it out on the landing. It was military green in colour with brown leather straps, and it was large enough to hold many things.

"Kooghey, hurry! Gather the clothes drying on the terrace. We need to rush back soon," said Jaikishen, as he moved around stuffing the holdall with clothes, woollens, a few vessels, sheets, blankets, and some provisions.

"What about the rest of our things, Pitaji?"

"We will have to leave them behind. Somebody who finds our things will use them, son."

"But, Pitaji ..."

"We shouldn't be so attached to our things, son."

Seeing Koogh's confused expression, he held his shoulders and looked at him squarely.

"Nothing is permanent, son. Today I have something, and tomorrow I could lose it all; what I can't lose is the love for my family, my values, skills, and memories. Nobody can take these things away from me. I know we have to let go of many things. The lesser baggage we carry, the faster we will move ahead. Any excess baggage will weigh me down. And it is only when I let things go that there will be room for other things to come in. God has a plan to fill our lap with new things, new friends, new school, new people, new experiences – A new home. So why grieve for what we leave behind? Just let go. Do you agree?"

Koogh gave him a slow nod. Jaikishen sighed and hugged him, "Now, let's get to work," he said.

"Yes, Pitaji," said Koogh and darted up the stairs.

. . .

By early evening, over 100 people known to Melaram had camped in his courtyard.

Women and children huddled indoors, while men stood guard at the doorway and terrace with their guns, sticks, and stones.

Melaram's neighbour, Qasim Ahmed, a handsome young man with light brown eyes, rushed into their house with worry on his face. He had got wind that a violent mob was approaching their neighbourhood.

"Salaam, *Chachajaan*. You all are in great danger if you stay here for longer than a few moments. These mobs are brutal and uncontrollable. And although you have guns, they will outnumber you. They will decimate you all. You have to evacuate and move to my home!"

The crowd huddled closer. Women gasped, and children started whimpering silent tears.

"How many people do you have here?" continued Qasim.

"We are more than 100 people, Qasim. How will you hide us in your home, son? I don't want to put Shaziya and the kids in danger. Save our women and children in your home. We men will fight to our last breath," said Melaram with folded hands.

Qasim had played in Melaram's courtyard with his children and enjoyed treats from his kitchen for so many years. He couldn't bring himself to accept Melaram's decision and shook his head vehemently. "I call you *Chachajaan* and respect you. I can't leave you here to die. I beg you, please, don't delay. We will manage. We don't have any time to think."

Gunshots rang through the air, and a raging fire blew up, followed by muffled screaming and shrieking of people in the distance. Men panicked while the women and children cried out aloud. Melaram looked at all the people under his shelter, and in a blink, decided to take Qasim's offer.

"Chachaji, I won't go without Koogh and his father," cried Geeta.

"Geeta, I understand, but for the sake of your other children and yourself, you have to come with us. My heart, too, is breaking to let them down like this, but I must protect everyone under my roof. God will watch over them," said Melaram, tears brimming in his old eyes.

Ratandeyi hugged Geeta and egged her on to pick up Bhollo while Soma carried Ghonni. Geeta relented with tears in her eyes and followed the crowd into Qasim's home. They all squeezed into every available space, and Qasim locked their gate and front door just as gunshots rang out again. The mob was closer this time. Melaram asked everyone to be silent and keep the children quiet.

Qasim put on his prayer cap and ran up to his terrace. He looked down to see a seething mob, armed with torches, swords, and sticks surround Melaram's home.

The mob hammered at the large wooden doorway furiously, kicking and pushing it until it fell from its hinges. The crowd stormed in and tore the house down.

Geeta hugged Bhollo close. Soma leaned against her - She had put Ghonni to sleep on her shoulder. They heard loud, abusive voices. Geeta prayed that Jaikishen and Koogh wouldn't turn up at Melaram's at this very moment.

The leader of the mob saw Qasim. "Where are they? Their beds and vessels are still warm. They ought to be somewhere here."

"They were here, bhaijaan. But I saw the family leave a while back."

"Bullshit. Do you take me for a fool?"

Shaziya came to stand by her husband, with their baby in her arms.

"What happened, bhaijaan?" she asked in a concerned tone.

"Bhabi, we are searching for the Melaram family. Your husband says they have left. You tell me, where are they?"

"Oh, those rats ran away a while ago. They must have gone to India."

"I hope you two are not hiding something from us," said the leader looking from Qasim to Saziya again.

"No bhaijaan, why would we do that. I am here with my husband and children. Why don't you come and check the house for yourself?"

Geeta's heart thudded so loud that she was sure the rioters, separated from them by a mere wall, would be able to hear it. Melaram raised his hand of assurance to his lips in the shadows. "Trust in God. Qasim will not let any harm come to us."

Outside, the rioters shifted uncertainly on their feet. "We trust your word, bhabi. Come
on, boys, let's get out of here and head onwards to the Ward 6 – there are loads of houses there. Let's ensure that we wipe these neighbourhoods clean," said the leader. They trudged out grumbling abuses and disappeared into the twilight shadows.

. . .

Jaikishen packed another small bag with a few of Geeta's valuables. The modest jewellery her parents had given her, money she had hidden away in canisters, the idol of her beloved Krishna and Radha, and the *Bhagavad Gita*, wrapped in glittering *gota*.

The sun kissed the horizon as Koogh reached the terrace to collect the clothes and also take his treasure box. He scanned the neighbourhood. *It seems empty.*

He listened for the familiar sounds of chatter, the radio, or the clanging of vessels. He heard nothing but a buffalo mooing in the cowshed behind their home. *He has got abandoned too! The silence feels eerie.*

Was that firing in the distance? There is danger looming around us as Gopinathji and Pitaji said. He picked the clothes off the clothesline. *Damn this independence. What is the point of it, if we can't stay where we want?* Tears sprung to his eyes as he tried to come to terms with all the changes in his life. His frail body racked with shivers. He reminded himself of Gopinath's advice - *be alert and brave if danger comes seeking me.*

He took out his treasure box and sat on the charpoy, sinking into it more than usual. *This charpoy's strings need tightening.* He then shook his head. *We will never need to tighten your strings again. What will come of you and the things we leave behind?*

He emptied the contents of his box onto the floor. The marbles rolled out, glittering in the early evening light. The coins were a total of two rupees and 95 paise, shining a bright silver. The lattoo with its thread wound tight around it stared back at him, with its point pointing pointlessly. His grand brass army of the Lion, the Cow, and the Peacock lay lifeless on their sides. Koogh picked them up one by one and smiled.

The day before, Vaid and Bhushan had got into a fistfight about each other cheating in the race. And Bhollu and Koogh had rolled with laughter. They were to play marbles that afternoon too. He peered over the terrace ledge, looking into the distance, hoping to see one of them. There was no sight of Vaid or Bhollu. Bhushan had already left with his family. *Maybe they did come looking for me and left after not finding me here. Or maybe they didn't come at all. I wonder if they are also leaving for India.*

Shots rang out in the distance again, reminding him of the impending danger. He hurried over to the charpoy and pocketed all the coins. He then put his avatars in his pocket along with 12 marbles and the lattoo.

Bhollu was the only one who knew where he hid the box, so he would find it if he came back. Koogh kept 50 paise back in the box and a few marbles, and a note.

Bhollu

I am leaving for India because Pitaji thinks we should be there. I am leaving some of my treasures behind for you. I hope you enjoy them and think of me when you play with them. I wish we could have played marbles and flown kites today one last time. Are you coming to India? If you come, please come and meet me. Your best friend – Koogh

He folded the note neatly and placed it into the box and hid it back in the wall. He felt sorry for himself and everyone he knew. He slumped back on the charpoy again - He would never see his school, Gopinath, his friends, and his kite fliers again. He didn't even get a chance to say goodbye. He pulled his knees to his chest and hugged them tightly. His eyes and face flooded as he cried silent tears onto his dusty brown cheeks.

Pitaji was right, I can't take everything, but I can take my memories with me.

Jaikishen's voice broke into his thoughts. He stood up abruptly, wiped his face, and turned to leave the terrace. Just then, something sharp whizzed past his right ear and hit the wall in front of him. A bullet! It splintered the wall and buried itself in the plaster.

Koogh cried out and fell to the floor, and lay there paralysed in fear. Some more bullets followed. Jaikishen heard the shots and Koogh's cry, and felt his heart stop. He raced up to the terrace, taking the steps two at a time.

"Kooghey! I'm coming, son. Lie down on the ground!"

He reached the terrace to see his brave little son wriggling towards the stairway on his belly. He reached out and pulled him down to the landing and then down to the stairway, and shut the landing door behind him. He was breathless as he held his son's small sweaty body, checking frantically for injury. "Are you hurt?"

"Bullets, Pitaji!" cried Koogh, out aloud.

"No, Pitaji."

Jaikishen hugged his son close, his heart still pounding. "Thank God! Why did you go up to the terrace?" he shouted.

"For the clothes, Pitaji."

Jaikishen bolted the landing door - even if someone climbed up to the terrace, they could not get to them. He took Koogh to the deodi and gave him a glass of water.

He stayed low and moved around in the dark, softly shutting and locking all the doors and windows.

When the house was secure, he went back to where Koogh was and pulled him onto his lap. Father and son breathed heavily in silence, clinging to each other, waiting for the rioters to pass.

In the shadows, Jaikishen stretched his legs out and looked at Koogh. "I want you to listen to me very carefully, son. These are dangerous times, and our only aim as a family is to come through it alive. To survive, we have to stay alert and together. If something happens to me, you have to promise me something."

"What promise Pitaji?"

"That you will somehow reach Babaji's place. From there, you will go with him and your mother, sisters, and brother to Jadanwala. And then you will go to India and take shelter in your Nanaji's house and take the responsibility of looking after the family and yourself. Is that clear?"

"But what will happen to you, Pitaji?"

"Nothing will happen to me. I am preparing you, just in case something untoward happens. You are my Commander-in-chief, aren't you? Do you promise to take charge?"

Koogh gave him an unsure nod.

"What are you thinking, son?"

"I'm thinking of my friends, Pitaji. And about Bharat Tauji and Gopinathji. What will happen to them? Will they also be coming to India? Or will they get killed?"

"Hush! Nobody will get killed. I don't know what their family's plans are, my son, but I know God will care for everyone. Who are we to worry about when he is in charge? For now, we have to do what is right to take care of ourselves. So we will lie low and be quiet."

Jaikishen's mind was racing with thoughts and worry.

"Pitaji, don't worry. I will show you how to sneak out from the back door to Bagga's house and Babaji's house."

"Your naughty times in these alleyways will come to good use after all," said Jaikishen tousling his son's head. *O God, please help us get to our family safely. I don't want us to die here, separated from them.*

. . .

They waited for some time before creeping out of the back door. Staying within the shadows, they fled into the night. They ran to Melaram's house, only to see the door broken and the house abandoned.

Jaikishen's heart leapt to his mouth, and he let out a gasp as his mind raced to the worst conclusions. Qasim's hushed voice called out to him, and he signalled them towards his back gate. Koogh followed his father to enter a darkened courtyard, smelling of body vapour. He blinked hard, trying to make out his surroundings.

As the door shut behind them, Qasim put a lantern close to Koogh's face. A collective sigh went around the room, as Geeta, Soma, and Bhollo rushed to meet them. Koogh hugged his family. *We are together!*

JUNGEE

. . .

Later that night, under the Army patrol's vigil, the group packed themselves into and on top of a bus. It was going to Jadanwala. As the engine started, Koogh knew that their journey to India had begun. Some people looked back at the fleeting neighbourhood that they had called home. The most who looked ahead had hopeful eyes and a quest in their hearts to reach a place that they could call home.

"Pitaji, you lost the bet with Bharat Tauji," said Koogh.

"Yes, son, I was wrong," said Jaikishen biting his lower lip, allowing his tears to flow.

The moonlit night offered them some light on the dark bus. When Koogh saw his father's face glisten with a stream of tears, he knew the worst was yet to come.

– – –

CHAPTER 4: HIT AND MISS

September 1947: The mammoth journey from India to India

I hope India will be a good place. Koogh sat pressed into a corner of the bus, near a window that wouldn't open. Perched cross-legged on his lap was Bhollo. She was drowsy and nibbled at a roti. He patted her sleepy head on his shoulder. Beside them was Soma and then was Tirloki. They were all sweating to the bone.

"Paaji, will we never go back home?" sniffled Bhollo, interrupting his thoughts.

"Bhollo, you have no idea of what a great adventure awaits you. We are going to a much better place and see what I have got along for you," he said, shifting to take out the avatars from his pocket.

Bhollo smiled, delighted to see their old friends. "You remembered! Oh, I'm so happy. Can we race now?"

"Not now, but tomorrow. It will be a different race with new rules. We are going to take these boys on their longest race yet - to India."

"Oh, Paaji, I want to be in that race."

"Okay. Since you are my favourite, you can choose the avatar you want first."

"I'm going to be the Lion," she giggled.

"Aha! So, you want to find new territory in India. Huh, Bhollo?"

"Yes," she said, clapping her hands with newfound glee.

"And I will be the Peacock and fly over you," said Tirloki with a cheeky smile, aiding Koogh's effort to make Bhollo feel better.

"Well, then I will have to be the Cow. Moo!" said Soma and tickled her sister.

"And I will be the commander-in-chief, making sure my troops are doing their job well," smirked Koogh.

"And how will we decide the winner?" asked Bhollo.

"The winner will be the one who goes through the whole race with a smile. The winner will be the one who doesn't trouble Pabbi. The prize will be the avatar itself."

"Will you give him to me forever?" said Bhollo kissing the Lion.

"Yes. So, are you going to win?" asked Koogh as the others listened in.

Bhollo nodded and growled like a lion, curling her little fingers to look like paws. They all burst into laughter, making the others in the bus turn around to look at them in wonder.

"I know you will win!" said Koogh with a hopeful smile, hugging his sister.

. . .

Jadanwala was a *tehsil* much bigger than Tandlianwala. The Army had set up a camp to control people's movement around a local cinema hall that had shut for business. Jaikishen and Melaram's group was a tiny segment of the thousands of people assembled at the camp. On arrival, they got labelled as refugees. Camp volunteers distributed portions of rice, dal, oil, salt, etc. based on each family's size. Jaikishen, along with the other men in their group, stood in line for hours to get their share. Tirloki and Koogh set up an improvised tent in the open grounds using sticks, sheets, and saris. At the same time, Geeta lit a small fire on the makeshift wood stove to cook *k-hichdi* for everyone. They sat to eat the meagre meal together.

"This is horrible," sulked Bhollo.

"This is the best I can make in these circumstances, and it is all that we will eat for the next few days. So, get used to it," snapped Geeta.

"I'm not saying I won't eat it, Pabbi," said Bhollo with a fake smile, catching Koogh's raised eyebrows. She looked down at the Lion in her small palm and ate the khichdi without any further fuss.

For the next five days, the number of refugees grew with each passing day. Koogh needed to dig deep into his energy trove to survive the subhuman conditions they lived in. There was no safety or privacy. The stench of thousands of unbathed, sweating bodies was obnoxious and prevalent everywhere. Open defecation added to it all and also started the spread of sickness. Further, the camp was fraught with frustration, quarrels, and theft. He saw people pawning jewellery and family heirlooms for necessities.

His heart wrenched each time he saw weeping lost and hungry children. There were so many of them. He'd try to help each time, but there was only so much he could do, being so little himself.

On the fifth night, the camp volunteers, who were at their wit's end, heaved a sigh of relief. Their ordeal was going to end, as Army officials did rounds on horseback, making announcements of the start of the walk to India. It was to start the next morning, under their protection. Koogh and the many thousand others broke into nervous energy. An uproar of sorts burst upon the camp. The adults chattered aloud about how to make a success of the journey. The old broke down, questioning the point of their life now that that leaving was certain.

Koogh helped his parents collect all their strewn possessions. Ghonni wailed in Soma's arms, but Bhollo smiled and was the only one who celebrated and braced herself for the great race that was finally going to start.

"The distance to India is about 200 kilometres. They say the trek has a varied terrain. The saving grace is a freshwater canal alongside most of the path," announced Jaikishen to his group. "We have to stay close together to ensure our safety."

Koogh spent a troubled night. He stretched himself and stood with his hands on his hips, watching the expansive milieu. The walk was to begin before sunrise. And as planned, it did. It started with a surge. Everyone was in a hurry to get going. More than 100,000 people were a part of the exodus that followed the army.

"Look, Tirloki," quipped Koogh, "They are like herds of cattle. Following their cowherd. Trusting in him to take them to fresh new pasture."

"We will join them too, Koogh," said Tirloki, rubbing his eyes open.

Tirloki was right. Koogh wondered how the little ones would manage. He woke them up on Geeta's cue and rushed to fill drinking water for the journey. Jaikishen packed while Geeta fed her family and sat to fuel her body with leftover rotis and pickles. Koogh returned to find that Melaram had organised a small horse-drawn carriage. The women and children loaded themselves and their things onto it, and they set off to join the thousands in the mammoth snake-like procession towards India.

"1 – 2 – 3 go!" exclaimed Koogh. The avatars glistened in the hands of the three contenders.

"Look after your avatar well, and be aware that I will be watching you all the time," said Koogh in a measured tone. All the children hooted, urging the horse to move faster.

"Pitaji, we should stay at the centre of the procession. We will be safer from possible attacks," said Koogh to Jaikishen from the carriage.

"That is a good idea, Kooghey. You are a good commander," said Jaikishen patting his son's head.

"Commander-in-chief, please!"

"Oh, Yes! Of course. But how are you a Commander-in-chief?"

"Pitaji, I am in complete control," he said, and then jumped off the cart and whispered in his ear. "I have made Bhollo believe that the walk to India is a race of my three avatars. Soma, Tirloki, and Bhollo are the team captains."

"You are quite the leader Kooghey," said Jaikishen.

Koogh and the rest of the children began the march with enthusiasm. They enjoyed the novel experience of riding in the cart and played singing games. But as the sun rose to its height, and the searing afternoon heat set in, it became more challenging to hold their heads up. Their faces were awash with sweat and dust, and the singing games didn't seem fun anymore. Seeing the sad faces around them, they realised this picnic was not fun at all.

By early evening, the horse was too exhausted to pull the cart any farther. Melaram had no choice but to abandon the cart. They loaded a few bags onto the horse's back and carried on walking. When the Army called an end to the day's march, they all fell to the ground like swatted flies.

Despite his tired condition, Jaikishen arranged for firewood and water for his family. Geeta prepared the *khichdi* once again. It got gobbled within minutes, without a word of complaint. That night they didn't bother with setting up tents and chose to sleep on the open grounds. The men formed an outer circle, while the women and children slept in the centre.

"I do not like this race at all, Paaji," said Bhollo in a tiny, tired voice, next to Koogh.

"The race has only just begun, Bhollo. Tomorrow will be even better. Remember, it is only if you smile through it that you can win," murmured Koogh, trying to keep his eyes open, "Are you crying?"

"No. I'm not crying at all. I'm smiling. See." She parted her parched lips a bit to show him her teeth.

"Good. It looks like your Lion is giving a stiff competition to the Peacock and Cow. I know you are going to win my Lion."

Bhollo attempted a small growl and slipped into a deep slumber on his arm. Koogh patted his little sister's head, pushing the sweat-stiffened hair off her face. He looked up at the velvety starry night.

"Look at how she is suffering. What wrong has she done to suffer so? Please forgive her and us if we have wronged. I know I shouldn't have pushed Vaid and kicked Bhushan that day. Help me to help my family, Krishna ...," Koogh whispered to the skies. Amid his dialogue with the divine, sleep overtook him.

The next morning, Jaikishen requested a neighbour to let the children take turns to sit on his donkey. By the time it was Koogh's turn, his feet had blistered, and the sun was beating down upon him from the afternoon sky. The poor donkey looked exhausted too. He looked at Koogh with his gaping eyes and let out a loud bray.

"Hello, Mr. Khoteya!" said Koogh, stroking his ride's back. The donkey shook his head, making all the tiny bells on his neck ring as if saying, 'I'm don't want to carry you!'

Koogh wriggled onto his grey back, which prompted the donkey into a short gallop.

"Oye, Mr. Khoteya, what are you doing? I will fall. Please carry me for some time," said Koogh stroking his neck.

The donkey brayed several times again, snorted, and finally began to plod along the trail.

Everyone had their heads covered, and eyes narrowed to ward off the fury of the sun. The afternoons became the bane for each traveller.

Koogh was uncomfortable, and he needed to work hard at staying atop the donkey's back. It was well worth it as his feet got the much-needed respite. His slippers fell off his feet, so Jaikishen carried them for him. He leaned against the baggage, while Jaikishen and the others trudged alongside.

Geeta walked with a wailing Ghonni on her hip, some steps behind them. She needed to keep slowing down to manage him, which annoyed Bhollo as she had instructions to keep pace with Geeta, even while the others moved ahead. But she had set her mind not to show her angst, so she walked a step ahead of Geeta, with an eager smile plastered on her face.

Jaikishen put a scarf over Koogh's head to protect him from the sun. Through the weave of the thin fabric, Koogh watched all the people passing by. Brown faces baked darker in the sun, covered in dust that stuck to their grimy skin. A graphic representation of their experiences over the last few days. Expressionless, moving in carts, on horse-carriages, on cycles, and foot. Silent, snapping, groaning, or crying. Sitting. Sleeping. Answering the call of nature. Walking. On and on. He sighed and turned his cheek to view the other side. It was no different.

He started counting people as they crossed him. Mr. Khoteya's bells, the footsteps, and the sounds of people formed a lilting rhythm. By the time he reached 100, he felt slumber creeping over him, and soon he was in a deep sleep.

Wild animals have a mind of their own, they say, and so do the domestic ones! Mr. Khoteya stopped to answer the call of nature. And chew some grass. And then for no reason, in particular, stepped up onto a pathway that took them to higher terrain. Koogh's body started to slide down the donkey's back, and he awoke with a jerk to readjust himself. He turned his head to look towards Jaikishen. The blurred face he saw was unfamiliar.

He rubbed his eyes and sat up, looking around for his father. There was no sight of him. Or his mother. Or anyone familiar. He panicked and broke into a cold sweat as fear engulfed him. Waves of people kept moving past, indifferent to yet another dusty, distressed child. Koogh called out to his parents, sisters, and brothers, but he got no response. Meanwhile, Mr. Khoteya kept strutting along, paying no heed to his cries. Koogh jumped off his ride to land onto the scorching ground.

He screamed jumping up in agony as his already bruised feet stung hard. He started running forward. Not seeing any familiar face, he ran back, scanning faces anxiously. After running back quite a distance, he saw Geeta. She was sitting on the pathway's side, and clutching onto her was a much distressed looking Bhollo and a wailing Ghonni. He rushed toward them. They, too, had got separated from the rest of the family. Geeta was a bundle of vulnerability. Seeing Koogh, her stretched nerves collapsed, and she wept so much that she fainted.

Koogh got back in command of himself. He put Ghonni on his hip and rushed with Bhollo to get water from the canal. He removed his shirt and soaked it in the freshwater and rushed back to Geeta. He wiped her face and neck with the wet cloth and squeezed a few drops of the water into her mouth. She stirred and sucked more of the water from his shirt. After a few minutes, she pushed herself to get up and hugged her children. She dragged herself to the canal with them and drank some more water. Once she felt better, she was ready to resume the walk. Koogh carried Ghonni piggyback, and he held Bhollo with a firm hand. She was beside herself with joy that Koogh was with her and not with the others. She beamed at him, and they walked together after that.

That evening they reached the camp-site exhausted, hungry, and covered in grime. Koogh's task was to look for the rest of his family. Geeta groaned and called out aloud for Krishna's mercy, as her children looked on. They had no provisions for the night. They walked to the canal and drank water, filling their empty stomachs. Worried that her children would wander off at night, Geeta tied them to herself with an extra sari.

Koogh awoke early, and although his body ached, he ran around the camp before people got afoot. After a good thirty minutes search, he found Jaikishen, who hugged him and wept bitter tears. He apologised for having separated from him, and they rushed to reunite with Geeta and the children. A pairing strategy got put into play after that, in which each one was responsible for another two. Koogh was responsible for Geeta and Bhollo. He took his job very seriously and watched their every move like a hawk.

As days passed, the human caravan was witness to countless instances of misery. Despite the Army's presence, the fear of attack was daunting, and the slightest loud sound put people on edge. Rations depleted, with stomachs being fed water and a few grains at the end of long tiring days. Sickness, injury, loud wails, tears, hostile expressions, and death were amuck. Koogh's limbs were sore even after a whole night's rest. His blistered feet bled, and he limped to keep pace. Many separated from their families, while many collapsed and gave up the journey and on life.

. . .

Meanwhile, Brij, who was in Lahore, somehow managed to reach Ludhiana. He arrived at Sharda's parents' doorstep in a messy state. Cries of joy broke out as the family rushed to greet him. The not-so-newlyweds were together again. Brij was happy, but he worried about the rest of his family. Almost two weeks had gone by since his arrival in India, and the rioting was relentless. He visited the refugee camp every day, hoping to find them. Each day he returned disappointed.

"Are you going to the bank today? They might give you a transfer," said Sharda, giving him a tall glass of sweetened milk.

He nodded. "I understand my responsibilities as a husband, Sharda. But my heart is so pained for my family that I do not feel inclined to do anything."

. . .

After the interview, Brij took Sansarchand, who was also posted as a policeman in Ludhiana, with him to the station. They stopped to speak to a railway officer on duty.

"Sir, we have been looking for our family for many weeks now. Do you know if any more people are coming from Pakistan?"

"Over 100,000 people have walked to India over the past

few days. Your family could be amongst them. They may have already reached. They may not have registered themselves yet, or they could still be on the way. Go to Khemkaran. A train will go there in the next few minutes."

With renewed hope, Brij and Sansarchand took the train. It soon pulled into Khemkaran. They scanned the thousands of faces standing on both sides of the train. Brij scoured the tracks while Sansarchand stood at the doorway to the platform. The Army and Police were herding people away from the train. There was a mixed feeling of anxiety and happiness on all the refugees' faces. They looked exhausted with tears of joy or relief, as they united with loved ones, hugging each other.

Brij's eyes clouded as he watched the emotional and physical states of all the people. He kept a lookout for a familiar face. Disappointment grew with every passing moment. All of a sudden, Sansarchand heard a shrill sound above the din, "Chachaji!"

He turned to trace the voice.

"Chachaji, Chachaji!"

He saw a young girl pushing through the thick crowd waving her arm at him in desperation. He couldn't place her. And yet she seemed so familiar! He called out to Brij.

"It is Soma!" cried Brij bursting into tears, jumping off the moving train.

The harsh sun had tanned Soma several shades darker. She looked hysterical to the onlooking crowds. Melaram and Jaikishen had also heard her cries. They didn't know who she was calling out to, so they ran after her. And then they too saw Sansarchand and Brij and pushed through the crowds to reach them, crying with joy.

"Pitaji, Chachaji," said Brij touching his father's feet. "Soma! I can't thank God enough for the moment you spotted us. Where are Pabbi and Chachiji and the children?"

"They are on the rail tracks. We all arrived this morning. We are exhausted, but we are all alive, and that is the grace of the almighty. It has been very tough, son," said Jaikishen in a weary tone leaning into his young son's strong arms.

Koogh was with Geeta, Bhollo, and Ghonni on the tracks amidst thousands of others, wincing in the hot sun. They looked like urchins, with dirty, tangled hair, sunburnt bodies, parched lips, and tattered clothing.

Koogh was wearing one of Jaikishen's shirts. It was so over-sized for him that it looked like he was wearing an ill-fitting nightdress. With hardly any energy in his body, he stretched his arm and moved towards his brother, weeping, tripping, and smiling all at the same time. The outburst of emotion at the family's reunion would have moved the most hardened heart. They hugged each other as tears of relief streamed down each of their cheeks. They had survived their worst nightmare yet.

. . .

Brij and Sansarchand took them to a local *Dhaba*. Provisions in the camp were exhausted four days ago, and most of them had eaten nothing at all. They all pounced on the food as it arrived on the table. Koogh alone ate more than 20 rotis.

"Don't overeat, Koogh. Your stomach will not be able to handle it," said Brij.

"But I'm still hungry. Can we take some food along?"

Brij wanted to explain that Koogh wouldn't have to worry about food running short again. But something in his brother's dark eyes stopped him. It was too soon, and his fears would take time to fade.

"Yes, of course, we can." Brij gave instructions to the waiter.

That evening as they lay in the damp barn, Koogh lifted the Lion in the air.

"The Lion is the winner," he announced in a small voice, much to Bhollo's delight. "You were an excellent little sister! As promised, you can keep the Lion. And because you cooperated so well, you also get a 25 paisa bonus."

Bhollo was beyond ecstatic as she clutched the Lion in her little palms and drifted into her dreams. Meanwhile, Koogh's stomach ached with cramps. The smells of the buffaloes in the barn added to his discomfort. He rubbed his stomach and his chest breaking into a cold sweat. He finally ran out of the barn and retched. After cleaning up, he lay limp on a haystack in the dark once again, sensing the various pains in his body.

There was silence all around him, but his mind was wandering. The partition had changed something inside him. He had felt like the Cow, responsible, and caring for his family's wellbeing. He wondered how that had come about.

A gnawing feeling was growing in the pit of his stomach. Their worries were far from over, and life, as it had been for them in their home in Tandlianwala, was behind them. Was it going to remain a sweet memory? Would he ever go back? He sighed.

"And is there any point in looking back now, Kooghey?" he said to himself aloud.

He stared in silence into the starry night, blinked, and shut his eyes.

– – –

CHAPTER 5: A HOME AWAY FROM HOME

1947 – 1953: Learning to live in Phagwara

The next few months after arriving in Punjab was a nomadic existence for most of the refugees that arrived in India. Koogh and his family too, moved from one temporary abode to the next. Jaikishen, despite several attempts, could not secure any form of income. As expected, their little kitty soon went dry. He had no choice but to land up at his father-in-law's house in Phagwara. Daulat Ram Mishra welcomed his daughter's family with open arms. And his home became theirs for the next few months.

Parsini, the local sweeper, cleaned the toilets every morning in the Mishra house. She was tall, broad, and middle-aged, with a perpetual smile plastered on her face. She wore colourful salwar kameezes, which were hand-me-downs of the ladies she worked for. She always tied her hair into a neat stiff bun, held together at the nape of her neck with pins. Her face had two distinct adornments on it – a red *bindi* set between her eyebrows and a gold nose stud.

"Namaste, Bibiji," said Parsini as she entered the Mishra residence, to an elderly lady walking down the lane.

The lady grumbled and hurried past with her nose covered, to avoid Parsini's excreta filled wicker basket.

"Why do you bother?" asked Koogh, who was playing marbles in the deodi.

"What do you mean, betaji?"

"People don't respond to you. So why do you bother to greet them?"

Parsini smiled. "I don't mind betaji. I like to be courteous."

"But it is such a wasted effort."

"No effort is ever a waste betaji. I am building my goodness points with God. I know he bothers."

"God doesn't bother either. If he did, he would not have made you a sweeper. He doesn't care about anyone, and if he did, he would not kill so many innocent people during the partition. He would not have taken away our home in Tandlianwala from us."

"Oh, betaji. I know the partition was horrible, and it saddens you to be here, and I can imagine how much you must miss home and your friends. I can't change what happened to you, but we all live our destinies laden with good, bad, and ugly experiences. Your family survived the partition, you have a roof over your head, and you have food in your belly."

Koogh nodded.

"Many others were not so lucky. Be thankful, betaji. And you will make new memories here, betaji."

Koogh shook his head.

"As for me, no work is bad in my eyes. It is the people who look down on others and create disparity. In God's eyes, we are all equal. And that is what I choose to believe. To be honest, I find it funny how people make way for me when I enter any space. I take pride in the work I do betaji because it feeds my family and me. And I am thankful for the generosity that all the homes show me on every occasion – it means treats, clothes, and money too for my family to enjoy. I am very indebted to the Mishras. So what if someone treats me poorly – that's not my *karma*. It's theirs. It's not my business to focus on how others are being. I focus on who I want to be. That is all that matters. Now, look how much time I've wasted yapping with you, boy!"

Koogh smiled as she rushed up the stairway to clean out the toilets.

...

One morning, Koogh was in the midst of a marble game with Bhollo, when Parsini stepped into the doorway. She huffed with excitement and asked him to call Jaikishen.

"Bhaisaab, there is an abandoned home in the Korian Mohalla, not so far away. I have locked it up for you. Would you like to go and see it now?" she said, breathing heavily.

Jaikishen agreed to go with her. Geeta asked Koogh to join him.

"But I'm playing a game, and I'm winning," sulked Koogh.

"That's okay. You can come back and play. Go with your father now."

"But ..."

"That's enough. Go!" screamed Geeta.

Koogh hated having to leave a game. He dragged his feet, walking behind Parsini and Jaikishen through the market way. They reached Korian Mohalla shortly. It was a small locality next to Bansawala Bazaar, situated at the centre of Phagwara. It had a lane of two, or three-level brick structures packed close to each other on both sides of it.

The house number under consideration, 16/2, had no nameplate on the outside. It had two sets of doors. The first was a netted double door opening outward, and the next was a wooden double door that opened inward. The inner door had a thick wrought iron chain at the upper end. Its last flat link had a slit, hooked onto a ring fixed on the door's frame.

A pompous fist-sized Godrej padlock glistened at them in the bright morning sun. Its stiff upturned position warded off entry from opportunists.

"A Muslim family's home, Bhaisaab," hissed Parsini, taking out the key from her cleavage. With discretion, she opened the padlock and pushed the wooden door open. "Welcome to your new home Bhaisaab!" she laughed out aloud.

Jaikishen and Koogh looked at her amused and then stepped inside, looking around. They found themselves in a 100 square feet deodi. At the left of the deodi sat a charpoy and cupboard, while to its immediate right was a staircase. Straight ahead was another door that led into a small roofless courtyard. Koogh stepped into it to get a clear view of the blue sky. At the courtyard's far-right were some empty wooden pegs while the immediate left was a tiny bathroom. And after this, on the far left was a tiny kitchen.

"There is no water source in the kitchen or the bathroom, Bhaisaab. You will have to fill water at the local well or the hand pump in the mohalla," added Parsini.

The house had signs of recent inhabitation. A brass bucket half-filled with water stood at the corner of the courtyard. Clothes dried stiff lay on a slumping clothesline strung across the courtyard. A faded hand napkin lay pasted on the floor. Cooking vessels lay unwashed in the kitchen with *masala* dried upon them. An army of ants seemed busy collecting their winter stash to the landing. A kitchen basket had some sprouting potatoes and a few shrivelled green chilies and to-matoes.

Beyond the courtyard was a living and dining area. On the

wall facing the entry was another door to the left and right of which were two built-in cupboards. The room had a single bed and two wooden armchairs. The walls were bare, and there was no electrical point. The living room walls and the rest of the house were white and seemed to have a recent paint coat. The 15-foot high ceiling had one solitary red brick in it.

"Allahditta," said Koogh pointing to the word written on it in Urdu.

"That's the name of the previous owner, betaji," said Parsini.

"Pitaji, why would he have written his name up there of all places?"

"He wanted to be out of reach, perhaps. Everyone has a reason for what they do Kooghey," smiled Jaikishen as he peeped into the next door.

The innermost room was a bedroom that had mud and clay flooring. It had one large bed, a lantern on a side-shelf, and an open Godrej cupboard. Clothes for a man, woman, and a little girl, hung loosely at the corners of upward-pointing hangers, onto fallen over stacks of clothes.

The staircase from the deodi had foot-high stone steps leading up to the first level and two toilets. A square hole in the floor looked down into the courtyard.

One side of the square hole was a narrow path that lay above the bathroom and kitchen, leading to an open space above the living room area. Two charpoys stood on their sides at the far end of the space. At the end was yet another brick-walled room set right above the lower bedroom. It was bare. A few *chattais, dhurries,* and *rajais* lay folded onto a charpoy in the corner.

Sight and sound travelled without any barriers in this

home, as all the homes in the lane had shared walls. Koogh smiled as he overheard the banter from neighbouring homes. He also saw some people cross over the short boundary walls from one terrace to the next with ease. Lack of privacy and safety were an accepted norm. *No wonder Allahditta left.*

"Pitaji, this house is bigger than our house in Tandlianwala. But I preferred that house. It had so much space for playing, and the fields, the canal, and the banyan tree. And my friends Bhollu, Vaid, Bhushan," said Koogh, his voice trailing off.

"Kooghey, there is goodness in every place and everyone if you are willing to open your eyes and look for it. Give it time, and this too will soon be home for you."

The resourceful Daulat Ram swung into action to get the house's papers put into Jaikishen's name. He then organised a clean-up and a *havan.*

"Why are we doing a havan, Pabbi?" To cleanse away any negative energies, Geeta had said in haste.

On the day of the havan, the family bathed and changed into fresh clothing. Koogh looked around at his family, sitting in prayer as the *pandit* chanted the mantras pouring melted ghee onto the burning sandalwood. They were all together like in Tandlianwala. Pitaji, Pabbi, Nanaji, Babaji, Bhaisaab, Bhabi, Soma, Bhollo, and Ghonni. He felt a warmth in his chest and then looked up at the red brick.

Krishna, can you make Allahditta find a house as we have found his? You could make him find our house and stay in it and use all the things left behind. But please make only Bhollu find my treasure box. The pandit put a tikka on his forehead and some flowers in his hand.

"Om swaha!" said the pandit, and they repeated in unison and offered the flowers at the feet of the deity.

"Geetaji, it is auspicious to start the kitchen with boiling some milk and cooking some sweet," he said.

Geeta started to get up, then thought again. "Sharda, please prepare some halva and set the milk for boiling, will you?" she called over her shoulder.

Her veiled, dutiful daughter-in-law Sharda rose without a moment's hesitation, "Yes, Mataji."

Geeta stretched her legs and smiled. *What a luxury to have a helping hand in the kitchen. Finally, my time is mine to own again.*

She started the new phase of her life by setting up her temple in the living room cupboard. She spread out a shiny cloth, and then on it, she placed her Krishna and Radha idols. The gota covered holy books got set on their left. And to their right, she placed a brass bell, prayer beads, cotton, *dhoop, Kumkum,* and pure ghee in a brass container. She offered the prasad from the havan to her beloved deity, lit a *diya*, and bowed her head to the prayer altar. When she finally looked up, Koogh saw a smile on her face. The whole family joined her with folded hands. There was no face in the room without tears in their eyes as they thanked the almighty for his grace.

. . .

And life was set into motion for the family. Geeta set up her kitchen with Sharda and Soma. According to Geeta, Soma had studied enough by completing her Prabhakar. She felt it best that she helped Sharda in the household chores and get ready for marriage. Brij and Sharda occupied the bedroom. Jaikishen chose to have his own space in the deodi - He wanted the convenience to leave for his morning walk to relieve himself with his cousins and friends in the open fields. He set up the charpoy and filled the cupboard with his knick-knacks, including ayurvedic medicines, stationery, books, and clothes. He also secured a job for himself at the local *mandi* at a meagre salary, much lesser than Geeta's expectations. She grumbled but decided to let him be. Depending on the weather, she and the children slept on charpoys in the living room or the terrace. Brij got a job at the Gorakhpur branch of Imperial Bank, and with a heavy heart, he bid farewell to the family and a pregnant Sharda. It was not right for him to take her along, Geeta had said.

Daulat Ram admitted the boys in Arya High School and Bhollo in the Government primary school. Koogh knew this meant there was no going back to Tandlianwala ever again.

. . .

Time flew, and things had settled into a routine for them, but Koogh could sense that something not so nice was brewing.

"How will we run the house on this money? Everything is so expensive," said Geeta. She shook her head as she looked at the money Jaikishen placed in her hands.

"Geeta, this is the best I can do. Brij will also send some money at the end of the month."

"And until then, how do I manage?"

"We will have to manage Geeta. I leave it to you."

"That is all that you can do, lift your hands and leave it to me. No respite for me!"

Frustration of a troubled life and penury since moving to Phagwara seeped into Geeta. She lost her patience and lived on edge at most times, losing her temper at disproportionate levels at the smallest of things. The children and Jaikishen often exchanged glances at her new emerging personality.

For Koogh, Phagwara brought with it adolescence. He ex-

JUNGEE

perienced change on several levels. A new home, a new school, and a new peer group of fifth graders to make his place within. And an awareness that his body was changing. At school, he befriended Rajkumar, Govind, and Mahinder. They were in the same class as him and lived in the same Mohalla too.

On *Holi*, the festival of colour, they promised Koogh a frolicking time. Koogh stuffed a sling bag with packets of purple, red, yellow, and green powder. He and his friends prowled the mohalla for any unsuspecting passers-by, threw colour on them, and hollered '*Holi Hai*.'

Kuggi, a boy of their age, and his friends played with *pichkaris* filled with coloured water from brass buckets. Each time Koogh and his friends went to throw colour on them, they squirted coloured water.

Koogh was unable to make contact with his coloured powder. He soon used up the powder in his hand, so he crouched to take out more colour from his bag. Kuggi picked up his bucket and overturned it onto Koogh. In all the excitement by accident, the bucket fell onto Koogh's head. His head spun with the impact, and he fell to the ground. Kuggi and his gang rolled with laughter.

"*Lalloo*, is that all you have?" sneered Kuggi.

Rage overtook Koogh. He instinctively grabbed a brass *gadvi* lying on the floor and hit Kuggi on his forehead. An instant gush of blood reddened his face. Kuggi ran home, shrieking for his mother.

"I'm not a Lalloo. You are. Now run home to your mother, you Lalloo," screamed Koogh after him, "Do you also want to try some brass?" said Koogh to the other boys, his aggression in full measure. They hurried with fright hither and thither, and Koogh collapsed, due to the loss of blood. His friends picked him up and rushed him to his house.

"Oh, my God! What has happened?" cried out Geeta, feeling faint at seeing the blood Koogh was losing.

His friends did a rough bandage with a soft *dupatta* and rushed him to the neighbourhood clinic with Jaikishen. Later that day, Kuggi's mother came to their home.

"Your son is a scoundrel in the making. How dare he hit my son? He has scarred him for life. Call him out now, so I can give him a tight slap," screamed Kuggi's mother, looking around to draw the neighbours' and eager onlookers' attention.

"Chachiji, Kuggi dropped the bucket on him, first," pitched Govind.

"Yes, Chachiji. And Kuggi laughed when he fell," added Rajkumar.

"Is that so?" said Geeta in a sarcastic tone.

"Yes, Chachiji, we speak the truth," and Mahinder.

"Nonsense! Don't concoct stories to cover up for that brat. Call him out. I will twist his ears and teach him some life lessons since you clearly can't," screamed the woman.

Geeta stalked up to the woman. "Now it's my turn to speak, and I can scream too! So watch your tongue. Look at what your son has done to my son. He has got a deep gash and has got stitches, and will need to miss school. Did I come to your doorstep, making a noise? No, I didn't. Because at a festival, children play and accidents happen. Please go home now," she said and slammed the door shut on her face.

Koogh looked at his friends through his sleepy eyes. They had stood by him. That evening when they came to check on him, he got them acquainted with his Avatar army. The racing games began once again, and their friendship grew, but so did their pranks. People came to meet Geeta to complain about

Koogh. Each time a fresh complaint came in, Geeta taunted him for the next few days. It got Koogh in check for a while, but then his urge to indulge in the fun bratty pranks with his friends would get the better of him yet again.

Although Koogh did well in Urdu and Punjabi at school, English and Hindi left him feeling inept. Both languages became his biggest challenge, and as the term progressed and studies intensified, his grades slipped. He was trying, but he could not keep up. He began to feel the pressure of performance due to Geeta's non-stop badgering. Jaikishen, in comparison, continued to have a mild-manner.

"So how is school shaping up? What sports do you play in school?"

"It's fine, Pitaji," said Koogh edgily, "I have enrolled in hockey and football training, after school."

"That's good – if you are consistent, you can join the school team someday. And how are your studies?"

"They teach a majority of the subjects in Urdu Pitaji, so I am managing to catch up with most of them."

"You call this managing?" taunted Geeta throwing his report to the floor in front of Jaikishen. "We are wasting our money by sending this *nikhattu* to school. He is becoming nothing but a rogue in the mohalla. Every day I receive so many complaints about him! I'm sick of defending him and he is so shameless that even punishment doesn't deter him."

Koogh breathed heavily, knowing this would not go down well.

"Stop shouting, Geeta!" said Jaikishen, picking up the report and scanning through it. "He is still a child, and he has been through a lot and joined in the middle of the school term. He is trying to cope. Give him time. It is only Hindi and English that are weak. We should get him a tutor."

"Oh my God!" she exclaimed, beating her forehead, "Of course we have to spend on *laat-saahib's* tuitions too."

"Pabbi, a friend of mine called Santosh, lives next to Paiyaji's house. She could teach him. She is a topper in studies. I could ask her help," pitched in Soma.

The very next morning, Soma and Koogh went to meet Santosh.

. . .

"I'll be happy to help, but I have a few conditions," said Santosh plaiting her hair with a red ribbon. "I do not want to waste my time if he is not serious, as I have my college studies too. He has to be attentive, do all the work I assign him, and no missing class."

"Yes, of course. What about your fees?"

"Nothing, Soma."

"But, you must take some *Guru Dakshina* for sharing your knowledge," said Soma.

"No. It doesn't matter to me, Soma. You can give me whatever you wish," she said and smiled at Koogh, who was awkwardly looking at her. "Can you speak?"

"Yes, of course, I can," he smiled, in his adolescent cracked voice.

Santosh smiled at her new student. Koogh was pleased as his tutor proved to be knowledgeable, and she had the patience to teach him the complexities of both the languages. With each class, his understanding improved and his respect for her grew.

. . .

One hot morning Koogh opened his eyes to Brij, peering down at him with a smile on his face.

"Am I dreaming?"

"No. I quit my job. I am back for good!"

"I missed you, Bhaisaab," said Koogh hugging his older brother.

Brij's return added to Geeta's woes. Her tongue acquired a razor-like sharpness. And her irritability took on a new measure, often landing choice insults and angry rhetoric on unsuspecting receivers, leaving them bewildered. A few days after Brij's return, she was on her way to the terrace to retire for the night, when he approached her.

"Pabbi."

Geeta ignored his call and brushed past Koogh, who was descending the stairs.

"Pabbi, I'm saying something, and you are walking away," Brij said, following her.

Geeta held her hand to her head, frustrated, "Can I get some rest, please?"

"No, Pabbi, I want to sort this with you."

She continued to climb the steps ignoring him. On reaching the terrace she made her way to her charpoy. *Sharda, is the only relief in my life, has thankfully made my bed.*

Bhollo and Soma were already lying on their respective charpoys, mid-slumber. Sensing a tense atmosphere, Koogh too hurried up to the terrace and lay down on his charpoy. Geeta was aware of Brij expectantly waiting as she gazed up at the starry, moonless sky. Tears pricked her eyes.

"I am feeling more tired lately," she said wistfully, "Life is a living hell. Work all day and scrounge to put a decent meal on the table. Only I know how I am managing this house. You cannot understand until you become a family man and have mouths to feed. Your father gives me Rs.50 in my hand every month. And you too have quit your job and come home. Tell me, how am I to manage? Money gets depleted so fast. Should I sell my jewellery too? Krishna, give me a solution because I don't see the light at the end of this tunnel, Brij. Please leave me alone," she wept.

"But Bhaisaab will get a job soon, Pabbi, and all will be well. Krishna will hear your prayers soon," said Koogh sitting up.

She folded her hands in his direction. "You of all people don't tell me what I need to do. And stop eavesdropping on other's conversations. Worry about your grades. If you want to ease my misery, stay out of trouble so that people stop coming to my doorstep about your misdoings. *Nikhattu*!"

"Pabbi, I was just ..."

"You were what?" she snapped at him, mid-sentence, "Are you wiser than me? Do you think I don't know how to handle my problems?" she screamed, pushing herself up on her elbows, making Soma and Bhollo wake up too.

"No, I ..."
"Then mind your business and don't advise unless someone solicits it."

She covered her face with her sheet, indicating that the conversation with Brij was over. Brij grimaced and shook his head before leaving the terrace. It was Koogh's turn to stare at the stars with vacant eyes, wondering at his mother's outburst. Yet again, she had belittled him.

Whatever I say is not good enough. Why does my mother hate me so much? Why is it that she yells only at me? I also spoke out of turn. I am so stupid. I should not speak at all. I don't know how to say the right thing anymore, with her. That is why she calls me a nikhattu.

He curled into a ball with his head covered, to cut out the sounds of frustration and judgment. He shut his eyes and entered into his dream world. He was racing with his army down the alleyways of Korian Mohalla with the Lion in the lead. The Peacock was flying above the homes, trying to keep pace. And the Cow lumbered along with the bells in his neck tinkling to a loud rhythm that grew fainter. They ran ahead and away from him, past the markets and into the fields and then flew into the sky, to the moon. He ran hard, trying to catch up with them, and then took flight from a hillock. All of a sudden, he fell into a bottomless pit screaming for help. He awoke breathless, as he felt someone shaking him. It was Bhollo.

"What happened, Paaji?"

"Nothing."

"Why did you scream? Did you have a bad dream?"

He turned away and shut his eyes.

. . .

Koogh was right, as the next month brought laughter back into the family. Brij got a job with the Bata Shoe Company and Sharda, and he became proud parents of a gurgling boy. They named the child Ravi and nick-named him Kuku. He became the centre of everybody's attention, and everyone got a new title. Jaikishen and Geeta became BABAJI and DADIMA. Koogh and Ghonni became CHACHAJI, while Soma and Bhollo became BUA. The whole family's mood got elevated with Kuku's arrival, and as he grew, everything he did was a reason to celebrate. Last but not least, Brij received his first salary.

Unfortunately for Koogh, Geeta's rebuking continued. His languages improved thanks to Santosh, but other subjects fell to borderline. To add to Geeta's anxiety, he started spending more time out of the house. And when he was home, he behaved like a recluse, staring at nothing, in particular, always sitting at his favourite spot at the far end of the terrace. Geeta threatened to pull him out of school due to his behaviour. "Why are you fooling yourself?" asked Soma looking at her brother with concern.

"What?"

"I said, you can fool others, but you can't fool yourself."

"I'm not fooling anybody or myself. I'm studying. Leave me alone."

"If you were studying as much as you pretend, your grades ought to be better. Santosh says you missed class again this week."

"I had to run some errands for Paiyaji. I never miss her class. I like studying with her. I'm trying. Should I stop trying also?"

"No. You should never stop trying, but you should be true to yourself when you are trying. There is nothing better than being true to yourself. You are so often lost in thought while the pages of your book flip away. What do you keep thinking?"

"Nothing. I was taking a break. I'm tired of all the questioning and criticism," said Koogh in a sarcastic tone, shaking his head.

"She is your mother, Koogh. Whatever she may say, she loves you."

"Rubbish. Please leave me alone. I don't wish to have this conversation."

"Well, someone has to, and since I am the only one here on

the terrace, I am choosing to have it. Our parents have their challenges, Koogh, and we have no right to judge them. Besides, what are you doing to help improve things? Where is your drive to make a positive change? On the contrary, you are using your books as an excuse to stay away from her and everyone else. You sit here for hours indulging in self-pity. I see you are receding into a shell. How is any of this helping you?"

"Are you done? If yes, leave me alone," he snapped at her, seething with anger. He ran his fingers through his hair, feeling incensed.

Soma stepped back, startled, and left the terrace with tears in her eyes.

'Damn! She is so right,' said Koogh leaving the terrace and slamming the house door to walk into the dusky evening to regroup with his friends.

. . .

The whole family broke into animated excitement about Geeta's younger brother, Chakkarpani's wedding. Daulat Ram chose Koogh to distribute the cards.

"*Puttar*, a doleful look doesn't suit a handsome face. Smile."

Koogh forced a small smile.

"That's better. And now I want you to go to the printer at the corner of the market. Pick up the wedding cards and distribute a card to each family on this list by evening."

"Consider it done, Paiyaji."

"And don't forget to smile as you do so. You are a *ladkawala* after all," said Daulat Ram, slapping his grandson's bony back.

PRIYA SHARMA SHAIKH

"And if I was from the *ladkiwala,* would I still be smiling?" asked Koogh.

"Why do you young people ask so many questions?" he said with folded hands, "Please spare me the horror of a socio-philosophical debate!"

Koogh got up to leave.

"And of course you would be smiling, because marriages are a celebration of happiness and love whether you are a ladka or a ladki," called out Daulat Ram behind him.

Koogh turned and smiled.

"Now that's the smile I was looking for," laughed Daulat Ram.

At the printer's shop, Koogh opened the bundle placed in front of him and took out a wedding card to view it. It was a simple white card that started with an OM at the top centre and all the information about the ceremonies written in red letters below it.

He looked at his list and rewrote it, dividing the names by location. He then repacked the bundle into smaller bundles for each location and set upon his task. He ticked each name on Daulat Ram's list and handed it to him by the evening, as promised.

"I'm impressed with your organisation and sense of responsibility, son! More work for you tomorrow!"

. . .

Chakkar's wedding was in May's sweltering heat in Hoshiarpur, and the baaratis set out for the big day. Koogh sat on the bus's last seats with his favourite cousins, Narender, Mahender, and Nirmal. Ahead of them, sitting and standing, were a hoard of over-dressed women, men, and children. Koogh rec-

JUNGEE

ognised most of them but preferred to keep to himself. Most of them were extended family. By the time they completed the choppy journey, all their readiness had become an absolute mess.

Chakkar, a rugged man of average looks and a hearing condition, dressed in a rich-looking sherwani, a heavy gold necklace, and a large golden turban, looked like a prince. He sat atop his decorated and well-groomed *ghodi.* In front of him sat his *sarwala,* a 5-year old boy called Gogii, dressed like a mini version of Chakkar.

"Gogii is so uncomfortable with the excessive baubles," said Koogh shaking his head.

"He is itching and crying and trying to get off the horse all simultaneously," said Narender looking amused.

"Mamaji, what is happening to your sarwala?" laughed Mahender.

"Laugh on you rogues! I'm going mental dealing with this brat. Gogii! My little love, I promise to give you extra goodies. Please be a good boy," pleaded Chakkar.

The opulence of Chakkar's wedding amazed Koogh. He had never experienced anything like it. After a sumptuous dinner, the girl's family sang and danced to foot-tapping mildly abrasive verses, teasing the groom and his family.

"They are hilarious. I haven't laughed so much ever. Our family's expressions have rapidly changed from smiles to scowls," laughed Narender.

"If this is how the girls' side will humour our family, there is no way I'm getting married. Pabbi will give them red hot hell!" grimaced Koogh.

"You won't have a choice, brother. *Masiji* is sure to get you

PRIYA SHARMA SHAIKH

married. Yaar, this kulfi is delicious," said Narender licking the melting treat off his fingers.

"Marriage for me is a non-starter," shrugged Koogh.

"Wow! How did that assumption make a place in your head?"

"Because she hates me."

"Who?"

"Pabbi."

"That's direct. But what have you done for Masiji to hate you?"

"I don't know yaar. Everything about me irritates Pabbi - My grades, speaking, clothes, hair, and friends. Everything. She spares no instance in insulting me. Thanks to her, my self-confidence is big zero," smirked Koogh making a zero with his finger and thumb.

"And why do you think she does that?"

"Because I am stupid. A nikhattu. These are her words! I'm the only one she shouts at," he said with a lump in his throat and abruptly left the dining area, dropping the curtain on the subject.

. . .

Narender entered the large room, arranged with gaddas's for the groom's family. Koogh was sitting at the window looking down at the wedding festivities.

After some silence Narender said, "Is it true that Masiji doesn't shout at anybody else?"

Koogh remained silent. He could see Geeta sitting alone in the crowd of people. For some strange reason, he felt terrible that she was alone.

"She does get upset with others, but nothing compared to me. That's my fortunate privilege," said Koogh.

"My God, brother, and what makes you believe that?"

"Because she does ... she doesn't have anybody else to lash out at," Koogh said, and paused to blink his eyes, "About her frustrations."

He felt a lump in his throat. He took a deep breath. "An epiphany is happening, Narender. Bhaisaab is much older and earning and is usually away from the house. Pitaji is discrete, and he has learnt how to stay out of troubles way. Soma and Bhabi are as dutiful as can be, and Bhollo and Ghonni are too little. I'm the only one she has to take out her frustrations on."

"What do you think makes her feel frustrated?"

"I guess the tough life she has led since she got married. And then the unsettlement and frugalness after partition. Look at the richness of this wedding. She is the daughter of Daulat Ram Mishra, a man of abundance, and our family condition is a mere apology!" After a pause, Koogh said, "And I haven't been much help either with my aloofness, rebellious behaviour and slipping grades. It is suddenly so clear."

Koogh sighed deeply. "It is not me; it is her destiny that makes her angry. And she doesn't know any better way to release her soured emotions," sighed Koogh wistfully.

He turned to look down at Geeta again. She was still sitting alone among the women. She appeared smaller than ever before, behind the silence of her dark glasses. His heart went out to her. *I want her to know that I understand her yelling and her complicated ways. And that from this day on, I will try my best to be a better son. It is time I become responsible.*

. . .

The next morning, Koogh awoke later than usual, to an outburst of hysterical jeering. Still half asleep, he rushed out to see the commotion and stumbled over a basket of mangos. The bride's father had arranged for huge baskets, filled with dozens of the 'king of fruit.' A competition was underway to see who could eat the maximum! The baaratis went berserk, eating one mango after another. Koogh had never seen such a lavish spread of the fruit. He was in shock to see such an odd spectacle of the courtyard as a yellow riot! Juice, skins, and seeds were everywhere. Faces, clothes, and hands of every one were full of yellow smears.

"Nice to see you smiling. The pandit won-he ate 35 mangos!" laughed Narender.

Koogh smiled and picked up a few mangos and pulled away from the crowd. He went from room to room, looking for Geeta. He found her listening in on a conversation with some ladies. He walked up to her and dropped the mangos in her lap, smiled, and left the room. He turned to see her looking at the fruit and then at him before merging into the yellowness.

There was something different in the way he looked at me. Geeta picked up a mango and smiled.

. . .

Four significant events happened in the family after Chakkar's wedding - Brij joined Brooke Bond, the tea company, as their Regional Sales Manager, and he moved with Sharda and Kuku, to Abhor. The family income came down yet again. Second, Brij and Sharda became parents to a daughter, Kusum, nick-named Pappi. Third, Soma got married in a humble wedding ceremony to Ram Lubhaya and moved to Nawan Shahar. With Sharda and Soma gone, the housework became Geeta's responsibility again. And fourth, Koogh completed his *matriculation* exams.

JUNGEE

On the way home, he wondered about what he had over-heard Pabbi grumbling to Pitaji, that morning. It was challen-ging to make ends meet with the money he got home. Jaiki-shen had looked down and sighed.

"How was your exam? And what plans?" said Santosh look-ing fondly at her student. He had grown so much. The little brat in shorts was now a handsome teenager with a bris-tly moustache and a shy demeanour. His squeaky voice had cracked too. And she now needed to tilt her head back to look up at him.

"It was okay, but I don't know what to do next."

"Then who will know? You are not a child anymore. You must have thought of something."

"I need to start working, but I have no idea what to do or where to start," said Koogh shifting uneasily. "I could be a *Prabhakar Ratan*, and then do a masters in English, like my Vimal Mamaji."

"Do you know that means studying very advanced Hindi and English studies?"

"Yes, I could try..." he said, his voice trailing off, feeling unsure.

"Do something that excites you. Let me know if you need help figuring things out."

. . .

Koogh asked around for a job among family and friends. He had no experience, or he was young, or there was no work for someone like him; is what he got as responses. For Koogh, the rejection reaffirmed his feeling of him not being good enough. The nikhattu!

He helped with odd jobs around the house and ate and met his friends and sketched. But mostly all he did was while his time away. Three months went by, and Geeta's taunts of frustration grew.

"You are not looking hard enough. Such a grown-up man and so lazy and shameless. We wasted money on your studies when all you want to do is eat free food."

"Pabbi, I tried …

"I don't see you putting in effort. You never have. That is why your grades suffered."

"Pabbi, my grades are poor only in English. Even Hindi has improved."

"Uff! Just stop talking. You are going to end up being nothing more than a *rickshawala*. Did you ask Soma's husband for a job?"

I don't want to work with Jijaji. Koogh shook his head and quietly walked away. Geeta had plenty of insults where that came from, and she didn't spare any opportunity to heap them on Koogh.

One hot morning, after hearing an earful from her, he went to the cowshed to get milk, as he did every day. He felt disturbed but strangely numb. He seemed to have learnt the knack of putting on a garb to hide his inner turmoil, which felt insurmountable. It made him feel smaller each day. He looked at the people at the cowshed while he waited in line. Most of them were older, holding their canisters, standing quietly, with their thoughts locked in their minds. Were they also portraying an outward calm, like he was? Was everything fine with anyone? Perhaps, not.

A familiar face appeared in the distance. Pappu, a friend from the neighbourhood, older by a few years, came up to

Koogh and hugged him.

Koogh snapped out of his dismal thoughts. "How are you?"
"I'm fine. So, what are you up to?"

"I am waiting to buy a litre of milk, with no real plan about what I should do for the rest of the day or the day after."

"Aren't you joining college?"

"No yaar. My family needs," Koogh paused, looking awkward, "I'm looking for a job Pappu."

"Hmm, I understand," nodded Pappu. Then as an afterthought, he added, "You've completed matriculation with science subjects, haven't you?"

"Yes."

"You just got lucky. There is a vacancy for a scientific assistant at Jagjit Starch Mills. Would you like to apply?"

"Yes, anything will do."

"Go and meet them," said Pappu putting his hand on Koogh's shoulder, "I will tell them to expect you. Go today itself."

Koogh thanked him and rushed home to share the news with Geeta. She was praying. He changed into a fresh set of clothes and went to Jagjit Starch Mills, a 15-minute walk from their home.

. . .

It was his first job interview, and he didn't know what to do or expect, so he did not feel nervous. The scientist-in-charge was Mr. Chatterjee. He was a thin, bird-like man with curly oiled hair. He had an inaudible whisper for a voice, which made it frustrating to talk to him. Koogh needed to lean forward to hear his questions and responded to him in an overly

PRIYA SHARMA SHAIKH

loud voice. Within half an hour of whispered exchanges and yelling, he landed the job at Rs.45 per month. He was to report to work the same evening for the night shift – from 6 pm to midnight. Chatterjee's brief to him was simple.

"You are to create a report of the density of crushed corn at various production stages until it becomes starch powder. You can leave the readings on my table to review them when I come into work in the morning. Please keep in mind that the precision of the readings is critical. A simple error can impact the finished product."

"Don't worry, Sir, I will take care," said Koogh, standing up tall.

...

Koogh joined work the same evening. He soon figured the task at hand. He was precise and diligently wrote the readings in neat handwriting at the top of every hour. Having so much time to spare, he leafed through the stack of old magazines and newspapers lying around Chatterjee's office, with the whirring girders' symphony as background score.

Koogh's adolescent days suddenly seemed to have a structure starting with class, lunch, study with Santosh, an early dinner, being at the mill, and turning into bed past midnight. At the end of the month, he had good reason to smile. The fruit of his diligence and precision became a reality when Chatterjee placed forty-five rupees in his hand and patted him on the back. *My first salary!* He couldn't stop smiling as he rushed home and put the money in Geeta's hand.

She teared up and looked at him, "God bless you with much more!" and then gathering herself, she said in a terse tone, "I'm warning you; stay put in your job. Don't be irresponsible, like your father." And then, as an afterthought, she put Rs. 5 back in his hand, "Don't waste it."

He nodded and exited the house without a word. He was happy that he could ease her life, even if mildly so. He felt a skip in his step after a long time and landed up at the neighbourhood stenography class. He used some of the money to enrol himself for a course in shorthand and typing, and then met Santosh and committed to studying with her for the Prabhakar exam.

Such a child! Santosh shook her head as Koogh smiled gleefully and slipped away.

...

Chatterjee was happy with Koogh and encouraged his thirst for learning. He gave him more magazines and books to read. The more you read, the more will your horizon widened, he had whispered. His boss was so right! The magazines showcased the phenomenal progress of the world. It felt so much bigger than the little world to which he belonged. He felt small, and the rest of the world seemed like a faraway dream.

Three months into the routine, Koogh grew restless. He knew something was not right. He was at 70 words per minute in his typing class, and he wasn't motivated to get any better. English seemed more arduous than he imagined and his work at the mill too did nothing to stimulate him. The continuous sound of the girders made him feel all the more dismal. He felt not unlike a wildflower - alive in the sunshine, but of little real use. The mill started closing in on him. He started feeling stuck. Like he was in an abyss.

One evening after capturing the Bomimetre readings, he sat with a vacant look in his eyes, at the magazines in front of him. The restlessness engulfed him. It felt like his heart was racing as if warning him about something. *A flutter, was it?* He got up to drink some water from the earthen pot, stretched, and sat down again. He took a deep breath and closed his eye-

PRIYA SHARMA SHAIKH

s. His mind suddenly got flooded with the Lion's image roaring, running towards the horizon as if chasing something. And then, all of a sudden, he made an abrupt stop and turned to look back at Koogh, with his piercing ochre yellow eyes.

Koogh's eyes opened with a start. And there he was! The Lion, in all his grandeur, walking down the narrow pathway of the mill. A heavenly halo surrounded him that made Koogh gasp and blink hard. He could not believe his eyes. And then he smiled. He realised he felt no fear.

"Hello, Lion. I'm happy to see you."

The Lion stared at him.

"Where are the others?" searching beyond the Lion.

The Lion was alone, and he stood still staring at him.

"Do you want to race? You and me?" he urged.

But all that the Lion did was stare. And then he roared and shook his head, making his mane bounce around him. Koogh stepped back, alarmed. And then, breathing heavily, he took small steps towards the Lion. As he got close, the Lion turned and padded away. Koogh sped up. And the Lion started running. Koogh laughed and chased him around the mill to the whirring girders' rhythm calling out his name. "LION! LION!" They ran to the front gate, where finally the Lion stopped. He turned to look at Koogh once more and roared. Koogh got startled and stopped. And then, just as he had appeared, he turned and disappeared into the night.

Koogh was breathless when he reached the gate, but there was no sign of the Lion. All he could see was misty shadows of the only naked street light. There was an eerie silence about the night as crickets and owls did their business, and a few dogs howled in the distance. He suddenly became aware of the loud sound of the whirring girders. He turned around and walked back into the factory.

What just happened? Where did he go? Did I imagine it all?

He collated his papers and set them neatly on Chatterjee's table under the paperweight. He glanced around at the dreary environment around him. The flutter returned once again. He sat down heavily, feeling a sudden emptiness and sadness engulf him. The Lion had appeared as a brief moment of excitement. A vision of something familiar and yet, unknown. He was back in his dull world with a thud. He was floating like a speck of dust, into nothingness. Into the abyss. His flutter grew. *Could I dare to desire a piece of the world beyond this?*

"Yes, I dare! Pabbi is not right, and I know I can make something of my life. I am not a nikhattu, Pabbi! I want to show you that I can, and I will," he said aloud. "But what will I do? And how? There are no easy answers," he sighed and shook his head, and began to walk into the labyrinth of a feeling-small storyline. *Stop this dreaming. This life is fine too. There is no need to be adventurous. Who am I, to desire such a radical change, and imagine a magnificent life for myself?*

A small voice beyond him said, "*Who are you not to dare?*" He looked up startled and searched for who had spoken. And then Geeta's voice echoed, "I'm warning you to stay put in your job. Don't be irresponsible like your father ..." He shut his ears and his eyes.

...

Despite the house being full of laughter and chattering, Koogh's mind remained clouded with the questions from the night before. He loved jokes and laughter, but he felt a strange restlessness within himself. He felt alone and stared into nothing in particular. *I'm sure nobody will notice if I left.* He discreetly slipped out to the terrace.

It was a chilly morning. He breathed in the crisp air deeply and scanned the dwellings in his grandfather's neighbourhood. So many beings like him with their thoughts, voices, and actions. All living the stories they were born into and stuck within their set paradigms, living the lies in their laughter, love, sadness, fear, anger, conquest, anxiety, and surprise. Living the script that people had written for them—wilfully deserting their dreams—being a shadow of their true selves—playing their parts, only to fit in—to belong to someone—and being unable to voice what they felt. Unable to change. Unable to truly live.

The chatter and laughter in the house below were in full swing when he heard Daulat Ram call out his name. He slid out of sight. He wanted to be alone. Anger seethed—he was angry with himself. *I want my life to change, but I don't know how and what to do. Why don't I get any answers? Must I let my life remain as is?*

He shook his head and looked up at the sky, feeling infuriated. But all he heard was twittering sparrows and the vegetable seller's call in the lane below. And the laughter. Tears pricked his eyes. He blinked and swallowed hard, to push them back, and breathed heavily. As his breath settled, he started humming his favourite ode from the feature film *Baiju Baawra – O Duniya ke rakhwale sun dard bhare mere naale (O, caretaker of the universe, listen to my pleas of grief)*. He started singing it. Softly at first. And then, as if his chest couldn't contain his pain, he sang louder and louder. He lifted his voice to the heavens, imploring the skies.

The neighbourhood stood still as the magic unfolded. The banter in the courtyard below stopped as they exchanged glances of amazement. People peeped out of windows and came up to terraces, standing agog at the depth and perfection of his melody, silently mouthing the grievous words along with him. The pain in Koogh's voice triggered many a tear to roll into streams of saline water. Koogh was in a trance, unaware of his audience, as he conversed with the almighty with wrath and desire like never before.

Daulat Ram stopped the others from rushing to him and came to the terrace alone. He watched his grandson silently until the song was complete. Just as Koogh caught his breath after the exhilarating crescendo, Daulat Ram appeared from the shadows.

"Paiyaji," said Koogh, still shaking with emotion.

Daulat Ram gave him a long embrace. "What a soulful singer you are. So much emotion that I have tears, and so does your audience. See!"

Koogh looked around him self-consciously and immediately sat on his haunches.
"Why are you hiding?"

"I'm embarrassed. I don't know what got into me. I couldn't stop myself."

"But it was amazing. Where did you learn to sing so well?"

"I like the song, so I sing it. I learnt it while listening to the radio."

"Hmm. But why is a young boy like you singing such a sad song?"

"I like the tune and the lyrics."

"Hmm. What do you like about the lyrics?"

"They are a prayer in the form of a song. It's beautiful."

Daulat Ram looked gently into Koogh's eyes.

"What is the matter, my Kooghey? Is something bothering you?"

"No, nothing," gulped Koogh and looked away.

"Maybe you don't want to share with an old man. But remember that woe kept within can devour your energy and weaken your being. You look so unhappy. Whatever is tying you down is nothing but a demon. Slay it with all your strength and bring change."

"That is the problem, Paiyaji. I don't know how to bring change."

"Keep thinking and searching. The answers will come since you are so eager to find them. Hopefully, sooner than later!"

Koogh pushed his hair back and breathed deeply. What could he say to his grandfather about his dilemma? If Geeta got wind that he wanted to quit, she would spit fire.

"All will be well, son, don't worry."

"Yes, Paiyaji."

"And if you spot an opportunity that has the potential to change things for you, seize it with both hands. However difficult and unreachable it may seem, you must gather the courage to take the risk and set yourself free from your self-created shackles. There is no limit to your potential son. You will know in your gut that it is what you want and then put all your energy to go after it," said Daulat Ram, jabbing Koogh's ribs.

"But what if I make a wrong decision?"

"No decision is wrong. Because when you make a decision, it has consequences. Because when you decide you make a choice, and your life is the consequence of all your choices, and some destiny too. Therefore, consider your options with a calm mind, trust yourself to evaluate them well, and choose what you think is best suited for you. At that moment, whatever you decide, will be right. Some choices will be good in the long run, and some not. You must make choices, nevertheless, again and again. Don't worry too much about the bad ones – instead, become wiser by learning from them."

"But what if I fail?"

"Are you better at playing marbles than most of your friends?"

"What? Yes, I am."

"And I'm sure you didn't get to be as good the first time you played."

Koogh nodded and smiled.

"As long as there is a good intention, you cannot fail. And if you do fail, then you can always try again. Be patient with yourself, son, and you will learn to win."

"I feel good talking to you, Paiyaji," said Koogh.

"As do I. You're special, and you will do great things some-day. Just keep believing in yourself and don't resist life's change while it happens. And, use your free time in the mill to exercise and get some muscles. You never know how it will come in use. Come down to be with the others, when you feel up to it."

...

On the first Saturday morning of January 1953, Koogh was all set to go for his typing class. Narender, who was visiting from Delhi, urged him to go with him to the films. The chance at some entertainment felt great. He hesitated and then agreed to bunk class. The film was *Do Bigha Zameen with* the storyline of an impoverished rickshawala named Shambhu Mahato. The film saddened Koogh. As he walked into the street, he bumped into someone and stumbled. He mumbled an apology and looked up to see a familiar face.

"Ajay! What are you doing in Phagwara? Didn't you move to

Jalandhar?"

"Yes, I did. My parents have some work here, so I tagged along. I miss this place. But, Jalandhar is nice too. So, no complaints. So what is new and exciting in your life?"

"I am working at Jagjit Starch Mill, close to our home."

"Oh! So, that means no college. It's good you're earning."

"Yes, but it's okay. I'm preparing for Prabhakar too. I plan to do my Masters in English."

"I didn't know you liked languages."

"I don't actually. So to speak my truth, I'm confused and don't know what to do. All is well, and yet it's not. I must sound silly, right?"

"I understand. I felt like that too. How do you feel about joining the Army? There is a recruitment camp in Jalandhar Cantt until next week."

Koogh blinked. "Army?"

"It's a government job. But of course, you'll have to leave home."

"Are you applying?"

"I did, but I got rejected," Ajay scowled, "But you may have better luck."

The rest of the way home, Narendar's discussion about Balraj Sahni's performance fell on deaf ears. By the time they got home, Koogh was sure he wanted to try his luck. His interactions with Geeta were to a bare minimum lately. But he felt life had brought him to an important cornerstone. He had to share his excitement with her. Nobody was in the courtyard or the living room.

Narender held his arm. "Don't rock the boat, brother."

"The boat is finally emerging from a storm, brother. I've done all the thinking I could. It's time to make a choice now. And I'm ready to face the consequences that come with it. Thank you. I'd never have known of the camp if I hadn't gone with you for the film," said Koogh and hugged his cousin.

Narender was not wrong. Geeta gave an unassuming impression to most people. A modern woman, they'd say. And she looked the part with her chic dark glasses and a lean figure in a well-draped starched sari. Some called her 'Classy' as she wore her hair in a neat bun at the small of her neck and adorned herself with simple gold earrings and bangles, and a thin tulsi-bead necklace. But in reality, Narender knew that his aunt was the undisputed matriarch that ran her home with a firm hand that nobody dared to challenge. She was illiterate, but she was clear about the boundaries of her world. Prayer twice a day was the only thing that softened her otherwise stern demeanour. She often got discussed in family circles, in hushed tones. He sighed and shook his head as Koogh raced up the stairs.

My Geeta Masiji's strong opinions are a harsh reality. I pray she understands him. But Koogh was on a different level of beingness. He felt a pervasive calm as his purpose was finally revealing, just like his Paiyaji had said, and Koogh was ready to claim it.

Deciding to go for the camp was Koogh's first decision.

He took the steps two at a time, his excitement rising with every step. Geeta was sitting on a charpoy at the far end of the terrace dressed in a purple and white sari. Sharda sat opposite her on a *mooda*. Geeta was scraping a basket of carrots, while Sharda grated them into tiny flakes in a large brass colander.

Koogh ducked under the clothesline and dodged the ceramic pickle jars holding down two white sheets. On them were slices of beetroot, turnip, cauliflower, and carrots; kept to dry to make the winter batch of pickle and *Kanji*.

Geeta had a straight face. Koogh's enthusiasm ebbed, and he felt uneasy, so he held back from sharing his news. He noted that he was sweating despite the winter chill.

"Bhabi, are we having *gajar-ka-halva* for dinner?" asked Koogh and grabbed a carrot from the basket and crunched into it, savouring its sweet juice.

Geeta muttered something under her breath and continued to peel the carrots.

"Your sweet tooth has not changed with age, I see. You are still a child at heart!"

Sharda was as demure as ever. After motherhood, she glowed all the more. Her beauty owed much to her pleasant disposition. Sharda hadn't studied much, but she believed in moving with the times. She lived to serve and make others happy and had adopted Geeta's regimen of veiling her face in front of the male elders. Koogh teased her about it when Geeta wasn't around. He was her go-to person for taking care of Kuku, six, and Pappi, who was still a toddler. Koogh loved the children dearly and felt happy when Pappi called him 'Cha-chaji' in her baby voice. She and Brij were visiting for a few weeks from Abhor along with the children.

"You know I love sweets, Bhabi," he smiled and sat down on the charpoy's edge, pulling his knees to his chest, as if hugging his news to himself.

"Did you go for your typing class?" snapped Geeta suddenly.

"Er... no Pabbi."

"Then where have you been all morning?"

Koogh looked down and sat up straight. "Narender dragged

me for a film."

Geeta shook her head with disgust. "And you didn't think you ought to have taken my permission? Just because you have started earning, you feel you can make decisions on your own, huh? We don't have money to spare, and you go and splurge on a film?"

"Narender paid for my ticket."

"And couldn't you say no, instead of choosing to miss class?"

"I'm sorry, Pabbi."

"Keep saying sorry all your life."

"I won't do it again, Pabbi. I can't anyway, as I never have any money."

"Are you taunting me, boy? How dare you talk to me about your money! Do you even know what all we have been through to bring you up? I should have stopped sending you to school, but I listened to your father. All that investment has been an absolute waste as you have no great future. And you have an attitude too. How dare you!"

"No, Pabbi, you have got me wrong. I don't need any money. I was just stating that I didn't spend any of our money."

"Enough! Don't you dare compromise your classes or your job in the future. Is that clear?"

He nodded and looked down. He twiddled with the carrot stump in his hands. His face clouded as the familiar feeling of self-doubt crept in. Feeling riled, he looked a—end the terrace, thinking about how to broach the camp's subject with her. But no ideas were forthcoming. His mind twisted into the self-limiting labyrinth, and he shook his head.

There is no point in these dreams. I should continue my job at

PRIYA SHARMA SHAIKH

the Mill and somehow do Prabhakar and get a better job. Then marriage, children, work hard all my life, get cursed despite all that I do, and then one fine day die—end of my life story. And here I go all over again! Urgh!'

He got up abruptly and looked at the far end of the terrace. Was that the Lion? It was him again. He was standing majestically on the wall. He was staring at Koogh with an expression of calm. Koogh moved towards him, but the Lion stepped down and disappeared down the stairs. He felt restless and paced the terrace. Several trails of sweat made hasty plunges down his back. His heart pounded.

If it was my destiny to stay here at the Mill, why did Ajay act as a messenger? Paiyaji had said I should do something if I want a change. I'd be fooling myself and be living a lie if I continue to exist as is. Meeting Ajay is a sign of change. It is time for me to go within and listen to my soul for answers. What do I want to do? Do I want to go to the camp? My answer is a big YES.

"Are you hiding something else?" said Geeta abruptly, giving Koogh a start.

"No," he said, biting his lip. "Pabbi, I ... I am going to Jalandhar, Chavni, tomorrow, early morning."

The dark glass framed slim steel jaw turned to look at him, and then heavenward. "What for? What is wrong with this boy? Where is your sense of responsibility?"

Sharda looked at Geeta and then at Koogh, feeling sorry for him. She could see that he had a stormy face.

"I know I have my class Pabbi, but I want to go to the military camp there."

Geeta stopped peeling the carrot in her hand and said sharply, "What military camp?"

"It is a selection camp, Pabbi. I want to go there because I

JUNGEE

want to join the military. I hate what I do at the mill. And I don't see how things will get any better for us if I continue working there!"

Koogh's words had poured forth in a rush. Geeta's gaze didn't move from her son's face, but her mouth tightened, turning pale at the corners.

"You listen to me loud and clear, boy! If you think you have become so big that you can make such big decisions on your own, you better think again! How dare you choose to get killed at the hands of some stranger's bullet?"

"The stranger will be an enemy, Pabbi."

"Enemy my foot! You are your enemy, and most of all, you are my enemy!"

"But ..."

"Be quiet! How dare you answer back!" she said and got up from the charpoy.

"Do you have no shame? Have you forgotten the memories of the enemy during partition? The enemy is not yours or mine. These are political games in which idiots like you are used as pawns to die like flies. We have seen enough bloodshed for a lifetime. Oh, Krishna! Have mercy upon me. Give this child some wisdom," she said, hitting her head with both her hands repeatedly.

"I'm not a child anymore, Pabbi..." pleaded Koogh.

"Your Pabbi is dead! And now go over her dead body to join the God damned military. Will you still go? Huh? I forbid you to go to that camp, and I don't want to discuss this any further. Have you understood?" she said, shaking him by his shoulders, tears streaming down her face.

"Mataji," said Sharda, who got up to get a hold of her, but

Geeta pushed her away.

"Pabbi, this is not right. You can't cry and make me change my mind. I am big enough to earn a living, so why can't I use my brains and think for myself?"

"If I think, I am considered shameless if I don't, I am a nikhattu. What do you expect of me?" he protested.

"I'm finished talking to you on this subject. Sharda, get everything to the kitchen," said Geeta, pushing Koogh aside.

She stomped off the terrace, leaving behind Koogh feeling enraged. Sharda looked at him sympathetically as she gathered her things.

"Why the military? Why don't you join a bank or a company like your bhaisaab?"

"It is not easy to get a bank job, Bhabi. And why is the military so wrong? It is a government job. After being confused for so long, I finally see a possible path to take. I'm just trying to get things better for all of us. Even then, I get treated like this." Koogh paced about in the small space between the clotheslines. "She doubts my decisions and makes me feel useless. Her way of treating me is sure to make me a nikhattu. She will be happy when her prophecy of me being the epic failure of the family will come true."

"I disagree. Mataji is strict and tough, but she loves you the most," said Sharda.

"I know she loves me, Bhabi. At most times, I don't let her words affect me, but I feel that this camp is my gateway to a better future. And for once, I will have my way!" said Koogh and stomped off the terrace, leaving Sharda agog.

. . .

Koogh refused to eat lunch and avoided interaction with

Geeta all day. He was distracted in class with Santosh too and rushed back to wait for Jaikishen at their doorstep. *I hope Pitaji will be more understanding.*

It was 5 pm, and Geeta had just finished her prayer at the family shrine when Koogh saw Jaikishen turn into their dimly lit narrow lane. Koogh stood up, watching his father. Time had not diminished Jaikishen's build, and his bluish-grey eyes, crinkled at the edges with age, never failed to smile. As always, he was wearing his white pyjamas, a white shirt, a sleeveless waistcoat that had large pockets, and a shawl draped around his shoulders. He looked tired after a long day of work at the mandi.

"Namaste, Pitaji," smiled Koogh anxiously.

Jaikishen looked at his young son's face and knew something was amiss. He put a hand on his shoulders, encouraging him to speak. "Namaste. What is it?"

"And you've finally arrived!" screamed Geeta before Koogh could say anything. Her evening prayers had not had the usual calming effect on her.

"Please tell your son that there's no need for him to go to the military camp tomorrow."

"Military camp?" said Jaikishen looking at Koogh, with wide eyes and a smile.

"Please give me a chance to explain Pitaji. The eligibility is matriculation and 16 years of age. It is a chance of getting a permanent government job. The camp is at Chavni. I will have to leave before dawn tomorrow. Please may I go, Pitaji," he pleaded.

Jaikishen looked at his son with raised eyebrows.

"I will miss my typing class, but I promise to make up the

day after," said Koogh.

Bhollo, Ghonni, and Kuku played marbles in the courtyard, as little Pappi watched on eagerly. Brij talked to Daulat Ram, who had dropped by a short while ago, to catch up on how life was treating him in Abhor. Sharda was busy cooking dinner in the kitchen.

"Your darling son has been sulking all afternoon, without any food. This mulish behaviour will not do in my house. Please tell him this clearly," Geeta bellowed on, walking about distributing prasad to everyone.

"I've told you before, never deny your body nourishment. You need the fuel to have a clear mind so that you can make mindful decisions," whispered Jaikishen to Koogh, as they entered the house. "Here is the pencil you asked for, Bhollo; I will sharpen it for you later," said Jaikishen to his awkward 14-year-old daughter. She took the pencil from him and was quick to step out of the centre stage.

Jaikishen handed over a cloth bag of vegetables to Sharda in the kitchen. He then eased his feet out of his *jootis* and hung his shawl on the peg and freshened up at the hand pump.

"What is the need to join the army? There are other ways for a man to make a living. None of the other boys in the locality are going anywhere. He will not go, and that is final," ranted on Geeta. She emerged in the courtyard with the prayer *thali* in her hand.

All heads turned to her, and then to Jaikishen, waiting for his reaction.

Geeta walked up to her husband. She was patient and silent as he moved his palms over the *diya's* flame and then put his palms to his face, thrice. She then gave him some prasad in his wet cupped hands. He mumbled a short prayer with his eyes closed and ate the prasad before entering the living room. He touched his father-in-law's feet and sat beside him and said, "Namaste, Pitaji."

"Namaste, puttar."

Koogh filled a glass of water at the hand pump for his father. Jaikishen drank his water in slow gulps, while the rest of the family waited, for what seemed like forever.

"I can't begin to tell you about the chaos at the Mandi today, Pitaji." Sharda sent Kuku to announce dinner in the hope of alleviating the atmosphere.

"Babaji, food is ready," said Kuku standing up close to his grandfather.

Jaikishen smiled at him and put an arm around him. "Not yet, son. Get me more water. I am very thirsty today. I have something for you." He put his hand in his waistcoat pocket and took out some toffees. All the children rushed to his side, keeping a wary eye on Geeta.

They grabbed their share from his extended hand and were quick to return to their marbles in the courtyard corner.

Geeta put her pooja *thali* in the kitchen and slapped her head with her hands in the living room. She walked up to Jaikishen with a furrowed brow. She turned to look at Koogh. He looked sheepish, with his head held down.

"You are the limit! Will, you ever say something to support me?" said Geeta looking pointedly at Jaikishen.

He held up his hand. "Stop worrying so much about something that hasn't happened. It is not easy to get selected in these camps. Thousands apply, and very few get selected."

"Then what is the need to waste time on a fruitless trip? Tell him not to go."

"He's young and curious. Let him see what it is all about for himself. Don't worry; he is not going to get selected. Kuku, tell your mother to serve dinner. I'm suddenly famished. Pitaji, you must have dinner with us."

"Your family has things to discuss, son. I should leave you all to it," said Daulat Ram, getting up with a heavy sigh. He walked over to Koogh and patted his back, whispered him good luck, and left.

Koogh saw Geeta sit down heavily and lift her glasses to wipe her tears with her sari. His weak moment crept up – *I am upsetting her so much. I should forget pursuing this.* He got up to explain to her, but she stomped into the inner room, grumbling under her breath and slammed the door shut.

A silence fell upon the household. Everyone ate dinner without much discussion. Koogh had a hurried meal and got ready to leave for his shift. He was going to be late. At about 5.45 pm, he went into the deodi to meet Jaikishen, who told Kuku a story about the Krishna and Sudama, while shaving Bhollo's pencil with a pocket-knife. Koogh touched Jaikishen's feet.

"Pitaji, I will leave for the camp at 5.30 in the morning."

Jaikishen nodded. "Come back soon tonight so that you can get some rest. Be confident and alert, and I'm sure you will do fine. God bless."

"Yes, Pitaji."

Sharda appeared at the doorway, with a cup of halwa in her hands.

"Have some *gajar ka halwa*. You are going for something new. You should eat something sweet before you leave." Koogh smiled and quickly gobbled a spoonful and then another.

"Thank you, Bhabi. I am so glad you all are here with us at this time."

He went to the living room to meet Geeta. She was praying with a rosary in her hand, lying silently on her charpoy in the dim room. Her body stiffened the moment she saw him in the doorway.

"Pabbi, I'm leaving for my shift. And I will go to the camp early tomorrow. I'm sorry I made you cry. I hope that someday you will understand me, and I can make you feel proud of my decision." He touched her feet and left for work.

In his rush to leave, he didn't see that Geeta had extended her hand to give him her blessings and then run out after him, peering from the wire-mesh door whispering a prayer as he receded into the mist. Jaikishen paused his story and smiled. He knew Geeta loved Koogh - More than he would ever know.

The temperature fell very low in the winter nights of Punjab. That night, he got home by 1:00 am, and like every night, Jaikishen opened the door to him.

"Wake me up at five, Pitaji," Jaikishen grunted and went back to sleep.

Koogh took off his slippers outside the living room and entered its warmth. He shrugged off his shawl and hung it on the peg. Usually, Geeta would acknowledge his arrival, but silence met him that night.

He made his way in the darkness to his charpoy and got into bed, covering himself with the thick rajai. He hugged himself into a tight ball to get warm in his freezing bed.

His mind raced with thoughts and emotions as he tried to sleep. Although his heart was heavy after the skirmish with his mother, he knew he had to give his luck a chance. He was happy that Jaikishen, Daulat Ram, and Brij had encouraged his decision to go to the camp. But then he remembered Jaikishen's words about the stiff competition. Ajay did get rejected. *What if I get rejected too?*

Geeta's bed creaked as she turned over. She lifted her head to look at Koogh's bed. Noting that he was back, she mumbled something and went back to sleep.

He understood her anger. She was worried about his safety. If he did get selected, it would mean that he would have to go away from home. Be in the midst of danger. Be at war.

Nobody in their family had ever done such a thing. Meeting Ajay at the cinema was luck. His sharing the information about the camp was also luck. But Koogh's decision to do something with that piece of information was the game-changer for him and hopefully for his family. His hands formed into fists as Daulat Ram and Jaikishen's words rang in his ears. His heart was beating furiously about what awaited him. *I will not let myself down. I will break my everyday life and get out of my comfort zone to create a new reality!'*

— — —

CHAPTER 6: MAKING A CHOICE

January 1954: Jalandhar Chavni recruitment camp

At about 6 am Koogh hopped off a running bus as it turned into the bus depot. Despite the bleak and dreary winter morning, people were going about their lives in Chavni, a small township in the city of Jalandhar. It was January and the coldest weeks of winter were already upon them. Temperatures threatened to go sub-zero. Sunrise was sluggish, merging the reluctant dawn into the foggy grey horizon. The fog usually hung heavy in the air late into the mornings.

Koogh's heart was heavy, unlike his footsteps. There was always so much resistance to change, more so when he was initiating it. He felt all the weight of his youth – was he reaching too far above himself? Would he do justice to his decision?

The few streetlights blurred his visibility down to a distance of two metres. He could hear people's footsteps much before they appeared from the fog. But he was familiar with the neighbourhood, so he walked with confidence. He turned a corner and jumped aside, startled. He had managed to stop himself from bumping into a woman sweeping the narrow gulley. Bent over, she moved her bristly broom in a loose rhythmic movement as she gathered the dirt and littered animal and human excreta. A hint of a smile came to Koogh's face as he saw two dreary faced children sitting in a squat ahead of him. They were defecating in an open drain on one side of

PRIYA SHARMA SHAIKH

the gulley. The sweeper woman was making jokes at their expense. They were too sleepy and cold to react. Bells rang in the distance, and Koogh shifted around the woman to hurry along. *Time waits for nobody.*

He was a picture of youthful vanity - clean-shaven, and his hair combed back in place. He was wearing what other village boys his age wore - a pair of white pyjamas and an oversized white shirt. He had worn a full-sleeved hand-knit sweater, and a grey muffler wound snug around his neck to cut the cold. On his feet, he wore an overused pair of blue rubber slippers. He walked with a quick step, as if with a purpose.

In a school nearby, a bell began to clang, summoning the students. Koogh slowed down as he walked past the school. Uniformed children flew past him, clinging on to their bags, racing to get through the gate ahead of each other. Mothers accompanying toddlers dropped them off with teachers at the gate, not before fussing over them, wiping food off their weeping faces, and adjusting their sweaters and caps one last time.

I wish I could go back to school again. Fly kites. And play all day. Koogh felt envious as he trailed his hand along the school wall, watching the children form neat lines for the morning assembly and prayer. Not so long ago, that had been him, with nothing to worry about except his homework and games. Becoming an adult brought with it responsibility for himself and his family too. *At first, this growing up business had felt like being in a straitjacket, but I had forced myself to get used to it. There had been no other way. Becoming responsible is what Pabbi wanted of me, and yet she got so upset.*

...

The fragrance of roasting spices burst through Koogh's thoughts, reminding him that he hadn't eaten much the previous evening. He saw a small group of men gathered around an eatery called *'Kake Da Dhaba.'*

A salt and pepper bearded Sikh sat on a stool behind the counter, with a friendly smile. He wore traditional Punjabi clothing - a bright blue turban, a pale white *kurta-pyjama, and* a black jacket. A leather strap was strung from his left shoulder across his torso, at the end of which lay nestled a small *Kirpan.* His twinkling blue eyes kept an eye on all his guests, and each time someone stopped at his eatery, he introduced himself.

"Myself, Kartar Singh," and he said to his guests and then proceeded to crack a joke in Punjabi, ending it with a loud, *Sat-Sri-Akal.* People hung around the counter to collect their food and catch Kartar's verbal pranks. They cracked up with laughter at each punch line to chorus Sat-Sri-Akal with him.

A puny assistant was at hand. He followed instructions and dished out fried balloon-like *kulchas* from a huge Dalda-filled *kadhai.* Kartar served them to his guests with spicy, sour *choley,* and sliced onions.

The sharp aromas of brewing tea and choley mingled, and made Koogh's stomach growl in response. He felt awkward as he lurked around the counter, even as a round of guffawing came to a close.

"One plate, please," said Koogh, above the din.

"*Puttar,* myself, Kartar Singh. Listen to this joke. A special one, piping hot, just for you. Raju failed his exams. So his father said, shame on you. Look at the neighbour's girl. She has stood first in class. So Raju said, Pitaji! Looking at her is all I have done this year! Sat-Sri-Akal."

The crowd cracked up while Koogh squirmed with embarrassment. Kartar Singh smiled and handed him a plate. Koogh took it and retreated to a bench at the back of the Dhaba. He could still listen to the merriment, but he did not wish to be part of it.

One of the onlookers said, "Sardarji, do you always make people laugh?"

"Life is to laugh at, puttar because it is like a hand of cards you get dealt. You never know what colours or characters will come your way. Winners play the game despite whatever they get. Twists and turns are a part of life, and I choose to enjoy my game of life by bringing laughter into my patrons' lives. They start their day with a laugh, and come back for more the next day. Everyone is happy," said Kartar.

Koogh blew on a piece of curry-dipped kulcha and stuffed it into his mouth. It was crisp and delicious and reminded him of home. His heart turned over, making his empty stomach churn, and the sounds of the Dhaba faded away. *Why am I disrupting everything? What if everything Pabbi said about me is right? What if I can't do it? What am I going to do with my life if I fail today? I guess I will do Prabhakar like Vimal Mamaji.*

A roar of guffaws from Kartar Singh and his gang brought his thoughts back. He looked at them with a hint of a smile. If only it were easy to laugh away his problems. *Maybe I can prove my demons of self-doubt wrong and see what lies on the other side.*

"Will you have another kulcha?" It was Kartar's eager assistant. Koogh shook his head and jumped up, sensing he would be late. He paid his bill and started on a brisk trot, leaving Kartar and his laughing crowd behind. *It is time - everything that happens today will decide my destiny.*

...

He reached the armed forces cantonment. Two tall, tough-looking uniformed guards manned the gate, performing a security check on everyone going through. Koogh got in, too, and followed the line of people ahead of him.

The place was a stark contrast to the cluttered market out-

JUNGEE

side, with cleanliness and order on in full display everywhere. The long pathway had well-tended *bael* and *neem* trees on both sides, and neatly-laid bricks marked the pathway. There were signboards surrounded by clumps of potted flowering plants. Some had philosophical messages on them, while others had directions or details of the tented workstations behind them.

Koogh tried, with difficulty, to mouth the English words as he hurried along. His challenge with the language made him conscious. He'd often held back in conversations for fear of making a fool of himself. The path finally culminated in a large open courtyard in front of a barrack. He took a deep breath and surveyed the activity unfolding in front of him. Hundreds of young men were there, murmuring, and being a part of what was happening. He had mixed feelings. A sense of comfort as they were of similar age. Fear, because he had no clue what to do next. And a nervous chill, because most of them had a better built than he was. Like him, they were there to try their luck at joining the armed forces. *If I get selected, some of these boys will be my fellow recruits and fight side by side to defend the country. But for now, each of them is competition.*

The enlistment criteria, as Ajay said, was straightforward. An applicant had to be male, between 16-18 years of age. He had to have passed the *Metric* examination and have physical and medical fitness.

The ground had three main areas, with rudimentary signboards declaring the sections for ARMY, NAVY, and AIR FORCE. The army line was huge and thick and snake-like at the start, with boys peering over each other's shoulders. It ended at the edge of the ground. The Navy and Air Force lines were much smaller. Alongside the registration was a second section for physical fitness. Boys in batches of ten got tested for field and track activities. They had to run and do rigorous rounds of exercise. The third section was for the medical examinations in a barrack that stood opposite the registration counter, packed

PRIYA SHARMA SHAIKH

to the gills, with boys pushing each other to complete their medical tests. Men in starched *khaki* uniforms walked about, shouting brisk instructions, trying to bring some method to the madness caused by the horde of young men in the three different spaces.

Koogh hadn't planned which line he would choose. He hesitated for a few minutes, standing still while people pushed past him, as this would be the decision that would set the course for his life.

The study of tides and continents intrigued him. Living in north India, he had seen the Indus River and her five tributaries - Sutlej, Beas, Ravi, Chenab, and Jhelum. He had studied the water bodies that surrounded India - The Bay of Bengal in the East, the Arabian Sea on her West, and the vast Indian Ocean to her south. Images in a magazine at Chatterjee's office, showcasing Bombay's famous coastal road, the beautiful curved Marine Drive, came to him. In the monsoon, the Arabian Sea tossed beside it with high waves. She as if romanced the shore, drenching gleeful pedestrians with her white spray. The water seemed mighty and powerful, and it had beckoned him ever since. He craned his neck beyond the boys waiting in line at the Navy counter. The official was busy writing down the candidates' details at the counter. A shiver of excitement ran down his spine. *Kartar Singh was so right. You have to laugh at life because you never know what's coming around the corner. An opportunity has presented itself, and here I am, stepping into a realm that I never knew existed before yesterday.*

Once he had processed his thoughts, he took his place in the Navy line without any hesitation - This was his second decision.

Koogh knew now that change happens and that if you allow it to flow with wonder, you never know where it could take you. He smiled as he imagined himself in the city of his dreams

156

- Bombay.

"Next."

The officer at the Navy counter didn't look up, but Koogh leaped to the counter.

"Name?"

"Inderjit"

"Full name?"

"Inderjit Sharma."

"What is your father's name?"
"Jaikishen Das."

"Where are you from?"

"Korian Mohalla, Phagwara."

"How old are you?"

"Seventeen."

"Have you done your Matriculation?"

"Yes, Sir."

"Proceed for your physical and medical examinations," the officer said mechanically, pointing to the field and barrack. He looked at Inder and paused to scan his thin frame.

"Is your weight okay?"

"Yes, Sir, why do you ask?"

The officer shrugged, a look of doubt on his face as he waved his hand.

"Next."

. . .

The morning after two-year-old Koogh had called the moon, the sun, Melaram's sister Parmeshwari Devi, had visited them from Mathura. She was a self-declared *Sadhvi*, the oldest in the family, and had unquestioned respect. She had shaved her head, adorned orange robes and *rudraksha* beads, and dedicated her life to Lord Krishna after becoming a widow. That morning she sat on a platform while her ardent devotees and the family sat on the floor when Geeta walked into the room and put Koogh in Parmeshwari's lap.

"Buaji, this is our youngest son. Please give him your blessings."

"What an adorable child! He has my blessings to have a long and successful life," she said with much delight. She smothered Koogh with hugs and kisses, but he resisted and pulled away. He rushed back to stand in front of Geeta's legs while everyone laughed.

"He is a real mother's boy, Buaji, and full of naughty tricks," beamed Jaikishen.

"Children have a mind of their own. He is lovely. What is his name?" she asked Geeta.

"His name is Gopal, but we call him Koogh," Geeta said.

Parmeshwar Devi smiled. "This boy knows how to get his way, and he is a fighter. Look at how bold he is. You should give him a strong name. Inderjit will be a fitting name for this warrior. It is the name of the victorious God of the skies and rain, Indra."

Geeta and Jaikishen smiled in agreement. And from that day, Gopal became Inderjit.

. . .

The physical fitness test followed the registration process.

Inder ran 100 metres, did 50 push-ups, and an exercise drill to test his stamina. He cleared the physical fitness round. *Paiyaji was so right about having a daily workout regimen - It has come to good use.*

Inder then went to the barrack for his medical examination. He waited for his turn in the long queue. Despite the cold weather, the boys had to strip to their underwear. Each of them got examined from head to toe.

The barrack was airy. It had a high ceiling and low hanging fans. Cobwebs between the blades were testimony that they had stood still for some time now. Framed photographs of august men and women of Indian history lined the walls. Inder recognised each of the faces known for their valour or thought leadership.

The round-spectacled Mahatma Gandhi. The leader of India's non-violence movement for freedom, *Bapu*, the father of the nation, dressed in his indigenous white loincloth, smiled back at him. The thin-lipped aristocratic first Prime Minister of independent India, Pandit Jawaharlal Nehru, had a hint of a smile while a red rose lay poetically ensconced in the buttonhole of his waistcoat. Shivaji, the mountain king of the western *ghats*, looked valiant brandishing his sword in the air as he rode his horse atop a mountain. Guru Gobind Singh, the tenth Sikh guru, who took on leadership at the tender age of nine, had a calm expression. The aggressive and outspoken Subhash Chandra Bose, dressed in the Indian National Army uniform, had a determined expression. CV Raman from the South Indian state of Tamil Nadu – India's Nobel Prize winner for his work in physics, stood out with a staid expression and a white turban atop his head. And finally, Rani Laxmi Bai, the brave queen who fought the Mughals on horseback, with her little son strapped to her back. Her courage to fight despite all odds had always impressed Inder. *Do I have it in me to do something commendable and inspiring, to make it to the wall of fame?*

"Please move ahead," said a stocky lad behind Inder.

"Do you know what the weight criteria are?" Inder asked, looking back at him.

Looking at Inder's frame, the boy smiled and said that he needed 50.80 kgs to pass the medical. Inder's stomach knotted up. *What if my weight isn't adequate? I am tough but maybe I am skinny.* He slipped away to find an unmanned weighing machine in the corner of the barrack. He stepped onto it and closed his eyes before looking down at the needle. He was underweight by a kilo!

He sat down with a deep sigh, holding his head in dismay, and broke into a cold sweat. The Lion appeared at the doorway of the barrack. Inder rushed towards it in anger. *Why do you appear? Do you come to see me lose?* No answers were forthcoming. Koogh dragged his feet and stepped out of the barrack.

It was the end of his dream, even before it had started.

CHAPTER 7: HEAD OVER HEART

*January 1954: Questioning the mind and
clearing the clouds*

The male-nurse signalled to Inder. He took a deep breath and stepped onto the weighing machine, bare-chested. His eyes looked calm as he looked straight ahead, unflinching. His slim and youthful body glistened in the beam of light from the window. The officer at the desk poised his pen over the register.

"Inderjit Sharma. Weight: 51.10 kgs. Height: 5 feet, 7 inches. Chest: 36 inches. Colour of eyes: Black. Next!"

Inder blinked. He held back a smile and got off the machine to dress in a hurry. He met the boy who had told him about the weight criteria at the barrack entrance. He shook his head with a smirk on his face. Inder put his hand on his shoulder and smiled.

"Can't stop to chat. Two litres of water means I have an urgent call of nature, brother."

Inder returned for the Ear, Nose, and Throat test. It had been a tough day at work for Doctor Anand Bhatia, dealing with all the candidates. By the time it was Inder's turn, he had no patience. He did a perfunctory check of Inder and put a cross against his name.

"Next."

"Sir, please ... what happened?" gasped Inder.

"Filthy, clogged ears!" he mumbled.

"I will clean them, Sir. Please don't reject me for such a small reason," Inder protested.

"We have enough candidates. Next!" snapped Bhatia.

Inder's application had come to yet another abrupt halt.

. . .

His face was crestfallen that evening, and the atmosphere at home was quiet. They discussed the day's events in small groups in the dim living room. Geeta heaved a sigh of relief but urged Jaikishen to get Inder's ears checked.

The very next morning, Inder visited Dr. Harbanslal, an ex-Indian National Army doctor. He was a talkative and merry natured Sikh with a quick-paced walk and an eager smile. As he treated Inder's ears, he inquired about the recruitment camp.

"Your ears are clean now, my boy."
"I wish I had known it is important to clean them. I would not have got rejected."

"So what stops you now? Go again and show him your cleaned ears. If you don't go, the answer is already NO. And give your Dr. Bhatia my regards. Tell him that I often think of the time we had together in INA," he said.

. . .

Inder immediately rushed to the camp and patiently waited for Bhatia to arrive. It was almost noon when he arrived. He brushed passed Inder, who jumped up to greet him. Inder waited again, but Bhatia didn't call for him. The aide took pity on Inder and prompted Bhatia to meet him for a few minutes. Bhatia seemed reluctant but then decided to summon Inder.

"Thank you for seeing me again, Sir," said Inder with child-like eagerness.

Bhatia grunted and switched on his work light to check Inder's ears.

"Sir, your friend Dr. Harbanslal, lives in my hometown," said Inder in a cautious tone.

"Which Harbanslal?"

"Your friend from the INA, Sir. He is the one who cleaned my ears, and he specially asked me to give you his regards."

Bhatia's frown changed to a pleasant smile.

"Well, well … what a small world. Please give Harbans my regards too. And do leave his address with me so that I can be in touch," said Bhatia.

He signed Inder's medical papers and cleared his name for selection as a recruit in the Indian Navy. Within minutes, Inder was holding a government warrant in his hands. He was to join training at INS Venduruthy immediately. His travel to Cochin by train was the very next morning.

. . .

That evening the atmosphere at home was that of gloom. Daulat Ram looked from one person to the other, with a grim expression. His daughter's weeping was incessant. Sharda and Brij stood beside her, trying to comfort her, while Bhollo and Ghonni looked on anxiously. Jaikishen held his head in his hands, looking rueful. They were all taking in the sudden change in Inder's life.

Inder sat in a squat staring at his mother, in the courtyard. His heart felt heavy. *Please try to understand why I need to do this, Pabbi.*

PRIYA SHARMA SHAIKH

"I didn't expect him to get selected in the Navy. He had spoken about joining the Army. But the Navy! The oceans are so vast and dangerous. How will he be safe in a boat in the ocean? What if it capsizes?" said Jaikishen to no one in particular.

Brij gave up trying to console Geeta. He had instructed Sharda to pack Inder's things. She had already laid out an old tin trunk in the courtyard, with few of Inder's belongings and toiletries in it. He asked Sharda also to pack a tiffin for the long journey ahead.

"Take note of all the family member's addresses and the neighbours number," Brij said to Inder and sat on his haunches in front of Jaikishen, holding his hands in his palms.

"Pitaji, your son is not a boy anymore. He is intelligent. He's chosen the Navy. Let us respect his decision. I know Cochin is very far away from home, and that his decision to join the Navy was not what you expected. But he will take care of himself and someday make us all very proud too! Let him go in peace with all our blessings. At this moment, that is all that we can do for him as his family."

Jaikishen thought for a few minutes and then gave a slow nod to his son.

Geeta slapped her head, "Why are you nodding your head like a sheep? What sort of a father are you? You are sending my son to drown in the ocean. I don't want him to die in the war. Oh Krishna, please get someone to understand what I am saying. We are pushing him into death's arms," screamed Geeta, her body jerking with tears.

"For God's sake, please stop fretting and making a scene like this, Pabbi," said Brij. And then emphasising each word, he said, "Nothing bad will happen to him. He is not going to drown. He is already a swimmer."

He walked up to Geeta and held her shoulders and shook her till she looked at him.

"Didn't you teach us how to protect ourselves and be brave like Krishna? You should be proud of your son. And he is not going to fight a war now, as India is not at war with any country. He is going to train; to prepare to protect our country, if the need arises."

She moved her tearful face away and pushed him, not willing to listen to reason. He pulled her back into a hug, and she wept bitter tears on the chest of her first-born.

Daulat Ram understood his daughter's grief and his grandson's desire. He put his hand on Inder's head. He had tears in his eyes as he ate his dinner slowly without looking up. Sharda had made his favourite *sabzi* of potatoes and peas with ghee smeared fresh *phulkas*.

"What are you thinking, son?"

"I didn't know it would hurt Pabbi so much, Paiyaji. Her worries are playing on my mind too. What would it be like to die at the hands of the enemy in a war?"

"Son, she is your mother, and she has her caustic ways of dealing with things. She doesn't know any better way. But, whether or not she may have expressed it before, she loves you. She is bound to feel upset as you are choosing not to pay any heed to her objections. But you don't have to worry. When she hears that you are well settled and doing well, she will be fine."

Inder nodded and hoped his grandfather was right.

"As regards war, you come from very courageous stock. And I know that if my people are under attack, I will be the first to come forward and fight as should you. It is a matter of pride to protect your homeland, son," said Daulat Ram and thumped Inder's shoulders.

"Yes, Paiyaji."

"You are going out into the world all by yourself, to a land that is unknown to us—new culture, new people, and no family around to fall back on for guidance. You will have only your internal compass to guide your decisions. Promise me that you will be present without distraction at all times so that you can take care of yourself under all circumstances."

"I promise Paiyaji."

His grandfather put his hand on his head, and Inder touched his feet and bid him goodbye. Sharda came to serve him his next *phulka*.

"Why are you eating less tonight? You have made a big decision today, and you are going to live alone now. There will be no Bhabi or Pabbi to serve you hot food. You will have to take care of yourself. You have suddenly become a man, Inderjit, so be responsible and eat up!" prodded Sharda, slipping a portion of *gajar-ka-halwa* into his plate.

"Thank you for everything, Bhabi," said Inder, looking up at her smiling face.

Jaikishen got up and paced the room. His son was going away, to an unknown address. They had to trust the piece of paper that was the government's warrant, which was also testimony to his Navy selection. Geeta had worked herself into a fever by 8 pm. She refused to eat and kept rambling about war and the ocean.

. . .

Inder finished dinner, washed his hands at the pump, and left the courtyard for his spot on the terrace for the last time. Jaikishen watched his beloved son's receding figure and had tears in his eyes. He knew that Koogh felt horrible to put his parents through so much pain, yet, he sensed that something in his being had hardened.

There was no turning back. Inder did a mental check of things he had intended to do.

He had stopped by to say goodbye to everyone. On hearing the news of his selection in the Navy, Chatterjee had beamed and quickly settled his accounts and wished him well. Santosh was beyond herself with joy that her student had finally found a meaningful purpose. His friends were happy for him too. His trunk was packed. All his boxes had got ticked, and he was ready to go.

...

It was finally time for goodbye, much before the break of dawn. Koogh bid farewell to his tearful family. Geeta refused to let go and clung onto him, hysterical, even as her body burned with high temperature.

"Kooghey, my son, don't go. Forgive me for all my rebuke and anger, I love you, my son, and I worry for you. That is why I get angry with you. Please don't leave me and go away, son. Please. I beg you. I don't want you to die."

"Pabbi, I promise I will make this separation worth it. Please give me your blessings."

He bent down and touched her feet and waited for her to touch his head. When her trembling hands finally did so, he got up. He felt an ache in his heart to see her so vulnerable. He breathed in deeply, picked up his trunk, and left without turning to look back, leaving behind his huddled family in the dark yellow misty shadows of Korian Mohalla.

My boy has become a man overnight! Panditji's prophecy of him having an adventurous life is coming true. Jaikishen smiled as he walked behind his son.

. . .

At the train station, Jaikishen and Inder walked to the compartment reserved for the armed forces. Inder found an open spot near a window and placed his trunk on it. He stepped out of the train to spend the last few minutes with Jaikishen. Other officials and fresh recruits were also getting into the train or standing in groups with their families.

A Sikh family was close to them. The young boy, who was the centre of the attention, exchanged a smile with Inder. It was an acknowledgment of their shared situation!

"A new journey is beginning for you, son! I'm so excited for you," said Jaikishen holding Inder's hands in his rough palms.

"Yes, so am I Pitaji. Everything happened so quickly. It all still feels like a dream. I wonder where this journey will take me, and when it will complete?"

"You will know when you are complete, son. For now, focus on starting and staying the course. Wherever you go, life will be great if you decide to make it great. Your village and family are your roots. They have given you your values."

"Wherever you go, remember to stay connected and live with those values. Some day they will give you the strength to achieve your highest potential."

"I still remember the lesson you gave me in Tandlianwala Pitaji. I cherish that and so many special moments we have spent together. And I am ever thankful for you being my father and your love for me."

"You are the best son a father could dream of, son. May God bless you."

The train gave its first hoot. Inder bent down and touched

Jaikishen's feet. "I will have to leave now, Pitaji. Thank you for having faith in me. Tell Pabbi I am sorry for the pain I've given her. I promise I will make her, and you feel proud."

Jaikishen hugged his son tightly, not wanting to let go, and then patted him hard on his back. His blue eyes sparkled as he fought back the tears. He hurriedly took out a bundle of postcards from his pocket and placed them in Inder's hands.

"I have written our address on each of these postcards. Keep sending them as often as you can, even if blank. I will feel assured that you are safe. Don't worry about your mother. She will be fine in a few days. I am already proud of you to have the courage to make such a big decision at such a young age. It is not my faith in you that has brought you here; it is the divine energy within you that has made you believe in yourself. Never stop believing in yourself, son, come what may. Your life is about to take off. And you need all the self-belief and grit you can summon, to take flight."

Inder nodded and stepped onto the train's footboard, and it jerked to a start. He stood at the doorway with a few other boys, all looking back at their own families, waving frantically, giving last-minute messages of love and respect. He kept looking at the receding figure of Jaikishen as the train picked up speed. Within seconds, he blurred into the morning fog. Inder stayed at the doorway, feeling the cold breeze on his face. He smiled as he saw the Lion running ahead along with the train. He was leading the way.

...

Inder went to his seat and opened the trunk, which contained a few clothes, a shawl, a towel, a tiffin, the Peacock, and the Cow. He placed the postcards inside and put the trunk below the seat. He patted his left pocket to make sure the twenty rupees were intact, and then put his hand inside his pyjama pocket to take out something.

It was the Lion.

. . .

Bhollo had slipped the Lion into his hand when he was packing.

"I want you to keep him now, Paaji. You are going to be like him now, aren't you?"

"Yes, I am going to look for adventure and the risks that come with it."

"I'll miss you, Paaji."

"I know. But we all finally will have to fly this nest and make our lives. I will write, and meanwhile, you be the perfect Peacock. Make the most of your childhood, my little sister."

"I'm not little anymore," she said and twiddled her ribboned plaits.

"Okay, then promise to take care of Pabbi and Pitaji, so that you can get their blessings before you get swept away by your groom."

She had given him a shy nod.

. . .

The Sikh boy sat next to Inder. He was slightly shorter and skinny and wheat complexioned, like Inder.

"Myself, Ajaib Singh Minhas, and I am joining the Navy. What about yourself?" he smiled and extended his hand to Inder.

"Me too. Inderjit Sharma," said Inder taking his hand awkwardly, "Where are you from?"

"I'm from a town called Daroli Kalan, where I lived until

this morning with my father, mother, and brothers. We have farmland."

"What made you join the Navy?"

"I could have assisted Papaji, or taken up a job like my brother, but I wanted to join the Navy. My parents were supportive. What about you?"

"My mother, unfortunately, is grief-stricken," said Inder sharing details of his family.

Within a few minutes of talking to each other, they found common ground in the sports they played, films and songs they liked, and, most that they would be recruits together.

"This train reaches Delhi early morning, and the connecting train leaves in the night. I am going to meet my brother in Meerut. You can come along if you like," said Minhas.

"You go ahead, I have plans in Delhi," said Inder, being conscious of not lightening his little kitty and not letting let up a chance to meet his favourite Vimal Mamaji.

. . .

Vimal opened the door to a dishevelled, unshaven Inder standing alone at his doorstep. He was immediately suspicious.

"Namaste Mamaji," smiled Inder and bent down to touch his feet.

"May you live long. Have you run away?" said Vimal, looking amused.

"No, Mamaji. I come bearing good news. I got selected as a recruit in the Navy."

"Congratulations. That's fantastic news."

"Indeed, it is! I am on my way to Cochin. My train is tonight.

I had time to spare, so I came to get your blessings."

"You have my blessings always. So, you finally found the answer to what you should do."

"Yes! The oceans beckon me. So, I decided to take the plunge."

Hearing about Inder's arrival, Narender, Mahinder, and Nirmal dropped in to meet him.

"Bombay? You, lucky guy! You can meet all the actors and actresses," said Mahinder.

"Yeah, right! Like they are waiting for me at the station."

"And what if you do meet them? Maybe there will be a film shooting, and you can bump into Madhubala," said Nirmal, dreamily.

"But I am not going to Bombay; I'm going to Cochin. Maybe later to Bombay."

"Whenever you go, I need a promise from you - if you meet Madhubala, please give her my love," said Nirmal with dreamy eyes.

"And if you meet Sadhana, give her mine," laughed Mahinder.

"Brothers, relax! He is going there to work, and not watch films, and least of all to meet film stars," said Narender, feeling happy for his cousin's sudden success.

That evening, when it was time for Inder to leave for the station, Vimal hugged him and pushed Rs.20 into his hand and took him aside.

"From now on, I will address you by your name, Inderjit! I'm so proud that you took a stand for yourself. And now that you have opened the door to something new, many more doors will open. You'll experience so many new things and places, befriend new people, study, and have fun. There will be so much newness around you that, at times, it will overwhelm you."

"Be mindful of what you are absorbing and let only what feels right, occupy your mind space, because your mind is the temple of the energy that flows within you. Protect it and keep it pure. It is the purity that you maintain that will give you clarity of thought while making decisions. And if something sets you back, consider your options and dare to get things back on track. Wallowing and self-pity won't help you. It is a wasteful exercise, and it will shift your focus from your goals. Just continue to be consistent in your effort with integrity and humility, Inderjit, and all will be well. Are you scared?"

"I am nervous, as my English is weak, and English is compulsory in the Navy."

"Well, what do you think you should do?"

"I don't know, Mamaji. You know English so well. How did you learn?"

"Nobody is born knowing any language. How do you think I would have learnt it?"

"I used to see you reading all those English novels. I guess I too will try to read the English newspaper and whatever novels I can get my hands on, and maybe watch films too and tune in to the English bulletin on the radio."

"You have all the answers Inderjit. The Navy will challenge all aspects of your mind, body, and soul. You have chosen to live on your terms. Good times will come, and so will difficulties. When they do come knocking on your door, be honest enough to acknowledge your weakness and be patient with yourself as you work on making your situation better. Set high benchmarks to get better each day and compete with nobody but yourself. I wish you all the best."

Inder felt enriched when his uncle bid him farewell. He rushed to catch his train scheduled to leave at 9 pm. Minhas would meet him directly at the platform.

. . .

Inspector Parminder looked up from the receipt book, "I'll ask you again: what is your name?"

Minhas and Inder sat shivering in the cold, tears, and fear in their eyes. Parminder's brows crowded, and he jerked his ink pen several times, as it refused to write. "This doesn't mean I will let you go free. You are coming with me to the police station. Pick up your things and follow me," he barked and jostled Inder up by his collar.

"Sir, please listen to us once," cried Inder falling at his feet, not letting him move. "My name is Inderjit Sharma, and he is Ajaib Singh Minhas. We are from Punjab, and we are Navy recruits. We are on our way to Cochin. We were to take the 9 pm train, but it got rescheduled to 6 am. Sir, I thought that instead of spending money going to Mamaji's place, we could sleep here. We are from Punjab, Sir, and we don't know city rules. Minhas, show your warrant to Sir," said Inder, still holding Parminder's leg.

Minhas quickly reached for his bag and handed a folded piece of paper to the officer.

"We received this from the Armed Forces recruitment camp at Chavni. Please read it once. Sir, I also have a similar warrant."

Parminder switched on his torchlight and scanned the document and then looked at the boys again. His brow crowded. He looked back at the warrant and mumbled something and then nodded slowly as his face broke into a sheepish smile.

"Harrumph! Well, this document seems valid. But you are still not allowed to sleep on the bench. There is a waiting room if you have no place to go. Come with me."

...

The next morning Inder and Minhas awoke in the waiting room. Parminder was still around. They greeted him warmly, and he walked with them to Banna's stall. The dreary Chotu was amused to see Inder and Minhas, who looked not unlike mere tramps.

"We will sail in an Indian Navy ship in the deep oceans," said Inder, hurriedly.

Chotu's eyes widened with amazement while Inder and Minhas laughed.

"Daroga Saab, we don't know if we'll see you again. It was a pleasure to meet you, Sir."

"The pleasure is mine. You are good, boys. You are going to serve the nation, and silly me thought you had run away from home. I'm sorry about the misunderstanding and being tough on you two," said Parminder looking embarrassed.

"You were doing your duty, Sir. You set a good example for us," said Inder.

"Goodbye, Sir," said Minhas.

The train's engine blew in the distance. Inder and Minhas boarded the train and turned to look back at Parminder, who waved at them and then comically saluted with a mischievous grin. They laughed and waved at him.

As the train picked up speed, they turned to look ahead with a smile on their faces. The early morning chill stung their faces, and the chilling breeze made their eyes water. Inder breathed in the crisp air, taking in the luminous beauty of the breaking dawn on the horizon. A new beginning awaited him —an unknown journey, that he was ready to embrace. The sun's fiery red rays emerged brighter with each passing moment, magically swathing the landscape with its light, making their faces glow, and showering its blessings, as if, on them. They hooted along with the train's siren and laughed, saluting the sun. Inder was finally onward bound towards a brand-new life.

— — —

JUNGEE

BOOK 2: THE LION

The Lion was young. He lifted his mighty head and shook his ochre yellow mane in the wind. Curiosity and leadership were his natural gifts. He knew they brought with them great joys and consequences too. He had committed to being noble, detached, and ferocious. He was true to the character of Narsimha, the incarnate of Lord Vishnu, fighting to protect good from evil.

He roared at the sun; as its rays shined onto his face blinding him as he set off gracefully into the horizon to explore the possibilities that lay ahead. He began to run, his heavy paws flying lithely over the ground, tearing through the terrain towards a faraway land, armed with courage and caution, looking for a territory he could call his own.

He had decided to leave his pride and forge a new path for himself, with a pledge to follow through. He knew that from here on, he was to be alone, once again. And he was willing to trust and believe in himself, to meet his greatness. He was finally running with a purpose, never once, looking back.

CHAPTER 8: NORTH TO SOUTH

January 1954: The journey of change begins

Inder was amazed at India's expansiveness as the train rattled along its rhythmic journey from the north towards Madras, in the southernmost state, Tamil Nadu.

Inside the compartment, Inder observed his fellow passengers. Unlike the few fresh recruits like Minhas and Inder, who were awkward skinny boys in plain clothes, there were tough-looking men in uniform or overalls, most from the Army. There were a few from the Air Force and Navy too. They were sitting in groups, indulging in the bonhomie and banter of old friends, stories, jokes, laughter, and songs.

Minhas dragged Inder to take a tour of the rest of the train. They walked through the general public compartments. Inder was intrigued to see many people so unlike any he'd seen before. Many of the men were dark-skinned and wore white cotton lungis like a long skirt, all the way down to their feet. Some had folded their lungis up to their knees, showing their hairy legs. Children played board and card games, while the women chatted animatedly in a language alien to him. One of the men caught his eye and addressed him at the next station.

"I speak a little Hindi. Do you speak English? I'm S. Babu. Where are you going?"

Inder blinked consciously and wondered where this conversation would go, considering his challenge with spoken English. "Myself, Inderjit Sharma, going to Madras. Navy." His voice sounded too loud to himself.

"Good, good! My cousin is also on a Naval ship in Bombay," smiled Babu.

Contrary to Babu's mostly average features, his wife, Lalitha, was beautiful. She had sharp features and big bright eyes. She wore chunky gold ornaments on her hands, ears, and neck, and her forehead had a red dot and the remains of dried sandalwood paste. She had bushy black hair, pinned back with a flower garland made of tiny orange flowers. Their daughters, Latha and Lakshmi, looked like twins. And like their mother, had *kajal* in their eyes, a small black dot on their foreheads and the dried sandalwood line. Their oiled hair was short and pinned back to reveal small gold earrings. They completed their look with identical frocks and sandals.

Once the train started, Inder and Minhas sat with Babu's family in their compartment. They talked about his business of cotton trade and the lack of impact of partition on South India.

"Do you watch films?" asked Babu.

"Yes, we love films," said Inder, exchanging glances with Minhas.

"For me, films are the best entertainment. NTR is the legend of South Indian cinema and Sivaji Ganesan too. Both are my favourite actors, and Padmini is my favourite actress. I don't see Hindi films that much. The last that I saw was Dev Anand's 'Taxi Driver.' I barely understood anything they were saying, but I could make out the story," said Babu sticking his tongue out and laughing, showing his sparkling white teeth.

Inder and Minhas laughed at his animated expressions. *Long live the diversity and* multiplicity *of India!* The rhythmic movement of the train soon got the better of Minhas, and he dozed off on Inder's shoulder while watching him play 'find the ring finger' with Babu's children who giggled, as their dark, prominent eyes danced with joy, each time Inder caught the wrong finger. After a while, Lalitha summoned them back to their berths to sleep, and the compartment was quiet. By the time the next station came, it was time for lunch. Inder and Minhas bid goodbye to Babu and his family and returned to their military compartment seats.

A Sikh sat opposite them, dressed in blue overalls, who had kept to himself most of the time. The name on his chest read, Maninder Singh. He, too, was a serving cadet in the Navy. He was eating a banana when Inder took out his tiffin into which Minhas eagerly dug in.

"Will you have some *paranthas* and mango pickle?" asked Inder, extending his tiffin towards Maninder.

Maninder murmured a thank you and helped himself.

"Nothing like home food, yaar," said Minhas closing his eyes with pleasure.

"Relish every bite of it. It will be some time before you get to eat it again," said Maninder, wistfully looking out of the window. Then turning to them again, "So, you are all set for a tough life, huh?"

"Yes, Sir!" said Inder and Minhas in unison.

"Good! Don't forget to write letters. Let your family hear about your new life regularly, so they are a part of your growth story."

The boys nodded obediently. Inder hardly got any sleep that night as the berth was very uncomfortable. The wind whipped his hair as he looked out into the darkness, seeing the distant lights of new homes in the villages, towns, and cities passing by.

I hope Pabbi is well. He sighed and took out a postcard to write to Jaikishen. At daybreak, the train stopped for 30 minutes at Hyderabad station. Inder stepped out, stretched, and found a post box to send his first communication home. On his return, close to his compartment, his attention got drawn to a skinny man with a wicker basket. He wore tight-fitting bell-bottom trousers, a colourful shirt, a yellow netted vest, and a red scarf tied around his neck. He was singing to the crowd gathered around him, bouncing around with agility to serve food from his basket. He was selling two pieces of white *peda* for 10 paise. Babu was standing nearby, and both he and Inder bought a plate each. The boy handed out a portion of a banana leaf to Inder and placed a serving of the *pedas* from one canister on it and put a milky paste on them from the other canister.

Inder shook Minhas up, "Wake up, and have some pedas."

Minhas blinked his eyes open and smiled. He put a piece into his mouth and instantly spat it out of the window, looking aghast. "What is this? It is not *peda*. It is not even sweet. It is sour! I feel like vomiting! They cheated you, brother."

Maninder, who was sitting opposite them, let out a loud laugh. "You are right, Minhas, they are not pedas. They are *idlis*, a south Indian delicacy made from fermented rice and *udad dal*. The white paste is coconut *chutney*." He laughed some more as Minhas's expression continued to be that of disgust.

"Your faces are a sight worth capturing on camera. But on a serious note, you're going to be experiencing a lot of new things. You should be open to all that the world has to offer. Life in the Navy will take you places not only in India but abroad too. The cuisine, the colours, the culture, the language, the people in each place will be different. Each of them has its own beauty – so keep your minds open to accept people and things as they are. And if you learn to appreciate the world in all its splendour, you will always feel at home, wherever you are."

He smiled at them and then looked out of the window and whistled at the boy, who ran up with a palm-full of idlis and a lavish serving of chutney.

"Yes, Saar! Do you want *idlis*? Best *idli chutney* Saar," he said, doing a jerky jig with his hand as he served the idli.

Maninder took a large bite and rolled his eyes with pleasure. Seeing him relish it so much, Inder dipped one idli into the chutney and bit into it hesitantly. He chewed slowly, savouring the new flavour his taste buds were experiencing, and finally swallowed.

"It's not so bad. I kind of like it," declared Inder and proceeded to take his next bite as the train started to leave the station.

Suddenly, they heard a clamour from the station. Before anyone realised, their compartment's windows were covered with faces and limbs of little boys and girls not more than 5 to 7 years of age hanging on to the bars of the window, even though the train moved to exit the station.

The kids pressed their faces to the windows, extending their hands through the bars begging for food or money. They all had soot-covered faces, broken teeth, hair stiff with grime, and tattered clothing. On Inder's window, a little girl hung on precariously. A stream of snot from her nose had coagulated on her upper lip. Her eyes were the size of cherries, and she had a beautiful toothy smile that lit up her smeared face. She peered in wonderment of the world on his side of the grill. Inder could see the innocence in her face - an ocean of untapped opportunity. She looked at him, wailing a heart-wrenching plea with practiced emotion, again and again.

Feeling sick in the pit of his stomach, Inder awkwardly ex-

PRIYA SHARMA SHAIKH

tended his remaining idlis to the little girl. She grabbed the food and took a bite, and offered some to the boy next to her. She didn't look at Inder a second time. As the train picked up speed, the children threw caution to the winds. They laughed, sang, and hooted as they hung on with unbelievable expertise. They didn't care that the passengers were gasping misgivings at the horror of the shocking mockery of human life - the children were literally on the edge of society. Inder looked away, knowing that he had no way to alleviate their condition.

They hung on to the next station, and just as they had appeared, they jumped off the moving train, and in a flash, disappeared into the world's shadows.

I have had so many unimaginable experiences within three days of leaving home – a far cry from my predictable and straightforward life back home.

— — —

CHAPTER 9: TOUCH DOWN AT TRAINING BASE

January 1954: Newness and possibilities abound

They changed trains for the third time in Madras. On the fourth day, on a humid morning, their train pulled in alongside Cochin station's platform. An endless line of dark-skinned bare-chested turbaned coolies, wearing checked folded lungis, waiting with bated breath, bounced into action as soon as the train slowed. The agile younger ones jumped into the train while the older ones ran alongside a window, making deals to carry the passengers' bags.

Inder looked shabby as did the other recruits when they alighted the train. A naval patrolman called Prithvi Mehta, an astute looking gentleman with a machine's stiffness received them. He took his role as the coordinator very seriously and maintained a straight face. In his immaculate creased uniform and every hair in place, he was the picture of neatness.

Prithvi greeted them briskly and conducted a roll call with each person to show their ID Cards or warrants. Then followed a quick briefing to the newbies, at the end of which they all boarded a 3-ton truck. The available seats got taken before Inder got on board, so he stood at the truck's edge and almost toppled out when it jerked to a start. He held on to the side and braced himself as it picked up speed to reveal the first glimpse of Cochin's beautiful landscape. Coconut trees and the bright pointy leaved green rice plantations swayed in the light breeze. The pathway was a mix of narrow, cramped lanes and wide roads with pockets of inhabitation nestled in the greenery in the form of pop-up stalls, vegetable and fish markets, schools, churches, and multi-coloured temples.

They drove up to a heavily guarded enclosure, with a sign that read in big, bold letters, INS Venduruthy. Inder was awestruck to see the neatness and orderliness at the various sections set along paved pathways lined with coconut trees and potted flowering plants.

As they arrived, Inder and the newbies stood in line for registration at the administrative office by producing their respective warrants once again. Shortly after, they got allotted their uniform and other utility kits.

"How are you boys settling in?" said Maninder peeking into Inder's barrack, as he struggled with setting up the mosquito net.

Inder looked overwhelmed. "I've never had so many possessions that I can claim as mine. It seems unreal!"

"It is for your pledge to serve the nation," said Maninder, helping him set up the net.

"It is going to take me a while to get used to this luxury. I'd love to see the expression on my parent's faces when they receive my next postcard," grinned Inder.

He settled his things into his allotted space, made his bed neatly, and rushed for the mandatory shave and haircut. After a quick bath, he slipped into his uniform. He felt very uncomfortable wearing the boat-neck tunic, but he dressed as instructed and looked at his reflection. He looked and felt different. He beamed at himself. *I am a sailor in the Indian Navy, and I now look the part!*

In a semi-circle on the grounds, Inder stood at attention along with the new batch of sailors as Nair, the Officer-in-

JUNGEE

Charge (OIC), took centre stage.

"Good afternoon, boys!"

"Good afternoon Sir."

"Welcome to INS Venduruthy. You begin your career with the Indian Navy today. You may stand at ease."

Inder got goosebumps. It felt surreal to be standing at ease as the OIC spoke about what they could expect over the coming days. He then led them on a tour of the base.

"All ten of the sailors' barracks are set alongside the channel. Take note of their brick coloured sloping roofs that allow for drainage during the heavy rains that hit the southern coast of India every monsoon," he said, pointing to the roofs.

"At the end of the barracks is the hospital, INHS Sanjeevni. Adjoining the barracks is the base office, behind which, facing the channel is the Basic & Divisional (B&D) School. Then comes the large ground, where you will have parades, and your daily physical training, starting at 6.30 am every morning. Opposite the barracks is the Administration Office and alongside that is the Commander in Chief South's Office, who is Commodore B. A. Soman. You will get to see him soon," he said, looking rather pleased.

"On the right of his office, is the Navigation & Direction (ND) School, Torpedo and Anti-Submarine (TAS) School, and Gunnery School, while to his left is the Communication School," he said, in an officious tone. "Behind the schools is INS Garuda, the aerodrome of the base. We have a cinema hall, that screens Hindi and English films too," he said and led them towards the channel.

"Here is the jetty school, the boat pool, and the nautical jetty. You will find docked sailing vessels and pulling boats like Dinghies, Whalers, Cutters, and Powerboats. You will get

187

to know the difference between these boats soon. The two jetties, alongside the boat pool, are used for Naval ships to come alongside, for your practical training, by the B&D school," said Nair, and looked at his watch.

"Very soon, the bugle will be played by the Quartermaster on duty. You will hear this sound at specific intervals throughout the day. You can know the time of day when it blows. The Hand's Call is the first to be played at 6 am. At 8 am, the Naval ensign flag gets hoisted by the signalman, duty officer, and bugler in the main parade ground."

"Then comes the Hands to Dinner call at 1 pm while at 4 pm is the Hands to Tea. The Naval ensign is then brought down at sunset with the bugle once again playing in the background. At 6.30 pm, the bugle for Hands to Supper will ring out, and finally, the Pipe Down call at 10 pm, which is the time for the base and all of you to call it a day. Is that clear?"

"Yes, Sir," said the boys, in varied intensity.

"So, can you tell me which call will get played some time now?"

"Hands to Tea," said a boy, while Inder tried to frame his response.

"Very good," said Nair with a smile.

After supper, Inder sat up in bed and looked around him. *My world has changed overnight. Unbelievable! I will never compromise this opportunity.* He smiled to himself and took out a postcard.

Respected Pitaji,

How is Pabbi? I have reached my destination safely. It is called INS Venduruthy, in Cochin. I am officially registered as a sailor with the Navy now. I will receive a salary of Rs.65. The base is beau-

tiful, and it is alongside the Ernakulum channel. There are 80 recruits in all, from across the country.

The Navy has already given me so much. I have three sets of uniform: shorts and singlets, a cap, a belt, a pair of boots, knee-high socks for parades, and a ceremonial uniform. I have also received a dhurrie, a mosquito net, a travel bag for transfers, two linen sets that include two sheets, a pillow with two covers, two towels, a few personal vessels - an aluminium plate and mug, and a steel fork and spoon. I have got allotted a coir bed and a locker for storing my personal belongings.

That boy I meet at the station, Minhas, and I share a barrack with 20 beds, with 18 others. Each group that shares a barrack is a division. My division is called Ashoka. This morning the barber of the base gave me a haircut. I am sure that all of you will have a hearty laugh if you see me now. I look like a scrubbing brush. My head feels very odd.

The food is good, but nothing like what Pabbi makes. With love to the little ones and regards to the elders. Your respectful son - Inderjit

Inder's eyes opened the next morning at 5.30 am. He jumped out of bed, itching.

"Despite the mosquito net I so many mosquito bites," gasped Inder scratching furiously.

"Bedbugs!" groaned Minhas switching on the torch. There were several tiny bloodstains on his sheet too. "I have been up almost the whole night, killing them."

After freshening up, Inder rushed to the sailors' galley to grab a mug of tea and then dressed in shorts, a vest, and canvas shoes for the first physical training on the grounds.

Inder outdid the rigorous routine's performance expectations, but he realised getting used to the humidity would take some time. He was dripping wet by the time their routine finished. After breakfast, they had their first set of skills training, including saluting, knots, and rope climbing.

. . .

Inder's first challenge was learning how to march. He couldn't seem to get his coordination right and kept lifting the wrong arm and leg and would end up tripping himself or someone else. The OIC for this part of the training was an Englishman called McClain. He was a tall, stocky man. He spoke minimal Hindi and was particular about getting the whole team to march correctly.

"You! What's your name?" said McClain.

"Inderjit Sharma, Sir," said Inder, standing to attention.

"You stay back, while others can go for dinner."

"Yes, Sir," said Inder. *I am in trouble.*

"At ease, Indianjit. Marching will teach you brotherhood and help you build team spirit, and perhaps someday, you may need to lead a platoon. So, watch me closely."

"Thank you, Sir," smiled Inder, relieved that McClain was compassionate.

"When you walk, your arms swing naturally, don't they? We move our hands to keep the balance of our bodies while we move. Marching is a more pronounced form of walking, with a higher swing of the arms. Watch how I march slowly at first, and then faster and finally a proper march," said McClain demonstrating as he spoke, "Don't worry about feeling a certain stiffness at first. It will ease once your body sets into the rhythm."

He made Inder practice multiple times up and down the parade ground.

"*Achha hai,* Indianjit. You will get better each day. Now run along and grab some dinner."

Over the next few days, Inder improved his marching skill, and soon he was in sync with his platoon. McLain was delighted with them.

"Good job!" he said, clapping his hands.

. . .

One sultry afternoon, Inder was returning from an exciting sailing exercise, where the OIC taught them about the various boats and the basics of ships and tides when he saw Joginder Singh doing a jig towards him. Inder smiled, looking embarrassed.

Joginder was one of the recruits in Ashoka, a tall and slim Sikh from Punjab. He wore a kerchief-turban that held his long hair in a knot at the top of his head. He played defence in Inder's football team and often made them win. He was a 'full of life' person with crazy antics up his sleeve, keeping everyone in splits. Inder soon befriended him.

"I've got a letter!" teased Joginder.

"You are a lucky guy! I have written so many letters to my parents but have received none," scowled Inder shaking his head.

"Urdu is not my strongest skill, but listen to this. My dear puttar Koogh! Is that your name?"

"That is my letter!" said Inder jumping at Joginder, who slipped out of his grasp, and ran around the mosquito-netted cots in the barrack, with Inder chasing after him. Inder tackled Joginder and snatched the postcard from him. It was over a month since he had left home, and he was happy to receive his first letter. He found a quiet spot under a tree to read it.

My dear Koogh,

May you live long and be happy always. I was so happy to receive your first postcard. I am so proud of your decision to take control of your life. I have some disturbing news to share with you, though. Your mother took ill due to the grief of your departure. We thought she would settle, but she refused to eat and kept crying. She started getting nightmares, and with each passing day, her condition got worse. Much against her wishes, we had to take her to the hospital. The Doctor says she has become weak. I know this news will sadden you, but I couldn't keep it from you. You focus on your work, son. We will do our best to take care of her.

Jaikishen

Inder was crestfallen. His brow clouded over, and his eyes were vacant as he stared at the words. *How selfish I am. What will I achieve if something happens to Pabbi!*

Joginder's smile faded as he approached Inder and sat cautiously beside him. "Sorry about the prank, yaar. What happened? Is everything okay?" he said, putting his hand on his friend's shoulder.

"My mother is in the hospital. I should go home. My dream is not worth her life, yaar."

"I understand, but this letter would have been written some time ago, Inderjit."

"Maybe her condition has improved. Do you think it might be a good idea to call someone in your neighbourhood to check before deciding to go?"

"Yes, you are right. I do have a phone number. I will book a lightening call right away."

"I'll come with you."

When Inder emerged from the phone booth, his smile said it all. Geeta's severe condition had improved, and she was back home and recovering fast.

"This calls for you to get me a *chota*," said Joginder hugging Inder.

. . .

Besides the absorbing course material and physical training, neatness and perfection were encouraged rigorously, from the first day as a requisite part of their lifestyle. Strict daily inspections of their living spaces and personal hygiene got conducted - beds made in a prescribed way, washed, ironed uniforms on hangers, arranged drawers, cleaned and polished footwear, crew haircuts, and clean-shaven faces, trimmed nails, and clean noses and ears. Social and official etiquette while interacting with seniors, also had an essential guideline. Anybody out of line got sent on a rigorous running drill. The obsessive need for perfection made Inder very particular and peculiar about how he led his life, body, and space, a habit that stayed with him for the rest of his life.

One morning, nine months after they had arrived at Venduruthy, McLain stood in front of them with a grim face.

"I have some news for you," he said in a dull tone.

Inder's stomach knotted with anxiety. *What had we done wrong, now?*

"I am happy to say that the Ashoka team has graduated the 9-month course at INS Venduruthy with flying colours. A word of caution for each of you: You cannot rest on your laurels and believe you have done your best. Your graduation is the beginning, and you have many miles to go, so there is no place for complacency. To create a great life for yourselves, make sure you choose the right ingredients - consistency and focus in your effort and putting your duty ahead of yourself. Push your limits so that you grow stronger and better with each day. Is that clear?"

"Yes, Sir!" said the boys in a loud synchronised chorus.

"Each of you has worked hard, and I can proudly say you are well-baked cookies today," said McLain candidly, "Go on and celebrate your first success, boys!" he said with a hint of a smile.

The Ashoka barrack burst into merriment until it was time for lights out.

. . .

The morning after, Inder went through the daily exercise and running routine and then went in for a shower. His body was still wet as he stood in his bath towel, in front of the chipped mirror. He stared at himself. He had grown. His chiselled muscles glistened as he flexed his arms in the dim light. His torso was taller and broader, and his short bristly hair gave him a tough look. He admired his reflection changing the angles to see which side looked better – *Definitely my left profile.*

He smiled as he saw the Lion appear in the mirror. He looked at ease, sitting on his haunches. *Was that a twinkle in those ochre eyes?* The Lion shook his mane out, stood up and roared, and then strolled out of the sailors' shared bathroom.

Inder blinked his eyes furiously, trying to contain his happiness. The evening before, he had celebrated two things – his graduation and the news of his first posting orders. He was to serve on INS Bengal, a minesweeper from the Second World War. She was alongside the naval docks in his dream city.

Bombay, I'll finally get to see you.

. . .

When he arrived in Bombay, the first thing to hit Inder was the humidity and the sweltering heat. He stood on the platform at Victoria Terminus Station, listening to the sounds of Hindi, English, and Marathi - another new language.

He felt amazed as the visuals he had seen in the films came alive as he stepped out. *So much to absorb!* Innumerable people went about their business in a bee-like buzz as they pushed past him. The intricate architecture of the station and buildings around it reaching up to the skies. He gaped at the double-decker bus, the tram, and the fancy cars that passed him. Mixed smells of mogra flowers, fish, and fried snacks wafted to him.

After much asking, he reached the Lion Gate, opposite the Prince of Wales Museum at Kala Ghoda, and as directed, made his way around the awe-inspiring dockyard to where INS Bengal stood alongside. He looked up at her stern and then across her length. She was formidable in comparison to the ships he had seen in Cochin. He breathed deeply and stepped onto the gangway to get on board with his bags in his hands. The sailor on duty greeted him warmly and made him sign the register.

Inder's sea-time in the Indian Navy began.

Life on board Bengal was like clockwork. He awoke at 6 am, exercised, and ate breakfast before aiding the Naval insignia's salute at the Quarterdeck and the national flag at Fox'l. He then completed his assigned duties, aided the pipe down of flags at sunset, ate his supper, and finally chatted with colleagues at the cowshed (sailors sleeping area) until the lights went out at 10 pm.

One stormy morning on Bengal anchored at sea, Inder greased some wires on the Fox'l when he heard an animated discussion on the starboard side. A small boat of the ship that had come alongside needed to get pulled up. The sailor in the boat was unable to hook the boat onto the lowered pulley. Everyone assembled, shouted instructions. Inder, too looked down at the embarrassed sailor. The Captain looked irritated.

"Sir, may I go down by rope and help?" said Inder to the Div-

PRIYA SHARMA SHAIKH

isional Officer.

"Are you sure? It is quite a height, Inderjit."

"I will do it, Sir, if I have your permission."

After getting the Captain's approval, the Divisional Officer gave Inder the go-ahead. Inder braced himself and then swung himself onto the rough rope and started climbing down while the crew cheered his bravado. He started hurrying his descent in his enthusiasm, and he miscalculated and lost his grip and slipped. The crew on board gasped, but Inder clung to the swaying rope. He slid to the bottom, holding on to the rope all the while. By the time he reached the boat, blood was all over his vest.

"Oh my God, Inder! You are so badly hurt."

"These peeled hands are for showing off. No worries. First aid will take care of it."

"Thanks for coming to my rescue, Inder! Is the Captain angry?"

"He is worried, I think. Just say sorry," said Inder and showed him how to hoist the boat, and they returned to the ship amidst cheers.

. . .

Bengal sailed to Ceylon - Inder's first international destination. On a visit to the local zoo, he stopped at the lion's caged enclosure. The wild cat's eyes were submissive, something unimaginable for the Lion he had known in his fantasy world. *I, too, had felt like the caged lion not so long ago. Life has changed so much within a year!*

. . .

After completing his tenure on Bengal, Inder returned to Venduruthy for the Radar Controllers Course - RC3 at the Gunnery School. For this, he got assigned to the officer-in-charge, Commander Dhinsa, at the radar control room at the coastal battery in Cochin. Officers visited the establishment for gunnery practice of 4," and 4.7" diameter guns and the Bofors anti-aircraft guns installed there.

"Inderjit, your tasks include calculating the range for shooting and setting the guns' elevation for firing," said Dhinsa.

Inder arrived every morning ahead of his reporting time, impeccably turned out, and performed all his duties as instructed.

"Your tenure here is complete – that means you have to move on," said Dhinsa.

"It was a pleasure to work here with you, Sir," said Inder looking crestfallen.

"Inderjit, I am pleased with your work ethic during your time here, and I am marking you as a commission-worthy candidate," said Dhinsa.

"Thank you, Sir. Sorry, Sir, but what does that mean?"

"Simply put, you are a boy whose progress is worth watching. I wish you all the best."

The dream of becoming 'worthy' got planted in Inder's head.

...

His next post was at the Radar Controllers course - RC2. A young cadet from another batch called R.G. Kumar drew his attention, every night. He would sit up in his mosquito net, reading some books.

"What do you keep reading RG? Are you studying for an exam?" joked Inder, after a few nights.

"Yes. I am studying for my exams in Maths, Algebra, Physics, English, Trigonometry, History, and Geography."

"So many subjects! Whatever for?"

"Passing the higher education tests will make me eligible to be an officer."

"An officer? Is that possible for us sailors?"

"Achieving anything great is possible, but it requires sacrifice and diligence."

Inder tossed and turned in bed all night. He awoke feeling groggy and with a new resolve of becoming an officer - This was Inder's third decision.

He issued books from the library and began his quest. Since he was a commission-worthy candidate, he also got encouragement and guidance from officers.

. . .

After RC2, Inder travelled to Liverpool to bring back INS Mysore, a British Cruiser. One afternoon, he rushed to grab lunch and bumped into someone.

"Sorry!" he said and realised it was his old friend, Minhas.

"Oye, Inder! Great to see you here, my friend. Which team are you with?"

"With the Captain, yaar. And I am to report in his cabin at 1 pm before his lunchtime. I have to eat my lunch before that."

"Isn't it scary to work for him?"

"No yaar, he is very nice. He lets me go when he doesn't need anything. And he encourages me a lot. I feel blessed."

"You were always the blessed one, my dear friend. Catch

you later."

. . .

Inder found a nook and opened his textbook to study, in the pool of light from the porthole.

"Now that is a sight, I wish I'd see more often," said a deep drawl. It was Rear Admiral Chakravarty, the Flag Officer-in-charge Western Fleet, along with the tall and good-looking ship's Captain and Inder's boss, Cdr. SM Nanda.

Inder bounced up and saluted stiffly. "Good afternoon, Sir!"

"At ease, boy. What are you reading?" asked Chakravarty.

"Geography, Sir. I am studying for the higher-education test, Sir."

"Excellent. What is your name?"

"Inderjit Sharma, Sir."

"He is my Coxswain, Sir. Very efficient and mindful boy. I'm happy to see he has a dream too," said Nanda, smiling at his protege.

"Thank you, Sir," said Inder, conscious of their proximity.

"Have you met Arogyaswamy?" asked Nanda. Seeing Inder's puzzled look, he added, "He is the education officer on board. He will be of great help to you."

"Right, Sir! I will meet him."

"All the best, Inderjit," said Chakravarty, nodding in agreement with Nanda.

"Thank you, Sir."

Inder saluted and watched the two men move down the corridor.

. . .

"You bookworm!" said a gruff voice. Inder looked up, startled to see Minhas's face beaming down at him.

"Scared you, didn't I?"

"Yes, you did! I thought it was one of the senior officers. It's going well, yaar. Cdr. Arogyaswamy is such a good teacher. He is so patient with me. He is teaching me Maths, Trigonometry, Physics, and English too. Why don't you also learn, Minhas? Someday you too can be an officer, yaar. It will be such a paradigm shift. Just imagine commanding a ship someday."

"Wow, what dreams you have, my friend! And I agree that we have to raise the bar for ourselves. But it's a Sunday, for God's sake. So, no lectures today. Drop your books, and let's go and see Liverpool!"

"What is the point when I don't have any money to spare?"

"You don't have to spend. We can see the sights, the beautiful girls, and window shop!"

"What's that?"

"You'll figure it out. Let's go see the world beyond India."

. . .

Mysore's workup was complete, and she started her journey to India. She stopped over at Gibraltar, Malta, Yugoslavia, Port Syed, and Eden through the Suez Canal. In each city, Inder relented to Minhas's coaxing. He found the architecture, people, and stores in each of the cities fascinating. He thanked Minhas for helping him see so much and teaching him the art of window shopping.

A good four months after being commissioned in Liverpool, Mysore finally harboured at the Bombay dockyard; and

JUNGEE

Inder felt prepared and appeared for the test. "The results will take a couple of hours," said the examiner, with a smile.

Inder felt anxious and used the time to visit the post office and send the monthly money order of Rs.100 to Jaikishen. He ate lunch and returned for his results.

You have passed, the duty officer had said very casually. Inder gasped with joy.

Yes! He gathered his report and rushed back to Mysore to meet his teacher and mentor Arogyaswamy.

"I'm proud of you, Inderjit!" said Arogyaswamy, the wise man that Inder had grown to respect so much. He patted Inder on his shoulder. "Your next milestone is to appear before the selection board at INS Angre. Clearing that will make you eligible for the upper-yard man course. Be immaculate in your turnout and read up on current affairs before you meet them."

. . .

Inder got up earlier than usual. He was to meet the selection board that morning. He felt a flutter in his stomach. He grabbed the Times of India and headed straight for the mess. The Congress Party's socialistic pattern drew his attention, and he scoured the article as he sipped his tea.

Captain Krishnan headed the selection board. In all, there were four officers.

"Good morning, Sir," said Inder, saluting stiffly.

"Good morning, Inderjit. Be at ease and please sit down," said Lieutenant Commander Dawson, one of the officers, "So, what are your views about a socialistic society for India?"

Inder blinked and swallowed. "Sir, in my opinion, a society is like a jungle that allows everyone to thrive and only the fit survive. You have to work hard to put food on the table for your family. Whatever be your craft, whether it is manufacturing or research or films, it is the ones that have the passion for keeping forging ahead despite hurdles that will succeed. It is a human prerogative to set new benchmarks to improve standards of living. That is how we progress and find happiness. In the Navy, too, when you work hard, you get noticed. And when the time comes, you are given responsibility. I have had tremendous personal growth in this learning process and am willing to go the extra mile to serve. But in a socialist state, it doesn't matter if you work hard or not. You get the same treatment. And that, to my mind, creates complacency and regression. So, socialism is not a way of governance for India."

Inder's eyes met Dawson's briefly. He had a smirk on his lips as he nodded slowly. Inder responded to the rest of the technical questions, but a niggling fear stayed with him when he left the board room.

What did Dawson's expression mean? His smile looked sarcastic. They probably had a hearty laugh at my expense. Inder walked straight out of the building without saying a word to the rest of the applicants.

On his return to Venduruthy, Inder changed trains at Arkunam Junction and bumped into Dawson, again.

"Good evening, Sir!" said Inder.

"Good evening. You did well, huh?" said Dawson with the same smile.

His statement and familiar smile made Inder's heart quiver with anxiety. Meanwhile, it was time for him to be on leave, so he bid goodbye to his friends and took a train to Phagwara.

...

He was excited about reuniting with everyone after two whole years. The weather was chilly, and his pace quickened

JUNGEE

as he entered the narrow lanes of Korian Mohalla. When Inder approached their lane, he saw Geeta at their doorway with a prayer thali in her hand in the fog. She wore a shawl and sweater over a white-bordered sari. He quickened his step with a smile on his face.

Geeta stood still looking towards him. He seemed familiar. She tried to collect her thoughts and strained to see the face but stood transfixed. *Who is that? O my Krishna, I forget too much lately. Is that Koogh? No, he looks like him. He looks different. And so much darker. That is not my son, for sure. This boy is taller, broader, and has such short hair, unlike Koogh. O Krishna, it is Koogh!*

"Pairi pauna Pabbi," said Inder, and leaned forward to touch her feet.

It was then that the clouds cleared, and she cried out aloud, bending to hug him, weeping tears of joy and calling out to Jaikishen and Ghonni all at once. She was overjoyed.

"Live long and happy, my son," said Jaikishen, happily embracing Inder.

Geeta repeated again and again, "Krishna is great. I just prayed for you to return, and here you are."

Throughout the day, she kept touching his face and head, not believing he was home. The prodigal son had returned anew! Coming home felt great. Every family member, including Soma and Brij and their respective families, assembled in their home to meet Inder. Geeta and Sharda prepared all his favourite treats. Oddly, he felt awkward and like a special guest in his own home. It felt good to be loved, but the constant attention felt overwhelming. However, although so many people surrounded him, his mind stayed preoccupied, and after lunch, he slipped away to his spot on the terrace.

I have worked very hard, then why do I fear failure? What if I fail and remain a sailor? Okay, stop! No, more negative chatter. I will not stagnate even if a hurdle comes. I will not give up.

He sat with his hand clenched against his forehead. He heard a sound at the doorway and turned to see Daulat Ram, hobble towards him! Inder rushed to touch his feet. "God bless you with a long and successful life. Look at my handsome grandson! Why are you making your old grandfather climb the stairs to meet you?"

"Sorry, Paiyaji, I just came up to look around. Everything is still the same. It is great to be back. You should have called out to me, and I would have come down to meet you."

"Well, I need the exercise." Daulat Ram patted Inder's shoulders. "I am happy to see you have toughened up. But your mind seems preoccupied. Is everything okay?"

"No, nothing at all, Paiyaji."

"As I've said before, you can't lie to an old man. Out with it!"

Inder smiled, looking sheepish. "You are right, Paiyaji. I appeared for an interview before coming. I am worried about the result. I feel I ruined it. But one of the interviewers said I did fine. Even though I keep reassuring myself that all will be well and that I won't give up, self-doubt creeps into my brain. I keep thinking that I will fail," he said, his voice trailing off.

"And what makes you think that way?"

"Because I haven't heard anything yet."

"How did you prepare for the exam?"

"I have never studied so much, Paiyaji. I know I could not have done better."

"Then, that was all you needed to do! Have confidence in yourself, son, and enjoy the journey called life. Ups and downs are a part of it. Don't worry about the results. Be like a brook that flows down mountains, valleys, and cities to merge into the deep ocean. It keeps going until it reaches its destination, as should you. Your job is to keep trying. And don't worry so much, the good news is on its way. Now come on and enjoy being with the family," said Daulat Ram. He slapped Inder's back fondly and pulled him down the stairs to join the guffawing below.

The next morning Inder awoke to Geeta, shaking him. "A telegram has arrived for you."

He opened it with bated breath.

Selected as Upper Yardman. Come to INS Venduruthy for Officers Training Course immediately.

– – –

CHAPTER 10: A LEAP OF FAITH

1959: An officer is also a gentleman

Inder was all of 23 in early 1959 when he reported as a trainee for the Upper Yardman Course at Venduruthy. His training at the B&D School was to be for nine months.

Apart from Joginder from Ashoka, his new course mates included Sud from Himachal, Gupta from Delhi, Tripathi from Uttar Pradesh, Martis from Mangalore, and Janardhan Deo from Orissa, each adding to the potpourri of Inder's naval experience. He felt awkward with the new joiners and kept a respectful distance from them when outside class. Seeing Inder's prowess in class, on the field, and at sea exercises, they slowly gravitated towards befriending him. Inder, however, kept his distance.

One morning, he finished his exercise drill ahead of the others and returned to his barrack. He tuned into Radio Ceylon. Mukesh's voice was singing, *"Kisi ki muskurahaton pe ho nisar"* from the film *Anari*. He sang along, unaware that his course mates could hear him from outside the barrack. They burst in on him. He felt embarrassed and stopped singing. However, they kept singing in a huddle and pulled him in. Inder smiled and let go of his inhibitions to join them. They sang, danced, and laughed in chorus. After that, Inder got declared the in-house entertainer. It became a ritual to make him sing their favourite songs in their spare time and when emotions challenged them. Inder felt at home.

Their friendship went up another notch when they participated in a 40-mile long Cutter Boat pulling race from Cochin to Alleppey and back. They trained rigorously for several weeks. All the hard work and team spirit paid off on race day, as their skill was unmatched. They were declared the unbeatable team.

Upon completing the Upper Yardman training, Inder, Deo and Joginder got transferred to Bombay for a 6-month sea attachment on INS Delhi, a fleet ship. Their tenure's main thrust was to learn navigation, watchkeeping, and fix the ship's position using the stars, sun, and other navigational marks. The Commanding Officer of the ship Capt. Pereira was very passionate about sailing. He added Joginder, Deo, and Inder into a Whaler crew along with Nandi, Patnaik, Chandy, and Lt. Guha as the Coxswain.

It was a bright and humid morning in Cochin when Pereira's boys took their positions in the Whaler near Tevara Bridge. At the shot of the gun, they leaped ahead of the other participating boats. The team followed Joginder's full and fast strokes and Guha's calls of encouragement. They pulled at a menacing pace, making their vests stick like a second skin to their agile, muscular bodies and shot through the water, winning by a considerable margin. Pereira was thrilled and celebrated the team gregariously with hurrahs and cheers by the ship's company, followed by drinks and a sumptuous meal.

Inder's tenure on Delhi was the culmination of his training as Upper Yardman, after which he travelled to Bangalore for the final leg of his journey to becoming an officer. He was to meet the Services Selection Board.

A day later, Inder and his course-mates, Martis, Joginder, Deo, Sud, Tripathi, and Gupta, received letters from the board. From the 06th of September 1960, they got commissioned as officers of the Indian Navy, with the rank of Sub-Lieutenant.

It was a night of celebration as they cheered each other in a victory dance in the sailor's mess. Before lights out, Inder took out a postcard.

Respected Pitaji,

Pairin pauna. It is a day of pride and humility for us as a family, as from tomorrow, your son will be an officer. My salary, too, will increase from Rs. 65 to Rs.350 per month and this is a significant milestone in my career in the Navy. I am moving from the sea into the vast ocean, where there will be deeper waters and bigger fish to work along with. There is no doubt that I will have to work very hard to stay abreast and keep pace with the bigger league. Striving for giving nothing short of my excellence to every moment has become my goal, and staying present to my goal is my sadhana, Pitaji. I seek your blessings and that of all the elders in the family.

Inderjit

. . .

Life as an officer brought with it several changes, getting used to, which would take time. The first change was that his locker from the sailor's ward got emptied, and his few belongings got shifted into the officer's ward, where he shared a room with Joginder. The room was airy with large windows, a bed, a study table, a chair, and a cupboard all to himself.

The second change was in his uniform. Although the colour of his uniform remained white, the style changed. His wardrobe now had a host of shirts, shorts, and trousers. There were also sets of light blue shirts and navy blue trousers for gunnery drills and various uniforms for different occasions and seasons. He wore his all-white uniform of trousers, half-sleeved shirt, belt, shoes, and cap and pinned his black and gold stripes-pad on his shoulders. He felt a surge of happiness, pride, and humility. His image in the mirror was evidence of the new phase of his life.

JUNGEE

He experienced the third change when he stepped out of his ward to walk towards the Officers' Mess for breakfast. The junior sailors on duty saluted him, stiffly, "Good morning, Sir."

"Good morning," smiled Inder, feeling awkward. The respect he received felt good.

The fourth change was the most radical for Inder, as it demanded a shift in his daily social etiquette. One part of his training was learning how to dance. The instructor, Mrs. Roy Milan, was a charming and elegant lady with all the world's patience. Each time she tried to teach Inder how to do the ball dance and pulled him towards her, he pulled back. He felt so nervous that he ended up with two left feet. "Inderjit, why are you so shy? Stop being so nervous, boy. It is an essential part of being an officer. What if your CO's wife wishes to dance with you at a party? You will be stamping her feet if you dance like this. Come on and watch my step."

"Yes, Ma'am," said Inder, blushing and biting his lip as she led him onto the dance floor.

Learning about alcohol and how to drink it was a part of the social training.

"Come and have a peg IJ," said Joginder.

"No, thank you," said Inder quietly.

"IJ, drinking is not compulsory, but it is a sign of being inclusive with your unit. The taste may not feel good to start with, but you will acquire it with time, and you will eventually have a preferred drink. You always have the choice to set your limit," said his supervisor, Roy Milan, who had eavesdropped on their conversation.

"I will keep that in mind, Sir," said Inder.

He concluded that although the Navy's social life had a lot

of merriment, he would make his presence on such occasions as discreet as possible. Get-togethers meant dressing as per code, holding a glass of whiskey in his hand all through the evening, and bobbing his head to the popular song, Tequila by the Champs. He steered clear of dancing.

The last and final change was learning to swim with the big fish – the intelligent, sophisticated, and well-spoken officers from the 16th course of NDA - the National Defence Academy! They were now Inder's course mates. Rumours of their snobbery had been doing the rounds. Inder decided to be cautious around them and try doubly hard to keep pace with their intellectual sharpness and excellent communication skills.

"Hello, friends, may I have your attention please," said Sub Lieutenant SK Das animatedly, at their first dinner at the officer's mess.

Inder looked towards the voice to see a slim man with a charming smile. *What a glib tongue he has.*

"I'd like to introduce you to us. We all have an official name that you are aware of, but what you don't know is our rechristened names," he said with a twinkle in his eyes. "So, let me have the privilege of reintroducing you to us. He walked around animatedly to introduce his NDA colleagues. "Raja Menon, one of the brightest of our course is called RAJA. The dashing Sushil Issacs is called IKE. Ram Gopal Kumar is called GULU. Our smart Sikh from Punjab, Jagmohan Sodhi, is called JUGGY. Buntwal Rao from Karnataka is called Bunty."

"And yours truly is SK Das from Orissa. I love having fun, sometimes at your expense, too – so watch out! They call me DAVY, and sometimes CHOTUDAS, too," he said, and everyone burst into laughter.

"But wait a minute, there is more. We have decided some names for all of you too. Janardhan Deo, we will call you JACK,

Joginder, you will be called TIGER, Sud will be pronounced SUD like mud, and thanks to his original home being in Pakistan and his eloquence in Urdu, Inderjit will be called PATHAN."

"But ...," protested Inder.

"Don't be defensive, Pathan. It is all in jest."

Inder played along for the moment. But later, when he stopped responding to Pathan, they too called him IJ.

One evening, the team was relaxing on the lawns in front of their ward.

"Hey IJ, I heard from Tiger that you sing beautifully. Can you sing a song for me? I can't remember its words, though. It's a romantic one, by Guru Dutt," said Davy. "That Choudhary and the moon something..."

"You mean *Chaudhvin ka Chand*," laughed Inder.

Davy chortled and urged him to oblige. Inder crooned the melodic track, and then another song and another. Soon the rest of the gang lounging around on the lawns joined in to listen. Under the nippy starry night, each of them got lost in their thoughts. Inder felt a warm fuzzy feeling to see his course mates be so comfortable around him. He could see that they liked him for what he was. He belonged and felt no judgment. They were a good set of men - Inder knew he would learn a lot from them.

Their technical training took them to a variety of bases. For the electrical engineering of power generation and its distribution, they went to INS Valsura in Jamnagar. For the understanding of engines, boilers, generators, and fire-fighting, INS Shivaji at Lonavala was their host. For supply and administration, they went to INS Hamla, in Bombay. And for their pre-watchkeeping technical courses, they came back to

Venduruthy.

Venduruthy was an altogether different experience this time, as his roommate was Raja, whose intelligence inspired Inder, as did his skill in sailing. On their first weekend, they set out sailing in a dinghy on the backwaters. Their sailing was thrilling but exhausting. They halted for the night, alongside the shore, and crashed on the floor of the boat. Inder awoke to the sound of giggles and chatter in Malayalam from a bunch of local kids.

Inder realised that he and Raja were their muse – they had been so exhausted and sweaty that they had slept bare-chested in just their shorts. He slipped on his T-shirt and waved to them.

"Raja, wake up. I need fuel to move. Ask these kids where we can get some breakfast," said Inder poking Raja, who stirred grudgingly.

"Ouch! My back is stiff as a rod, man," groaned Raja. He turned on his back and waved to the gigglers. He talked to them in Malayalam and got directions to the closest eatery.

"Kerala is the only state that mandates education for every gender and class of society, because of which they produce some of the brightest minds in the country," said Raja slurping on the remains of his sambhar.

"Impressive, but, sadly, they don't understand Hindi at all. It is the national language, yaar."

"They believe they need to know English as that is the most widely spoken language globally. They learn it from the beginning of school, so they speak it reasonably well, although with a strong accent. Good enough to get them jobs overseas," he smiled.

After breakfast, they set sail again, but by the time they reached Ernakulum, the high tide had made it impossible for the boat to proceed.

"The tide is weaker along the shore, Raja, so let's steer the boat to the coast and row along with it," said Inder.

"Good idea, IJ."

They went on for a while until it was dark again. By about 10.30 in the night, Inder couldn't pull the boat any further, so he got off and climbed onto the channel's parapet and started walking on it, pulling the boat's head rope. Raja meanwhile steered her clear from the bank of the channel. A bunch of sailors returning after an evening drink at the mess saw Inder pulling the boat in his shorts and jeered at him – they were unaware that Inder and Raja were officers. Inder ignored them and kept pulling on till they reached the boat pool. It was 1.30 in the night when they secured the boat to the jetty. Inder was exhausted. He dragged his feet to their room and flopped onto his bed.

"An expedition gone wrong is what you could call this. I don't know how we will wake up for gunnery. Why haven't you switched on the light IJ?" said Raja staggering in after Inder. He switched on the light and gasped to see Inder's blistered hands bleeding! He shook him hard. "IJ, you need medication, mate!" But Inder was out like a light.

...

Inder did get first aid the next morning, and although he felt weary in class, he rushed back to pack as they were to leave for Coimbatore. Their training there included the firing of small arms and the 4" gun firing at the coastal battery. It required him to do hours of shooting in the hot sun for a whole ten weeks. There was no time to tend to his blisters, and Inder was one to take copious notes, so the blisters healed themselves.

"This course is tough, and the humidity is killing," said

Inder to Raja.

"We aren't anyone to complain, IJ. We'd better gear up. I hear training is going to get even more intensive from here on."

Raja was so right. What followed was an overdrive of learning at the various schools at Venduruthy. By the end of which, Inder acquired knowledge and practical experience of anti-submarine torpedoes and rockets, sonars, torpedoes, depth charges, drawing charts, navigation, early warning radars and navigational radars, gyros, magnetic compasses, the functionalities of a ship's operation room, the various types of transmission and reception sets, electronic warfare, messaging using semaphore flags and lights, coding and decoding secret messages. He also got an understanding of the war course, which involved taking note of a developing situation at any time and deciding the use of force based on the options at hand. The batch got divided into syndicates of friend and foe in wartime situations and got asked to suggest the most suitable course of action.

...

A couple of weekends before the end of their training, Jack burst into Inder's room in his usual exuberant manner.

"Hey, IJ, our training is ending soon. God knows when we will be able to do anything fun together again. Let's see the countryside on bikes during the upcoming Onam holidays. What say?"

Inder looked up from his notes, folded his arms, and smiled, "Where to?"

"Trivandrum. We'll borrow or hire, yaar. Choose a finger – one is yes, and the other is no," said Jack sticking out his right-hand index and middle fingers for Inder to choose.

"How do I know you won't cheat me on the answer? I don't know which finger is which?"

"Should I make chits?"

"Looks like you are not going to take no for an answer. What do I have to do?"

"Nothing. I will make all the arrangements," grinned Jack.

. . .

They borrowed cycles from the base and set off before sunrise on the 24th of August – it was a Thursday, and the boys had been given a long weekend to the 27th. Having started early, they soon crossed the bridge over the Ernakulum channel and put in several hours of cycling. Past noon, they got off the road and walked up to a home nestled in the foliage.

"Let's get some water from here," said Jack, wiping his sweaty face.

A beautiful young woman dressed in off-white silk and gold bordered sari opened the door. She had gold ornaments on her neck, ears, and hands. Her forehead had a red dot, below which a fine line of dried *Chandan* held the place of pride. Her hair was in a loose plait, and from it hung strands of fresh mogra flowers.

"What can I do for you?" she said with a warm smile.

"Ma'am, we are naval officers under training at Cochin's base, and we are on a cycling trek to Trivandrum. We have run out of water. Can you be kind enough to give us a refill, please?" said Jack.

"Yes, sure. But why just water? It is Onam today. It is a very auspicious day for us. You are welcome to have a meal with us too. My name is Laila. And you are?"

"This is Inderjit Sharma and I am Janardhan Deo."

"Welcome," she smiled, making way for them to enter the house.

"No,...," Inder hesitated.

"This is a God sent offer, IJ. We don't say no to home-cooked food!" whispered Jack.

The house bustled with people, amid chores for the festival. They paused when they saw the awkward-looking strangers, dressed in shorts, T-shirts, and sports shoes at the doorstep. Laila requested them to remove their shoes and led them into the living room.

The moment she was out of sight, Inder looked around them. It was a beautiful, neat home with wide divans and armchairs and several artifacts. Inder pointed out framed images of Marx, Stalin, and Lenin on the walls.

"Jack, I believe we have landed ourselves in the house of the prominent communist leader, Ms. Gopalan. I have read about Ma'am. She is one of the founding members of the communist party in Kerala."

This time it was Jack's turn to look awkward when Laila returned. "Your prestigious family might not appreciate that we are uninvited."

"Nonsense. We feel blessed to be able to serve anyone on Onam."

"But our attire is ungainly Ma'am," said Inder feeling embarrassed.

"It's okay because I too have had friends that trained at the Cochin base, so I understand," she laughed. "Onam is our New Year, and a celebration of the harvest in Kerala. So, all are welcome."

"You should see how the locals celebrate. They have boat races called *Vallam Kali*, tiger dances called *Pulli Kali,* and masked dances. Men and women dance to offer worship and food to Lord Vamana, the incarnate of Lord Vishnu. You must try to catch some of the festivities, but only after you have eaten," she smiled cheerfully, as a battery of people arrived bearing trays of food.

They set a large banana leaf in front of Inder and Jack and served small portions of various preparations.

"This is Olan, made of white gourd and black peas in a coconut gravy. And the white gravy is Avial, again a coconut-based mixed vegetable, and that is Thoran, a leafy vegetable cooked with chilies and coconut. And these are chutneys and home-made pickles. All of them can best get eaten with hot steamed rice," she beamed.

Inder remembered Maninder's advice and savoured the new flavours that titillated his taste buds. The food was delicious. They completed the meal with a delicious *Payassam*. It reminded Inder of the rice kheer Pabbi made on festivals. He wondered how she would adjust to an environment like Kerala. He smiled, thinking of the tantrums that would ensue if she was expected to eat out of banana leaves.

They thanked Laila and her family for their gracious hospitality and resumed their journey. At Alleppey, they caught the famed boat race and tiger dance and later caught a Malayalam film, called *Sreekovil.*

"That was a great experience, Jack, thank you," said Inder as they walked into the gates of Venduruthy the next evening.

"Anytime, my friend. I'm so glad you liked it," said Jack putting his arm around Inder's shoulder.

. . .

PRIYA SHARMA SHAIKH

Their tenure at Venduruthy soon came to an end. It had been the most wholesome year for Inder. He felt technically enriched, and for the first time, he felt socially comfortable. His reservations had flown with the winds. He sealed lifelong friendships with Davy, Jack, Raja, Avnish, Bunty, Gulu, Tiger, and Ike. Not only did they peg his benchmark of learning higher, but they had taught him how to be comfortable in his skin. He felt ready to face the ocean.

On completing the training, Inder and Ike got posted on INS Khukri as watchkeeping under-trainees. Inder was excited as securing the watchkeeping ticket would give him the qualification to hold independent watch of a ship at sea. On the morning of his first day, Inder settled his things and went with Ike to report to the ExO, Lt. Cdr. Bhardwaj. He acknowledged their salutes and introduced them to the other officers on board and the ship's Captain, Lt. Cdr. Batra.

Ike got assigned to the navigating officer who reported to Batra. Ike's placement would give him excellent hands-on training and also help him build relationships with the bosses. On the other hand, Inder got an independent charge of the Quarterdeck, the lowest deck in height from the water level, which gets dirty with the soot from the boilers and the sea's spray. Inder's responsibility was to manage its upkeep and manage the sailors of the Quarterdeck. Inder felt slighted, but he consoled himself - *Every job is essential. I will do my best.*

He worked tirelessly on his always hot, dirty, and grimy workspace – and left no opportunity for complaint. Alongside he also underwent the watchkeeping training under the guidance of one of the ship's watchkeeping officers. However, he was always busy, and his workspace was away from where the senior officers sat. Ike, who spoke glib English, had a lot more confidence to perfectly blend in with the seniors. Inder felt socially excluded. He pushed away negative thoughts so as not to lose focus. He found respite in befriending the pleasant natured Bahadur Kavina, who was assigned to manage the Fox'l and signals. Three months had gone by, and Inder's gruelling training was coming to a close. He had an unlikely visitor at the Quarterdeck, one afternoon. It was Ike.

"IJ, I got my watchkeeping ticket," beamed Ike.

"Congratulations. I'm so happy for you, Ike."

"What about you, my friend?"

"You are fortunate to have been at such close quarters with them, Ike. I can't imagine them coming into this grime to share the good news with me. I will go have to and get it myself."

Inder quickly finished his day's duty and rushed to meet Bhardwaj. *This is it! said Inder in his mind.*

"Good evening Sir," said Inder anxiously.

"Inderjit, your diligence and sincerity have been highlighted by the Captain. However, he has categorically stated that you will need more navigation, TAS, and gunnery training. He has decided not to award you the watchkeeping ticket," said Bhardwaj, and handed over the report to him with pursed lips.

In a sweep, Inder got left behind, while his course mates moved ahead in their training. His hands felt cold as he stood there, momentarily, looking at the report in his hand.

"Right, Sir," said Inder in a small voice and quick nod, before exiting Bhardwaj's cabin.

He rushed towards the cowshed, brushing past one of the sailors under his command, completely ignoring his eager greeting. He sat down heavily on his bunk with his face in his hands as his mind raced with thoughts of his time on Khukri.

He felt cheated. Small. Not good enough. And once again, the labyrinth of self-doubt entwined his mind. He doubted his ability to achieve anything meaningful. The hopelessness overtook him, and for the first time after joining the Navy, in the shadows of his bunk, he wept silently and bitterly.

Why? Why, when I have worked so hard? My knowledge of TAS, navigation, and gunnery is up to the mark. I know my stuff. Then, what went wrong? My English? Or that I am not socially active. They excluded me even though I tried, or maybe it is because I came from the lower deck. But how can that be held against me? I have worked so hard to get this far.

Answers were not coming to him, and he felt like he was ablaze. He wiped his face and looked at himself in the mirror. His eyes were bloodshot, and his face was clouded over with emotion – an image he had never seen before. *Is this what I want to see myself as - a pitiful, hopeless man? No, that is not me! Then why did this happen? And what do I do?*

He suddenly remembered Vimal's advice – "If something sets you back, consider your options and, dare to get things back on track. Wallowing and self-pity won't help you."

He breathed heavily, not knowing what to do with himself. The Lion appeared in the reflection. Inder frowned turning to glare at him. The Lion looked away. With an attitude like never before, Inder lay face down in the narrow corridor of the cowshed, heaved his body on his hands, and started doing push-ups, ignoring his colleagues' jeering. Sweat poured from his face and body onto the floor as the Lion watched him push himself to finish a set of 100.

Once done, Inder got up and ran to the Quarterdeck and stood there breathless with his hands on the railing. His heart pained, and his mind was awash with his thoughts. He felt alone and helpless. He stared at nothing in particular as his thoughts raced. And then he shook his head. *I am not pitiful and hopeless, I didn't come this far to give it all up. But I don't know what to do.*

He looked at the horizon. His breath settled, and the rapid heaving of his chest set into an invisible rhythm. In the pause he had allowed himself, the beauty of the sunset drew his attention. He gasped at the slow dip of the orange-red sun towards the water, and at the dancing spangles of purple, gold, and orange, created on the ripples of water as if they were in a mad dance together. The moment spoke to him, as if caressing his being ... of the thoughts the day gone by, and what was to be.

What beauty you create, silently doing your karma with detachment day after day, nurturing us despite all the ills we do in the world. And you don't seek acknowledgment of your power and beauty - you are powerful and beautiful, nevertheless. You set, only to rise again, shining your glorious light upon all of us alike. It is in your this beingness that I see hope. I will not play victim and let a small blip jeopardise my life. My efforts went unnoticed, which pained me, but I am committed to knowing where I fell short, and rise again to get back on track and be in control to give my best to the world. I promise to do my karma until my journey is complete. Nobody can take this promise away from me.

This was Inder's fourth decision.

...

Inder stepped onto the deck of INS Brahmaputra, with a smile. She was an old frigate packed with some of the best specialists, under the charge of Capt. Yesudasan. The next three months flew by.

"You should have got awarded your watchkeeping ticket sooner, Inderjit. You knew it all already. I wish you all the best," said Yesudasan with a smile.

"Thank you for your wishes and acknowledgment, Sir," said Inder - *My moment of receiving the watchkeeping ticket is finally here.*

Inder's got his first assignment as an independent watch-keeping officer at INS Rajput, under the command of Captain Jack Shea. Inder knew that this was just the beginning.

The usual time it took to rise in rank to a Lieutenant was three years. Inder reduced this period by doing additional training. In 1962, eight years after leaving Phagwara, at the age of 26, and with seniority of five and a half months, he rose to be Lieutenant Inderjit Sharma.

— — —

CHAPTER 11: A COMMITMENT FOR SEVEN LIFETIMES

1962 - 1963: A feeling and responsibility of a new kind

Patanjli Prasad was a man of quick action and a well-read intellectual. He had served the Indian Railways from the time of the British Raj. His wife Sarla and he lived at NF40 Quilla Mohalla in Jalandhar. They had four sons and four daughters. Patanjli doted on his wife, pampering her with every convenience and comfort. He fondly addressed her as Priya. Sarla was a loving and caring woman with the energy of a bee.

As a couple, they believed that education was the only wealth they could give their children, and they spared no opportunity to follow a rigorous study regimen. Patanjli travelled a lot. Sarla, despite her paralysed right limbs, had taken it upon herself to make no compromise in the upbringing of their children. A typical day for everyone started at 5 am. They all had to freshen up, pray, have breakfast of boiled eggs and hot sweetened milk, and study for two hours.

Their first-born was the stocky, Dinesh, articulate, brilliant, and handsome. Then was the historian Sharat, quick with his wit and a heart of gold. Dinesh and Sharat were married to Kusum and Kirti, respectively. Four beautiful daughters followed the boys – Rekha, the oldest of the four, Manju, who was also married, Mukul, and Meena. The tail-enders were two boys, Rakesh and Sunil. All eight children were excellent in their studies, making Patanjli and Sarla feel incredibly proud.

Rekha was the ideal daughter in every way - she was intelligent, beautiful both inside and out, pious, and simple-hearted. Her qualifications and grades matched those of her older brothers. She lived to please the people she loved and found joy in the smallest of things. She was closest to her sister Manju. As kids, the two would race to the Shiv temple to join the evening aarti every Monday. Her favourite film hero was Dilip Kumar, and her favourite film was *Doctor Kotnis ki Amar Kahani*. She was fascinated by the beauty of the Hindi film actress, Meena Kumari. After watching her performance as Karuna in *'Dil apna aur preet parayi,'* she had secretly renamed herself and scribbled *Karuna* in her books. At home and among her friends, she was called Munni. Reading was her hobby, and one of her favourite stories was that of Sara.

. . .

There was once a handsome warrior named Alam, who had won many a battle. During one such war, he got severely wounded. On his way home with his men on horseback, he stopped at a village well.

A young maiden, dressed in a white flowing dress and flowers in her loose hair, came to the well, humming softly. He had never seen anyone more beautiful. She was ethereal, with soft eyes and rose coloured lips. He couldn't take his eyes off her, but his injuries overcame him, and he sank to the floor.

When he opened his eyes, he was in the village medic's home, and assisting him was his daughter - The same ethereal beauty! Her name was Sara.

He stayed at their home until he felt better. Sara tended to his wounds as he groaned through the many days and nights. When he recovered, he asked for her hand in marriage.

To his surprise, Sara said no. Do you not love me? He pleaded to her. I do, but I need to be with my aging parents. Her duty was unquestionable. Broken-hearted, he bid her farewell and went on his way.

Sometime later, Sara's town got attacked by bandits, and the village men got outnumbered. Just as she gave up hope, Alam arrived on horseback with his men and joined the fighters to quash the bandits.

When all was at peace, he said: 'I wish to marry you, Sara, and take your parents along with me to my palace.' She wept with joy and conceded to his proposal. The story ended with him carrying her away on his horse into the horizon.

Rekha finished reading the book for the umpteenth time. She smiled shyly at the thoughts going through her mind and looked at her friend.

"Indra, I've decided."

"Now what, Munni?"

"I'm going to marry a warrior."

Indra Burmikhana rolled her eyes and made a funny face at her childhood friend, who stood confidently under one of the school arches, with her hands on her hips, a smirk on her lips, and an exciting glow in her eyes.

"And what if he dies in the war?"

Rekha made a face at Indra and then thought for a moment and said, "But we will all die sooner or later Indra. Isn't it better to die a brave death? My husband will be strong and will face any danger that approaches him with bravado, and he will take me away to a faraway land."

"Your dreamland is beyond me. Snap out of it and get back to your studies, unless you wish to flunk tomorrow's exam."

"I am prepared for the exam, Indra. But seriously, what do you think of my dream?"

"It is romantic. But what about all your admirers here? Have some pity on them also."

"I can't help it if I am such a beauty. It is their problem if they are in love with me."

She twirled around and added, "I don't like any of them as much. So much talk of the moon and stars. Most annoying. Besides, Mummy has strictly warned me of the "consequences" of going down the love path. So, no love-shove for me!"

"Consequences?"

"Yes, those ahem-ahem consequences," said Rekha giggling consciously, "Hey, let's get some *kulfi*."

The kulfi seller stopped his bicycle and opened the casket on his carrier, filled with different flavours of the delicious frozen milk treats. He gave a kulfi stick to each of them.

"Mohan Bhaiya, you sell the best kulfi in Jalandhar. How do you make it?" asked Indra.

"Mother makes it with milk and sugar and loads of love. I'm a mere seller," said Mohan.

"But you are doing the hard work of selling. What a waste this delicious kulfi would be if you didn't sell it from street to street. You are a good son, so don't underplay what you do," beamed Rekha.

They paid him ten paise each and skipped away, licking the melting treats.

"I wonder how he freezes it to such perfection?"

"He uses large crystals of salt and hay to reduce the water temperature to make ice and then puts the filled moulds into them to freeze them—simple chemistry. You should pay more attention in class, Indra," winked Rekha.

"Thank you for the wisdom, smarty pants!" said Indra sarcastically.

"You are welcome, darling."

"You know, Munni, marrying a warrior is fine, but the ancient horseback warriors don't exist anymore. Now we have the Army, Navy, and Air Force. Do you remember Puttu?"

"Yes, of course, I remember Puttu, your cousin."

"He is in the Army. What a tough life he has!"

"What do you mean?"

"His wife may as well not be married. Most of the time, she has to stay back with her in-laws while he gets transferred all over the country or is at the front protecting our borders. You will be like a babe lost in the woods if you marry a warrior like that."

Rekha processed the new piece of information that could potentially derail her dreams.

"Marry a Naval officer. They travel too, but not as much. And a little separation will only make the hearts grow fonder. What say?"

"Yes, yes," said Rekha with renewed excitement.

"They wear white uniforms and look so good and are very modern too."

"Chander Rekha Patanjli, the wife of a Naval officer sailing on a ship ... Dip, dip, dip!"

Indra smiled at her friend, skipping along the streets, with her melting kulfi in one hand and bag in the other, beaming up at the sky.

. . .

That conversation was from some years ago, when Rekha lived in a hostel in Chandigarh, pursuing her Bachelor of Science at Punjab University. All of 5 feet tall, she was now a lecturer and examiner of Biology and Chemistry at the University. Her sincerity and intelligence had landed her the coveted government job. Her interest in the Navy had grown ever since, and she devoured every news article she could get her hands on.

Patanjli heard much praise about Inder from his cousin and spoke to Rekha about him. "The boy's name is Inderjit. He is a Lieutenant in the Navy; and has travelled abroad several times. She says he is handsome too." Rekha's face lit up. *It is a sign.* She insisted he take her proposal to him immediately. Patanjli smiled at his daughter's enthusiasm and decided to take the first bus to meet Inder.

. . .

On the same day at Inder's home in Phagwara, Jaikishen said, with pride, to Geeta, "It's time we get him married. Our son looks so handsome and well-groomed."

Inder was on leave again. He animatedly played a game with Kuku and Pappi on the terrace as his parents watched. Geeta smiled while running her sandalwood prayer beads through her fingers, murmuring mantras.

"The hawks are on the prowl. Proposals have been coming in, but I haven't found anything suitable. Sevadeyiji's niece, who lives in Jalandhar, is one. Her name is Rekha. But she is too highly qualified. B.Sc., B.Ed. And to top that, she is working at the University, teaching young boys too! I say, what use is so much study going to come to when a girl has to manage the house and children after marriage? It's okay to study, but too much of it plants ambition in girls' minds, and the house and children get neglected. I wonder at the brains of the parents of such girls! Bah! Such a girl won't fit in my home for sure," quipped Geeta, shaking her head.

"Why are your thoughts in the medieval ages, Geeta? Have you seen your son lately? He is an officer in the Indian Navy now and is earning well too."

Inder felt a warmth as he listened to his dear father.

"I have never earned more than Rs.100 per month, and he earns much more. He needs a smart partner in his life who can improve his life further. How can an illiterate woman match his stride?"

"Why not? Earning a living is a man's job, and women going to work should not be encouraged. It increases unemployment in the society. I say, what is wrong with women who didn't study? Look at Sharda and me. Am I not a good wife? That is what God made a woman for - nurturing her family and managing the home, while the man provides for the household by earning a living. I want to have a demure, pious woman for my son. Educated girls have too much of an attitude about household chores. It is about time that I got some help. I need some respite too."

"Geeta, you are so wrong."

"How many times do I need to say that you need to stay out of household matters?" frowned Geeta, "Nobody, but I will decide on the bride for my son."

She got up to leave the terrace and then turned around, "Besides, whoever he marries, will not be travelling the high seas with him. She will be here with us."

Jaikishen rolled his eyes and shook his head while Inder overheard their conversation. He didn't say anything. He had developed a quality of listening to everyone, but finally doing whatever he felt was right. His father was right. Choosing a life partner for marriage was a big decision. As a Naval officer, his life could be at risk if he went to war, so he was clear that he wanted to marry a qualified girl who could be financially independent. *Rekha. Hmm. Perhaps she is the one.*

. . .

The next morning, Patanjli, dressed in a dark suit and a matching felt hat, approached Korian Mohalla. He walked quickly and had an air of curiosity about him, as he scanned the surroundings keenly. He stopped at the Sharma household. Pappi opened the netted door and peered her little head out, looking up at him, trying to guess who he was.

"Namaste betaji!"

"Namaste," said Pappi in a suspicious tone.

"You must be Kusum. Is your Dadaji home?"

"Yes, he is home. But what do you want from him? Are you from my school?"

"No, my child. Are you worried because you have been naughty in school?" he laughed out aloud.

"Who has come, Pappi?" called Geeta from the inner room.

"Who should I say has come?"

"Tell them Patanjli Prasad, from Jalandhar."

On hearing his name, Jaikishen came rushing from the living room and opened the door with enthusiasm.

"Pappi, what are you doing, child? Sorry, bhaisaab, please do come in," he gushed, "Go and call Chachaji quickly," he said to Pappi.

"She is a lovely child with a curious mind. I enjoyed her pertinent questioning."

. . .

Patanjli's visit to the Sharma house went off well. Inder entered the living room, touched his feet, and sat beside him. He responded to all of the questions that Patanjli asked and agreed that they would visit their home in Jalandhar to meet Rekha the next day.

Inder decided that Sharda, Tripta (Bhollo), and Somnath would meet Rekha. Geeta was predictably sceptical. "I disapprove of the girl. And what is the hurry? You don't have to show your desperation," she scoffed.

Inder smiled.

"Why don't you come along? You should select your bride," said Somnath, Bhollo's husband, to Inder as they walked to the bus stop.

"Somnathji, I find the custom of going to see a girl very disrespectful."

"But how will you select a wife for yourself like this?"

"I'd rather get feedback from people I trust. When I go to see her, it will be to say yes."

Patanjli was disappointed that Inder didn't come himself, but Rekha was willing to be patient. They liked her instantly. She looked beautiful and was pleasant-natured. On their return, Inder met them at the bus station and immediately took Somnath aside.

"Well?" said Inder, and Somnath smiled, amused at his brother-in-law's excitement. "Would you have married her?"

"Yes. Rekha is good looking, qualified, and very sweet-natured. You are a lucky man."

"Thank you, Somnathji," smiled Inder, feeling a rush of anticipation. *I will marry Rekha.*

This was Inder's fifth decision.

Two days after, Geeta and his cousin Mahinder accompanied Inder to Jalandhar.

. . .

That morning Rekha woke up after a restless night. It was a pleasant spring morning. She could hear familiar sounds of the morning as she lay awake in bed. Her father murmured shlokas and rang his little brass prayer bell as Sarla tinkered around in the kitchen. The early morning light lit up Manju's sleeping face. She looked as radiant as ever with smudged *sindoor* in the centre of her thick black hair. *I hope I look as beautiful as Manju when I get married.*

She leaned forward and whispered into Manju's ears, "Manju!"

"Hmm."

"What if they don't come?"

"Oh, gosh! Have you slept at all, girl? Of course, they will come."

"But what if he doesn't like me?"

"How can anybody not like you, Munni? You are everyone's favourite."

"Hmm. But what do you think I should talk to him about?"

"What makes you think Mummy will let you have a conversation with him?"

"Then how will I know what he's like?"

"Goodness can be seen in the eyes. Catch a glimpse when

you get the chance."

"Aankhon hi aankhon mein ishaara ho gaya, baithe baithe jeene ka sahara ho gaya," sang Rekha and tickled her sister making her squeal.

She bathed and dressed in her favourite beige *salwar kameez* with a light pink printed *chunni*. Soon it was time for them to arrive. She dragged Manju to the window on the first level, overlooking their lane and craned each time a cycle rickshaw appeared.

"I will see him first, and if he is as good as *bua* said, I will just die with happiness. Manju laughed at her sister.

"Manju, my hands are trembling with excitement. I can't wait. Please tell me that he will like me, my darling sister."

"You are beautiful, Rekha, of course, he will like you and say yes. What if he is ugly?"

"That is not possible. He is going to be the most handsome man ever. You wait and watch - you're all going to be so jealous. Also, I'm going to get a view of him before anybody else does. So, you are allowed to sit here, but you will not see him. Promise me that. Wait, I don't trust you - come here, let me close your eyes," said Rekha putting her palms on Manju's eyes.

"What are you doing? I won't look, Rekha. I promise. Let me go, please."

"Damn! I can't look out while holding your eyes shut. I will blindfold you until I see him," she said and tied a scarf across Manju's eyes.

It was 10 am when a cycle rickshaw pulled up outside their lane and from it descended two men and a lady in dark glasses.

"It's them, Manju. I can't see much of his face from this far, but he is wearing dark shades, black trousers, black shoes, and an olive-green T-shirt. He looks so good, Manju. They are now walking towards the house," squealed Rekha continuing to peep out.

When they walked closer, she got a glimpse of his face and shrieked and then buried her mouth in her chunni, hugging her sister with joy.

"Let me see too, Rekha," Manju protested.

Rekha relented, allowing her to take the scarf off Manju's eyes, so she could also get a glimpse. Manju saw him just as they were at their doorstep. They both jumped up and down, hugging each other until Sarla called out to everyone from the kitchen below.

Sarla, Patanjli, Dinesh, Sharad, Kusum, and Kirti welcomed the guests at their doorstep and ushered them into the court-yard. Chairs and two *divans* had got arranged in a U formation, with a table in the centre. Inder's family sat on one diwan with Geeta in the centre, while Patanjli and Sarla with Kusum and Kirti sat on the other divan. Dinesh and Sharat sat on the chairs. They chatted about the journey, the weather in Jaland-har, life in the Navy, his ship, and his travels. Sarla watched Inder, noting his every word, expression, and gesture.

The courtyard was adjoining the kitchen. Rekha heard every word they spoke. Meena, Sunil, and Rakesh kept an on-going commentary of all that was happening outside.

"He has learnt to fire big guns and torpedoes, Rekha Bhenji," said Sunil in an excited voice.

"The warrior and his wife!" said Rekha with a nostalgic smile.

"He has been to so many countries, Rekha Bhenji," said young Rakesh.

"England, Thailand, Japan, Malta, Vietnam, China, Egypt. Wow!" said Meena.

"He will take me away to a faraway land," danced Rekha in the kitchen amidst her excited brothers and sisters.

"He lives in Bombay. Imagine you will also live in Bombay. Wow yaar, you may get to see Dilip Kumar and Meena Kumari after all," said Manju.

"Yes, Bombay, here I come! When can I go and see him, Manju?"

"Mummy will call for you soon. Have patience, girl."

"You are a lucky girl, Rekha. He is a great catch, just like Buaji said," said Meena.

"I'm also a good catch for him," winked Rekha.

"Rekha, come here, my dear one," called out Patanjli.

Rekha froze and couldn't move. Manju and the others pushed her out of the kitchen. She entered the courtyard awkwardly. When she walked towards them, she felt as if the whole world was looking at her. She sat next to Patanjli on the edge of the *divan*. Inder was sitting in front of her.

"Inderjit, this is our daughter Rekha. She is pure at heart and is one of my most precious jewels. Rekha, why don't you cut some apple for our guests," said Patanjli to Rekha.

Rekha picked up two apples and a knife from the plate on the table and sliced them carefully. Inder had been looking at Patanjli as he spoke of Rekha. He then discreetly steered his eyes to look at Rekha for a brief moment. She was peeling an apple. *She is beautiful. I wish she would look up for a bit.*

Just then, Rekha lifted her hand to move a strand of hair that was bothering her. As she moved it, she stole a glance at Inder. *Finally!* He held her gaze for a brief moment. They were transfixed as one, as if for eternity. A surge of warmth flooded Inder's being, and, at that moment, he knew she was the right girl for him. He gave a hint of a smile, and she blushed. Their stolen moment, amidst the chatter of both the families, made Rekha's hands tremble. She pursed her lips to stop smiling.

She got up to serve Geeta, then Mahinder. When she came to Inder, he took a piece and looked up at her and smiled.

"Thank you."

She stood frozen, and the universe came to a pause yet again. Her lips trembled as she tried to conceal her joy. His heart knew he was in love. When she sat down, she saw Inder talking to his mother from the corner of her eyes, while her family waited with bated breath.

"Bhaisaab and Bhabi, we are pleased to offer you *shagan* of Rs.1.25. Your daughter is now ours. But the marriage is not possible any time soon as Inderjit has to report back to duty. The date for the marriage will be sometime next year," said Geeta with a warm smile.

"Wadhaiyaan Priyaji - Rekha wadhaiyaan!" said Patanjli jumping up to hug Inder, and the house broke into a celebration.

Amidst the din around her, Rekha looked up at Inder, now her fiancé. He looked at her and blinked his eyes, smiled, and turned to Patanjli. "I will be boarding the train to Bombay from Jalandhar next Saturday."

"Okay, son. Rekha will come to see you off with Dinesh and Kusum."

. . .

A week later, it was a bright sunny morning when Inder walked into Jalandhar Station with his bags to board the train to Bombay. Rekha was already there with Dinesh and Kusum. Inder blushed when Dinesh teased him about how anxious Rekha had been to get to the station ahead of time. He was conscious that Rekha was looking at him unabashedly while he talked to Dinesh.

In Rekha's besotted eyes, Inder was picture-perfect with his rectangular-shaped face, chiselled high cheekbones, sharp jawline, and cleft. She was in a trance, watching the beads of sweat glimmering above his beautifully shaped lips. When he smiled, his eyes danced, and his cheeks blushed to a tinge of rouge. *I am hook, line and sinker in love!*

When it was almost time for the train to leave, Inder shook hands with Dinesh and stepped aside with Rekha. They were with each other up close for the first time. As he looked at her, the crowd surged around them, but the two of them stood transfixed, smiling and blushing as their eyes talked, and their bodies simmered with the tingling current between them.

She was a tiny package of delight, dressed in her white *chudidaar kurta*, staring up at him. She looked beautiful - her eyes and hair were pitch black, and her full lips painted a perfect matte pink. He sighed deeply, looking at her taking in the twinkle of her eyes and the curve of her smile. *Oh, the boundaries of an arranged marriage!* He shifted awkwardly, trying to act normal when he wanted so much to kiss her.

"Stop looking at me like that," he teased.

"Should I be looking at someone else?"

"No," he said with a small laugh, surprised at how possessive he felt of her already.

"You are also looking at me. What do you see and feel?" she looked into his eyes searching for the love she felt for him.

"I see beauty, in your eyes, Rekha. And I feel like holding you in my arms and never letting you go. And ..." he looked visibly embarrassed. "I can't believe I said that! And I don't know how this is possible, but I am in love with you already," said Inder with a softness in his eyes.

The engine hooted in the distance, breaking their trance. "I will have to go now," Inder said gently.

He stepped onto the train and turned to stand at the doorway and held out his hand to Rekha. She grasped it, instantly feeling a surge of warmth rush through her body at the first touch of his firm but gentle handshake. She wanted him to envelope her in his strong arms.

The train jerked to a start moving slowly, but Rekha refused to let go of his hand, holding on tighter as she walked along with the train.

"I love you too, Inderjit. I want to come with you."

"I wish," he laughed, trying to pull his hand away.

At this point, Dinesh saw what was happening and ran up to them. "He will be back soon, Rekha," he said, pulling her hand away from his, "Goodbye Inderjit. See you soon for the wedding."

Rekha stood there feeling weak in her knees, her heart beating fast, feeling breathless, waving to him until the train blurred into the distance.

Inder sighed heavily and went to his seat with a smile on his face. He relived his moments with Rekha again and again. Her smile, her wit, and above all, the naughty look in her eyes. He was humbled to see love written all over her face. His hand tingled with the warmth of her touch. *What a beautiful and magical feeling is love.*

. . .

Back in Jalandhar, Rekha pined for her new-found beloved.

She treasured the memory of their two meetings, reminiscing every moment and imagining him everywhere she went.

A few weeks after he had left, Indra peeped into the terrace room and made a loud sound, startling Rekha, who screamed and then hugged her friend and burst into tears.

"I'm sorry, Munni. What happened?"

"I miss him."

"Oh, my dear sister! Hasn't Inderjit written yet?"
"No, and I'm so angry. Is this love?"

"Yes, this is love for sure."

"But how do you know that this is love?"

"Because I have seen it in the films. You smile unknowingly, you cry for no reason, and get lost in your thoughts continually. If this is not love, then I don't know what is, Rekha?" she said, wiping Rekha's tears.

They hugged each other and sat down on the charpoy, nibbling the roasted peanuts that Indra had got along.

"Look at my luck. I meet the perfect man and then, poof! He is gone away some thousands of miles away. I don't even have a photograph!"

"It's barely been a couple of weeks since he left. He must have got busy. Life in the forces is busy, Munni. Maybe he is travelling. Be patient, my dear, and before you know it, you will be married."

"Rekha," said Meena in a shrill voice, waving a letter from Inder at her. Rekha excused herself and ran to the Shiva temple to sit under the banyan tree and look at his handwriting's neat small lettering. She ran her finger over the writing and pressed her lips to the letter before opening it. Inside was a black and white photograph of Inder dressed in a suit.

"Sigh! You, winsome monster! How am I to survive with you looking at me through your dark eyes?" she giggled.

"My Rekha ... it started ... She read the two pages covered back to back, again and again, first with tears, then with a smile, and then aloud. It was the first of many letters that followed. Their pen-courtship taught them a lot about each other - her studies and job, his trip to Singapore, his ship, the shopping he had done for them, their friends and family, and when they would marry. Inder wanted to get married soon, but Geeta dilly-dallied about the date, saying the stars are not yet aligned. Patanjli wrote to Inder.

Dear Inderjit,

I hope this letter finds you well. You are a soldier, my son, and if a war broke out, I wonder if you would look for the stars before you retaliate. Humans have made customs to enrich our lives with culture. Still, if customs come in the way of our lives and progress, it is detrimental to our existence; superstition and unreasonable customs cannot have a place in an intelligent mind like yours. Each day is right in the eyes of the Almighty, provided you decide to make it so. Please let us know if you can't keep to your commitment to decide what is best for Rekha's future.

Best regards - Patanjli

Inder responded to Patanjli immediately, to confirm the wedding for 13 October 1963.

. . .

Inder and his hundred-plus baaratis arrived in Jalandhar a few days before the auspicious day. They set up base at Janjghar, a place designated for wedding families, not too far from Rekha's home.

"Can I get a peek at him, Manju?"

"No, Munni. The bride and groom can't see each other a week before the wedding."

"Who has made these silly customs? And why are we silly enough to still follow them?"

"Ignore the small irritants, Rekha, and stand up and make a noise to change only the bigger things that matter. That has been my policy. If you still wish to break custom, I can ask Sunil to take you to meet *Jijaji*."

"Sigh! No, let it be. I have waited so long; I can manage a few more days."

"That's my girl."

Both the families immersed themselves in the several fun-packed ceremonies associated with a Punjabi wedding. The Patanjli household got decorated with lights and flowers. A *bawarchi* got hired to cook treats for all the days leading up to the wedding.

Rekha, dressed in yellow, sat with outstretched hands, watching her cousin Indu draw intricate *mehndi* designs on her palms. Alongside them, the in-house *dholaki-chamcha* experts accompanied the ladies of the family on sing-along wedding songs. The formal *sangeet* ceremony happened the evening before the wedding, at which family and friends dressed in colourful finery danced to catchy songs late into the night.

. . .

On the morning of the wedding, Inder awoke with a smile on his face. He had dreamt of Rekha. Time had flown since he first met her, and through the countless letters, his love for her had grown. He was exhausted from the night before, and so he took the chance to laze a bit longer as he waited for his turn to bathe. That morning, in separate functions held by their families and friends, Rekha and he were smeared from head to toe, with *batna*, a paste made of gram flour, curd, turmeric, and pure ghee. Rekha's Mamaji, Amritlal Salwan, and his wife Swaran brought her *chooda* and slipped it onto both her wrists. The followed her *Kaleerey* ceremony in which all the married women of the family tied tiny golden ornaments onto her bangles. Rekha was in the seventh heaven, revelling in everyone's pampering and all the colours around her.

"Your henna has such a deep colour, Rekha. You are going to get so much love from your husband," teased Meena.

Rekha smiled and blinked her eyes naughtily, admiring the deep maroon colour that the mehndi had left on her palms. "Please apply red polish on my nails Manju and border my feet with *Alta*."

As the evening approached, Inder dressed in black trousers, a white shirt, and a black-tie. The pandit wrapped a pink *pagdi* on his head and then carefully tied on the *sehra*, which dropped a curtain of flowers covering his face. He looked at himself in the mirror – he liked what he saw – his happiness reflected on his face. *My Rekha will be mine for life today.*

At the scheduled time, Inder climbed onto a horse with his *sarwala*, Bhollo's son, Gugla. Most of the baaratis walked ahead and indulged in frenzied dancing as the bandmaster conducted his troop of musicians to play popular tunes. Inder was amused and embarrassed at their histrionics.

Rekha's skin glowed with the oiling and ritual baths. When she wore her wedding outfit, baby pink, and golden *gota* work-filled salwar kameez, her family gushed at how lovely she looked. She felt gorgeous – *I am finally going to marry the man of my dreams.*

Patanjli and his family welcomed the baaratis at the *milni* ceremony, wherein the men of the two families exchanged gifts. Then followed the *jaimala*, where the bride and groom were to garland each other.

Inder's face was still covered with his flower tassels when Rekha came to stand in front of him. There was a cacophony around them. But Inder's mind was lost in the beauty that stood in front of him. *Rekha looks stunning.*

Her head covered with a light pink and *gota* border dupatta, and *teeka* shimmered in the lights. Her hair was parted in the centre, giving her broad forehead a glow. She looked like a queen. Inder smiled at himself behind his sehra and then lifted it. She looked up to see him. They caught each other's eyes and blushed. He congratulated himself for having decided to marry her, and as he stood there soaking in her beauty, Rekha suddenly lifted her arms and put the jaimala around his neck.

The crowds booed him and said that he shouldn't have let her get away with garlanding him so quickly. His face was aglow with happiness, and he tried to garland her, but Rekha's brothers instantly lifted her out of his reach. Inder looked away to conceal his amusement. Rekha grew impatient and irritated with her brothers and sisters as they teased Inder. She insisted they put her down so she could get garlanded. The two families broke into laughter. Rekha got set in front of Inder again. This time he put the garland around the neck of his much relieved and smiling bride. Inder and Rekha's wedding ceremony concluded late at night with Patanjli and Sarla doing the *kanyadaan,* and the couple took their holy vows, taking seven circles around the fire.

Early next morning, Inder dressed in a black suit for the *bidaai*, while Rekha wore a red and gold sari that Geeta had sent for her. Rekha's family insisted that Inder sing a song before leaving. He was hesitant, but when Rakesh and Meena insisted, he agreed to oblige and sang '*Tum ek baar mohabbat ka imtihan to lo*' from the film *Babar*. Hearing his melodious singing, Rekha was beside herself with joy. *He is all good!*

Inder, Tripta, Somnath, and Rekha were to travel in a borrowed car covered with flowers, and an elaborate 'Just Married' prop stuck to its bonnet. Rekha's smiling face became the talk amidst everyone assembled to bid her goodbye. Inder felt happy that she was not weeping like girls typically did when leaving their parents.

"Rekha, stop grinning so much," said Manju, hugging her sister close.

"Why? I can't help that I am so happy, Manju."

"You, crazy girl."

"Yes, I'm crazy about Inderjit," she said naughtily.

Inder entered the car and sat next to her. Rekha rejoiced at finally having him to herself. His tight muscled arms brushed hers, and her body tingled with excitement at his closeness.

However, her happiness was short-lived, as Tripta entered the car and sat on her left, while Somnath sat in the front seat with the driver. The rhythmic movement of the car ad tiredness from the night before made Rekha feel sleepy. She soon dozed off on Inder's shoulder. When she awoke an hour later, his arm was around her.

"Sorry! I dozed off," said Rekha, feeling embarrassed.

"No problem," said Inder and moved his arm abruptly to sit up straight. "We should be reaching soon. Your hair has got all messed up. You might want to cover your head," he said awkwardly and looked out of the window. *He looks upset. Is it because I slept??*

The October sun shined at its peak as they reached Phagwara, and silken clothing made Rekha sweaty and weary. Her makeup, like her hair, was a mess too. When the car stopped, she straightened her clothes and hair as much as she could before stepping out. Rekha realised Inder looked impatient.

Is he still upset?

He led the way a step ahead of her, down the narrow lanes towards Korian Mohalla. Onlookers peered and cheered from their windows and terraces all along the way. Rekha felt special, ad she smiled and waved at everyone as her eyes met theirs.

"Stop doing that, please," said Inder. His continued curt demeanour made her oddly uncomfortable.

"Why are you so irritated?"

He didn't hear her over the ambient sounds. Just then, they reached the house, and in her dark glasses, Geeta was waiting at the doorstep with an aarti plate in her hand. A few other family people stood behind her. They peered over each other's shoulders to get a glimpse of the welcome ceremony.

"Namaste, Mataji," said Rekha with a smile.

"Radhe Krishna. Namaste," said Geeta. She put a red tikka on both their foreheads and a piece of prasad in their mouths. Inder and Rekha bent down and touched her feet.

As they stood up, Geeta leaned forward and twitched Rekha's chunni to cover her face. "Keep your face veiled from now on, please," she muttered. "Welcome to our home."

Rekha awkwardly looked towards Inder for guidance, but he had turned to speak to Jaikishen. Geeta instructed Rekha to step over the threshold and tip over a raw rice bowl with her right foot. "This signifies that like Goddess *Lakshmi*, you bring with you good fortune into our home," explained Geeta.

Rekha then stepped into a plate of red liquid. She followed instructions and walked into the house to leave behind a trail of red footsteps. The veil felt uncomfortable, but she went with the flow of the ceremony. But as the ceremony persisted,

PRIYA SHARMA SHAIKH

she started feeling upset. She liked looking into people's eyes as they talked, but a sheer fabric now obstructed her world view. She decided it was a hindrance that she could do well without. *It's okay for now, but I will tell Inderjit this won't do for me.*

She got moved to sit in the inner room. Several relatives, friends, and neighbours walked in and out, greeting, talking, laughing with each other all at once. A cacophony of sorts surrounded Rekha. The people who came to see her were women. Each of them followed the same process of *muhn-dikhai* - lifting her veil, smiling, introducing themselves, commenting about her looks or jewellery or sari, placing a *shagun* envelope into her lap, and dropping the veil over her face. Each of them made her feel good, but the endless flow and the overt proximity of so many strangers overwhelmed Rekha. *I feel like a mannequin on display. Where is Inderjit?* From the living room sounds, she guessed he was outside with the male guests and family members.

"Bhabhi, its time for some games," teased Tripta and guided Rekha to the living room. "Tradition calls for newly-weds to play games together. You have to find a ring immersed in a large bowl filled with milk and rose petals. If you win, you will have the upper hand in the relationship."

"That's silly. How can that prove anything?" said the veiled Rekha, feeling flustered.

Tripta didn't hear her feeble voiced protest. A large pitcher was set in the living room. Inder sat on one side of it, and Rekha opposite him. She could see his hands from under the veil, and she so wanted to lift her veil and say aloud - *Enough of this circus and leave me alone with my husband.* But then she thought again. *Not just yet. Not with so many people around. These small moments shall pass. I will be patient.*

"Mamiji, you have to win," said little Kusum, sticking close to Rekha.

"Come on, Inderjit," teased the menfolk.

Rekha was amazed at the mounting disharmony between the men and women screaming and urging the groom and bride to win. When the game started, Inder rolled up his sleeve and frantically moved his hand in the pitcher. Rekha was reluctant. She dipped her hand slowly into the milky water. With all the cheering, Rekha felt the pressure to perform too. So, she started moving her hand about, pausing each time Inder's hand touched hers. He grabbed her fingers playfully, and from the shadows of the veil, she could see that he looked at her. She giggled. He pulled his hand away and resumed the frantic search. Then, she suddenly felt his fingers slip the ring into her hand. *He found it and gave it to me!*

She raised her hand out of the milky water victoriously, to show off the ring.

"*Phittey-munh*! What a pity!"

"Inderjit is going to be a hen-pecked husband."

"Losing to your wife! Man, that is the pits!"

"What war will you win if you can't even win against a woman?"

Inder laughed at the comments, but Rekha was shocked at the outrageous insinuations. She wanted to lift her veil and give them a piece of her mind. And then she thought again and held herself back.

A sinking feeling was entering Rekha's heart. Brought up in a modern home, she was always engrossed in studies and never got exposed to the tradition of veiling that persisted in some sections of society. Least of all had she expected to be married into a house that practiced it. *When Inder met me for the first time, Mataji was wearing dark glasses. She seemed such a modern woman. And Inder is an officer in the Navy. How does he think this is okay?* Her inability to express her displeasure of the ceremonies upset her. And for the first time, the happy-go-lucky bride that left her home with unabridged happiness felt tears stinging her eyes. She blinked hard to stop herself from making a spectacle of herself, trying hard to believe she was happy to be married to Inderjit. *All will be well; I just know it.*

Meanwhile, Inder stayed in the next room all day, getting entertained and teased by the rest of the male guests, and he had no clue of Rekha's discomfort.

When the day ended, Rekha was left by herself in the room. She lifted her veil and looked around the dimly lit room, with its tiny window and unmatched furniture. The flooring made her feet muddy, while the faded linen laid out for their first night made her feel sick. *Where are the flowers and scent and floating lace curtains and candles? And where is the romance? Was all of that just a lost dream?* Strains of chatter and raucous laughter from outside drifted through the door. *They are still teasing him.*

The experience of her marriage to the man of her dreams had turned into a disappointing anti-climax. She sat on the bed by herself, uncertain of what to say and do. Her mind raced with thoughts of ambiguity. *What will my life with Inderjit be like?* She thought of her parents and the comfort of her home, and tears plummeted down her cheeks.

A sudden opening of the doors startled her. She wiped her cheeks in a hurry and pulled down her veil. It was Inder. He shut the door behind him and locked it, muffling out the sounds. He walked up to where she was sitting. Her heart thudded. He gently lifted her veil to reveal a very sweaty and tearful Rekha. She forced a smile and blinked her eyes hard as he lifted her face. He looked at her fondly in the shadows of the candlelight.

"My Rekha! I have waited so long for this moment," he said, with the warm gaze she was familiar with.

"Me too, Inderjit. I have had a..." she protested feebly and stopped, as he leaned closer. Her anguish turned to a gasp at his closeness. He clearly cannot tell that I have been crying. *It's good.* She didn't want to ruin their union with her complaints. It had to wait for later. She stood up and, without any hesitation, put her head against his chest.

Inder felt overjoyed. He let out a small laugh, and instinctively wrapped his arms around her. He breathed in the fragrance of the flowers in her hair. "You are so beautiful, Rekha. And so delicate."

"Finally, the words I wanted to hear all day!" she sighed deeply and clung onto him, swooning in the comfort of his strong arms. Her heart raced, not sure what to expect next. *If he kisses me now, how am I supposed to respond?* Inder too contemplated what his next move ought to be. *I should kiss her now, or perhaps, in a little while.*

He moved the few loose hair strands off her face. His firm yet gentle hand held her shoulders, and then slipped to her neck and back. She shivered in excitement as her veil fell to the floor, and her bun collapsed over her shoulders.

It all felt so romantic and so new to Inder. He closed his eyes and held her tightly against him. He opened his eyes to look at her, as did she following his cue, both of them breathing and sensing and feeling together. His head then bent down, and he tenderly kissed her on her forehead, her eyes, and her nose. He looked at her once again and pressed his lips in a gentle kiss on her quivering lips.

And in a flash, all her misgivings were blown away, like dandelions in the wind. She breathed heavily, letting out a delighted giggle, and closed her eyes. The closeness and firmness of their moment of union felt just right, and they responded to each other, magically submitting to the grooves of each other's bodies and blending into the rhythm of the romance they had dreamt of.

He gently guided her onto the bed, to begin a new chapter in their lives.

— — —

CHAPTER 12: LOVE BLOSSOMS IN BOMBAY

1964: Finding warmth in the depths of his iceberg

I nder and Rekha took leave for a month for the wedding. They decided to divide the time between her home and his. This 'home-neymoon' had several benefits but a drawback too - lack of privacy! Rekha noted that Inder stayed in a reserved mood at home. Especially during the day. She tried to probe him, but he would get conscious of the people around them, and he'd brush her away, saying, "Nothing is the matter." She decided to give him time to open up to her. Inder, too wanted to share some thoughts, but somehow the time never seemed right or adequate. But when they were alone or shut out their families in the night, they created beautiful moments of love. Progress was slow, but it happened with each passing day, and for both of them, that felt good.

Inder introduced Rekha to his Avatars, narrated mythical stories of each of them, and shared their significance in his growing years.

"So, are you the Lion still or now have you become the cow?" asked Rekha, fascinated by the figurines in her hand.

"The Lion, I believe, as there is a lot more to explore still," he said dreamily, rolling onto the charpoy.

"That means even I can explore," she smiled playfully.

"You got me wrong. I mean explore, in my work – I wish

to face more challenges and to achieve more. On the personal front, I have arrived," said Inder pulling her towards him.

. . .

"I don't like this veiling. I feel like an animal," said Rekha, pulling him into the inner room, after they bid goodbye to the last of the wedding guests.

Inder looked uncomfortable. He wasn't sure how to react to Rekha. "It is our family's tradition to protect the women of the house from any vile eyes. Women veil themselves from male elders of the family and, of course, outsiders too," he said, awkwardly.

"Do male elders of the house have a vile eye Inderjit?" she said, looking curious.

"No, Rekha. That can never be the case."

"I thought so too. People make traditions, and they should change when they don't apply anymore or make people un-happy. Tell Mataji that I don't wish to veil myself."

"You should tell her if you so much want to," smiled Inder.

"Oh!"

"Rekha, this home has some unsaid rules, which could be different from your home. Since you are new here, you will need to make your place before bringing in change. Give it time, and either you will adapt, or we will learn from your ways. Also, you won't live here forever. In my opinion, it's okay to inconvenience oneself to give elders some happiness."

"But is that fair that I keep the peace with others but cause turmoil in my own heart? I feel miserable behind this veil. I keep banging into people. I feel ..."

"Chachaji, can we play Ludo?" barged in Kuku, and their conversation came to a pause.

"Yes, sure. Your Chachi will love that," said Inder and then turned to whisper to Rekha, who looked visibly disturbed. "When we are together outside the house, you don't have to veil yourself. We have very little time together here, Rekha, and I want to spend this time in a happy state of mind. I don't wish to waste any of it in an altercation of any kind. Let's just go with the flow for now. We have our first lunch invitation in an hour."

Rekha nodded, looking unsure. Inder noted that she didn't say anything after that, but he knew she wasn't at peace. He understood her anxiety and wanted to ensure she was comfortable and cared for, and yet he knew he didn't want to rock Geeta's boat.

. . .

Everybody was excited to get to know the newlyweds and get an update on their lives. Invitations flowed for breakfast, lunch, and dinner at the homes of relatives and friends in Phagwara, Jalandhar, and other neighbouring towns. Everyone wanted to outdo the other in their showcase of the proverbial Punjabi hospitality.

All their hosts served great food, and they stuffed their tummies, what with the persistent soliciting of "Have some more!" from their eager-to-please hosts. And every conversation was laced with similar questions – What was your journey to become an officer? Which armed force is better, and why? What was his first salary, and what is his salary now? Did you get scared while sailing in the ocean? Which countries have you travelled to? Will Rekha go to the city with you? Where will she stay when you sail? What about Rekha's government job? Will she quit? Tch, tch! What a waste!

Geeta complained that they were not spending enough

time at home. But Rekha and Inder continued honouring the obligations, which had a three-fold effect. First, they both spoke the response to each question like it was a script. Second, they felt sick at the sight of food, groaning each time a new invitation presented itself. Third, and most importantly, their travels to the various places by local buses, rickshaws, and on foot allowed them to talk freely.

Yet, although he shared so much, Rekha sensed she knew Inder only on the surface.

"Why do you suddenly go so quiet?" said Rekha, sitting snugly next to him in the crowded bus. They were travelling to her home to spend some time with her family.

"What?" said Inder, looking startled.

She smiled at him. "Are you thinking of something, or are you holding back some...?"

"No. Why would I be holding back?" he said as his brow wrinkled, and the hint of a cleft appeared.

"I don't know. I often catch you thinking. Is there something I should know?" Rekha said with a concerned look, trying to study what his eyes were not saying.

"No," he snapped, and looked away, shaking his head.

Rekha wondered what to make of his sudden reaction. She began to speak, but he abruptly got up and moved towards the doorway. She walked up behind him, trying to hold his arm. He pulled away and got off the bus as it stopped, and walked a step ahead of to her home in Quilla Mohalla.

. . .

As soon as they entered her home, he met everybody warmly. They were given a beautifully arranged bedroom on the top floor of the house. It had fresh linen, flowers, and incense. As soon as they entered, Rekha shut the door and hugged him.

"I'm sorry if I upset you," she said, looking into his eyes.

He smiled and kissed her gently. "Rekha, before we left, Pabbi was upset that we were leaving for so many days to Jalandhar. And I didn't want to cancel coming here as that would upset you, and everyone here. There is no other problem."

"Oh! Why didn't you tell me?"

"I had to say no to one of you, and in this case, it had to be Pabbi. She had such a small face when I said we were leaving. I don't like making her feel small. There is always a better way to do things, and I didn't give it due attention. Anyway, we are here now, so let us enjoy with your family."

"Our family," Rekha corrected.

"Yes, our family. Mummy, Papa, and everybody else is so nice, and these arrangements make me feel special. And you don't need to apologise to me about any..."

There was a loud knock on their door. "Jijaji, let's play Antakshari. Please, don't say no, Jijaji," said a shrill voice.

Inder opened the door to find Rakesh, Meena, and Sunil with a tray of chilled Rooh Afza and snacks. After they had eaten, Meena said the rhyme to start the singing game.

"Baithe baithe kya karein, karna hain kuch kaam, shuru karein antakshari lekar prabhu ka naam," said Meena. She stopped at Inder.

"Aha!" laughed Rakesh, "Jijaji, please sing a song with the letter M."

Inder smiled and sang, *"Main zindagi ka saath nibhata chala gaya, har fiqr ko dhuein mein udata chala gaya."*

"Wow, Jijaji, you are too good," said Sunil.

"Jijaji, do you smoke?" asked Meena with a naughty expression.

"No," he smiled.

"And drink?"

"One drink and only at official parties," he laughed, looking consciously at Rekha. "Meena, now you sing with the sound, Y."

Rekha smiled. *He looks happy. Oh! My tall, dark, and handsome husband. I love you so much. Sadly, he had to say no to Mataji. Maybe if she came with us, but she would disagree. Stop these ifs and buts, and just enjoy this moment.*

Their stay at Jalandhar was the most romantic and fun time of their home-neymoon. They went for films and ate *chaat* and *kulfis* in the market. Slowly Inder got to know the family during the numerous cards, singing, and jokes sessions.

"RFekhaFa, hFasF jFijFajFi kFissFed yFouF yFetF?" asked Meena, in F-language.

"MFanFy tFimeFs," said Rekha, and they all laughed at Inder's confused expression.

Love, respect, and laughter were omnipresent in the Patanjli home. And Inder joined in fully releasing the child-like fun side of himself that he had long forgotten, in Tandlianwala. He felt at home. He looked at Rekha with warmth – *My Rekha is filling my life with the nectar of love.*

Patanjli and Sarla exchanged glances. They had chosen well for their daughter.

...

It was soon time for Inder to resume duty. Rekha came to see him off at the station along with Dinesh and Kusum. Inder's heart felt a tug, knowing he had to leave her behind, not knowing when he could be with her again. *I love her so much. I'm going to miss her.*

"Write to me, take care of yourself, and I will call for you soon," said Inder, as Rekha stared at him with a smile. When it was time, Inder hugged her, said goodbye to everyone, and boarded the train. And then, Rekha jumped onto the train, just as it started.

"What is wrong with you? How will you get off?" gasped Inder, at her brazenness.

She shouted and waved to the amused Dinesh and Kusum, "I have my monthly pass."

She turned to embrace Inder, who laughed and shook his head at her surprising behaviour. Their hearts and eyes once again filled with emotion for one last time. They romanced in the narrow corridors of the first-class bogey. Till Ludhiana, Rekha clung onto Inder, not wanting to let go. Until he reluctantly pulled away.

He kissed her forehead. "Thank you for this bonus time. I want you with me forever, Rekha. Promise me that you will be strong. You have your family here with you while I am going to be alone. Let me leave with the memory of your smiling face."

Rekha smiled at him and got off the train. She held his hand until the train jerked to a start, and let go, with a prayer on her lips. Inder's heart felt heavy. A part of him was left behind with Rekha. He opened his bag to get a peek at a framed photograph of her. There she was with the now-familiar glint in her eyes and well-shaped, ready to smile lips. He sighed deeply and put

PRIYA SHARMA SHAIKH

his suitcase away and looked at the receding maize fields with a smile on his face. It was time to return to his first love - the Navy.

...

Rekha stayed in Jalandhar to continue her job and tried to balance her time between the University and Geeta's obligations. Every other week when she arrived at Korian Mohalla, her real-self came to a pause. Jaikishen interjected, but Geeta stood firm, refusing to retract her decree of veiling, house chores, and supervision each time she left the house.

Rekha conceded, but she was restless as she was living a dual life. In the little time she got, she wrote to Inder. His letters came filled with all the happenings in his life and that he missed her. She'd start reading each letter eagerly and end with staring at it blankly.

She looked at her reflection in her hand mirror. The red sindoor in the parting of her hair shone brightly.

Not as beautiful as Manju, but I am very much married, like her. But am I happy? How can I be happy when I can't be me?

...

One chilly afternoon, the sun bore down giving Rekha some much needed warmth as she sat cleaning a pile of dishes in the courtyard, with a bundle of coarse rope smeared with ash.

"Why are you doing all this alone, Rekha?" said Meena, who was visiting.

"I don't know, Meena," said Rekha in a resigned tone. "Being here without Inderjit, doing endless chores is a far cry from my dream marriage. I miss Mummy. She tirelessly cooked and worked for so many of us, despite her paralysis, without a word of complaint." Rekha's eyes welled up. "I realise now how

I took her love for granted. Unconditional love is only possible by a mother. But 'this' reality of marriage is perhaps how it is, for many a married woman. Marriage is not just love and fun – it is a lot of work too. Most of all, it is caring selflessly for the people you love as Mummy did for us."

"But Rekha, someone from the family, including Pitaji, always helped Mummy."

"You are right. But Inder's family is now mine too, and therefore working for them is not what bothers me. But contempt in the garb of tradition does. I may be wrong, but I feel small here. I am the most educated person, but that has become my biggest bane. Mataji's stereotypical belief is that because I am educated, I am *badmash*. She just won't listen to reason and doesn't understand my need to set papers or correct them or make a lecture plan. She thinks I use the University as an excuse to shirk housework. So, she gives me more chores. But, whatever I do, I just can't seem to please her," she said, breathing heavily.

"What nonsense! I am going to ask Mataji why she is mean to you."

"No, please don't. I can speak for myself."

"But, Rekha, you have never done so many chores."

"I love Inderjit, and for him, I want to find a way to manage this new life. I know I'm falling short in some ways. But don't worry, I get loved by everyone else - my students, all of you, and Inderjit, in his letters. I'm tougher than you think I am, Meena. My time to change and assert myself is not now. Until then, I will find joy in cleaning this *patila*."

. . .

It was more than six months since Inder had left, when one evening on her return home from college, Rekha saw her

PRIYA SHARMA SHAIKH

younger siblings peering over something. It was Inder's letter, and they had opened it! Rekha was aghast. She snatched it from them. Compared to the first two sentences, the rest of the letter blurred - *I have arranged for accommodation. I want you to come to Bombay at the earliest.*

On the 26th of May 1964, temperatures soared to 44 °C. An unveiled Rekha met Geeta and Narender (they needed to have a man along!) at Jalandhar station, to set off on their journey to Bombay. Geeta scowled.

"Mataji, Inderjit will be very embarrassed in the Navy if I wear a veil. His respect matters to me a lot, as I'm sure it does to you too. What do you say Mataji?" said Rekha with a calm smile.

To Rekha's surprise, Geeta nodded her head slowly. They shared a cabin of four with a young attractive Punjabi girl called Soni Gupta. She, too, was going to Bombay. She befriended Rekha instantly and chatted continually.

"What are you reading?" asked Rekha.

"Leo Tolstoy's *War and Peace*. I've read *Anna Karenina* too. He is fascinating."

"That is a fat book!"

"Yes, I love it."

"You are mighty brave to go to Bombay all by yourself. Are you going on holiday?"

"No. I am enrolled for my Masters in English at Elphinstone College - Their faculty is the best! I want to be a journalist and, eventually, a writer. I will be staying with my uncle until I find a place to stay. What are your plans, Mrs. Sharma?"

Rekha smiled, "Call me, Rekha. I'm not sure what will happen to my government job."

"Can't you get a transfer to Bombay?"

"I don't know. For now, being with my husband is paramount," said Rekha wistfully.

"Stay away from her," grumbled Geeta to Rekha, the moment Soni stepped out to go to the toilet. "Such girls are a bad influence," she said, shaking her head.

"Bad influence on who, Mataji?"

"On you, who else?"

"But what makes you believe that I will get badly influenced, Mataji?"

"I don't have the patience to explain everything to you, Rekha. Just don't respond to her when she talks. Eat your dinner and go to sleep early," snapped Geeta in a firm voice.

Geeta decided that Rekha and Soni would sleep on the two upper berths while she and Narender took the lower ones.

Soni turned to Rekha while arranging her blanket. "Rekha, there are enough and more colleges in Bombay, and there will always be a need for teachers."

"Let's see," said Rekha, glancing down.

Geeta was looking up at her pointedly. She immediately pretended to yawn and turned to lie on her back, looking up at the compartment's ceiling. *Here I am heading towards Bombay. Away from the things and people I love - my family, friends, students, Quilla Mohalla, and all my favourite eateries. But nothing matches the joy of being with Inderjit.* She smiled as thoughts of him came to her, and she closed her eyes.

Rekha awoke the next morning to sounds of vendors selling their wares inside and outside the train. They had reached Karnal. Narender was not in the coupe, and Geeta was sitting with her back to Soni, beading her rosary and mumbling prayers. Soni had already freshened up. She opened the window and bought a newspaper from a passing vendor. She poured herself a cup of tea from her Eagle thermos and sat back to take a sip.

"Oh no!" she said, looking up to see if Rekha was awake.

"What happened?" asked Rekha peering from her berth.

"Nehru has collapsed. His condition is serious, and he is under strict observation. He suffered a severe heart attack last evening."

Early the next morning, closer to Bombay, Rekha borrowed the Times of India from a fellow passenger. The headlines screamed, 'JAWAHARLAL NEHRU IS DEAD. Sudden End Follows A Heart Attack. THE LIGHT IS OUT.'

. . .

The news spread like wildfire, and people from across the country congregated to get one last look at their leader. Heads of government from across the world sent in condolences, and the national flag was to be at half-mast for the next ten days. The whole city was abuzz with talk about - who would lead India next.

Inder's heart was filled with mixed emotions, grieving for the country's loss, and excited to be with his beloved. He had already moved into his flat, which he shared with Lt. and Mrs. Gupta. He had been having visions of Rekha roaming around it. Keeping Geeta in mind, he had stocked up vegetables and grains and woke up early to prepare a simple meal of ladyfinger and lentils without any onions and garlic, how Geeta would like it. He took time off and arrived early at Bombay Central station to receive them.

As he made his way through the crowded platform, he

was aware of the looks of admiration he got from passers-by. However, he was only concerned about Rekha and Geeta's reactions - this was the first time they would see him in uniform.

The train rolled in alongside the platform at the scheduled 10 am, and Inder's heart started beating faster. He couldn't help himself grinning in anticipation, even as he craned his neck to look at each compartment that passed, trying to catch a familiar face.

Narender stood at the doorway with their bags to hail a coolie, while Rekha peered eagerly over his shoulder, scanning the crowds for Inder. She knew he would be there.

Inder spotted them and called out to Narender over the din, waving out. Rekha's head turned to trace the voice. There he was. Her excited gaze met his, and he blushed.

He moved towards them with enthusiasm, smiling and wiping his sweaty brow and upper lip with his handkerchief. His heart raced with happiness to see Rekha after so long, but he consciously stayed clear of any display of affection. Geeta considered any public displays of affection inappropriate social behaviour.

"My son! You look all the more handsome in uniform," exclaimed Geeta, as Inder bent to touch her feet.

"I am happy you like it, Pabbi. It is so good to see you all," he said, hugging Narender.

"You look great, brother," said Narender, happy to see his cousin looking so well turned out.

"Welcome to Bombay," he said, turning to look at Rekha, who stood smiling as she watched his every move. "Hope you had a comfortable journey."

"Yes, we did. Thank you," Rekha smiled, overwhelmed with the joy of seeing him. She shivered at his touch when he took her bag from her hand and guided her elbow towards the exit. "It was a bitter-sweet journey, as you can imagine. Pandit Nehru's news was shocking."

"Yes. The entire nation is mourning. What was the sweet bit?"

"Oh! I met a girl called Soni. She said I could look for a teaching job in Bombay," said Rekha, catching his strong hand.

He pulled away immediately and moved ahead with the coolie. She wanted to tease him for pulling away, and she wanted to hug him tightly. Then she remembered his sudden aloofness in Jalandhar.

He is indeed a different person around his family, more so in Mataji's presence. I wish I could do a magical statue to everyone and be left alone with him for our reunion after six months!

Outside the station, humidity and heat played havoc on them as sweat trickled down their bodies, and their heads burned as Inder looked for a taxi. After much difficulty, he managed to engage one. Geeta got in first, and Inder helped the driver load the bags. Rekha stole a quick hug before sitting next to Geeta. Narender sat with the cabbie, while Inder squeezed in next to her. Their bodies simmered, and they foolishly smiled as they held hands under her dupatta. Inder pointed out places to Geeta, who was visiting the city for the first time, just as Rekha squeezed his fingers.

"Just you wait," he whispered.

"I can't wait," she whispered back.

The taxi made its way to the city's southernmost tip to enter Navy Nagar's green haven.

"This place has parks, schools, a service canteen, a hospital, and a provision store. Defence is a cinema hall, there is a

United Services Club, a Golf Course, a sports stadium and an Olympic sized pool too. There is a temple, too, Pabbi," said Inder to Geeta.

Inder's shared home was a small but cosy flat. He got a few fleeting moments of privacy with Rekha before leaving for work. As soon as he left, Geeta took charge. She decided what they would eat, how they would sleep, and when and where they would go sightseeing.

"This house is like a matchbox and that too shared with another family! When will my son learn?" she said to Narender, and then looking at Rekha, "You better veil yourself from Gupta when he returns."

"Mataji, veiling is not a custom here," said Rekha.

"There is no respect for traditions in the cities, I tell you," Geeta grumbled under her breath, and looked at Narender. "These are the problems we don't foresee when we village folk leap towards the city."

"But Masiji, Inderjit has taken the family's graph up. Aren't you proud?"

"I am, but traditions and culture are a consideration too, aren't they?"

"What is more valuable for you, Mataji, traditions, or the happiness of the people who love you?" said Rekha smiling at Geeta.

"I am going for a bath," said Geeta, ignoring Rekha. "We will get back to Punjab soon, and there we can get back to tradition!"

Rekha's eyes fluttered in disbelief. *Going back - What does she mean? I dare not ask. Living away from Inderjit in Punjab is not the life I want. I cannot be faceless behind a veil, mistrusting the family's men, and living a life of permissions. Is this what Inderjit also expects of me?*

Throughout the day, Geeta ignored Rekha and made matters worse by filing Inder's ears with a string of negative things about her when he returned home in the evening. He listened patiently and nodded. Rekha looked towards Inder for consolation, but he offered nothing.

"What's for dinner?" he asked.

"Er ... *Moong dal, potatoes with peas* and fruit custard."

"Wow, let's eat."

He enjoyed the meal and blinked and smiled at Rekha.

"I loved the food, and I love you," he said hurriedly in a hushed tone when she was clearing up in the kitchen and gave her a quick hug and kiss. She got startled and dropped a few steel bowls that clattered endlessly in different directions.

"Now what have you done?" said Geeta, rushing into the kitchen.

"Nothing, Mataji," giggled Rekha, as Inder scooted out.

She hung onto the stolen moments of love. But that was that. Before she knew it, they turned off the lights, and it was time for all of them to sleep in the same room until the sun rose next morning, and all the chores that, by default, became her responsibility, started once again. She tried her best to please Geeta by being respectful and not engaging her in unnecessary conversation. But her efforts were in vain.

Rekha had visited her aunt in Bombay many times before. And she had had so many dreams of regaling Inder with tales of the history of Mumba-Devi, see the artifacts in the Prince of Wales Museum, watch films at Eros, shop at Colaba Causeway, hop onto a boat ride from Gateway of India, kiss him in the big shoe at Hanging Gardens, go for a carriage ride on Marine

JUNGEE

Drive, make sandcastles at Chowpatty, and so much more! But none of it happened.

Geeta didn't want to go out too much. Plus, she had food restrictions of no garlic and onion. Alcohol was taboo, of course, and she did not eat out of glassware - as glass is made of bones, she said! On the fifth day, Rekha was dismayed when Narender returned to Delhi, but Geeta chose to stay. Inder thought nothing of it. Geeta's high-handedness with Rekha and complaints were relentless, as was Inder's silence. On the contrary, he was gentle and cared for all her needs. The low morale, ongoing chores, and lack of time to have a complete uninterrupted conversation with Inder eventually got to Rekha.

My mind feels like the looming black monsoon clouds rising on the horizon. Where is the time for us together? Why can't Inderjit sense what my need is and doesn't he feel the need to be with me? She initially seethed with anger but then chose to withdraw. Her conversations became transactional, and with each day, her frown deepened. Inder sensed her stiffness and, when home, he spent his time studying, eating quietly, and talking to Geeta. They were living in the same home but in separate cocoons.

"What vegetables should I get from the market?" said Inder, startling Rekha as she sat staring vacantly at the newspaper.

Rekha shrugged. "Ask Mataji."

"I'm asking you."

"I don't get to make decisions in this house, and you don't care to express your opinion, so please ask her," she said plainly.

"What do you mean?"

"Mataji is the matriarch of this home, Inderjit, and she takes the final call on all household matters," she said with a tired expression.

"I'm sensing you find something wrong with that."

"There is never anything wrong or right. It is always a matter of perspective. Just don't ask me, as what I say will get overruled anyway."

Inder looked baffled. "Rekha, can you please explain your attitude to me? I don't understand the problem here, but I sense there is one."

"Don't you see that Mataji is constantly telling us how to run our lives - what we should eat, where we should go, what we should do or not do, when and where we should sleep. Like we have no mind of our own! So ask her what vegetables you should get," she said.

"Rekha, she is my mother. I know she is difficult, but trust me, she is not vengeful. She is just illiterate and has old-fashioned ways of being, and she doesn't know any better way. It is beyond her to understand your values or city life. And, I don't wish to provoke her at this age and convince her to be someone else." Inder searched Rekha's face, hoping she understood. "I want to make this trip an opportunity for her to have a nice time for a change. As I said, give it time so that you can create a case for her to learn from you, but meanwhile, you have to adapt."

"I agree that she is your mother, and she should get our utmost respect and care. Even I want her to have a good holiday," Rekha said, sitting up so he could see she meant well.

"And believe me, I have been nice to her and tried to understand her point of view. But, how can she insinuate to my face that educated women are *badmash*? How is it okay that she constantly finds faults in me despite my doing all the work? How is it okay that she tells you my faults and has no word of praise? And what am I to make of my husband, who does not say a word in my defence?"

She thought she had said it all, but her misery overflowed. "Is it fair to me, Inderjit? And why should I get used to something that is not right for me? Like, insisting I veil when it is against my value principles. How does she not realise that we have met after so long and that we need some privacy? Then this morning, she said that she and I would be going back to Phagwara! Has she discussed this with you? I want to stay with you."

"Rekha, we have our whole life ahead for privacy. You're not going anywhere. I have got this house for you. And whatever she may say about you is immaterial. I don't believe any of it. I listen to her venting because it makes her feel good."

"And where do I vent? She is clearly in the wrong, and by not asserting yourself on my behalf, so are you. What stops you from standing up to her diktat when it comes to me when you get away by asserting for yourself."

Inder looked away. A pregnant silence ensued. "The days of her stopping me are long gone, Rekha. She came from an environment of criticism and judgment, and that was not fair to her either. She came from a rich home, but she led a tough life of poverty for years after marriage and partition. She is maybe throwing her weight around as a mother-in-law to assert her sense of power once again. She feels a need to be bigger as she has felt less in her life before. Hence she has set customs, that are difficult to adopt by a free-spirited soul like you," he sighed. "I understand you, Rekha, and I am here to listen to you if you wish to talk to me. But please help me by trying to understand her limitations too. I have grown up to put respect for my elders ahead of myself. You, too, will have to adopt that practice and adjust until you have garnered enough trust to assert change. If I stand up for you now, she will hold a grudge against you and say that you caused a divide between her and me. And I don't want that to happen. Like me, let her be the way she chooses to be."

"But she holds a grudge against me anyway. And letting things be is putting dust under the carpet. How long can that go on?"

"I don't know, Rekha," he hushed, as Geeta awoke from her nap.

"What is the matter?" asked Geeta.

"Nothing, Pabbi. What would you like to eat tonight? Should we have tea?"

"Yes, tea will be nice. Get some *karelas* for dinner," said Geeta looking at the rains bursting from the sky and lash against the windowpane. "Lord Indra, please stop this rain."

"The rain is needed, Pabbi. Without it, crops and people cannot survive," smiled Inder.

"Radhe Krishna! These rains are too scary for my liking. I feel it is time to return to Phagwara. Please book tickets for Rekha and me."

"Rekha will stay here with me, Pabbi," said Inder in a steady tone.

"Are you out of your mind? It is not appropriate for her to stay in a shared accommodation like this," declared Geeta.

"It is all that was available, Pabbi. We will manage."

"Not with another man living in the same house. Have you thought of her safety when you go sailing?"

"Gupta is a married man, and this is the Navy cantonment. It is safe here," said Inder, in a patient tone.

"Nonsense. I have decided, and that is that."

"Mataji, I can manage to stay alone," protested Rekha standing at the door, looking anxious as decisions were being made about her future.

"How things have changed! I'd be sick if I talk back to my elders."

Rekha looked at Inder and spoke to him in English. "I do not wish to go back. Inderjit!"

"I never took my husband's name, either. There was so much respect."

"I am capable of living alone, just like I did when I was in the hostel. And if you can't take responsibility, I will," hissed Rekha, ignoring Geeta.

"What is she saying, in English?"

"Nothing, Pabbi," said Inder, his brow furrowing.

Rekha looked at him with disbelief and then at Geeta, who looked, blissfully unaware of the trouble she had started. Rekha stomped into the kitchen, while Inder walked into the balcony and leaned out to let the rain wash away his pain.

How do I make Pabbi understand that I want Rekha to be here with me?

...

The next evening, Rekha rushed to open the door to Inder and stopped him at the doorway. She and Geeta would be accompanied by a senior sailor, who was also going on leave to Punjab.

"Have you got the tickets?"

"Yes," he said in a solemn voice, trying to move past her.

"Are you happy that I'm going back?" she asked, holding his

arm.

"I got this accommodation for you, Rekha. I need not have done all this if you were to return."

"Tell me, will you be happy if I go back?"

"No. I want you to stay, but Pabbi is right that you can't stay here alone when I'm sailing. You have your job too. It has been a big mistake," he said and brushed past her.

"I am not going to allow anybody to say 'this' has been a mistake. Not even you," said Rekha.

She snatched the tickets from his hand and walked up to Geeta, who had just finished saying her evening prayers. Rekha put the tickets in her lap.

"Good! When do we leave? But wait, what is this? These are only two tickets. Isn't that boy going with us? Where is his ticket?"

"Mataji, Inderjit could get only two tickets. The first ticket is yours, and the second is for that boy. He will take you home safely."

"What about your ticket? There is some mistake, Rekha!"

"There is no mistake, Mataji. I will come with Inderjit later," Rekha said, in a calm tone.

Inder's mouth opened in astonishment as he watched Rekha turn around, with the third ticket crumpled in her hand. She walked out of the room to brew some tea and torched it on the kitchen burner. After he stood his ground and left Punjab, it was the first time someone stood up to Geeta.

. . .

Geeta left. Rekha and Inder began their married life. They

made love, talked, discussed, debated, disagreed, frowned, and then made up. They saw the city together, watched films, took walks by the seaside, relished Kwality ice creams and Inder heard all of Rekha's stories.

Inder learnt of Rekha's willing piety to lend a helping hand to the poor and oppressed, uplifting them and empowering many with education. Her warm, friendly nature touched many lives - her heart was pure gold.

And Rekha learnt that Inder found joy in the smallest things. His day's highlight was gorging on the desserts that she painstakingly made for him - cakes, puddings, kheer, semiyan, and fruit custard; just about anything sweet! She also realised that the fun life she had imagined herself being a part of in the Navy was quite different in reality. Life for Inder was routine. *Or is it that he chooses to lead a simple life?*

"Don't you meet any friends regularly?" asked Rekha one Sunday morning.

"I used to. But most of my course mates are posted all over the country or busy with their lives. Understandably, it is difficult to make time now. And I don't feel the need to meet anybody regularly."

"Relationships have to be cultivated for them to sustain the tides of time."

"I did when I was younger and had more time. The only relationships I wish to cultivate now is with the Navy and you," said Inder.

...

A few weeks later, Rekha brushed her teeth one morning while Inder applied shaving cream on his face. He set the brush down and picked up the razor.

"We have to attend a party this evening," said Inder casually, lifting his hand to shave.

"What ..." said Rekha blubbering with foam in her mouth, her eyes shining.

"Wear one of your good saris as all the senior officers and their wives will be present," he said, holding his left cheekbone with his hand and moving te razor smoothly towards his chin, to reveal a clean-shaven strip on his cheek.

Rekha quickly rinsed her mouth and jumped with joy, "Finally, a party! What all happens at these naval parties?"

"You meet people, talk to them, have dinner, and that's that. Some people drink, but you should not. Some people dance too, but you should not – I mean not with anybody else," he said, looking at her pointedly and then back at his image in the mirror, "If someone asks you for a dance, politely say, no thank you," he said, proceeding to shave his other cheek.

"But why shouldn't I drink and dance?"

"Because girls from good families don't," he shrugged and moved his razor to his chin.

"But if other wives do, so should I, and if I can't do so even when you are around, then when can I?" she said, prodding his underarm, causing him to jerk and nick his chin.

"Ouch! Look at what you've done - stop being a child, Rekha! It is just an official party. We are going because my Captain has invited us. Stop overreacting. And anyway, do you even know how to dance?" he said, reaching out for a piece of paper to blot the bright red blood.

"I'm sorry, darling." She scowled. "I don't know how to dance, but you could teach me."

"No. I don't like dancing, and it's not easy to learn," said Inder smugly.

"Do you even know how to dance?"

"It was part of my training. I want an omelette for breakfast," said Inder, walking out.

She followed him out of the bathroom with a forlorn expression and watched as he meticulously took out his crisp white uniform from the cupboard and hung it on the door handle, and neatly laid out his undergarments, socks, belt and sparkling white shoes.
"What happened to you?" said Inder.

"I'm upset, Inderjit. I have never attended a party. Pitaji didn't permit me in college as they were known to have women who smoked, drank, danced, and wore Western clothing! It wouldn't be of much help in improving my future, he had said. And now you have issues too. If your Captain hadn't said so, you would not have taken me at all. Why do I need to take permission all my life?"

Inder looked at her, kindly. "It is not about taking permissions. I don't enjoy dancing, and I don't want to share you with any other man. And an evening can be enjoyed without drinking too."

"But I want ..."

"Rekha, you are my wife, and I don't like the idea of you drinking and dancing with other men. I'm a little selfish there, but you can dance with me. Okay, I promise I will teach you. Can we stop arguing now? I'll be late for work," he said and walked into the bathroom.

"So possessive and such a fighter. Jungee! That's what you are! I will call you Jungee from now on. It is the ideal name for you!" she said, outside the shut bathroom door.

Well, at least I am going to a party. That is a start! I wonder how I should dress for the occasion – my silk sari or maybe the zari chiffon. The phulkari chudidaar kurta would be better for dancing, though. That's if I get to dance at all. I'll make a high bun. No, a braid. Damn! All this is so confusing. But I will dazzle you with my looks tonight, Jungee darling – just you wait.

She winked at her reflection.

. . .

Inder came home that evening and quickly changed into the evening uniform, including black trousers, a white half-sleeved shirt, a black cummerbund, his stripes, and black shoes.

He called out to Rekha as he combed his hair, worried that she would be late. "We leave in 5 minutes," he said and hurried into the living room to sip his tea.

Rekha emerged from the bedroom dressed in a light green silk sari. Her hair swirled into a high bouffant, and her two inches high silver stilettoes added to her look's glamour. Inder's mouth dropped open. *She looks dazzling.* He held her waist and twirled her around, close to him, and smelled her mild perfume.

"I will be the luckiest man at the party," he said and gently kissed her lips.

"Thank you. Nice uniform, Jungee," she blushed.

"This is the Red Sea rig. And even though you are looking so stunning, you can't call me Jungee in public, okay?

"Okay, Jungee."

"Shall we?" he said, secretly tickled by his new nickname.

. . .

The party was in the ballroom of the mess. It was a grand well-lit room, with huge windows that overlooked the Arabian Sea. Rekha's head started moving to the music's beat playing in the background as they entered. She took in the sounds of chatter, laughter, and the clinking of glasses. Officers and their partners standing in groups talking to each other with a drink in their hands filled the room. Waiters walked about with trays laden with drinks and snacks. Some couples were already dancing in the centre near the live band.

Inder introduced Rekha to his colleagues Lt. Dubey, Lt. Tripathi, and Lt. Cdr. Joginder Singh, the Executive Officer (ExO), and his commanding officer, Commander Mukherjee. He had a stocky build and a warm disposition, with a ready charming smile.

As planned, when any officer asked Rekha to dance, she smiled and politely declined. Just then, Mrs. Mukherjee walked up to Inder. "IJ, you may have the pleasure of this dance with me," her eyes twinkling as she held out her hand for him to take.

"Sure, Ma'am, it will be my pleasure," said Inder taking her hand awkwardly. He led her to the dance floor, while Rekha stood there with her eyes wide open. *So, he can dance after all. And he can dance with another woman!* She narrowed her eyes and grimaced.

"Close your mouth, darling."

Rekha turned to face a tall, slim woman, who looked like a filmstar. She wore a beautiful black chiffon sari, and her hair was in a loose low bun.

"Sorry?" said Rekha startled.

"I'm Meeta. You are Rekha, IJ's wife, right?"

"Yes. Hello."

"And this is your first Navy party."

"Yes. How did you know?" said Rekha, keeping one eye on

Inder, as he moved around the dance floor with Mrs. Mukherjee.

"You are looking at everything and everyone with such wonder, and you had a smile stuck on your face until your husband got kidnapped."

"Oh!" Rekha felt gauche and gave a sheepish smile.

"It's okay. There's always a first time. Make it memorable," Meera laughed. "So, do you like Bombay?"

"Yes, very much."

"I think it's highly overrated."

"Why do you say that?"

"Well, we still don't have any proper accommodation, everything is so far away, and all these parties are just so boring."

"I like it here because I get to be with Inderjit."

"The proverbial Sita! So, where is your beloved Ram right now?"

She sighed deeply, "Dancing!"

"And, here comes someone to ask you for a dance," she said, winking at Rekha.

"Oh, no!"

"Oh, do say yes, Rekha."

Rekha turned to find Sub-Lieutenant Das, a well-built, handsome officer, smiling at her.

"Good evening, Ma'am. May I have this dance?" he said with a flattering courtesy.

Rekha's stomach became a knot. She looked over her shoulder at Meera, who encouraged her to go ahead. There was no sight of Inder in the crowded banquet hall.

"Sorry I don't know how to dance. Please dance with someone else."

"Well, Ma'am, it would be my honour to tutor you," he paused and held out his hand. "And I won't take no for an answer," he said and took her hand and led her to the dance floor.

He turned to face her and held his arm up. "This form of dance is called the ball dance. You are to hold me on my right shoulder while I hold you by your waist and hold your right hand up in my left hand, like this," he said, demonstrating her position.

He then placed his hand around Rekha's waist. She blushed and pulled back as he was a stranger! But Das was all politeness, so she complied.

"Now listen to the beat of the music, and get a sense of it."

"Okay," said Rekha, bobbing her head to the beat.

"Great! Now, when I say go, I will take a step towards you while you take a step back. I will lead you, so don't worry. Let's go!" Das said and moved towards Rekha.

She stumbled over his toes and bumped into him and tripped over her sari. Das was a patient teacher, and each time she stumbled, he covered up with a smile and encouraged her to keep moving. Finally, they were swirling around the dance floor without a fault to the music's flow! She giggled with the joy of having learnt something new. She was having such a lovely time until she caught sight of Inder glaring at her.

"My husband ... he's waiting for me. Thank you so much for being such a good teacher," she said, abruptly leaving Das's hand and stepping back, bumping into another couple, apolo-

PRIYA SHARMA SHAIKH

gising and feeling ruffled.

"Sure, Ma'am, it was my pleasure. I hope you had a nice time," he said, but Rekha had turned and hurried through the crowd of dancers towards Inder's stiff withdrawing figure. She followed him into the balcony outside the banquet hall and grabbed his arm. "Jungee, I..."

"I told you not to dance with anyone," he said in a hushed tone, his face shadowed in anger.

"I said no, but he was so..." she said, still smiling.

"But you couldn't. Right?" snapped Inder, "Please leave me alone."

"Leave you alone? And where do you suppose I go? I don't know anybody here. And why the double standards. You were dancing too."

"She was my CO's wife – I couldn't say no," he seethed.

"And, Das was nice and respectful, and even I couldn't say no, as he dared to ask and had the patience to teach a senior officer's wife," shot back Rekha.

"Oh, you are incorrigible," he said, looking away with a huff.

"As are you," she said, looking away from him.

They spent the rest of the evening in a sour mood, with both of them ignoring each other until it was polite to leave. Inder walked out of the mess with Rekha a few steps behind him, scowling and dragging her tired, blistered feet.

"Nice evening, huh, IJ?" It was Mukherjee.

"Lovely evening, Sir. We had a great time. Thank you," said Inder standing to attention as Rekha looked awkward.

"At ease, IJ. And has your lovely wife had a nice evening

too?"

"Yes, thank you," said Rekha, with a forced smile.

"Good. Have you seen Dharini yet, young lady?"

"No, not yet," said Rekha awkwardly.

"Well, we are going to correct that mistake tomorrow, aren't we IJ? Make sure you do, since it is a Saturday. Good night."

. . .

Rekha awoke the next morning to find Inder in a headstand by the door. He was sweating after having done a rigorous workout. She scowled at him and went straight for a shower and dressed in a pink and white chudidaar kurta to visit Inder's ship.

Rekha was fascinated to see so many ships of different sizes at the dockyard along the jetty. Men dressed in a variety of white uniforms went about their business with an air of infectious sincerity. Rekha looked up at Dharini, standing at the foot of the gangway. She was a massive ship in height and width. Inder held out his hand to help her get on to the gangway. She stayed close behind him, watching him deftly navigate his way and greet the sailor on duty.

"Good morning, Sir. Good morning, Ma'am. Welcome aboard INS Dharini," said the young sailor.

"Good morning," smiled Rekha, looking around in wonder.

Inder took her to the wardroom, where they met his colleagues Dubey and Tripathi. Inder left her with them and went to meet the Captain.

"Good morning, Sir. Reporting on my status, Sir," said Inder.

"Good morning IJ. Has the radar wiring been completed?"

PRIYA SHARMA SHAIKH

"It is in perfect working condition now, Sir."

"And how are the new boys shaping up?"

"Sir, they are now familiar with the ship's working. I will test their skills when we sail."

"Good job! Has Rekha come in with you?"

"Yes, she has, Sir."

"That's jolly good! It is essential to keep your wife engaged with every aspect of your life, IJ. Help her blend into the Navy so she also considers it as her family, as you do."

"Aye Sir," said Inder and headed back to the wardroom to meet Rekha.

"Come," smiled Inder, "I'll take you for a tour."

After walking through a few corridors, Rekha stomped her feet and stopped.

"What is it?" he said in a hushed tone, looking around consciously.

"Are we just walking around, or will you also explain things?"

"It is a lot to explain. It took me so many years to learn everything about a ship."

"Rome got built because people started working on it. I have no desire to become an officer like you, so I don't need to know all the details. But it would be nice to know some basics. So, bring on the guided tour, officer," she whispered.

"Yes, Ma'am," said Inder holding back a smile. "A ship is a self-sufficient manmade island of steel that can float and sail on water. She provisions for her crew to live here, as they do at home."

"Are there bedrooms for everyone?"

"There are a few cabins for the Captain and the senior officers, but the rest of the crew has bunk beds for sleeping. And that is where camaraderie gets built. There is a dining area too, and big ships like Dharini also have a wardroom for recreation."

"That is where I had tea," said Rekha.

"Yes. The ship's right side is called the starboard side, and the left is the port side, which has green and red indicators, respectively when sailing. When ships cross each other at sea, they always do so to their right sides - so two green lights cross each other."

"What is that area called?" asked Rekha, pointing to the front of the ship.

"The front of the ship is called Forecastle or Fox'l, and the back is called the Aft or Quarterdeck. The Fox'l holds and lets down the anchor to hold a position in the water. The Aft houses the propeller, which spins at high speed to move the ship forward. Here you will also find the Quarterdeck, which is the lowest and filthiest part of any ship. It gets flooded with soot from the funnel and water from the ocean, making it muddy and greasy and very difficult to keep clean. I have spent many hours in the Quarterdeck during my early days as an officer," said Inder, wistfully.

"Oh!" said Rekha. After an awkward silence, she looked up with squinted eyes, "What is that up there?"

"That is the Radar, on top of the mast of the ship. It works as an antenna. There are various types of radars – the surveillance one is usually the highest antenna, and then there are navigation and gun systems' radars. The surveillance radar can pick up a contact way beyond the line of vision, which can then activate the guns system radar to pick up the contact too, and if she is an enemy vessel, we engage the target."

"How do you know she is an enemy, Jungee?"

"If a ship fails to give the code, she is identified as an enemy vessel."

"Interesting. All the doors on this ship are so oddly built."

"There is a reason they look that way. A ship has several compartments, separated by watertight doors, bulkheads, or hatches lined with tough rubber, which seals the door with a latch called a cleat. The watertight doors prevent the free flow of water from one side of the ship to the other. If a hole develops in one part of the ship, you can seal the compartment around the hole, and only that compartment gets flooded. The ship will tilt to one side with the water's weight, but water will not seep through to other areas. We then maintain a balance by flooding the opposite side of the ship too! So, despite a flooded section, she can keep moving."

"How fascinating!"

"Indeed. Each of these windows called portholes is also of toughened glass and has a steel cover that also keeps it watertight."

They re-entered the ship's inner chambers and walked down a narrow corridor to a raised square in the floor, "This is a hatch, which will take us to another level of the ship."

"Levels, as in floors? How many floors does a ship have?"

"It depends on the size of the ship and the number of people on board. Dharini has four levels as she has huge storage areas that provide fresh and dry provisions, toiletries, medicine, and essentials, including water, fuel, etc., for the fleet at sea. She has cranes and booms to lift and move things around. INS Rajput, where I served as an independent watchkeeping officer, has three levels, but she is much smaller than Dharini.

JUNGEE

However, Rajput is a warship with guns, torpedoes, and depth charges, etc."

"Were you trained to use the guns?"

"Yes. We are trained for war, to hit first, hit hard, and keep hitting."

"Gosh! That sounds harsh."

"War is not a time to pull punches, Rekha."

"I don't like guns, ammunition, and war – we ought to stop them!"

"Nobody wants war. But war is sometimes the only choice, and all forces prepare for that unfortunate eventuality. India has never attacked any country or waged war with anybody. But all kinds of tribes, countries, and conquerors have invaded her as she is a land rich in culture, treasure, and opportunity – Moghuls, French, Portuguese, British. They fell in love with our land and chose to make India their home," said Inder.

"Today India is a melting pot of many civilisations. Unfortunately, this process has eroded our original knowledge, culture, and wealth, and over time I'd dare say, our self-esteem too," said Inder leading the way up a stairway.

Rekha looked at Inder with admiration, as he turned to extend his hand to her.

"Apologies for the digression! But our job is to protect our homeland. And we will have to take action when wartime comes, or we could get hit. "

"War gives me the jitters. So many soldiers die, and we waste so much money. And I worry about your safety if we ever go to war."

"Worrying won't save me or my ship – proper training, regular practice, and focus will. Here we have reached the bridge; it is the Captain's workstation."

Mukherjee was talking with two officers, bent over a large chart unrolled onto a table. He looked up from the chart and smiled at Rekha warmly.

"Welcome aboard, young lady. So, how do you like your husband's first home?"

"Fascinating. Thank you so much for letting me be here."

"It's our pleasure to have you. Isn't Dharini an amazing piece of work?"

"Oh yes, she is wonderful," gushed Rekha.

"I'm glad you like it. Let me introduce you to the bridge, the high command centre, where all orders are received, and decisions are taken, implemented, and recorded. These boys, including IJ, play with the stars and the sun's position to know exactly where we are in the ocean vis-à-vis the land."

"Do they use a sextant for that?" asked Rekha.

"Jolly good Rekha! IJ, you have an intelligent wife. Physics student?"

"Yes," blushed Rekha.

"Excellent. IJ will explain more details to you, as I have to get back to work. I hope you enjoy the rest of the tour."

"Oh, sure. Thank you."

Inder whispered, "3-4 key people manage the Bridge of a ship – The Captain himself, his second in command, the ExO, the Signals Officer, the Watchkeeping Officer, and the Quarter-master, who stands at the wheel steering the ship as per the Captain's orders."

"How does the ship get the power to sail at high speed?"

"On diesel fuel, which generates the steam in the engine room, which runs the propellers and gas turbines on the shafts. This generates power, which makes everything else on the ship work. As I said, this is a self-sufficient island."

"It is all so amazing. Is Dharini your second ship Jungee?"

"As an officer, I first served on Khukri, then the Brahmaputra, then Rajput and Dharini. Each of them was a new learning experience – its form, purpose, functions, and people. There is so much I have learnt from colleagues, Rekha, whether they were senior or junior, great or tough to work with, and from their varied cultures. Living on a ship taught me how to coexist because you don't get to choose your colleagues. What you do get to choose is your manner in accepting them and learning to work with them."

"This feels like one big family with everyone doing their duties and the Captain at the helm, like a father," said Rekha in amazement.

"That is a good analogy. I believe I have done my job well," said Inder.

She looked up at him and smiled, and caught him staring at her warmly. She blushed and fidgeted with her dupatta. "What is it?" she murmured.

"I'm a lucky man."

"You can't be more right, Jungee, you are truly a very lucky man," she whispered, flicking her hair and walking ahead while he followed, holding back a laugh.

...

Rekha watched as Inder ate his breakfast of two fried eggs, toast, and milk. "How are you so handsome?"

"What do you mean? I just am."

"Humility is not one of your virtues. Can we go to watch *Leader* this evening? It has my favourite hero Dilip Kumar in it. I simply love him."

Inder's brow crowded, and he continued chewing his toast and egg with a straight face.

"What time will you return?" she said in her continued excitement.

"We are not going," he snapped.

"Why not?"

"Because I don't want to see it."

He finished the rest of his breakfast in silence. Rekha followed him to the washbasin, and he shook his head.

"I didn't know you could love another man," he said sarcastically.

"Officer, do I smell fumes of jealousy? Shame on you, fighting with your wife for such a little thing! Well, he is my most favourite actor and your being jealous is not going to change that," she said grabbing his cap, and putting it on she dodged him around the house.

"I will be late for work, Rekha!"

"Only because I don't want you to blame me for being late," she handed out the cap, and then snatched it back before he got a hold of it, giggled and finally gave it to him. He scowled, turned to the mirror and placed it on his head and straightened his uniform.

"You are my real hero, Jungee. Nobody is as good," she sighed and hugged his back.

"Don't call me Jungee."

"Trying to dominate me, huh?"

He looked at her questioningly and brushed her hands off his body.

"Is that all you have, officer?" she smiled naughtily.

Inder looked at her with a straight face, then picked up his bag and headed to the door. He slammed the door shut. Rekha's smile faded. He was gone. He hadn't played along with her after all. He was annoyed. Again. *What is this habit, of sudden withdrawal, without any apparent provocation, and then being all wound up? Urrghh!*

She had tried to seek entry into his moments of silence with her light-heartedness, but he wouldn't let her in. The more she tried to get him to open up, the more distant he became.

He would continue to carry her shopping bags, move her to the road's inner side when they walked together, open and close the lift door for her, and help with chores, all in complete silence. And then he would unwind in a snap as if nothing had happened at all.

A few days before, they had been to a bookstore in the Colaba market. She had sighed, looking at all the packed bookshelves, taking in the freshly printed textbooks' smells. She had flipped through the biology and chemistry textbooks for senior school and graduate studies. The syllabus was similar to what she taught.

As they had manoeuvred their way out of the market, past vegetable and fruit stalls, an idea was taking hold of Rekha. "Do you think I could get a job in some college here?"

Silence.

PRIYA SHARMA SHAIKH

"Which are the good colleges in Bombay?"

Silence.

"Soni, that girl in the train, I told you about ...," Rekha continued, trying to draw Inder's attention as she dodged a fisherwoman with a basket of fish on her head.

Silence.

"Soni had mentioned Elphinstone College. I could apply there. What do you think?"

He stopped walking when they reached the bus-stop. "Are you listening to me at all?"

"I heard all that you said, Rekha. We live in Navy Nagar, while all the colleges are at Fort and beyond. It is not safe for you to travel on a bus."

The bus had arrived just then, and they pushed to clambered on. They edged around and made a place for themselves on the packed bus. Inder placed Rekha with her back against the railing and stood guard with his arms braced around her, as she gasped and anxiously avoided the press of the crowds. He looked down at his delicate wife fondly but said nothing. In his protective manoeuvring, Rekha could see his love for her. His anxiety was not unfounded.

There had been several such instances. Rekha walked back to her room, reminiscing the events of the morning. She had not pursued the subject of teaching after that trip to Colaba, but it had stayed on her mind. Rekha picked up the latest Femina and crunched on some Spangles and Quality Street chocolates. She replayed the morning's incident all through the day until she fell asleep. The doorbell jolted her from her siesta. She had overslept and cooked nothing for the evening! She rushed to open the door. Inder stood there looking at her in a groggy state. It was Inder and quite unexpectedly he

JUNGEE

looked very excited.

"Hello ..." she started, but before she could say anything further, he grabbed her hand and pulled her along, running down the stairs.

"Where are you taking me? Let me brush my hair, at least."

"You look just fine," he said as they reached the building entrance. Glimmering in the evening sun, with all the poise of a big prowling cat, stood a brand-new grey-blue Lambretta scooter.

"Is this yours?" she asked, looking at him with wide eyes.

"It's ours," he said with aplomb.

"Oh, my God!"

"You like it, huh?" he said, watching her walk around it. She touched the seat, pressed the horn, ran her fingers over the light. She found it hard to believe; they owned the scooter.

She looked up at him with a glow. "I love it. Let's go for a ride."

"Dressed like this?"

"Does it matter?"

"No, it doesn't," he said and started the scooter.

Rekha perched herself pillion, with both her legs to one side and put her arm around Inder's slim waist. They sped through the streets of Navy Nagar, Afghan Church, Cuffe Parade, and finally got on to the picturesque Marine Drive. The evening breeze played with Rekha's hair, making her forget all her misgivings, as she rested her chin on his shoulder. *I live for such moments.*

Inder loved the view – the buildings on one side of the road

291

PRIYA SHARMA SHAIKH

overlooking the beautiful Arabian Sea. But it wasn't only a beautiful view; it was also one of his long-standing dreams. It had been a long way to finally be working in Bombay, buy a scooter, and ride it along Marine Drive with his beautiful wife. The sparkling waves lashed a spray of water onto their faces, and they squealed aloud. *What a perfect moment!*

"Why don't we have some *chaat* at Chowpatty?" suggested Rekha.

"Your wish is my command," he said and parked at the beach. They gobbled *pani-puris* and a *bhel* each at a makeshift stall.

"They have the best bhel in the city! I wonder how they make it so delicious."

"Puffed rice, boiled potatoes, onions, tomatoes, green chilies, coriander, lime, and salt. I can make it too, but I can't replicate the joy of this experience at home," said Rekha after swallowing the last mouthful of bhel.

They walked towards the water, sharing a bottle of Coca-Cola. The sun moved towards the ocean, slowly painting the sky in magical blends of purple, pink, orange, and yellow.

"Shall we sit?" asked Inder.

"Yes."

Inder stared into the distance in silence, as he sipped on the soda. He felt awkward, and yet he was aware of the closeness he felt for Rekha.

"What are you thinking of, Jungee?"

"I'm sorry about this morning. I have not been an ideal part-ner for you."

"I never said that," she said, looking at him with a comical scowl.

"You didn't, but you must think so," he said, and looked away, to gaze into the distance again. "I've grown up avoiding conflict with Pabbi. And I believe it has stayed as a way I deal with conflict to date. I escape it and push my feelings under the carpet because I get insecure around conflict. Not always, just sometimes."

"Like today?" asked Rekha letting some sand pass through her fingers.

"Yes. When I can't express my perspective with conviction or feel I might lose control of a situation, I get on edge, lose congruency, and am not at peace."

"I see! Now that you say this, I remember you seemed irritated when we first went to Phagwara together. Were you on edge back then too?"

"Yes, I think I was. Rekha, I know Pabbi's conservative way of life. And from whatever little I knew of you by then, you seemed modern. I was anxious about what she might say to you if she saw you waving at the neighbours. Anyone that is traditional and pious are smiled upon by her, and she scorns modernity. I just wanted to protect you, but amongst so many people, I just didn't know how to say it better than just snap at you not to wave."

"I understand, Jungee. What do you experience when you have these feelings?"

"I become offensive, or I just clam up. But it doesn't stop there. I start having little memories from the past, which rapidly take me down a spiralling labyrinth. Memories of mediocrity, limiting beliefs of me not being good enough, and me fighting to find direction as an adolescent," Inder paused and turned to look at Rekha, as his lips tried to find the right words.

He then took a deep breath and said, "I was 17 when I joined the Navy, Rekha and I didn't join as an officer. I started as a lower deckhand. As a sailor." He felt vulnerable at suddenly being so open, but he was unable to hold back anymore. Rekha held his hand, and her loving gaze encouraged him to continue.

"I was so naive then. I had left home, trusting just myself to discover the unknown beyond my comfort zone. I could barely understand English, let alone speak it. I was shy, and I felt awkward and left out. But I was determined to discover new horizons and abilities within me. And destiny's plans for me were more than I had ever imagined. I became an officer. As a rookie, I had gained a reasonable amount of confidence. I made good friends too. And yet, I found it hard to fit in amongst strangers. I often felt judged. Judgment is a dangerous weapon, Rekha. People use it to cloud your mind and make you believe you are inadequate. I sensed undertones from some senior officers and got disregarded on some occasions too. That made me keep a distance from people and focus just on my work."

"And that did a lot of good for you. But do you still feel judged?"

"Not anymore, but sometimes when I sense conflict, those memories do get triggered. I showed you the Quarterdeck that day. After slogging it out there for six months on board Khukri, my watchkeeping ticket was held back by the Captain. That held me back in my course, while the rest of my batchmates went ahead. I was in dismay at first because I knew my stuff, and I knew I had done a good job. And yet I was side-lined. I felt targeted. I felt alone. And I cried tears of defeat." Inder sighed and paused.

"And then I wiped my tears too," he gave her a cynical laugh, "Maybe I haven't learnt my lesson of rising above my insecurities, and that is why those shadows still resurface and make me be this person that you find difficult to understand."

"What do you think makes you hold onto those memories?"

"I guess I feel sorry for myself, and I take solace in blaming someone to have put me through those times. Feeling like the victim."

"And who did you find to blame?"

Inder sat silent, looking at the horizon. "All the while, I have blamed externally – Pabbi, and others that made me feel small. But now, as I talk to you, the reality is that I have no one but myself to blame." He paused.

"Now that you've come to this awareness, how does it make you feel, Jungee?"

"When I allow someone to make me feel inadequate, I give them wings, and I arrest my flight. I should not have yearned for external validation. But I didn't understand this then. My friends did tell me I was silly - You are good at your work, and you need not be so self-conscious of others, they'd say." He paused again, reminiscing that time.

" I should have listened and been content being the diligent, hard-working village boy!"

"What else did those moments teach you?"

"That my life's journey is my mountain to climb. Alone. And that I have to take responsibility and continue to have the courage and belief in myself to face my fears and obstacles. That will help me deal with any conflicts," he said, sighing deeply. "I am more aware now, but I still fail sometimes, like this morning," he said, feeling sheepish and looking at Rekha.

"Is there anything else on your mind?"

"Sunsets are truly magical. They always give me hope of a new tomorrow and a chance to start afresh. It was a beautiful sunset like this one, when I stood on the Quarterdeck of Khukri with my emotions in turmoil, knowing I would get left behind from my other coursemates as they got their watchkeeping ticket. And as I looked at the sun and her brilliance on all of the world, I realised my first few lessons of adult life."

"And what were those lessons?"

"That it is wrong for me to expect a reward just because I have done a good job. Whether I get rewarded or not is immaterial, my *karma* is, and it should persist, nevertheless. It taught me humility, grounding, and patience. When things don't happen as expected, the time is not right, and I need to have patience and be kind to myself while I stay the course; until the time is right. And detractors are bound to come to test my resolve. My aim should be to learn from every experience and become the wiser. So, after everyone moved on, I decided to change my paradigm. I used the contempt I received as fuel," he smiled.

"That sounds powerful," Rekha mused. "How did you do that?"

"I grew even more motivated to excel in whatever I did. I worked harder. I kept my head clear of the internal and external chatter. I made a conscious effort to improve myself on every social parameter that had also perhaps kept me back. I did finally garner the necessary acknowledgment from my seniors, and I got awarded my ticket." Inder looked at her. "It also made me good enough to have you as my wife."

Rekha blushed. Inder's gaze softened, and he said, "When I'm at a loss, I sometimes still feel the weight of all the past baggage. And I usually prefer to walk away until I have sorted my thoughts rather than inflict my bad mood on anyone or get into a traffic jam of opinions. Perhaps it is my way of processing my momentary insecurity."

"Hmm. Tell me, what does security mean to you, Jungee?"

"Something unwavering, that inspires me with confidence, and to believe in myself."

"And who or what in your life today gives you that feeling of confidence?"

"The Navy. She offers me limitless possibilities. She is like the ocean, with the power to encompass all that flows into her. Pitaji has been my biggest strength, and you."

Rekha sat up and looked straight at him. "Great! I'm going to try something, and I want you to think before you answer. When you say yes to being insecure and avoid conflict, what are you saying no to at that moment?"

"Peace of mind – I lose my presence."

"And how important is presence for you?"

"It is my *sadhana* or my purpose to be present to give excellence to every moment so that I have no regrets. I don't like it when I am pushed to the rails by my insecurities."

"Right. You have had the training to fight your enemy head-on, Jungee. You know how to use weapons to defeat them. You will agree that you can't defeat them by avoiding them. You say your insecurity disturbs your peace. What could you do to fight that insecurity?"

He paused and looked at her. "I could think of the things and people that give me security. The Navy. Pitaji. You."

"Absolutely. Why do you feel secure with Pitaji?"

"I have complete trust in him."

"But, with me, when you sense conflict, you walk away because you don't wish to spoil the mood. What do you think is the measure of trust you have in me?"

"I do trust you, but ..."

"The fact that you say a but means that trust has yet to develop, and that is because we are just married. Now, you know I love you, and I think the world of you; if you wish to build trust with me, what could you do instead of walking away?"

"Fearlessly share my thoughts and be open to listening to your point of view too, like I am talking to you today. And if there is a conflict, I will deal with it and, or learn from it. I will stop feeling weighed down, and instead, be present to find viable solutions that suit the moment." He grinned. "What a revelation this evening has been, Rekha. Can I call you darling?" he said with a smile, looking awkward.

She smiled and said, "Do you promise to do that?"

"To call you, darling. Well, of course."

"Well, that too. But I meant, do you promise to stay present in any situation and handle potential conflict by fearlessly sharing and listening?

"I do. I commit to believe in myself to handle any conflict – internal and external in the now. Do you believe in me and love me?"

"Completely and unconditionally. Your life story was worth hearing and learning from, Jungee."

"I don't have too much that I can claim as mine, Rekha. I have two treasures; first is my dream of making something meaningful of my life in the Navy. I wish to develop fortitude and character that nobody can take away from me, and prove to myself that I was not wrong in believing in me. I want to be that man. I'm getting there, slowly, but surely."

"You are already that man, Jungee and I'm so proud of you. And your second treasure?"

"You. And I hate sharing you with anyone. Your intelligence, energy, spirit, self-respect, and loving nature is admirable, Rekha. It has been on my mind that you wish to teach again, but I worry about you travelling on a crowded bus. But I am sure we will find a way for you to teach again since you desire it so much. This morning I was jealous of you 'loving' Dilip Kumar, the actor! In retrospect I knew my reaction was silly, but I did not want to admit it or discuss it and feel judged; so I walked away. I am embarrassed."

"Don't be. I admire your being vulnerable with me. This has been the most beautiful evening since I arrived in Bombay. Thank you for a beautiful voyage, Jungee."

"The scooter is great, right?"

"No, silly! Into your thoughts," she said, holding his hand warmly.

"Oh, that! Yes, I am so glad for this conversation. It just flowed. I was thinking of turning around to apologise from the moment I left home this morning. When the scooter got delivered, I rushed home early to share my joy with you. I love you, my darling."

"I love you too, Jungee," said Rekha with a mischievous grin.

"That is all I need," he said, jumping up and holding out his hand to her. "Hurry darling, so that we catch the evening show of Leader at Maratha Mandir."

"Someone is full of surprises today," said Rekha grabbing his hand and scrambling up.

As they ran hand in hand, Inder felt light as a feather - Having this impromptu vulnerable conversation with Rekha was his sixth decision.

They wobbled in the sand, all the way to the scooter. The beautiful Bombay skyline shimmered as the sun melted into the sea, and the pink twilight gave their celebration of new-found love the perfect backdrop.

— — —

CHAPTER 13: TAKING COMMAND

October 1964: Learning to believe in the plan of the universe

Inder joined his colleagues assembled at the Fox'l for the daily 9 am meeting. It was a humid October morning, and sweat trickled down every face on the deck. After the customary salutes and greetings, Joginder, the ExO, held centre stage as the team reported on assigned work from the previous day. He then proceeded to give duties for the day to each department head. After the meeting, Inder gathered his team of senior sailors for a quick briefing. He was overseeing the work of his team when Joginder called out to him.

"Captain would like to meet you as soon as possible, IJ."

"On my way, Sir," called back Inder, wondering what the matter could be.

...

"Good morning Sir," said Inder in a crisp tone, to the Captain and saluted stiffly.

"Good morning IJ. At ease. NHQ has called for you, and that means we won't have the pleasure of your company for long," said Mukherjee, finishing his coffee in one gulp.

"The loss is mine, Sir. It was my honour to work with you, Sir."

PRIYA SHARMA SHAIKH

"You have to report to Vizag. You will be the Captain of a ship."

"It is my honour, Sir," said Inder, feeling a zing run through his body.

"The ship is INS Sharda. It is an anti-smuggling patrol boat operating between India and Ceylon. She performs an important function of watching out for smugglers and miscreants and other nefarious activities in those waters."

"Aye Sir," said Inder, now feeling not unlike a defused light bulb.

"Your base will be Madras. Sharda is under repair in Vizag at the moment. You will report to Vizag, and once she is fit, you will sail her to Madras."

"Aye, Sir. When do I have to leave?" said Inder, without hesitation.

"As soon as possible, are the orders," he said with a dispassionate tone, looking up at the young Lieutenant in front of him, feeling regret that he was to let him go.

"I will make the necessary arrangements to handover charge, Sir."

Inder saluted and left the cabin.

The Navy had hardened him over time by internalising the wisdom of detachment. He tried hard to be true to the present moment. But his mind was a maze of thoughts. His face was ashen by the time he reached his workstation as he tried to come to terms with the change that had fallen upon him. *I'm signing out of Dharini. Why this punishment? Where did I go wrong now? Why is it that despite whatever I do, I get dispensed? And Rekha. What about her? She stayed back to be with me, and now with the new posting and no indication of any family accommodation, where will she stay? She should have left with Pabbi.*

JUNGEE

. . .

Four months had flown by, and they had settled beautifully into married life in Bombay. Their relationship had achieved a maturity that they had both dreamt. And suddenly, in a snap, it was time for a change. He sighed deeply before entering the house.

Rekha was curled up in an armchair in the living room, reading The Illustrated Weekly, while their newly acquired Murphy Radio played a familiar Hindi film song on low volume. A bread and butter sandwich lay half-eaten in a quarter plate, on the side table. He smiled - She loved a lavish spread of Amul butter in her sandwich. *She looks like such a picture of comfort and peace. I don't have the heart to disturb her.*

Rekha sensed his presence and jumped up to hug him. "I have made your favourite onion *pakoras,* for tea," she said and ran into the kitchen, while he entered the bedroom to change.

She served him the snack and tea and plopped in front of him. "A penny for your thoughts, Jungee darling," she said, raising her eyebrows at him curiously, "Is all well?"

"You like living in Bombay, don't you?" said Inder, staying away from the topic of is transfer.

"*Ho*, Bombay *mala khup awadhta,*" she said, in an awkward Marathi accent.

"Where did you learn to speak that, and what does it mean?" he laughed while chomping a pakora. "Oh my God, this is delicious!"

"It means – Yes, I like Bombay very much. I learnt it from Ratna while she was doing the dishes this morning. She was quite amused at my pronunciation."

"It's time to learn some Tamil," said Inder taking a sip of his tea.

"What do you mean?"

"Okay, so I do have some news for you."

"Tell me."

"I have got transfer orders. I will be captaining a ship called INS Sharda and will operate on India's southeast coast to aid the coast guard's efforts to stem smuggling and miscreant activity in the region. Welcome to the ever-changing life of a naval officer," he said with a solemn voice.

"I didn't know the Navy does such work too. Will I go with you?"

"Of course. I have already bought your ticket, darling."

"Great! And where to are we going?"

"Madras, which is one of our major ports on the country's southeast coast, in Tamil Nadu. We leave this Saturday for Vizag and then after a while, to Madras."

"Wow! I am excited. They say the food there is different. New people and a new house."

"I don't have any update on our housing arrangements yet – we will need to share accommodation again."

"I am used to that. I can show off my saris and clothes anew."

"What do you mean?"

"Well, nobody there has seen any of my clothes, so in a way, I have a fresh wardrobe, right? So, I don't have to worry about my clothes repeating for a while. Phew! I'd run out of new ones if we were to continue to stay in Bombay!"

"I love your nonchalant approach to life, Rekha," said Inder laughing out aloud.

"Life is to be taken lightly, Jungee."

"Yeah," he said with an uncertain smile.

"Okay, out with it. What is on your mind?" Rekha said, looking pointedly at him.

"To speak the truth, I am disturbed about this posting. What am I to make of a role as commanding officer of a patrol ship? My course mates are on bigger vessels, where their performance will be visible. They will have the potential of growth, while I will be in a far-flung insignificant post. Most of my work there will go unnoticed by the top brass of the Navy, Rekha. I have been wondering all day what I did wrong now. Of all the officers, the Navy decided to send me there. I feel demotivated."

"I can see you are upset, Jungee," she said, treading cautiously. "But, I wonder, what sort of an officer would be suitable to perform this role at Sharda?"

He breathed in slowly and looked away. "Someone responsible, I guess. With integrity and the clarity and courage to take action when required." He paused and looked back at her sharply, realizing how her question had led him to his answer. "I am told I have all these qualities. Come to think of it, since someone has to do the job, so why not me!? Maybe, something good will come out of it."

"So, when do we pack?" she said, reaching out for the last pakora.

Inder grabbed it and winked before crunching into it, with a laugh.

. . .

On arriving in Vizag, Inder set Rekha up in his friend Lt. Dharam Singh's house, and reported to the Eastern Naval Command, to receive his orders and meet Lt. Nair at INS Sharda to take charge. Inder's first observation was that she was a small boat.

"Welcome aboard, IJ," said Nair and took Inder to his compact cabin. "She is all of 40 feet in length. There is limited artillery of 30 rifles and a 30mm gun each on her fox' l and aft. I have put all the details in this handover file. You will primarily patrol in the waterway of Palk Strait, which connects the two large water bodies on either side of India - the Bay of Bengal, on the east coast, and the Indian Ocean on the west. The narrow passageway that Palk Strait passes through lies between two famous places - Dhanushkodi, a fisherman's village at the southeast tip of India, north of Palk Strait. And to its south is Talaimannar, the closest location to India from Ceylon's North West coast. These places serve as terminus points for the ferry service between the two countries. Along this ferry way are large reef shoals, making it impossible for large boats to navigate those waters. Sharda being a small ship has been deployed in the region, and our job is to assist the government in squelching the smuggling of imported goods and precious metals. These spuriously get dumped on Tamil Nadu's shores and sneakily make it to India's grey markets."

"Fascinating. Do you have any advice for me?"

"Well, IJ, let me say this; it will be a different experience for you. We did not join the Navy for this role. And because there are no peers to talk to or learn from, it can get boring. The team is familiar with the ship's workings and operations in the region, which is good for you. The ExO, Sub Lt. Saxena, unfortunately, is on leave temporarily. He is a perfect guy and will be good company for you once he returns. He should be back in a month. His replacement is Sub. Lt. Appu Kutan, who hails from Kerala. He is a funny one and will add life to the otherwise dull routine of patrolling. Loganathan, the Chief Mechanic, hails from Tamil Nadu. He is very humble and meticulous with his work. Then there is G. Singh, the quiet and pleasant natured Sikh. The rest of the 27 members of the crew are junior sailors. A good set of boys! Come, let me introduce you to them."

The crew stood to attention, in three rows of nine men on the deck as Inder approached.

"Boys, meet your Commanding Officer, Lt. Inderjit Sharma."

"Good morning, Sir," they said in unison, giving Inder a stiff salute.

"Good morning. At ease, boys," said Inder, feeling a sudden sense of responsibility for the 30 men standing in front of him. The three senior men stepped forward. Inder walked towards them to shake each of their hands.

"Sir, I am Appu Kutan, your ExO. I look forward to serving with you, Sir."

"Likewise, Appu."

"I am Loganathan Sir, welcome on board, Sir."

"Thank you, Loganathan."

"Sir, I am Singh, your Bosun."

"Looking forward to it, Singh."

Inder smiled and did a quick scan of the rest of the men behind them. "Thank you for the warm welcome, boys. I understand from Lt. Nair that you all know the waters and the patrolling drill well. I will depend on your experiences to help me come to speed with the operations of the region. We will sail to Madras in a week."

"Yes, Sir," they all said in unison.

...

Within a week of their arrival, Sharda got set to sail. Inder sailed, while Rekha took the train to Madras. Loganathan came to meet Inder in the bridge.

"Good afternoon, Sir." Inder was reviewing charts with a pensive look on his face. He didn't respond.

"Sir ..."

"Oh! Loganathan. Excuse my preoccupation."

"You look worried, Sir. Could I be of help to you in some way, Sir?"

"Oh! I am worried about the accommodation for my wife in Madras. After trying all my sources, I have not been able to find a place," he sighed.

He looked back at his charts absentmindedly, "I will have to send her back to Punjab. So, yes, I'm all ears if you can point out any blind spot that I may be missing."

"I can understand, Sir," said Loganathan. After a pause he smiled and said, "Sir, if you don't mind, you can stay at my home. I live at my mother-in-law's home, in a suburb called Tambaram. It takes 45 minutes by local train to get there, from Madras. It will mean daily travel for you, but you can be with her when you're not sailing. Sorry, Sir, if it is a silly suggestion."

"No, you don't have to be sorry at all. It's worth considering. I will ask my good lady if she is comfortable with the idea."

"Sure, Sir. When we reach Madras today, I could take you to see my house."

"Thank you, Loganathan," said Inder, looking somewhat hopeful.

JUNGEE

...

The sun receded into the background casting shadows on the neighbourhood, just as the windowpanes shimmered with the golden light. Inder's pace quickened after he collected the change. He had stopped to pick up some vegetables and fruit. His daily 15-minute walk from Tambaram station to Loganathan's home had got familiar. It was a small town lined with ground-level brick dwellings, colourful temples, and a Church. He hoped Rekha felt settled into their temporary arrangement.

Loganathan had introduced Rekha and him to his family, a week ago, on their arrival in Madras. None of them spoke Hindi or English. Their unsuspecting hosts had met them with awkward toothy smiles. His wife, Saroja, a simple lady, was dressed in a traditional long skirt and blouse. Her hair was in a bun tucked neatly at the nape of her neck. On her waist was perched their daughter, Saraswathi, Saras, for short, a toddler with silver anklets and bangles and short curly oiled hair. Saroja's brothers Bala and Chandru, both strapping teenagers, shook Inder's hand. Saroja's mother, the house's lady, with barely a few strands of white in her long black hair, looked fit and very curious. They had launched into a discussion at their arrival, and finally, Saroja's mother had turned to smile at them.

It had been Inder and Rekha's turn to exchange awkward glances. It was up to them to choose whether they wished to stay with them or not. Rekha knew that the only other option was for her to return to Phagwara. She smiled at the family in front of her and nodded her willingness to stay with them.

The family had immediately swung into action. They had cleared a large room for them. It had a large window, almost the size of a door with a brightly printed curtain. Their room looked onto the main street, which had flowering trees. A lone bulb dangled from a wire in the centre of the room. Their baggage got set against one of the walls, and Loganathan had helped Inder spread out two mattresses with fresh sheets and pillows. They had finally set up a mosquito net tied to nails in the walls.

...

Rekha greeted Inder with a smile at the doorstep. *She looks happy.*

Inder handed a bag full of provisions to Chandru and greeted his mother. After a simple meal of rice and mixed vegetables with Loganathan's family, Inder and Rekha retired for the night.

"This is a minimalist living arrangement, darling, but it is clean, we have privacy, and most of all, it is safe. I am at peace," said Inder, stroking Rekha's hair.

"Hmm. I am intrigued by the culture of Loganathan's family. Their food is nice too. But I miss our food. Aunty keeps smiling and nodding each time I look at her. She's funny."

"She probably finds you amusing. You are different from the women she has seen here, darling. And you are her son-in-law's boss's wife. I'm sure she is happy to have us here."

"She doesn't understand me. But I will get by. Saroja showed me the church today. It was beautiful. It felt so peaceful, Jungee," said Rekha, as Inder enveloped her in his arms.

...

Inder made a few trial trips around Madras and returned home to Rekha every evening.

"My body is aching due to sleeping on this mattress," groaned Rekha.

"Perhaps we can pad up the mattress a little," yawned Inder,

"I'll request Loganathan."

Rekha scowled.

"Why the scowl? We don't have any other options, my darling."

"I know. But what about my pains?"

"I'll get you some medication from the hospital. I know it is not easy to stay cut away from the city and like-minded people. My chatterbox has to be in forced silence."

"And you are going away soon too."

"Yes. I'll be away for a few days. Would you rather go back to Punjab?" he teased.

"Why do you ask when you know my answer?"

"Well then toughen up, darling," he said, sitting up and looking at her pointedly. "Trust me - I have thought through this decision. I am working all day and coming up and down by train. I could easily stay on the ship instead, but I come here because I don't want to leave you alone. I am selfish because this is the only way to have you near me. You have me hooked for life, darling."

Inder reached out to her, and she responded by holding out her hand to him.

He pulled her close to him. He hugged her tightly, not wanting to let go, believing that this was the perfect world that he could provide for her. So what if they didn't have a house to themselves. So what if they didn't have comfort. So what if they didn't have any friends around them. So what if the food was not the way she liked it. And so what if he had to sail, leaving her behind for days.

They were one when they were together, and that is all that mattered to Inder.

. . .

The Resident Naval Officer, Commander Nair, gave Inder orders to start his first patrol. On 18th December 1964, he awoke well before the cock-a-doodling sounds that rang through the locality every dawn.

After a quick workout, he got dressed, while Rekha prepared a glass of milk for him. Alongside the glass, she set a spoonful of sugar and cardamom, which was prasad, that she had prayed over at the Mother Mary shrine in the courtyard. He ate the prasad and kissed her warmly before embracing her.

"Goodbye, darling. I will be away for a week. Look after yourself for me."

"I will. Don't worry about me, Jungee. You take care of yourself. I love you."

. . .

He arrived on board Sharda at 7 am and immediately called for a meeting with Appu, Loganathan, and Singh to check for the ship's readiness before proceeding to sea.

"Good morning Sir," they said in their varied voices, all of which sounded familiar to Inder.

"Good morning, boys. We are taking our maiden voyage together as a team. We will sail to Palk Strait. Do you have any questions or updates for me?"

"No, Sir."

"Good. Loganathan, how are the engines' routines?"

"All routines are complete, Sir - the engines are in order."

"How is the generator?"

"All good there too, Sir."

"Singh, have the checks on all the ropes and boats been done?"

"Yes, Sir. All are in place."

"Good. Appu?"

"Yes, Sir."

"Have you checked the leaking hatch?"

"Yes Sir, the shipwright sailor is on the job."

"How much time will it take? Please closely monitor and see if he needs any special assistance. Do we have an adequate quantity of rubber for him?"

"I am keeping a close watch on the progress, and he is drawing the rubber from the store – it should be okay in shortly, Sir."

"Do you have an adequate quantity of light bulbs for the mess decks, quarterdeck, engine room, and other areas?

"Yes, Sir, we have adequate stock. I recently replaced the bulbs, so there should be no problem with lighting."

"Do you have adequate provisions, fuel, and water?"

"Yes Sir – water tanks are full, and we have fuel for 15 days of sail."

"Excellent. We have orders to sail at 10 am."

"Aye, Sir."

As planned, at 10 am, Sharda pulled away from the jetty, and set sail towards Palk Strait. The waters were rough due to the north-east monsoon in the Bay of Bengal, so Inder made a stop at Nagapattinam after 18 hours of sailing.

On the morning of 20th December, he set sail again. By

then, the sea had started to get choppier, but Inder persisted along the East coast to finally enter Palk Strait. He experienced difficulty patrolling the area, and all his attempts to get past Dhanushkodi to Mandapam remained futile.

"The rough weather can be dangerous for the ship. Appu, steer her towards Kachchatheevu," said Inder fidgeting with his pen, "Have you been to the island before?"

"No, Sir."

"Sir, I have been there. It is a small disputed territory between Ceylon and India. It is a very peaceful place, Sir," said Loganathan. Inder nodded as Loganathan continued, "There is only one structure on the island - an ancient, unmanned, St. Anthony's Church. Nobody lives there, but every day before embarking on their fishing escapades, fishermen from both the countries, go there to offer prayers. They believe a visit to the church will give them a good catch."

Southwest of Kachchatheevu, Inder set the anchor. The island was smaller and flatter than he imagined, with barely any trees on it. Inder took out the tony boat to go ashore with a few of his men. On reaching the island, he walked up to the church, situated to the island's northeast side. It was a dilapidated brick structure about 20 feet in width and 30 feet in length, with a cross placed at its deep end. It was a bare room with no windows and no lighting. The only light that came in was from the doorway, which cast long shadows of Inder and his men as they walked in.

"Is this it?" asked Inder, looking around. *It is uncanny how faith makes its way into people's minds, and generations follow.*

"Yes, Sir. This is it," said Loganathan. "Around Christmas every year, the fisherfolk from both countries put up a *mela* to celebrate the festival together," said Loganathan, "It is a great event, Sir, attended by many. It is a great binder for the people who let go of rivalries and misgivings from the past and enjoy."

Inder breathed in the salty air and felt the sense of peace that had Loganathan had described. Looking around at the simplicity of the surroundings, he felt humbled. His hands folded in prayer, and he mumbled to the almighty for the safety of his ship, crew, and Rekha.

. . .

At about the same time, across the strait, in a humble shack, on the island of Dhanushkodi, Ravi's eyes blinked open. He felt very chilly, and he instinctively snuggled closer to his mother, Susheela. The breeze coming in from the crack in the window felt colder than usual. He curled into a ball against the warmth of her body. She turned and pulled him into a snug embrace, murmuring before going back to sleep.

Seven-year-old Ravi was the only one awake. In the darkness, he looked from above the covers at the front door of their tiny home. His thoughts wandered to his father, Rajan, who had been away for three days. Ravi wondered what had kept him. He had prodded his mother earlier that day and got a smarting spank across his bare back.

"Did I not tell you that he has gone fishing and I don't know why he hasn't come? The next time you ask, the slap will be on your face."

"But *Appa* said he would come back last evening," said Ravi rubbing his shoulder where she had spanked him.

"Go and ask Kali Anna," said Susheela, pushing worrying thoughts out of her mind.

Susheela had a wiry frame, but she was tough. She had sharp features and a natural cleft in her chin. She had a charming smile that lit up her face when it appeared. It seldom did. She worked hard, cooking and cleaning their home, repairing

PRIYA SHARMA SHAIKH

Rajan's fishing nets, sharpening his knives, and weaving wicker baskets to add to their income. To add to all the chores that never seemed to end, she was also the caregiver to her father-in-law, Bali, whose body was paralysed from his neck downwards, making him completely bedridden. Her mother-in-law Latha, although kind and quiet, was in weak health and, therefore, of no real help to her. As she cooked, her thoughts went to Rajan - *It is unlike him to be at sea for more than the usual two days.*

Ravi loved his father, who he called, Appa, the most. They played catch in the sand and hide and seek amidst the island's ruins. Rajan told him stories of their ancestors, and the ocean and Ravi hung onto every word, in awe. When Rajan sailed in with his catch, Ravi waited on the shore, jumping excitedly and helping him carry the caskets of still jumping fish, making sure that none escaped back into the water. They'd go to the market together to sell the fish, and at the end of the day, Ravi would climb onto his Appa's muscular shoulders and feel on top of the world.

"Appa, don't you get scared sailing in the ocean?" Ravi had asked a few evenings before.

"No, my *Kutty*, the water is my playground. My boat is the queen of the ocean, and I am her King. I fear nothing."

"Not even death, Appa?"

"Kutty, death is the final destination that we all race towards, so why fear it?"

Ravi had blinked, looking at the dark ocean. "Then when will you take me with you, Appa? I also want to learn how to sail and catch fish."

"When the time is right, my kutty," said Rajan pulling him down and looking at him seriously, "Now it is your time to study and take care of Thatha and Patti so that you collect a whole lot of blessings from them. Can you do that for your Appa?"

"Yes, Appa. But can you take me sailing once?"

"The next time I return, I promise to take you for a spin. Will that make you happy?"

"Yes, Appa."

Like thousands of other fisherfolk, Ravi's family lived on the pristine beaches of Dhanushkodi Island, situated southeast of the famed Rameshwaram temple in Pamban. The locals considered Dhanushkodi to be sacred because of its shape like Lord Ram's bow.

Rajan was a fisherman of strong lineage.

Like him, his ancestors had been fishing in the waters surrounding Dhanushkodi - Palk Strait and Gulf of Mannar from the beginning of time. Rajan had curly hair and a glistening dark body that had been toughened and weathered by the ocean in his 30 years of life. He had a deep scar on his cheek, earned as a child when playing with a fishing knife. Bali had taught him fishing on the very same motorboat that he now sailed in. It was a beautiful vessel painted in bright hues of blue, red, and white with multicoloured deco on her sides. Inscribed in bold in the curly Tamil script – *Katal Rani* or Queen of the Sea, her name, was on both her sides.

Katal Rani was 30 feet long, with a red flag at her bow and stern. The boat's centre had a thatched hood to cover the engine controls and steering wheel and made for an ideal place to sleep and cook when the sun bore down at sea. His fellow fishermen, Mutthu, Sampath, and Ananthan, all tough-bodied men, had become his best friends over time and never failed to join him on each fishing trip. The four of them were the most enviable team on the island, as they always managed to pull in the best catch.

Lying snuggled next to his mother, Ravi didn't know that all the years of experience and strength of the four men on Katal Rani got tested on that very fateful day; that they tried their best to overcome the disaster that arose from the depths of the ocean.

. . .

After spending the day and night at Kachchatheevu, Inder set sail for Mandapam early the next morning. Sharda experienced head-on sea, which made her toss around dangerously, making it impossible to proceed.

"The sea spray is coming on too strong, Sir. It is terrible."

"Nature is not making way for us, Appu. Steer back to Kachchatheevu," resigned Inder.

"Sir, we have lost all radio and wireless connection," said Loganathan, looking dismal.

"We will try Mandapam again tomorrow. Get everyone to stay indoors and enclosed in the bridge until things settle down," said Inder looking pensive.

Early the next morning, Inder tried once again to go to the sheltered port of Mandapam. He managed to reach the waiting area outside the port and waited for the naval pilot to show up and take them alongside. He honked several times to alert the pilots to come to them. But the pilots were not expecting Sharda or any vessel at the bay in the bad weather. Inder had no choice but to return to Kachchatheevu to spend the second night.

The next morning on 22nd December, Inder made another attempt to go to Mandapam, and this time he sighted the pilot coming towards them in a tony boat. "Sir, what are you doing in these waters in such a storm?" gasped the pilot.

"I have orders to be at Palk Strait, so here I am," said Inder.

"Oh, I see."

"The sea has been very rough, and we tried to come in yesterday, but nobody was around to take us alongside, so we went to Kachchatheevu, which served as a haven from the storm."

"Apologies, Sir. But don't worry, we will go safely alongside now."

"Has the storm ebbed yet?"

"Not yet, Sir."

The Pamban Rail Bridge, the longest water bridge in India, was constructed by a German engineer during the British regime, opened to allow Sharda to pass through to go alongside the Mandapam jetty. Meanwhile, the sea became rougher, with winds at a velocity of 100 miles an hour. Inder thought it best to stay put at Mandapam for the next two days.

. . .

As *Katal Rani* approached deeper waters, the sea became rougher. Rajan was tired of the harassment from the Ceylon border authorities, so he had decided to steer his boat past Palk Strait into the Bay of Bengal. The sea continued to be choppy the whole day, and by the time it was evening, it worsened. The moon played peek-a-boo as the dark clouds rushed through the sky, glinting silver each time there was a crack of lightning.

"This is a disruptive downpour. I have a bad feeling about this. We should turn back," said Rajan, standing with his hands on his hips at the bow.

The vessel's excessive rocking made him unsteady, and

PRIYA SHARMA SHAIKH

Sampath standing close behind him reached out to steady him. They both held onto the side of the boat, each feeling the ocean's immense turbulence in their bodies.

"I agree, *Anna*," said Sampath.

"Nah, you scary-boobies, it's a passing storm. Anna, you know it happens in December. This stew is delicious and spicy! I love it, Ananth. From now on, you are the official cook," said Mutthu ignoring the angst on his friends' faces as he furiously licked his fingers and palms, ensuring that every grain and ounce of the gravy got polished off the banana leaf in front of him.

"There is no sight of the horizon or the skies," said Ananth, getting up to join Rajan and Sampath.

"Show some patience, all of you. Let us wait until morning," said Mutthu, wiping the curry off the banana leaf.
"I pray that you are right, Mutthu," said Rajan looking pensively at the heavens, "Okay, we will wait until morning."

Rajan awoke early the next morning and surveyed the horizon and the skies. He was sure that the weather spelled trouble. He hurriedly woke up the rest of his crew, who agreed that things were not good.

"It looks like we're amid a *Curavali*. Turn back without further delay. Be on full alert and move fast."

Rajan turned the boat around, steering it himself as the waves got fiercer. He throttled the engine at the fastest speed possible, while the others looked on anxiously, bracing themselves for the journey back home.

...

That afternoon, Susheela got ready to take her Latha to the railway station to put her into the train for Mandapam. She had wished to visit her older sister, who lived there. Latha hugged Ravi goodbye.

"Where are you going, *Patti*?" said Ravi, looking at his grandmother.

"To meet my sister, kutty. She is not well. I'll be back tomorrow," said Latha.

"Bring me pink candy and some tamarind," whispered Ravi into her ears.

"I will get your goodies, but you be a good boy and look after *Tata* and don't trouble Amma. And don't forget to receive me at the train station tomorrow with Appa."

"Okay, Patti," said Ravi, hugging his grandmother's legs.

"I love you, my *Kutty*," said Latha, getting up to leave.

"Be with Thatha till I return," said Susheela, tightening her bun and straightening her skirt.

"Yes, Amma."

After walking some distance, Latha turned back to look at Ravi. He was sitting at the doorstep of their home. He waved to her. She smiled warmly, blew him a kiss, and followed Susheela towards the train station.

As soon as Susheela got back, Ravi ran towards the beach and parked himself on the jetty. Oddly it was deserted. He was there for Rajan's return. It was the third evening since he had gone to sea. He ought to have returned in time for the evening market. *Maybe Appa won't go to the market today since it is raining so much.*

The skies were grey, and the waters were at a high tide making all the boats alongside toss around and bang into each other. The waves soon covered the jetty, forcing him to move onto the beach. He sat craning his neck now and then hoping to spot Rajan's boat in the horizon, while his little hands made a sandcastle with a moat around it. He painstakingly decorated it with shells and leaves. Once done, he strolled along the beach and picked up shells and pocketed them.

The clouds had been crowding the sky all day, burst at the same time with a continuous rumble of thunder. Cold heavy rain poured, and Ravi ran for shelter under a broken structure. He watched his sandcastle get washed away. His gaze didn't move from the jetty. He waited in vain as the grey day turned into night. His eyes clouded, and he sniveled. *Where are you, Appa?* He then reluctantly stepped into the rain and ran all the way home.

. . .

Rekha was yellow.

She stared dismally at herself in the tiny hand mirror. All her scrubbing had yielded no result. She made a funny expression and giggled as Saras imitated her. Although everybody in the Loganathan home continued to care for all her needs, they kept a respectful distance after Inder left. She felt alone and like a misfit. She guessed this was for two reasons. The first being their lack of understanding English and her Tamil. The extent of Saroja's vocabulary was *Yes, No, Go Church, Food.* For the talkative Rekha, the real conversation was absent. The second and more obvious reason was that she looked and dressed differently. Rekha borrowed a long, printed skirt and a short, fitting blouse from Saroja. And she rubbed turmeric paste on her skin before bathing, just like Saroja did.

Unfortunately, she left on the turmeric for too long, which stained her pale skin, yellow. Rekha decided she would live with a yellow colour. And in her enthusiasm, she oiled her hair and made a tight plait, and finished the look by tying a string of orange flowers onto her braid. Dressed in her new avatar, she joined the family in a squat to eat food off the banana leaf. She mixed the rice and sambhar thoroughly with her fingers and made a ball of the mixture before popping it into her mouth. These efforts did show results - the Loganathan family smiles turned into laughter. *It is a good sign. But how do I converse with these beautiful people?*

That evening, the dressed-like-a-local Rekha visited the church with Saroja. She was the happiest being there, sitting with her head covered, listening to the priest's Tamil sermon. She didn't understand a word, but she felt at peace kneeling on the pew with her eyes shut, and hands folded in prayer.

Although she had started liking the food they made, Rekha missed *Kulcha-Chola, Kadhi*, and *Rajma's taste*. On her way back with Saroja, they stopped to buy provisions. Rekha saw Rajma beans on sale! She bought some and announced that she would cook dinner for everyone. Since most of their baggage was locked away in a warehouse, she had to make do with cooking in their vessels. The obstinate Rajma beans refused to cook on their makeshift slow cooking firewood stove – she missed her Hawkins pressure cooker. After two hours of cooking it and listening to Saroja's mother grumble in the background while Saroja squirmed awkwardly, the rajma finally seemed to be done!

Saroja took a polite helping but didn't ask for more. The rest of the family had got too tired of waiting and had already eaten the leftover sambhar and rice from lunch. Rekha felt miserable. She nevertheless eagerly served herself and sat quietly at her window, feeling happy that she would finally eat something that she loved. She took one bite and realised why Saroja didn't ask for a second serving – it was horrible and semi-cooked. Rekha rushed back to the kitchen to sprinkle salt on her food and grab some green chilies and pickle to make it palatable. With tears in her eyes, she ate her meal while watching life in the town pass by. Tomorrow, she would try again for her and Inder. Because despite all the odds, it was a better bargain.

. . .

Susheela had also been anxious about Rajan. She asked the other fisher folk about him as they returned home. They had seen his boat going out of Palk Strait, while the rest preferred to play catch with the Ceylon authorities. Susheela's stomach knotted with worry as she heard their descriptions of the rough sea. She walked home in a daze and started cooking the evening meal, just as the thunder and downpour started. The evening progressed, but there was no sign of Rajan. *And where is that rascal, Ravi!* She banged her vessels in anger.

When Ravi returned home, drenched, she was standing at the doorway, wringing her hands, sick with anxiety. He looked crestfallen, and despite his wet face, she could see he had been crying. Her throat felt a lump, but she snapped at him for being late and immediately proceeded to wipe and change his clothes. She then sat him down for dinner and grumbled under her breath for the rest of the evening, blinking away her tears now and then.

"Selfish and stubborn! He won't listen to anybody! Tch, tch, tch! Why did I have to fight to marry him? I don't know what demons got into your head, Susheela, that you agreed to his wooing! Stupid! Stupid girl – that is what you were and what you still are!" she said and slapped her forehead in exasperation.

"All that he desires is to have the best catch. Be the hero of the village. The King of Katal Rani. King, my foot! How intelligent is he to risk his life, his boat, and his friends just for fish? Amma is with her sister, and he has gone fishing even when the weather is rough. Ufff! And I am to deal with all the burden at home. Alone! Very nice arrangement. And who is going to eat all this curry? What a waste! And what am I to do now that he has not come home? Stupid man! And stupid me to believe he will change! Continue to live in a dream, Susheela!" she said, shaking her head at nobody in particular, as she fed Bali small balls of rice and fish curry.

Ravi listened to his mother's rant as he ate. His eyes were stinging with tears, but he too blinked them away. *I know Amma loves Appa and is anxious about his safety.* After eating, he went to the door again and peered into the stormy night. The rain was still falling hard as lightning cracked the black sky, as thundering persisted.

"And you stop looking out of the goddamned door again and again. Appa is not coming home tonight. Get into bed," she screamed as tears brimmed her eyes. She hurriedly blew out the lantern to lose her tears in the shadows. She lay down in the darkness, as tears of worry dampened her sheets. Ravi could barely sleep and kept looking at the front door, expecting to hear Rajan's muffled footsteps at their doorstep. Finally, his tired body slipped into slumber.

Now, snuggled against his mother's warmth, he looked above the covers at the front door and listened keenly. The only sound he heard was of the ocean, the howling winds, and the shivering of their home walls and windows.

"Come home soon, Appa," said Ravi, in an empty whisper.

Just then, he heard flapping - It was a heron! It had come in through a crack in the window. At first, he wasn't sure what to make of it, but then he saw another heron step in.

"Amma, see what has come," he said, waking Susheela, pointing out the herons.

Susheela didn't want to believe what she saw, but she knew it was confirmed when she saw the look of worry in her father-in-law's eyes. She screamed, holding her face in horror.

"Curavali! Rajan! O Rameshwara! Please save my husband."

"What happened, Amma?"

"This is the sign of a big cyclone, kutty. The birds have come here for shelter. And your Appa is still at sea. O Rama, what will happen to him?"

Ravi shook his head even as his eyes widened, and he tried to measure the circumstances that had fallen upon them.

"Nothing will happen to him, Amma. He is the King of the ocean, and his boat is the queen. Don't worry about him. He will save himself. Let us save ourselves and Thatha. We must go to the temple. Appa said it is the safest place."

Susheela looked at her son and gathered her wits. *Ravi is right. What would Rajan do?* She quickly packed a few essentials and the few rupees she had at home into a small bundle, which she tied onto her waist. They had only one cork tube in the house, which she put around Ravi. She hung a wicker basket on the back of her head. Once geared up, she yanked Bali's cot out of the hut corner and instructed Ravi to help her carry it to the temple.

It took them a while to get to the temple due to the cot's weight and the lashing rain. They reached the temple which had already got crowded with several other fisherfolk, who helped Susheela bring Bali inside. The downpour became heavier. It seemed like the skies would split apart. The fisherfolk assembled in the temple stared at the ocean with empty eyes, fearing the unknown and wondering what was to be.

...

In the early hours of 24th December, the weather hadn't improved. Since the crew didn't have much to do, Inder decided to pay a short visit to Rameshwaram on the crew's insistence. It was a 45-minute train ride from Mandapam. They took the first train out, and within an hour, they were at the shrine's entrance. His artistic mind was fascinated at the detailing and grandeur of the structure and its variety of sculptures. He walked through the long ornate corridors and finally sat to relish the *prasadam*.

Pabbi would like this place. Someday, I will bring Pitaji and her for a darshan. So many people have come worship even though it is a Thursday. Although I am here, why is it that I don't feel reverence in me? He bit into the delicious ladoo from the dried leaf bowl in his hand. *It is not that I don't believe in God. I was too much of a brat as a child with not a moment to spare for Godliness. And later, when so many hurtful things happened, I probably believed that God wasn't caring for me. I never feel the need to pray, except when I'm challenged and need help. But shouldn't I have a give and take relationship with God? Shouldn't I feel like praying even in good times, or every day, as Pabbi does? Why don't I feel the need for it? If I don't feel the need, why did my hands fold in prayer in the church at Kachchatheevu? Maybe because it felt surreal being at such a unique place of worship, and there was no pressure to perform a ritual. It was just me, and my moment with the almighty, and prayer had come straight from my heart. I felt a momentary connection. Perhaps, I will pray when I am comfortable to feel that connection.*

Once they were outside the main shrine, Inder sat to wear his shoes. As he pulled on his socks, his eyes fell upon an inscription written in English on the door of the sanctum sanctorum *'The greatest service to God is to serve humanity – by Swami Vivekananda.'* The words struck a chord instantly, and he pointed the board to his crew, who were busy giggling at Appu's antics.

"Yes, Sir, very true," said Loganathan.

"But is it realistic, Sir?" said Appu with a grin, as others looked on.

"Why not? If you cherish other's lives as much as your own, that is true humanity. God resides in every living being, and when you help or show compassion and kindness to others, you are in service to God." Something shifted in Inder as he spoke. "I don't pray," he paused and then said softly, "yet."

"You are right, Sir," said Appu, while the others nodded their heads in agreement. "Sir, can we explore the town tonight and get back to the ship in the morning?"

"No, Appu, we will take the train back as planned. We must get back to Sharda."

. . .

Later that morning, an anxious Latha bid farewell to her sister to make her way back to Dhanushkodi. She had managed to buy tamarind and cotton candy for Ravi the previous evening and held it in a small bag in her hand to give him at the station. She got herself a seat in one of the packed wooden coaches of Boat Mail Express, the age-old rickety metre gauge train. She looked out of the barred window at the grey skies with foreboding.

Latha usually enjoyed riding in it. *Today the train feels different.* Latha grimaced. Following her fellow passengers' cue, she pulled the windows shut to keep the pouring rain out. The air in the cabin felt damp and heavy, as did the conversations. She felt claustrophobic, even as the train left Mandapam station.

"Winds are at a velocity of more than 100 miles per hour," said a young man.

What does that mean? The winds are hitting hard today, and the skies are spewing fury.

"Dhanushkodi will be at high risk," said a lady, sitting close to her.

"Fisherfolk will be in danger. I am going to evacuate my family," said another man.

JUNGEE

The plump and stocky engine driver, Mani forged towards Dhanushkodi. For the first few minutes, the journey seemed fine. As they got farther out above the sea, the waves leaped higher, and the rain got ferocious. The winds and rain lashed at the windows of the train, eventually breaking them. The rising waves smashed into the cabins, to drench all 150 of the screaming passengers. People cried and coughed, clinging to each other to avoid getting swept away each time the waves entered and then receded with a surge. Mani panicked midway on Pamban Bridge as the waves grew to a height of 4-5 metres. He stopped, thinking it was best to turn back. Then he thought again. Since he had come this far, he felt it was best to get past the bridge soon. He forged ahead once again. People screamed with fear and rage.

"We should go back! - The engine driver is a mad man. He will kill us all! - Help, help! - Somebody, anybody, please help me - Oh lord Rama, help me!"

The ocean around them seethed and swelled, black with turbulence. Latha looked at it and turned her head away, terrified. It looked like it was preparing to punish Mani's decision to move ahead. The waves rose higher with each passing moment, reaching more than 6 metres in height, enveloping the entire train each time. The Pamban Bridge, battered by the massive waves force all along its length, shivered, as if frightened. The train stopped again. Mani was unable to move in any direction.

Latha coughed and gasped for breath, pressed between several other passengers as they braced themselves to deal with the next wave.

She saw a wave rise in the distance and approach them with chilling certainty. It rolled over the surface of the ocean and gathered intensity. It soon became a wall of water more than

7.5 metres high – taller than a coconut tree!

Latha bowed her head and joined her palms, tears running down her face. "O Rameshwara, look after my children and Bali."

One hundred fifty voices reached a crescendo, before nature's fury silenced them.

. . .

At Dhanushkodi Island, Susheela, Ravi, and Bali and several hundred others have spent hours in the temple by now - they were exhausted and scared. But the downpour refused to relent, and the ocean completely overtook the landmass. It repeatedly beat the temple walls as people screamed out and prayed for mercy to the deity. But the water level inside the shrine only rose rapidly.

The temple is sure to get submerged. Susheela knew they had no option but to get out, failing which they were sure to drown. Susheela rechecked Ravi's tube's harness. She had upturned the wicker basket and used a sari to harness Bali's body onto one side of it, another sari to harness herself next to him. She used the third sari to tie Ravi to herself. She finally turned to Ravi with tears in her frightened eyes.

"My *chinna paiya*, you are a courageous and intelligent boy, and you know you will be just fine. We are going out into the storm now, as the temple will soon be underwater. That means we will be in the open ocean. You have to stay close to me. Nobody but yourself is going to save you. You will have to fend for yourself, my kutty." She hugged her son, praying over his head and wiped his face clean, admiring his beautiful face.

"Whatever happens after this, always know that your Appa, Thatha, Patti, and I love you and want you to become a great man someday. You will have a lovely wife and adorable children to whom you can tell stories about us. Promise me you will take care of yourself."

"Why are you saying all this, Amma? Why will I tell stories to my children? You will tell the stories to them. Amma, like Patti, tells me stories," he said with confidence in his eyes as he wiped his mother's tears, "Don't worry, Amma, nothing will happen to us. I will take care of myself."

"Very good, my kutty. Appa, let us get ready for a fight for survival. I am sorry, but I can't do better, Appa, and I am sorry that I yelled at you last night. Please forgive me, Appa," she wept, hugging the frail body of her father-in-law.

Bali looked at Susheela and Ravi with tears in his eyes. He knew she was doing her best and that things were not good and that Rajan should not have gone to sea, and Latha should not have gone to see her sister. He prayed for everyone's safety and shut his eyes.

A huge wave crashed over the temple, submerging all of them. Susheela kicked hard and soon emerged between the temple pillars, with Bali and Ravi trailing behind her. They gasped for breath, between coughs and tears, and then before they could react, the waves growled again and tossed them into the air and threw them back down. Limbs flailed. They screamed. Within seconds, all the harnesses and planned co-ordination were in vain, and Rajan's family and hundreds of others were washed away into the folds of the dreaded Curavali.

...

Lord Indra's fury knew no bounds. Inder and his men reached the jetty just after noon, amidst lightning that definitively crackled through the thunderous black clouds that loomed menacingly low. Inder leaned into the wind and slanting rain, fighting to move up the gangplank, gripping the ropes with all his strength.

The ship's atmosphere was chaotic, as the men animatedly discussed the outcome of the storm. Inder's demeanour was a contrast to his panic-stricken soaked to the bone crew. He stood on the deck; his muscular form defiant against the storm. He clenched the railing to steady himself and surveyed the sea with slit eyes, even as the water slashed his face and body. In his twelve years of service, he had never seen such a storm. The waves in the distance rose to heights of six to seven metres, lashing at Sharda and making her toss around dangerously.

He stood stoic, processing the gravity of the situation he was dealing with, running through the measures he could take to ensure Sharda's safety and her 30 men under his charge. He knew it would be difficult to stay alongside without being damaged. And then, as if to reinforce his judgment, he saw S. S. Irwin, a larger ferry boat, breaking all her ropes and wires, being pulled into the open sea by the tide. The horrifying spectacle snapped Inder into action.

As the Captain of this ship, I hold the responsibility for her safety and that of everyone on board. It is a cyclonic storm, and it is too dangerous. I should evacuate my men. I'll stay guard with the ship as long as I can, and go down with her. At least my crew will be saved. He suddenly saw the Lion standing at the edge of the ship. His mane was drenched in the rain, his eyes flashing as he stood firm against the elements, looking directly at Inder. Inder's brow crowded as he thought again and shook his head.

If only I remains on board, Sharda will sink for sure. And the way the waters are raging, my boys too have nowhere to go. I cannot attempt to do this alone. We will have to employ a team effort, and only then will Sharda, and all of us stand a chance of survival.

"Sir, please come inside," yelled Appu, peering out from the bridge door.

JUNGEE

Soaking wet, Inder entered the bridge and called for a team briefing.

"Boys, from now on, every man on board is on red alert, until I say otherwise."

He wiped his face and head with a towel and said, "I want all hands on deck until further notice. Everyone has to wear a life jacket. We are dealing with an emergency that calls for the collective might of all our minds and strength. Singh, I want your men and you to harness yourselves and ensure that Sharda is tied more securely to the jetty. Appu, start the main engines, and keep a watch that they don't shut down for even a moment. I will personally take the wheel. I want you to update me on the ropes' stiffness - You have to tell me when they are going slack and tight. Nobody will sleep tonight until things are under control. Are we clear?"

"Aye, Sir!" boomed the team.

All 30 men on board Sharda sprang into action. Ropes got secured, the engine started, and on cue from Appu, Inder began to move the ship forward and backward along the jetty. This action instantly reduced the stress on the ropes. Despite the frantic bobbing all through the stormy night, Sharda stayed unharmed and afloat.

. . .

The announcement of an approaching cyclone had come in three days after Inder left. At first, Rekha didn't pay too much heed to it. But, when each passing bulletin gave updates of its movement and fury towards Tamil Nadu and Ceylon's coast, she panicked. Rekha held onto every update that crackled through. She listened from one news bulletin to the next, praying that she wouldn't hear any bad news about Sharda.

"Sharda must be in another area, or else there would be

news about her on the radio," said Rekha to Saroja, with an unsure smile.

Saroja looked at a much oiled, yellow, and anxious Rekha with sadness. Rekha knew she didn't understand anything she had said. There was no telephone at home or in the vicinity. Rekha had no connection with Inder or with the Navy. She battled all the negative thoughts that preyed her idle mind, and mumbled a small prayer, as she watched Saras trace the alphabet in a notebook.

On the fifth day after Inder had left, the news confirmed that the cyclone had struck India's southeast coast.

Rekha sat in silence, staring blankly at the radio. When Saroja brought her food and water, she left it untouched. Saroja was worried about her and tried to take the radio away from her. But, Rekha grabbed it right back with a childlike stubbornness. It was her only link to the outside world.

. . .

At daybreak, the sea became miraculously calm. The howling wind ceased to make its presence felt, and the rain was down to a drizzle. Inder and the crew had stayed awake all night. Exhaustion was all over their faces. Inder freshened up and returned to the bridge.

"Singh, get some sleep."

"Only after you get some rest, Sir."

"I can't rest until there is an all-clear. I need some tea and breakfast," yawned Inder, rubbing his bloodshot eyes.

"I will get Yadav to serve you, Sir," said Singh.

Yadav, the steward, brought him a hot cup of tea and an omelet sandwich. After devouring his breakfast, he took Appu and a sailor with him in a tony boat to survey the port's damage.

The devastation left him stunned. Anonymous naked dead bodies of people and cattle swelled with water floated belly up, while boats lay wedged high up in fallen trees' branches. Clothes, huts, vessels, furniture, wicker baskets, vehicles, carts, and toys floated aimlessly entangled and enmeshed.

Inder wondered abstractly how the sea had calmed down so soon after so much destruction when he felt a cold realization sink in. It wasn't over! He yelled to rush back to Sharda. The sailor pulled hard on the oars to move between the rubble. Inder sweated fearing they would get tossed in the storm any minute.

They got back on board in the nick of time, just as the fury of the storm resumed. The boys on board were flustered. They were all exhausted, and from the night before – none of them had the physical energy left in them to continue the fight. Inder's brow crowded with worry. *How will we survive?*

Could he find a way not to get swept away like S. S. Irwin?

. . .

Rekha awoke with a gasp. It was the nightmare once again! A calendar, flapped in the wind, with 25th December 1964 on it was magnified. Sharda rocked up and down in a heaving ocean and drifted away into the open water. Inder, dressed in a long white robe, fought a sea demon with a silver sword. The demon breathed flames at him. He dodged them, but he appeared tired falling this way and that, and yet he wielded his sword at the fire-spewing demon. "Oh, my dear run away," she was saying. "Run!" She awoke with a start. Rekha remained restless the whole night, tossing and turning until she heard the cock in the distance. Rekha lifted the mosquito net and went to the living room, where Saroja was still asleep. Rekha touched her gently.

"Saroja," she whispered. Saroja turned to look at Rekha.

"Merry Christmas," said Rekha, with an uncertain smile on her face, "I don't have a gift for you. I pray Mother Mary blesses your family and that your husband returns safely."

"Merry Christmas," said Saroja, smiling in her sleep. She sat up and stretched and mumbled something to Chandru in Tamil.

"Saroja, it is also my birthday today." Saroja smiled. She didn't understand. "I was very moved by midnight mass last night. I want to take communion and be a Christian, Saroja."

"Christian? Father Phillips ...," said Saroja looking puzzled.

Just then, the familiar beeps before the news bulletin started on the radio. Rekha instinctively turned up the volume. *'Good morning. This is the News Bulletin in English from All India Radio. The cyclonic storm in the Bay of Bengal has caused unprecedented devastation in the coastal region of Tamil Nadu. Over 4000 lives have been affected. Rescue operations in the region have proved impossible. Telephone connections and electricity have got disrupted in the region. The Boat Mail Express from Mandapam to Dhanushkodi got twisted like a rope in the cyclone's fury. It is an estimate that the lives of all the 150 passengers on board are lost. The ferry boat between India and Ceylon, S.S. Irwin, has been swept away from the Mandapam jetty, with the water current. The Indian Naval Headquarters have reported that INS Sharda, patrolling the region, has gone missing, and all attempts to connect with her have failed. The Prime Minister, Lal Bahadur Shastri, has expressed deep...'*

Rekha screamed out aloud and burst into tears. She felt the earth falling away beneath her feet and fell to the floor with a thud. What she had dreaded all this time had come true after all. Saroja rushed to Rekha's side as Chandru ran to call the local medic.

When Rekha awoke the neighbourhood, Dr. Sudha, was examining her. She had suffered a paralytic attack due to stress, she said. Rekha ought to go to the Navy hospital in Madras for suitable treatment, she said and prescribed some medication for the interim.

Rekha was in no condition to travel to the city as she couldn't walk or talk properly. Her limbs had got twisted, and her stomach felt sick all the time, making her throw up whatever little food she ate. The subservient young Chandru rushed to Rekha's aid each time she threw up and cleaned up after her without any hesitation.

Rekha decided she would wait another few days before she would travel. Rekha repeatedly wept while her mind raced with the possibilities that lay ahead for her. *O Mother, is my Jungee alive? Is it all over after all? Will I be left here alone in Madras? How will the Navy inform me? Nobody knows I am in Loganathan's house. What will my life be without Jungee, O Mother Mary, help me with answers? How will I go back to Punjab in this condition? I will have to send a telegram to Papa to pick me up. What would they say when they see my twisted body? Maybe, I'm overthinking. And maybe, they have just lost connection with his ship. Or maybe not.*

Dr. Sudha came to revisit Rekha. "You need medical attention, Rekha. Crying will finish your energies. Eat your food properly as your body needs fuel to heal. Your condition will worsen if you don't take care and go to hospital."

...

Inder started doing the forward-backward movement of Sharda, all day. It was evening when the sea finally subsided, and the winds dropped too. Things became peaceful once again. It was evident by then that a cyclone had crossed Mandapam.

"Sir, thank God you got back in the nick of time – it could have proved very dangerous."

"Yes, Appu. Instinctively I felt we should get back. We were at the epicentre of the storm. It could have been fatal for all of us, had we stayed on a few moments longer."

Waiting for the weather to improve was the only option for Inder. Singh entered the bridge and announced a visit from the local customs officer, Mr. Shankuni Menon.

"Captain, we urgently need your help."

"Sure, Mr. Menon, how can I help you?"

"Dhanushkodi is the last station of the Indian Railways. We do not have any contact with them, and we don't know what the situation is like over there. Irwin was our only hope, but she too is destroyed. We had lost all hope. But then I was informed that your boat survived the storm and hence my visit.

"Yes, we saw Irwin getting swept with the waves."

"It has been terrible. The railway line is destroyed after Mandapam too. There are thousands of fishermen stranded in Dhanushkodi. Since Sharda is a small ship, you are the only one that can help us rescue them by sailing through the shoal ridden waters."

"I can imagine the state of the destruction. The Navy will help. Appu, please try to reach the RNO again."

"Sir, I have been trying continuously, but I'm afraid I cannot restore radio connection."

"All phone lines are down, too," said Menon.

"Hmm," said Inder looking pensive, about the grave situation presented to him. "If we are to go to Dhanushkodi, we will need to approach it from the northern side at the jetty located there," said Inder looking at the charts.

"Sir, unfortunately, that will not be possible. The port superintendent said that the railway bridge is damaged. We cannot open it. We will have to approach Dhanushkodi from the southern side," said Appu.

"Hmm. I understand the gravity of the situation, Menon, I will help you, even though I don't have official Navy orders. Appu, get the ship's company ready. We sail immediately."

This was Inder's seventh decision.

"Aye, Sir."

After sailing for two hours, Sharda reached the southern side of Dhanushkodi. Since there was no jetty, she could not go alongside. Inder anchored as close to the shore as possible. He got Appu and a few more sailors to swim ashore with their life jackets.

When they returned, they brought back the first piece of information about the grave situation in Dhanushkodi. There was complete devastation. The jetty lay smashed to smithereens; the railway line had got uprooted. Thousands were rendered homeless, and countless were missing or dead.

Inder and his crew worked with the fishermen to launch an abandoned fishing boat. The fisherfolk made announcements amongst the thousands gathered on the beach. *The Navy ship Sharda will save us*, they said. A mad scramble stemmed in an instant, to get on the boat first. A few leaders in the frenzied crowd, after much travail, managed to get some order. The most vulnerable people, including the elderly, women with babies, children, and the physically disabled, were put in the first boat that left Dhanushkodi to board Sharda.

. . .

Susheela opened her eyes to see the sky overhead. I'm alive! She gasped, realising she was floating in the middle of the water, tied to the wicker basket. The sea seemed calm. She moved about, looking desperately for Bali and Ravi, and then shrieked with excruciating pain in her right leg – she couldn't see it, but every move hurt. Dead bodies floated in the water around her. Her eyes filled with tears as she realised that the saris she had used to tie them to the wicker basket were still intact, but there was no sign of them. She shouted out their names as loud as she could, scanning the faces of the bodies she paddled past. She knew in her heart that she had most certainly lost them forever. She leaned her head against the wicker basket, floating in the water, weeping silent tears. Everything was over for her. The shore seemed so far away, and her bruised tired limbs and broken heart had no will to do the long swim back.

A boat filled with people. Rescuers! Survivors! Her heart leaped with rekindled hope, and she kicked hard at the water and started swimming towards the shore, with the empty wicker basket trailing behind her.

...

Inder was on the deck, supervising as the people came onto the ship. He was horrified at their annihilated conditions. Shriveled bodies due to the prolonged exposure to water. Older adults with gashes and breathless toothless, crying mouths. Most had open wounds or broken limbs and ripped clothing, while children cried of hunger and pain. Fear was a common emotion written all over their pitiful faces, making several of them ramble incessantly.

"Sir, they are saying that they have come back from death. They are very thankful for our help, Sir. They are saying you are a guardian angel," said Loganathan. The crew listened and sighed. Inder turned to address his boys.

"Alright, boys. I know you are tired but let's snap into action, to perform this duty. These people need our help, not our tears. I want all hands on deck to provide them the food we have prepared, first-aid, spare clothing, and space to rest. Let us get on with our jobs."

Sharda set sail with the first batch of rescued people, towards Mandapam. One child stood alone by the railings, looking out at sea.

Inder walked up to him and tried to turn him around to face him. But he turned away. He had several wounds. A fresh bandage on his head covered most of his swollen face.

"Go and eat some food, son."

The boy shook his head, blinking his eyes furiously to hold back his flowing tears.

"Come now; you are a brave boy. What makes you cry?"

"I have lost my family," he spat. "I am brave. But what good is my bravery when I could not save them? What will become of me now?"

Inder remembered how scared he had been when he separated from his family during the partition walk to India!

"Life is sometimes difficult to understand, son. But when the going gets tough, you have no option but to reach out to your inner strength to become stronger. The authorities will take care of you. And perhaps your parents are there too."

"My Appa said that when he is away, I am the man of the house."

"Yes, your Appa is right. So, find the courage and eat so that you can have the strength to find your Appa. What is your name?"

"Ravi," he said, turning around to look at Inder with an unsure smile.

Inder took the first shipload to Mandapam on the evening of 26th December. He tried again to call Cdr. Nair. The phone rang, and Nair answered!

"Good evening, Sir, this is Lt. Inderjit Sharma reporting from Mandapam."

"Oh my God, IJ! It is such a relief to hear your voice. We had given up all hope, thinking that you were swept away in the storm. How are you? There has been no radio and telephone contact, too."

"I am fine, Sir, and everything is under control. I have an important matter to report."

"Shoot IJ."

Inder briefed him about the conditions and his independent call for rescue action. "Sir, I believed it was my duty to rise to the occasion and help the people of Dhanushkodi on behalf of the Navy. I am happy to report that we have rescued 120 people on our first trip."

"Fantastic news, IJ! The Navy is proud of your decision. I commend your action."

"Sir, with your permission, I would like to continue the rescue operations."

"Please continue the good work and keep me posted whenever possible. I will try and send additional help as soon as possible."

This conversation was the first piece of information, which India got about the devastation in Dhanushkodi. News shot like lightning across all national dailies and radio – *'The devastation is unprecedented, INS Sharda is safe, and her captain, Lieu-*

tenant Inderjit Sharma, is leading the region's rescue operations.'

Things slowly started improving. The radio connection got restored. The Pamban Bridge got manually opened, allowing Sharda to approach the jetty on the northern side of the peninsula. The turn-around time of the rescue operation got reduced, allowing more rescue trips per day. The supplies on Sharda got replenished by the local administration at the cost of the state government. NHQ sent INS Magar, a massive ship compared to Sharda, to help Inder, but she couldn't manage the logistics on board. For over two weeks, Inder continued his rescue operations, taking the count of rescued people to around 2500.

On 10th January, Mahalingam, one of the electrical sailors, went on leave. Inder asked him to visit Loganathan's home to inform Rekha of their well being. He returned from the break two days later and updated Inder about Rekha's condition.

"Sir, Maam and Loganathan Sir's wife wept with happiness at the news that all was well. She is still not good, even after visiting the hospital. But, Maam felt motivated to get better, Sir."

Tears pricked Inder's eyes. He was shocked to hear the news and felt miserable that he could not care for her when she needed him most. He felt guilty for putting her in such a condition. He looked up at the skies imploring the almighty, and with tears in his eyes, he put his hands up in prayer. *Have mercy on us, oh Krishna! Give my Rekha and me the strength to endure all the perils that you have set for us.*

. . .

The government of India went all out to provide aid and care for the rescued people. Thousands took refuge in the relief camp at Mandapam. Susheela limped into the camp.

Her hand instantly covered her nose to avert the unbear-

PRIYA SHARMA SHAIKH

able stench. The place was a mess with people lying around in a disorderly manner, holding their heads with vacant eyes, crying, and groaning in monotonous tones that nobody listened. Nurses and doctors on duty ran about their administration of medication and care while volunteers distributed food packets. A desk at one corner of the camp kept a register of all the camp people. Susheela scrolled through the scores of pages anxiously.

"This child," she stammered, bursting into tears, "Ravi Rajan is listed as an orphan. He is my son. He is not an orphan. Please help me - where can I find him, brother?"

The man at the desk smiled. "God is great! All will be well, Ma. Orphaned children are all behind me. There are hundreds. Your son hopefully is one of them."

"Thank you, brother; you are an angel of hope. God bless you," she wept, folding her hands in front of him.

She walked hurriedly through the lines of children lying around in sickly and bruised conditions. It was hard to decipher the mutilated and bruised faces. And just as she was coming to the end of the section, she saw a familiar pair of shorts. She peered harder. The child was sleeping on his stomach with his hand covering his bandaged head. She went up to him and slowly moved the hand off his face and then cried out aloud as she recognised Ravi. He was severely bruised and swollen. She hugged him weeping bitterly. "Oh, my Ravi, Ravi, Ravi! Thank you, God, for your mercy. I'm sorry that you had to go through all this alone, my kutty, my chinna paiyaa."

"Amma, Amma!" Ravi too wept, "I drifted away with the waves Amma. I was so scared that I won't see you again. Everything feels broken Amma and so many people were dead and hurt," he wept, "Sharda ship saved me. I was in the first group that got rescued Amma. The Captain told me I would find you here."

"Oh, my dear kutty, I so missed your chatter."

"Amma, where is Thatha?"

"I lost him too. If he has survived, wherever he is, I hope he gets care."

"And Patti?" he asked hopefully.

"I don't know, kutty. I pray that your Patti decided not to travel that afternoon."
"Is Appa dead, Amma?" cried Ravi.

"Hush, son, I don't know. I have just come here. I have not yet looked for his name in the register because I wanted to find you first. We will check with the authorities."

When Susheela collected herself, she took Ravi with her to the desk to look for Rajan's name. He was not listed. Ravi started crying, and Susheela hugged him, weeping herself.
"The ship is still doing rescue operations. Have faith, Ma," said the desk clerk.

"Pray, kutty. Pray. It is all we can do. Appa will be safe – I just know it."

. . .

Appu walked up to Inder with a message from NHQ. They were orders to help the Ceylon government rescue their fishermen stranded in the Gulf of Mannar. They were to take them to the southern side of Talaimannar. Sharda headed south as per orders. On his very first round, Inder encountered Ceylon Navy's frigate ship, Gajababu. She instantly challenged Inder on the radio.

"What ship? Where bound?"

She was not informed of Inder's movement to Talaimannar, due to which an ugly situation could have emerged. Inder responded quickly. "I'm INS Sharda, and I have orders from Naval Headquarters to assist Sinhalese fishermen stranded at Gulf of Mannar. I am taking them to Talaimannar."

"Noted. Carry on. Over," crackled back the voice.

Sharda proceeded to the west jetty and operated in the area rescuing over 550 people over the next two days. Amongst them were several Indian fishers too whose boats had been stranded or damaged at the Gulf of Mannar. They also were taken back to the rescue camp at Mandapam.

As the last batch of people alighted Sharda at Mandapam, a man with a gashed and broken leg turned to Inder with tearful eyes and a firm handshake.

"Thank you, Sir."

"It is our honour," said Inder, noting the deep scar on his right cheek.

"I hope I find my family – without them, I have nothing to live for."

Inder patted his shoulder and nodded. "Hope was your motivation to survive, and it will make you find them too. Go in peace, friend."

. . .

Inder received a message from the commanding officer of INS Magar, Cdr. Bhushan, keeping the RNO, CNC East, and NHQ in a copy.

"IJ, you kept the naval flag flying high - I was a mere spectator."

Their last day at Mandapam finally came, and Inder and his team got showered with blessings and tearful gratifications. "Sir, you should get a *Swaran Padukam* by the President of India," said one of the port pilots, and the rest heartily agreed with him.

Inder received a signal from the Chief of Naval Staff, Admiral Chatterji. He beamed as he read the message and assembled his boys. He scanned theme with pride and noticed how messy they looked in dirty uniforms, and hair and beards longer than the prescribed norm.

"I have with me here a message from the CNS himself, and it is my pleasure to read it out to you, as it is as much for you, as it is for me as your proud Captain. *Your untiring efforts and devotion to duty under adverse conditions have saved a number of lives during the recent operations of Dhanushkodi. I congratulate your team and you for all the fine effort, which is in keeping with the highest traditions of the service. WELL DONE!*"

Inder sighed and folded the message and then looked at his boys, "I'd like to share something with all of you today. I had dreaded my appointment to Sharda. But today, I stand here feeling humbled and proud that I am the commanding officer of this glorious team. It is destiny that each of us was to be present for the service of so many people. That is why we returned by the last train from Rameshwaram. Let us put our hands together and clap for the exemplary teamwork each of us has displayed during this momentous time in human history. But for your tireless efforts, we would not have been able to rescue over 3000 people. It was an impossible task without each of your efforts. Thank you very much for all that you have done. God bless each of you. Let us celebrate with some much-deserved *bada-khana* now!"

The crew cheered and hugged each other with tears in their eyes, while Appu clicked pictures and started his antics, making everybody laugh.

...

It was 21st January 1965, a little over a month since Inder

PRIYA SHARMA SHAIKH

had left Rekha at Tambaram. While standing at the train's doorway, his thoughts went to how Rekha had learnt how to adjust to his temperament and kept him anchored with her stimulating conversation when he got appointed at Sharda. Maybe *something good will come out of it*, he had concluded. The events of the weeks gone by were a testimony of the good that came out of Sharda's maiden trip.

He looked at the skies, at the wonder of the almighty.

Despite the odds, everything worked out well, Krishna. God's greatest service is to serve humanity - was it a simple coincidence that your message came to me just before the time it was most needed to be put into action? Thank you for the opportunity. I feel a surreal connection with you. He smiled at Loganathan as the train pulled in at Tambaram.

. . .

Rekha was lying in her room, lost in thought when she heard muffled voices in the living room.

"The good news is that she is much better, Sir."

"Thank you. Loganathan ... indebted ... grace and hospitality."

Rekha looked up. She didn't recognise the long-haired, bearded man in plain clothing, enter the room. As he approached, his body odour made her nauseous. She struggled up to leave the room and stumbled as she rose. Inder caught her arm to steady her, but she pulled away, crying for help.

"Rekha! Darling, it's me. Don't you recognise me?" he said, with tears in his eyes.

She turned around to get a proper look at him. *It is Jungee.* She fell into his arms and burst into loud tears against his chest.

"Jungee! I was so worried, and alone," she wept bitterly,

clinging onto him tightly.

"Hush my darling," said Inder, hugging her tightly, feeling shocked at seeing his beautiful wife's pitiful condition, "I'm so very sorry for all that happened to you. You didn't deserve this. Everything will be okay. I'm with you now."

All the horror and anxiety of the previous weeks welled up and overflowed. After what seemed like an age, their hearts were one again, talking to each other without any words.

. . .

On returning from work next that evening, Inder took Rekha to the hospital for a complete check-up. While they waited for their turn, he told her about his experiences at sea. He also shared that that Lt. Cdr. Green, a newsreader on the English bulletin of All India Radio, had interviewed him that morning.

"I feel overwhelmed by the sudden attention from so many friends, family, colleagues, the government, the media, and superiors in the Navy.

Rekha hugged his arm, "There was a reason that you were to be at Sharda, after all. Your team and you deserve the praise and recognition. There is one problem, though."

"What?"

"I bid goodbye to a dashing man, and the Navy has returned a bearded greyhaired man."

He laughed. "Yes, we all need to go to the barber. All my boys are in such a mess too. They all worked so hard, Rekha," sighed Inder.

The nurse called out to them to meet the doctor. As they entered his cabin, he reached out to shake Inder's hand vehemently. "Aha, well, if it isn't Lt. Inderjit Sharma! Congratulations on a fantastic job done. You are a celebrity."

"Thank you, Sir," blushed Inder.

"And now that you are back, I am sure Rekha's paralysis will improve too. The tests show considerable improvement. But it will take some more time to completely correct itself, as she has become very weak with all the stress," he said and beamed at them. "So, how are you both celebrating?"

Inder and Rekha exchanged looks, "Let us see – we will do something."

"I'm not just talking of your glorious return, but also that you both are going to be parents. Your lovely wife is pregnant."

Rekha and Inderjit looked at each other and gasped with joy.

"The first trimester is the most important time for the baby," continued the doctor, "You should ensure Rekha gets good care. Keep her happy and make certain she eats well; she takes her medication on time and takes long walks once she is better."

Inder and Rekha's faces were aglow as they left the hospital - A new dream was born!

— — —

CHAPTER 14: UNPRECEDENTED REALISATIONS AND VALIDATIONS

September 1965: Becoming a parent brings in so much more

Inder started praying. He set up a shrine in his home with Rameshwara, Krishna, Durga, the Ramayana, and a brass oil lamp. After bathing, he lit the lamp and had his first of a lifetime of conversations with God.

One morning, Rekha looked outside the window at the swaying boughs of the Gulmohar tree. Its orange flowers had blanketed the ground around it. She smiled and talked to her unborn child about the freshness of colour. She rubbed her visibly, pregnant stomach gently.

She was in her third trimester. The Doctor had pronounced that she and the baby were in perfect health. She bought some like delicate printed fabric and set to work stitching baby clothes on her Singer sewing machine. She had never been happier, she thought, as she bit into the pulp of a mango slice.

Who is that under the Gulmohar tree? Is that someone waving at me? She strained to focus. It was Sarla, Patanjli, and Meena. Rekha wept with joy at meeting her family after so many months. So much had happened! Inder was thrilled too, and relieved that they were there to give Rekha the much-needed care while he got back to patrolling duties once again. And indulge her they did, fulfilling every one of her food cravings and aiding her efforts to stitch and knit clothes for the baby.

It was the end of August 1965, when India sensed some activity from Pakistan. All the armed forces were on high alert. Sharda too got deployed to carry out security patrols for any possible dangers outside Madras harbour.

While Inder was at sea, on 01 September 1965, Rekha went into labor sometime after dinner. At 6.30 am, on 02 September 1965, she gave a final push, and her baby slipped into the gloved hands of Surgeon Lt. Cdr. Kohli.

"Congratulations, Rekha, you have a beautiful baby girl. All her toes and fingers are intact," said Kohli, holding the baby up by her feet for her to see. He waited for her to cry, and when she didn't, he slapped her tiny buttocks, and she wailed weakly and then after gasping, loudly.

"Doctor, please don't...," protested the exhausted Rekha, straining to look at her baby.

The nurses whisked her child away for cleaning and wrapping. The painkillers that the Doctor had given Rekha kicked in, and she fell into a deep sleep. When she awakened, she found herself in the general ward. Patanjli was holding her baby in his arms, whispering into her ears. He put the baby next to Rekha. "Mama, I'm your baby girl," said Patanjli speaking like a baby.

"Congratulations, Rekha, and thank you for making us proud grandparents," clucked Sarla.

Rekha beamed, admiring her baby, unsure of how to hold her. But when Patanjli put the baby in her lap, the right posture came to her naturally. She kissed her daughter gently. "Does Inderjit know?"

"Yes, he has sent a message - *Congratulations. My love to Ladli.*"

Inder was ecstatic when he got the news and rushed to Vizag, late that evening. Being a father felt oddly unfamiliar. He had a quickness in his step as he proceeded down the dim hallway of the hospital, the heel of his shoes going click click click on the tiles. Inder was showered with wishes by everyone on entering Rekha's ward. He moved to her bedside and smiled warmly. She looked tired but beautiful. Nestled on her arm was the baby, sound asleep. Rekha turned the baby's little round face for him to see.

Inder's face lit up with a smile of fascination – *My daughter!* She wore a long white and pink printed cotton dress. She had thick dark hair, pink skin, and rose-pink lips. Her face was an unexplainable calm as she lay with her eyes shut and tightly clenched fists. She held the keys to his hearts from the moment he set eyes on her.

"Ladli," he exclaimed, touching her forehead gently, "What a beautiful gift, Rekha. Thank you."

When Inder returned for patrolling, early next morning, images of Rekha and Ladli kept coming to him. Overnight he felt a sense of responsibility for their wellbeing. Patanjli and Sarla said they would stay on for the next 40 days to settle Rekha into motherhood, while Inder continued to sail.

. . .

Rekha brought Ladli home with Patanjli after a few days. Sarla and Meena, along with a few naval wives, welcomed them with *aarti* and *tikka.* Everyone gushed at the new member of the family. Meena and Patanjli distributed sweets to the guests as they all fussed around Rekha, giving their opinions of how the baby should be cared for, fed, and cleaned. Rekha listened to everyone but trusted her favourite childbirth book, by Dr. Spock.

Ladli's red tikka, in the centre of her forehead, shone like a burning flame to Rekha. She was by now madly in love with Ladli.

"Mummy doesn't she look like goddess Durga with the tikka and her clenched fists, ready to fight against the evils of the world," she said, mistily smiling as Ladli opened her eyes.

"A mother's love has no bounds!" laughed Sarla. "And you're right – Shakti and Shiva are in all of us, and in your little daughter too."

Rekha enjoyed nursing Ladli, holding to her belief of mother's milk being the best. She was very protective of her, too, and didn't trust anyone with bathing, dressing, and nappy changing. She would talk to her, and Ladli would open her black eyes to look up at her mother and gurgle. Rekha was smitten.

Sarla cautioned her to stop staring. *"Nazar lag jayegi,"* she said with concern.

"There is no such thing, Priyaji," said Patanjli, "Family and friends can never think ill for a child, least of all the child's mother. God watches over children all the time."

"But children fall ill too, don't they?" argued Sarla.

"Must we talk of negative things when we are blessed with the presence of Shakti herself?" said Patanjli, silencing Sarla's protests of Rekha doting too much on the baby.

Along with Rekha, the rest of the family were just as besotted by the baby. Meena stitched a new frock for her every day. Patanjli carried Ladli into the morning sun every day, to strengthen her bones. And Sarla made certain that Rekha ate the healthiest food. And the caretaker for Ladli called Raju, ran errands for Rekha through the day.

When Ladli was two months old, Sarla, Patanjli, and Meena

returned to Punjab, and Rekha moved back to Madras to be closer to Inder. They lived with Inder's coursemate, Lt. Joginder Singh, and his wife Raj, who had also delivered a baby girl.

Every evening Inder rushed home to play with his daughter, take pictures of her, take her for walks, carry her in his lap when she cried, burped her, and dressed her up after Rekha gave her an evening sponge. He loved keeping her amused by talking to her when she awoke. She would hold his finger tightly and look up at his lips intently. And when she did something new, he celebrated and boasted about it to his friends.

"Okay, so she is turning over, which means she is growing just fine," said Joginder one evening to Inder. "But, have you decided on a name yet? You and Rekha keep calling her different names, Ladli, Reena Tapki, Priyadarshini, and Nanki. What's it going to be?" Both men were sitting together, watching over their babies with uncharacteristically soft expressions.

"I like Nanki, although Rekha keeps changing her mind. See, she is turning her side again, and she may just show you her commando crawl too."

Joginder laughed. "She is adorable, my brother, as is my daughter Sukanya. Angels."

"See! There she is doing the commando crawl," laughed Inder, "Come on my darling. Come on!" said Inder getting down on all fours encouraging Ladli to go on, "She is going to be a tough one when she grows up, I tell you," said Inder with glee.

. . .

The train stopped at Delhi, and Inder rushed to grab a cup of tea for Rekha and himself. They were on their way back after celebrating Ladli's first Diwali in Punjab. He saw a new side of Rekha on this trip – she had done the unthinkable! The whole

Sharma family got into a state of shock and grief.

The day before they left, Rekha had served Jaikishen lunch in the living room, while he debated some money matters with Geeta.

"Pitaji," said Rekha, and she set the plate in front of him. She then touched his feet gently and lifted her veil.

He had looked at her, not entirely understanding what she was doing.

"Pitaji, you are my father, and I will not veil myself from you or anybody from today. This doesn't mean I disrespect your traditions or you; it just means that I respect myself, and I will not do anything that makes me feel less in my own eyes."

Jaikishen had looked startled. His eyes had darted towards Geeta to gauge her reaction, but not before he smiled and blessed Rekha. As was expected, Geeta had broken into a state of dramatic exclamations, rebuking Rekha and calling out her preposterous act.

Inder had watched the whole incident from a distance. He had got upset with the unsuspecting theatrical, as Rekha had not mentioned her plans to lift her veil. His eyes had narrowed, but he said nothing and walked into the inner bedroom. Rekha had joined him with Ladli, who was fast asleep cradled in her arms. She shut the door behind her and breathed heavily, looking at her husband's figure sitting on the bed, even as Geeta went on about how grieved and disrespected she felt. An uncomfortable silence ensued.

"Jungee."

His mind was awash with turmoil, and he had not turned to look at her.

Rekha persisted, "I don't regret what I have done, and I am glad that this is behind me. I can finally be myself without any fear."

"Rekha, look at how much you have upset Pabbi. I'm all for your forward-thinking, but this was not the way," he had said.

Rekha stood with her back to Inder, rocking Ladli, looking at herself in the mirror, unwavering in her resolve, even as the living room's outbursts continued.

"What other way was there, Jungee?" she finally said, with a cold sigh. "And when would it have been a perfect time? I have tried to tow Mataji's line for more than two years because I love you, but unfortunately, there seems no end to her tunnel of unreasonable expectations. It had to stop. And this was the only way, and the perfect time. Trust me, I thought through this before finally doing it."

"But…"

"Pitaji is my father, and you know that I respect him the most, in this house. I also find him sensible, and I refuse to believe anymore that he could have a vile eye for me. It is sickening to even think of it. If you have your values of not disrespecting your mother, I too have been brought up to have self-respect, and my resolve is not to displease myself and not be tough on myself. Not anymore. I am ready to bear the consequence of this because it serves my need of self-respect."

"Rekha, I hate that we will be leaving them with such a bad taste after we have had such a good time here with Ladli."

"The good thing is that this happened while everyone was at home and also that we will be gone tomorrow. Time is a great healer. Mataji will be fine in a few days. But, if it is a problem for me to stay here tonight, I will leave for my father's home right away."

"Don't be ridiculous, Rekha. You never have to leave and go to your father's house to seek shelter, ever." He had got agitated. "I don't understand what brought about this tough side of you all of a sudden. It is very unlike your loving nature."

"It started when I held Ladli in my arms for the first time. My softness and obedience were taken for granted, Jungee. And I was leading a life of duplicity. I want my daughter to see me live a life free of any hypocrisy, doing the things that give me happiness because it is when I am happy that I can make her happy and you happy. I have never had more clarity," she had said, with a new calm over her face.

Inder shuddered as he remembered the incident. But when they'd left home that morning, although things were not amicable, the atmosphere had settled. Geeta had blessed them when they touched her feet to say goodbye. Rekha had been right once again.

. . .

A young man with a slight stubble stood at the tea stall. There was no sign of Banna.

"Aren't you Chotu? Do you remember me?"

"I'm sorry, my memory fails me."

"Well, it was long ago. Where is your father?"

"There he comes," said Chotu pointing to an older and leaner Banna walk up to them.

"Namaste bhaisaab! I had tea at your stall years ago. I'd got caught by Darogaji for ..."

"Sleeping on the bench. Oh, yes! It was more than ten years ago if I am not wrong. Right?"
"12 years, to be precise."

"You were going to join the Navy. Chotu, this is the boy I used to tell you about."

"I can't recollect you, but your story of being so young and courageous has been a part of the several lectures that I got growing up. What is the Navy like, bhaisaab?"

"It is fantastic. I am an officer now and have travelled across the country and the world. Joining the Navy was the best decision of my life. I'd like two teas, please."

"Coming up. Also, give our guest a box of the laddoos. Chotu is also considering what to do next. I am keen that he joins a bank. What do you think?"

"Let him decide what he wants to do, bhaisaab," said Inder and then looked at Chotu, "Think of the things that make you happy or how you want to make the world a better place. It could be better sanitation, finance, education, music, art, infrastructure, or armed forces. Find out more about the field by talking to people in the field. And then take a leap of faith. Whatever you decide to do, do it with complete focus, humility, and consistence. And be patient with yourself, as becoming successful takes time."

"And what if I don't like what I choose?"

"If you have thought hard enough at the start, it is unlikely. But if you still meet with disappointment, it is never too late to course-correct – it is your life after all. Just don't make excuses for your failure, and don't look for easy ways to succeed."

"Thank you, bhaisaab, I will remember your advice," smiled Chotu.

"All the best!" said Inder walking away with the teas and laddoos.

. . .

Rekha and Inder were barely settling in as parents when they realised they were pregnant again. The Doctor advised Rekha to stop nursing Ladli immediately. This proved challenging for both Rekha and Ladli, so Inder stepped in to wean her away.

While Rekha was anxious about not nursing her baby anymore, Ladli shrieked loudly, wanting to reunite with her mother. Inder patiently tended to her protests and strictly forbade Rekha from entering their room. Inder tried to feed her with a bottle, but Ladli pushed the bottle away. After a whole day and night of tears and tantrums, when Ladli awoke the next morning, she was ready to cry again, and Inder was ready with yet another bottle of warm milk.

Ladli looked at it with a tearful expression and turned to look at the doorway for Rekha. Not seeing her mother there, she looked at Inder dolefully and then at the bottle in his hand, and finally reached out. Inder put it to her mouth, holding her head up gently in his arms. She guzzled the much-needed nourishment and finished the whole bottle. Rekha watched with tears rolling down her cheeks from behind the curtains.

"This had to be done, darling, as just as you love Ladli, there is another baby in the making. You cannot deny that child the nutrition it deserves."

"I understand. It saddens me that we had to force Ladli to give up something she loved."

"How could it have been done better? She would never have stopped wanting to be fed by you, and you would have continued to relent because of your love. Sometimes you have to make tough decisions. At least she was with me while going through it."

"Yes, seeing her with you was the only relief."

Inder gulped and looked at Rekha, "Darling, this moment feels like an epiphany. You were right about lifting your veil when you did, and I acknowledge you for having the courage to do so alone, and being as respectful as you could at that moment. Pabbi will eventually understand."

. . .

On Republic Day, 26 January 1966, the RNO received a signal from the Chief of Naval Staff.

"Congratulations, my dear Inderjit! The President of India will award you the Ati Vishisht Seva Medal for your service to the nation during the rescue operations at Dhanushkodi. The award will get presented later this year."

"Thank you so much, Sir!" blushed Inder, shaking Nair's hand.

She was thrilled when Inder shared the news about the award with her at lunch. Later that afternoon, the Naval Officers Wives Association had organised a get-together, which Rekha attended along with Ladli. After the meeting and games were over, Rekha sat to feed Ladli some laddoo and gushed about Inder's award.

"Your Papa is getting an award, darling Ladli. You are so lucky for us."

Ladli drooled and gobbled the sweets as a few senior officers' wives looked on.

"What is the celebration, Rekha?" said Rupa, immaculately dressed in a chiffon sari.

Rekha gushed with joy and shared the news with her as two other senior officer's wives, Usha and Nandita, looked on. Usha smirked, contemptuously adjusting a strand of loose hair into her high bun. "Oh really! Congrats! Although I can't believe that they gave him an AVSM for the rescue work at Dhanushkodi. It's like he has won some major battle. He just happened to be in the area, and so he had to save people. Why an award for that?"

"I couldn't agree more. There's honestly nothing heroic about the rescue operation, Rekha!" said Rupa, smirking and looking at the others. "The Navy gives awards to anyone and for anything nowadays," she concluded, rolled her eyes, and shook her head before sipping on her Fanta.

Rekha's mouth fell open in shock as she looked from one lady to the other. "But ... he could have lost his crew and the ship and died himself. It was his presence of mind and intelligence that ..."

"I'd simply call it luck, Rekha. What is the intelligence in saving people once the storm has stemmed?" said Nandita laughing and cutting Rekha, mid-sentence, "I mean come on. Don't be so naive and get sold on every story your husband tells you."

"Yes, anybody could have done the same," said Rupa.

"Rekha, which batch of NDA was Inderjit in?" asked Usha with a curious expression.

"Shhh! He is a lower deckhand," whispered Rupa to Usha.

"Oh...oops!" said Usha.

"I don't know you, ladies, personally, but I know that you are senior officers' wives. What inspiring and encouraging words I am receiving from you. I can't believe it!" said Rekha, with collected calm.

"Well, ...," started Nandita.

"Excuse me, but I believe it is now my turn to speak," said Rekha in a steady tone even though her heart wrenched with anger and her eyes welled with tears, "Instead of celebrating my husband's success with me, you belittle him in front of me. Yes, he joined the Navy as a sailor, but he worked hard and became an officer and also did his officer's training with the NDA's 16th course. And what do you know, today he is the youngest decorated officer of the Navy despite the disparagers that tried to stem his growth. I am so proud of him, and thankfully so is the Navy, and I am glad she measures her men's merit dispassionately. Lastly, my husband doesn't need to tell me stories to impress me. I love him nevertheless. Good afternoon ladies."

She looked at each of them in the eye and walked away gracefully, with Ladli tucked on her hip, leaving them behind with their mouths ajar.

. . .

Before going home, Inderjit called to speak with Jaikishen and Geeta on the neighbour's telephone. After a long pause, Inder heard Geeta's voice on the line, "Inderjit?"

"Namaste, Pabbi. How are you? Where is Pitaji?" he said in Punjabi.

"He has gone to meet Chachaji, puttar. It is so nice to hear your voice. How are Rekha and Ladli?" she said with emotion in her voice.

"We are all fine. I want to share some good news with you, Pabbi. Thanks to your blessings, I will be awarded by the President for my work during the rescue operations. I got to know this morning, and hence this call to share the news with you."

"Fantastic news, my son! You have made me so proud. Your father will be thrilled to hear this news," said Geeta, her voice quivering with tears and happiness, "Live long and happy."

"I am happy I could make you feel proud, Pabbi," said Inder, "Give my love to everyone and regards to all the elders," he said and put the receiver down with a smile on his face.

. . .

When he got back home, he went to his shrine, while Rekha ironed and folded Ladli's clothes.

Thank you for bestowing this honour on me. Give me the wisdom and strength to keep me on the path you have set for me, always. Rekha smiled at her husband's new-found piety.

He cradled Ladli to sleep in his lap while Rekha served him a bowl of fruit custard.

"Congratulations and celebrations again, Jungee darling. This is my treat for your award," said Rekha.

"You are the best, Rekha. I love it!"

"Look at what all came out of your dreaded posting to Sharda! So, are you satisfied with your achievements and ready to be the Cow now?"

He gently pushed the hair off Ladli's face, "When I am with this one and you, I am the Cow, but the Lion within me is still restless to discover more. This is just the beginning, Rekha. Let's see what destiny has in store for me. How was the NOWA party?"

"Umm...it was nice," she said vaguely, continuing to iron.

"It's not you to hum and haw. What happened?" said Inder, laying Ladli on the bed.

Rekha recounted the incident to him. Inder shook his head. "Forget it, Jungee. Some people just cannot see goodness coming to others. I gave them a piece of my mind. You know me, I'm not one to sit quietly and watch people mow all over me."

"The shadows of the past never really leave you," said Inder, shaking his head.

"They find a way to creep back into your present. I am at the cusp of being a decorated officer, but people like them want to pull me back. They want me to believe I am still not good enough; the lower deckhand should get reminded that now and then. He should remain in that paradigm, no matter all his efforts! Isn't it more important where I am today? Yes, I rose from the lower deck. And I know I am not any less than my NDA course mates? The Navy doesn't think I am less."

Inder looked down. Rekha held his hand. "What are you thinking, darling? Talk to me, Jungee."

"Destiny may have placed my crew and me at Dhanushkodi at the time of the storm, but I know that each of us felt privileged that we could be of service when it was most needed. We didn't work to get rewarded. All we cared about at the time was doing the best we could for those people. It was the small but important and timely decisions that made all the difference in that operation—returning to Sharda by the last train that left Rameshwaram, securing the ropes properly and running the engines all night, rowing back to the ship in the nick of time, starting rescue operations without NHQ's orders. We collectively saved so many lives. Many more would have died had we not acted in time." Inder paused to look at Rekha. "It baffles me, to think, why would they feel such contempt? It makes me lose trust, and that pains me." He got up to leave for the kitchen and then turned back. "But I shall refrain from caring about what anybody thinks or says. I trust my karma; I know it will speak for me. There is an intriguing piece of wisdom that Krishna shares with Arjuna in the battleground of the Mahabharata - *Karmanye vadhikaraste, ma phaleshu kadachana, Ma karma-phala-hetur-bhurmate sangostva akarmani.*"

"What does it mean?"

"That I must do my karma, without being attached to the result. Worrying about victory and making it the purpose of my karma is futile. Do you remember our conversation when I got posted to Sharda?"

"Of course, I do."

PRIYA SHARMA SHAIKH

"Ever since, I have ceased being attached to glory or recognition. If it comes to me, great, and if it doesn't, I will continue to do my *karma* nevertheless – do my best, however insignificant the role, even when nobody is watching. Being present, being in the flow, while bringing my best self to whatever situation life brings forth is my purpose, Rekha. And I feel a limitless divine energy flow through me, making me believe in myself and making me live my purpose with clarity. And with divinity is on my side, no storm is formidable enough to pull me down."

"Life seems to have been your biggest teacher Jungee," she sighed deeply, hugging him, "Is your mind at peace now?"

He sighed deeply, "It is, and I'm sorry you had to experience this on my account. Yes, I am wiser each day. I now choose the battles I want to fight."

He smiled and added, "At the risk of sounding pompous, that day in the storm, the work we did was nothing short of divinity. So, if anybody wants to belittle it, I choose to rise above such noise."

"That's my, Jungee."

He nodded and touched Ladli's warm cheeks, looking at her sound asleep.

"The biggest reward I had to come back to claim was to be her father," he said, blinking away the tears in his eyes, "And on that happy note, let's have some more custard."

"At your service, officer."

. . .

"Jungee, I have decided to name her Priya," said Rekha.

"Why Priya?" said Inder letting his struggling daughter crawl off from his lap to play with Timmu, her beeping rubber rabbit.

"Two reasons – the first is that my father calls my mother Priya with love, and he has always loved her so much. Second, the Kuruvillas have two daughters - Priya and Laila. I want our daughter to be like them – beautiful, confident, and loved by all."

"I like it, but doesn't Priya mean darling? Everyone will call her darling."

"Well, that means all people will love her. And that is a good thing, right?

"Point."

"We finally agree on a name. Priya. Priya. Priya," said Rekha.

Ladli turned to look at Rekha and smiled and proceeded to jump on her haunches to the squeaky sounds of, Timmu.

"She approves," smiled Inder.

. . .

The next morning Inder said goodbye to Rekha and Priya and opened the front door.

"Jungee."

He turned. Behind him was Priya, sitting in a squat on the floor.

"Jungee," she said again and clapped her little hands.
Inder looked astonished. "Rekha, come quickly, Priya has just said her first word," he exclaimed.

Rekha came running in, "What? What did she say?"

"Jungee," he laughed, "Just imagine! Who would have thought that my daughter will also call me Jungee?"

"Jungee," said Priya.

"Darling, say, Papa!"

"Papa," said Priya, reading Inder's lips.

"Excellent, Priya. I am your Papa," he said, pointing to himself.

"Priya, say, Mama," pleaded Rekha, waiting expectantly.

"Mama, Mama," said Priya, again watching her mother's lips move.

"She is saying all the words."

"Looks like she will speak before our second baby is born," said Inder, kissing Priya on her forehead.

That afternoon, Inder went to the Municipal Corporation in Vizag and registered his daughter's name as Priya Inderjit Sharma.

After that, just as her parents had predicted, Priya spoke clear English words and chattered nineteen to the dozen, managing to get her way with everyone. She had her parents wrapped around her little finger.

...

Rekha and Inder became parents to their second child, a baby girl on 15 September 1966, in the same bed, in the same ward of INHS Kalyani, Vizag, with the same Surgeon Lt. Cdr. Kohli! Exactly a year and 13 days younger to Priya, she was a delightful child, with infectious energy about her. Her attractive black eyes were alert from the word go. When Priya came to the hospital to see her little sister, she looked forlorn, as she had been away from her mother for three whole days. She walked up to Rekha's bedside and saw the baby in the cradle and smiled with glee.

"Mama, small baby."

"Yes, darling, she is your small baby. Your little sister. Isn't she beautiful?"

"She is like a beautiful doll, Mama," said Priya touching the baby's toes.

. . .

A few evenings after Rekha returned home with her second baby, Inder arrived to find her in the kitchen.

"Hello, darling," he piped cheerfully, with Priya on his shoulders.

Rekha didn't respond.

"What happened, Rekha?"

She showed him the letter she had received from Phagwara that morning, with tears in her eyes. The message was that of regret that Rekha had given birth to one more daughter.

"How can she be so nasty about my child and me? How can she make such a shallow remark about my ability to bear a son? Does she not know that the man's sperm decides the sex of the child?" said Rekha, in an unusual raised voice and raised eyebrows.

Inder sighed and put Priya down. "Go and play with Raju darling," he said, and turned to Rekha, "I'm sorry, on her behalf. She is illiterate, Rekha, and with a very narrow world view, darling. Her map of the world and its metrics are very different from yours, and I know for sure she doesn't understand the science of reproduction."

"So, does her illiteracy give her the licence to be hurtful to her son and me? I have spent the whole day feeling miserable, and that has got the baby cranky too. She has just gone to sleep. I am exhausted."

"I understand darling. But can't you instead choose to ignore her to avoid feeling miserable. I know that Pabbi does not mean ill. I will write to Pitaji to explain to her..."

"I will deal with the conflict head-on when it comes my way. I won't skirt it. That was the promise you had made to yourself and me, right?"

"How can I have a conflict with my mother, Rekha? I request you just ignore such eccentricities from her, darling. We can't change the people around us. But we can manage our reaction to them. So choose to not get affected. Right?"

"This is contempt towards me, yet again. She has disturbed my peace of mind. And all you have to say is - ignore her? You just made me feel so alone, Inderjit Sharma. I have nothing more to say to you," she yelled and left the kitchen, as she heard the baby crying.

Rekha, and Inder, had no time to stay upset with each other. And yet, although the matter remained unresolved, they were forced to bring life back to normal as there was always so much to do with two little children at hand. Their time got filled with feeds, baths, storytelling, walks in the park, bedtime duels, nappy changes, cleaning, cooking, photography, crying, gripe water, burping, sweet nothings, accidents, and so much more.

After much deliberation, Rekha and Inderjit named their second daughter, Mala.

...

In the winter of 1966, Inder and Rekha took a trip to Delhi, along with the Priya and Mala. Inder was to receive the *Ati Vishisht Seva Medal* (AVSM) from the then President of India, Dr. Zakir Hussain, in a grand ceremony at the Rashtrapati Bhavan. He was allowed to bring along one more family member for the ceremony, and without any hesitation, he chose to invite Jaikishen. Narendra's family provided them the warmth and hospitality. Rekha left the children in their care and accompanied the beaming Jaikishen to the award ceremony.

Jaikishen looked on with folded hands and tears in his eyes as Inder marched up the centre of the hallway to the President. He did a stiff salute to Shri Hussain, who pinned the medal above his left pocket, congratulated him, and shook his hand. Inder saluted and marched off.

A tea party at the President's private garden followed the award ceremony, hosting all the award winners and their respective families. Inder shared his experience with the President one-on-one, who listened intently and nodded his appreciation with a smile and said, "Come, let's get a picture with your family, Inderjit."

Inder held his breath as Jaikishen, Rekha, and he stood around the President. The photographer said, "SMILE, PLEASE." Click, and the frame got captured.

In Inder's life story, thus far, this was one of the most significant milestones.

— — —

CHAPTER 15: GEARING UP IN A NEW HORIZON

1970: Training in the snow fields of Russia

The humidity was at a high, as was the temperature, during March 1968. Sweating profusely, Inder gathered his notes and rushed home. It was almost a year since he had arrived with his family in Cochin. It always felt good being at INS Venduruthy. The Long Gunnery Course, intensive training in ammunition, was finally coming to an end.

"Papa, I am Mary, and this little sister of mine, is my lamb," Priya shrieked, jumping up and down next to Inder, urging him to pick her up as he entered the house. Inder obliged instantly, while Mala clapped her hands at them, in her nappy and embellished cap, bouncing on her haunches.

"But you are not Mary. You are Priya."

"Wait, I'll show you," said Priya wiggling out of his lap. She skipped out of the room, and sure enough, Mala dawdled after her.

Priya laughed uproariously. "See Papa! See, my lamb is running after me."

"She is taking her rhymes too seriously," said Rekha at Inder's confused expression, "She is a real drama queen. Malati and I are on our toes all day with her games and chatter."

Inder looked amused and picked up Mala to wipe the drool

off her face, "What fun you must have with these two."

"I do, but Mala is exhausting me! One look away, and madam is up to her antics. Look at this!" she pointed at Mala's forehead for Inder to see. "In her attempt to follow Priya, she fell into the gutter today."

Inder laughed out aloud. "She will be fine. This one is surely a risk-taker like me. I, too, had fallen into a gutter when I was a toddler. Look at her knees. They always have scabs! She is my Rana Sanga, the great king of Mewar that had several injuries on his body."

"Oh, she is naughty. She chases the dogs and cats that pass by and gets het up when they bark or mew at her. Malati says she ran after a snake the other day and tried to get a hold of it. Priya, on the other hand, screamed the house down. Thankfully the poor snake slithered away."

Every evening Inder came home to his three angels taking turns at drawing his attention about all that happened while he was busy mastering firearms. He felt happy.

"Get ready to pack up, darling. My tenure here is over."
"But it's not even been a year! What and where is the new posting?"

Inder bit into a ladoo and grinned, "Life in the Navy darling, where change is a constant. I will join as Squadron Gunnery Officer on INS Rajput, in Bombay. Say your goodbyes."

. . .

Mala awoke to new surroundings. She woke Priya up, curled up next to her. They walked out of the bedroom hand-in-hand, sleepy-eyed and tousle-headed, bumping into stacks of boxes and cartons.

"Mama!" cried out Priya, leading Mala around the boxes.

"Priya, Mama is in the kitchen. Come here, darling."

They followed the sound and cautiously peeped into the kitchen.

"Good morning, my darlings. We have come to Bombay. Do you like your new home?"

"No. There are too many things," said Priya grumpily.

"I like it, Mama," smiled Mala, hugging Rekha's legs.

"Malbachnooo," she said, bending to kiss Mala, keeping her wet hands away, "That's because we've just about arrived, Priya. Mama is making breakfast for Papa. Will you please help me?"

"I will help you, Mama," said Mala, as Priya looked on grumpily.

"No, I will help Mama," chided Priya.

Inder came into the kitchen in his uniform. "Good morning, my angels. Come, let me show you our new home," he said, while Rekha laid the table for breakfast.

Inder got allotted an independent two-bedroom flat in Navy Nagar in Bombay. It was spacious, with an extra study room, a servant quarter, and a large living room with a six-seater dining table, a big balcony that overlooked the play area below, French doors, and plenty of windows. Inder was delighted with the fresh air and sunlight.

"I love this house. My first task is to employ some help, as it will be difficult to manage time for the girls with all the housework. I'd rather spend time playing, reading, and teaching than getting embroiled in the endless chores."

While Inder ate his breakfast, Mala and Priya sat on opposite sides of him to drink a glass of milk. Mala gulped down her

JUNGEE

glass. Priya frowned at her and then proceeded to look doleful, nursing her milk. She tried to find an excuse to get out of drinking it. Her wish got granted when the doorbell rang, and she jumped up to open the door. And Mala followed, of course. At the door, looking down at them, stood a slim young woman dressed in a sari and a tight bun. She had a broad smile on her face.

"Hello, baby! Where is mummy?" she said in Hindi.

"Mama, an auntie has come to meet you," called Mala, while Priya sized her up.

"An auntie at this hour?" said Rekha peering to look out of the kitchen's back door.

"Namaste, Memsaab. My name is Anandi. Do you need a maid?"

"Yes, I do," said Rekha concealing her joy.

She said she was a Maharashtrian in her mid 30's, and that she had been working in Navy Nagar for several years. Her husband Ganpat and she could move in immediately. This was music to Rekha's ears! Anandi got instantly recruited at Rs. 25 per month.

. . .

"I decided to put my skills of stitching and smocking to good use. I had some spare money from last month, so I bought some fabric, thread, and lace, Jungee," said Rekha, to Inder one evening as he bounced Priya and Mala on his ankles.

"Mama made these nighties today, Papa," said Priya doing a twirl. Mala joined the twirling Priya.

"Wow! They're beautiful! Girls, stop twirling, or you will feel dizzy. I also want a nightie."

The twirling girls fell to the floor, giggling. "Are you a girl,

Papa? How can you wear a nightie?" laughed Priya.

Inder laughed and tickled Priya as she squealed with laughter.

"Mama is making frocks with matching hairbands for us," said Mala, "We will wear them to Reena's birthday party."

"You girls are so fortunate," said Inder, remembering how rarely he got new clothes as a little boy.

"Jungee, I got talking to one of the mothers in the garden today. She was also there at the National Yachting Championship yesterday. She said all the officers were saying that Soli Contractor and you make a formidable team. She asked me how long you had trained?"

"I learnt sailing when I joined the Navy."

"No wonder you won, Jungee," said Rekha with admiration.

"But like any sport, you have to practice to do well. Soli and I started training when I joined Rajput. We both love sailing, and we trained consistently."

"And it showed. Between managing the sails and the steering, you both were perfectly synchronised. Admiral Chatterjee was all praise too."

"He was and he looked quite amused, giving us the unique silver beer mug trophy."

"Anju also said something that has got me thinking; instead of a college, I could consider teaching at a school. I have been stuck about teaching at a college because I used to teach university students in Punjab. But I love teaching, so why should it matter if I teach college or school kids?"

. . .

Rekha set her mind on doing her research and zeroed in on

JUNGEE

the only convent school in the area, called St. Joseph's High School at R. C. Church, about 15 minutes' walk from their home. The very next morning, she dressed in her favourite slacks and tunic. Priya and Mala accompanied her in matching pink and white frocks, lace socks up to their knees, and shiny white pointed buckled shoes.

It was a sultry day. The trio was a bundle of sweat and thirst when they reached. The school was bustling with familiar sights and sounds that made Rekha smile. Students dressed in beige and white uniforms recited some text on stands in a large hall; teachers walked with a pile of notebooks in their hands, while children played in the field alongside. *What joy it would be to work in a place like this.*

A tall, thin, bespectacled office clerk dressed in a dull blue uniform stopped Rekha outside the Principal's office.

"Yes?" he said with authority, holding his hand up against the swinging half-doors.

"I am a science teacher. I would like to meet the Principal. I wish to teach here."

He pointed her to a bench, "Please wait here, Madam."

The school gong rang loudly, startling Mala and Priya. Rekha smiled, "That bell is to tell everyone that one period is over."

"What is a period, Mama?" asked Priya.

Rekha, took out a hand mirror and adjusted her lipstick and combed her hair. "Well, in school, you have many subjects to study, so they divide the day into short periods of time to study each subject. One period has just finished, and the next will start."

"Mala, don't look under the door. The Principal will get upset."

"Why will she get upset? I am just looking. Mama, she is wearing a long white cap."

"Hush! Be quiet, Mala."

After waiting for 15 minutes, it was time for Rekha to see the Principal, a short pleasant-looking woman. She wore white habit and silver cross with pride and flashed a million-dollar smile at Rekha and the girls as they approached her desk.

"Good morning, Madam," said Rekha.

"Good morning. You can call me Mother or Mother Helen, whatever you are comfortable with."

"Oh, thank you, Mother," smiled Rekha while Priya and Mala exchanged glances, whispering to each other.

"Priya, why is Mama calling her Mother?"

"I don't know. Shh!" said Priya holding her index finger to her lips.

"Thank you so much for seeing me without an appointment, Mother. My name is Rekha Sharma, and these are my daughters, Priya and Mala. Children, say good morning to Mother."

"Good morning, Mother," said Priya, half giggling. Mala too wished her, and then both of them covered their mouths to conceal their giggles.

"Oh my! What lovely little ducklings you have following you around, Rekha," said Mother Helen.

The girls giggled evermore.

"What are you two giggling about?" she said, smiling down at them as they fidgeted with the edge of her desk.

JUNGEE

"Why are you calling us ducklings, and why is Mama calling you Mother?" asked Priya, suddenly feeling a little self-conscious.

"Why are we calling you, mother, when she is our mother," said Mala, going to Rekha.

"She calls me Mother, because I am everyone's mother, and you two look like identical baby ducks that always trail behind their mother in the pond," she laughed. She then turned her attention to Rekha and said, "Lovely girls you have. So, I understand you wish to teach here."

"Yes, Mother, I am a science teacher. I have done my B.Ed. from Punjab University and had a government job as a lecturer, which I quit after marriage as I wanted to be with my husband. I wish to resume teaching."

"What science subjects can you teach?"

"All science subjects – General Science for juniors, and Physics, Chemistry, and Biology for seniors, with lab experiments. But I have one problem. As you can see, my children are small; I can only teach thrice a week for about an hour."

"Okay, we offer only Rs.200 per month for part-time work."

"That will be just fine, Mother."

"Wonderful! Can you join from tomorrow?"

"Oh, yes!" said an overjoyed Rekha, "Thank you so much, Mother."

. . .

That evening Rekha rushed to open the door to Inder, with Priya and Mala squealing after her.

"Mama will be a teacher," blurted out Priya, as soon as the

door opened.

"And mama made us call another aunty MOTHER," said Mala, climbing onto Inder like a monkey.

"What?" said Inder looking amused as Priya also climbed onto his arms and back.

"Yes, Jungee, it's true," said Rekha hugging Inder and taking his briefcase from him, "I got a job at St. Joseph's. It is a girls school, and I will teach science to higher secondary students. I am to start work tomorrow."

"That is fantastic news! But how will you manage these monkeys?" Priya had taken off his cap and jammed it on her head by now, while Mala also tried to get a grab at it.

"I will take them along since it is a matter of an hour. While the children play in the grounds under the supervision of Anandi, I will teach."

"Wow, darling, you are unstoppable," he said, looking at Rekha with newfound respect.

. . .

Mother Helen was impressed with Rekha's dedication and work during her part-time assignment, and after a few weeks, she offered her a full-time job for Rs. 400 per month.

"I wish I could, Mother, but I have to decline your generous offer regretfully. I cannot leave my daughters with the house help for the whole day," said Rekha, looking wistful.

"Let's see. Priya is three and a half years old. We can put her in the nursery, but Mala is only two and a half. The school's admission policy means that Mala is too young for admission, but we are so desperate for a good science teacher that I will take the liberty to waive the policy. You could come and go along with them. Will that work?"

JUNGEE

Rekha was delighted and agreed to join as a full-time teacher when the school reopened for the new academic year in mid-June.

. . .

The month of June 1969 was a time of change for Inder and his family. Rekha joined St. Joseph's as a full-time teacher. It was their first day of school, and they had to leave home at 8.30 am with Inder. Rekha wore a white and black polka-dotted sari, while the girls wore green and white checked frocks, which was the uniform for kindergarten.

"Children, today you are going to start school," she perked, biting into a boiled egg.

"Why do we have to go to school, Mama?" said Priya, looking drowsy, nursing her glass of milk, while Mala was already half-way through.

"To learn things, darling. Mama and Papa also studied in schools when we were young like you. You will meet children of your age who will study and play games with you. It will be great fun."

"But where will we study?" asked Priya, looking cross with this change in routine.

Mala put down her empty glass with a victorious flourish and wiped her milky white moustache from her upper lip with the back of her hand.

"Very good, Malkin. Come on, my Peachy, finish your milk."

"No, first you tell me," Priya persisted, her glass of milk standing tall as ever.

"In class, in the hall and the garden. Now drink your milk, darling" said Rekha, getting impatient.

Priya looked at Mala and smiled with her eyes opened wide, feeling hopeful about school. She then drank a big sip.

Inder joined them at the dining table. His breakfast plate lay arranged the way he liked it, on a table mat, and the cutlery was all neatly set up. On the plate were arranged two fried eggs, four slices of bread, a slab of Amul butter, and six peeled almonds. Alongside stood a glass of hot milk and a bottle of marmalade.

"So today is your first day at school, huh girls!"

"Yes, Papa," said Mala, showing off her empty glass.

"But I don't like school," said Priya, almost in tears.

"Good girl, Mala. But why don't you like school, darling?" laughed Inder.

"Don't laugh at me."

"Okay, I won't. Why don't you want to go to school?"

"Because I have to get up early and drink this milk," said Priya, tears welling her eyes.

"Milk is good for you, darling," said Inder.

"Priya is a good girl, just you watch, Jungee," said Rekha, anxious that Priya would eventually not drink it. "Come on, Peachy, my darling, let's show Papa how quickly you can drink it."

"In your class, you will have many other children like you, and there will be a teacher too. Remember to be respectful to your teacher because she is there to care for you and share her knowledge with you," said Inder.

"Okay, Papa," said Mala, listening eagerly.

"Mama is also going to be a teacher in the same school. But

you can't go and meet her when you want, as she will be busy teaching other older children," said Inder.

"But she is my mama first," said Priya, touching the glass to her lips.

"She will always be your mama first, Priya. But you can't disturb her, as she is going there to work. And you can't call her 'Mama' - You have to call her Mrs. Sharma or Miss."

"Mrs. Sharma," said Mala to Rekha and giggled.

Priya looked at Mala with a frown and set down her empty glass.

"Good girl! When I come back this evening, tell me stories about your school, okay?"

"Okay, Papa," said Priya as she got up to straighten her uniform and carry her bag.

"I will see you both during recess. I have made sandwiches for lunch. Anandi put the tiffin in my bag and the children's snack boxes and water bottles in their bags," said Rekha tying her bun as she munched on her share of peeled almonds. "Come on, let's go girls. Bye Anandi."

The beaming Anandi bid the family goodbye at the lift. They trooped to Inder's scooter. Rekha sat sideways in her sari, and to keep her sari pleats intact, she made Priya, much to her further displeasure, sit astride between Inder and her. Mala had the advantage of being tinier - stood in the small space in front of Inder holding onto the handle.

They rode through the humid sunny streets of Navy Nagar with Mala enjoying the morning breeze on her face chatting away with Inder while Priya sweated and sulked in between her parents.

Rekha trooped into the school with her ducklings dawdling

behind her. She dropped off the disgruntled Priya and an eager Mala with their class teacher, the slim and smiling Mrs. Goese; and rushed to the staff room to drop off her bag, collect the relevant textbook for her first class of Physics for standard 10; and walked into the chattering assembly that miraculously hushed into silence as soon as Mother Helen took the podium mike.

The 9 am siren rang in the distance as a beaming Inder headed towards Lion Gate.

What a day it is. My small family has reached a new milestone. Rekha has resumed teaching, and our daughters have started school.

. . .

A few days later, Inder was at his workstation when he received a call from the ExO, Lt. Cdr. Hardev Singh. A signal had come in from NHQ.

"Inder, congratulations!"

"Thank you, Sir, but what is this for?"

"You have been selected as one of the officers for a classified Project called AK-25 in Russia. You are to report to INS Angre immediately."

"Oh, thank you, Sir," beamed Inder.

Inder rushed to INS Angre at the given time. In the briefing, he got to know that two Divisional Commanders had got appointed for the secret 25th missile boat squadron. The first was Cdr. B. B. Yadav (Babroo) as head of Div-K251 and, the second was Cdr. A.R. Parti (Amrit) as the head of Div-K252.

"IJ, glad to see you here, mate."

"Likewise, Ike. I'm intrigued about this project," said Inder looking around the room full of officers.

"Do you recollect that news about the Egyptian Navy action using a small Komar class missile boat acquired from Russia?" asked Ike.

"Yes, I remember reading about it in October 1967. She had fired a missile from within Egypt's harbour and sunk the large Israeli destroyer INS Eilat, outside her harbour. That action shook the world news, and I guess every Navy wanted to know about the Russian made weapon systems," said Inder.

"And I guess so did the Indian Navy. I'm sure this project is to gain superiority in warfare," said Ike, while Inder nodded his head.

. . .

Inder returned home that evening to a barrage of stories from his angels. There had been a fancy-dress competition in school, and Rekha had dressed Priya and Mala as an Indian groom and bride, respectively.

"Papa, we won the first prize," squealed Mala jumping up and down, showing off their prize to him.

"Congratulations! Rekha, where did you get these lovely costumes?"

"Maganlal Dresswala on Marine Drive. I had gone there with a few teachers."

"And why is my Piyu sulking?"

"Because I wanted to be the bride and look pretty. Mama made me the groom, wearing a pagdi!" she howled.

"Well, you make a very handsome groom just like your Papa; when I married Mama."

"When? Where was I?" said Priya, looking confused.

"When we got married, darling. You and Mala were not yet born. You look like Papa, so Mama made you the groom."

Priya's face lit up. "Then, I am happy to be the groom. Papa, you know this Mala is so silly. She is supposed to put the garland on me, but she didn't do it only. Mama had to make her put the garland on me, and then I put the garland for her."

"Why didn't you put the garland, Mala?"

"Because Mama said it is my garland."

They all laughed.

"Oh, what a long and tiring day it has been," yawned Rekha, stretching herself.

"I have some good news and bad news."

"Good news first, please."

"I am part of a select group of officers working on an exclusive classified project."

"That is excellent news, Jungee," she said, sitting up with excitement, and then holding her breath, she said, "And the bad news is ...?"

"That the project training is for 11 months, in Russia, and you all can't come along."

. . .

That night they lay in each other's arms, with thoughts about their lives in the year ahead came to them.

"What will life be like without you for so long, Jungee?"

"Difficult, but not impossible. All will be well, darling. I have complete faith in you. And the girls and school will keep you busy."

"Won't it be freezing in Russia?"

"Yes, but the Navy is investing so much on the project, I'm sure suitable clothing will get provided. We will also buy a few things from Chor bazaar - I believe you get good jackets there. Let us not fret too much about what is to come, Rekha. Just let us go with the flow and trust each other to manage," said Inder hugging her tightly.

"Okay, darling. Good night," said Rekha.

Inder slipped into his dreams. The Lion was walking through thick snow, leaving a trail of paw prints behind him as snow showered on the deck of a ship that silently glided into the midnight sky.

. . .

Inder joined 350 others, including the team of officers under Babroo and Amrit, the squadron crew, the technical position crew, and several sailors, in rigorous training to learn Russian from interpreters from Jawaharlal Nehru University, Delhi.

Inder found the language easy to learn and worked hard to memorise the alphabet, words, and understanding of the grammar. The team slowly got acquainted with each other. The Navy provided them with the necessary winter gear to face the challenging weather conditions of Russia.

. . .

The job at St. Joseph's proved to be more than satisfying for Rekha. Like the rest of the staff, she grew to love her Mother Helen's efficiency, resourcefulness, and warmth. Her piety was supreme, and her enthusiasm to look after the poor and needy became an inspiration for Rekha to emulate.

One day Rekha sent the girls to a birthday party from

school. She stayed on to correct a set of journals that were to be handed over to the students the next morning. She bit into a cold samosa from the school tuck shop and drank the rest of her warm Coca-Cola after completing her work.

On her way out of school, she heard Mother Helen conducting mass at the school church. Rekha stepped in and sat on the last pew listening to her sermon. She looked around and took in the beauty of the various representations of the story of Christ on the walls and pillars. Memories of her days in Tambaram flooded back to her. Mass concluded, and she rushed to meet Mother Helen near the altar.

"Rekha! What are you doing here at this hour? Where are your girls?"

"I was correcting journals, Mother, and the girls are at a friend's birthday party. I heard a bit of your beautiful sermon from outside and decided to stay and listen. May I ask you something, Mother?"

"Yes, you may. What is on your mind, my child?"

"Mother, I wish to take communion. I have wanted to for a while now."

"And what made you wish so?"

"There was a time not so long ago when I had almost given up on life. I had started going to church while living with a family in a small south Indian town called Tambaram. My husband went missing in the Dhanushkodi cyclone in December 1964, while I was pregnant with Priya. I had got paralysed due to the stress. Those were dark times, Mother, and there seemed to be no hope. I would fear for the worst. I used to sit on the local church's pews for hours, praying for his safe return. I believe it was Jesus who brought him back to me. My condition improved, and Priya was born eight months later," said Rekha, her eyes welling up.

"Hush, my child. I see you're still holding onto that memory. How is that serving you?"

"As a little girl, I wanted to marry a warrior, but when my husband was in danger, all I wanted was his safety. I was worried, sick. I know I shouldn't think of the past, Mother, but I often wonder, why did I suffer so much when I have harmed no one?"

"Everyone has their share of suffering, Rekha. What do you think?"

"You are right, Mother," sighed Rekha, looking sad.

"I can understand, my dear. You know Jesus got crucified on a cross. And he was made to carry that cross up the mountain to where he got crucified. It was heavy, and he was wounded, and yet he kept going. He bled, facing the rebuke and wounds that people inflicted upon him, and all he said was, *Forgive them, Lord, they know not what they do.*' His weeping mother looked on helplessly. He had so many miracles to his name, yet he did not stop this from happening to himself. Why do you think he did that?"

"I don't know, mother. I had often wondered why he had to suffer when he was the son of God."

"He accepted it because he wanted us to know that if he could have the courage to bear his suffering, so can we. What is destined for us will happen, Rekha, whether good or bad. We have to accept the bad as we do the good. We don't question or deny the good fortune when it happens to us, do we? So, when misfortune happens, why do we shun it and blame others and ourselves? We should move on without holding grudges in our hearts for the people or the situation that brought us harm."

"True, Mother, I don't like any harm coming to my loved ones."

"We are all loved ones of the Lord, my child. And yet he gives us crosses to bear. Some of us have big crosses to carry Rekha, and some have small ones. He wants us to accept them and learn from them. And when we are in the darkest moments of our life, it is then that he is the closest to us."

Mother Helen paused and looked at the statue of Christ. She sighed deeply. "After the darkest night comes the morning, shining its light upon the tiny weeds and the huge banyan tree on the shrubs' flowers in the wild and the rich manicured flower beds; on all sentient beings. Think about that unconditional love, my child, and try to understand it. You will always have peace in your heart. You need not take communion to pray here, Rekha. You are welcome to be in the church whenever you wish to. Pray and sing along, or simply soak in the beauty of the peace it offers. Cheer up, Rekha! By the grace of God, you have a beautiful life and a lot to be thankful for. Enjoy all the beauty that you are blessed with, my dear, and accept the flow of life, while trying to understand why things happen to you."

. . .

On the 25th of June 1969, Patanjli passed away in his sleep. Rekha was devastated. She rushed to be with her family in Jalandhar to perform the last rites and returned with a heavy heart, leaving behind a grieving Sarla. The time for Inder to leave for Russia was coming close, and Rekha had been anxious. Not once did managing the kids, or the house or her job daunt her. But the thought of letting Inder go made her weak. She hugged him on her return, not wanting to let go.

"Anandi is around."

She buried her head into his chest and mumbled, taking in the smells of his body.
"What?"

"I said I don't care."

"Ya lublu tebya," whispered Inder.

"What?"

"It means 'I love you' in Russian."

"Which Russian girl are you going to say that to?"

"No, my darling. I can't have enough of you. No other woman can ever take your place. I learnt it today, and I was blushing in class at the thought of your expression when I say it to you this evening," he said, kissing her forehead and hugging her back warmly.

It will soon be a difficult time for my Rekha once again.

. . .

Before leaving for Russia, Inder took leave and met his parents in Phagwara and then to Jalandhar to meet Sarla. When Rekha opened the door to him a week later, standing along with him was a smiling Sarla.

Mother and daughter embraced and opened their hearts to each other. Priya and Mala looked on and eagerly listened to the endless chatting and stories they shared. Inder felt at peace that Rekha would have her mother's company and emotional support while he was away.

. . .

It was the end of August when Inder bid farewell to his family. Along with the rest of the crew, he was to take a chartered Air India flight to Moscow. This was his first experience with flying. Once in the aircraft, he was greeted by the air hostess, a beautiful lady dressed in a neatly draped sari. "Namaste and welcome aboard, Sir."

"Namaste. Thank you," said Inder awkwardly.

He put his handbag and woollens away into the luggage bin and took his seat next to the window. He was fascinated with the staff's warm hospitality and how things got neatly packed into small spaces. He listened to every word of the safety instructions, and when the aircraft taxied on the runway and picked up speed to take off, he braced himself, holding the arms of his chair tightly. He looked out of the window at the waning lights of Bombay. *My little family is probably sound asleep by now.*

"Sir, would you care for some orange juice this evening?" said the smiling air hostess.

"I will. Thank you," smiled Inder, taking a sip of the fresh juice. *Wow! What luxury!*

Inder's journey was long. They first stopped briefly in Tehran and then flew non-stop to Moscow. They switched to a much larger Aeroflot aircraft, which took them east towards Khabarovsk, a few hundred miles north of Vladivostok, on Russia's east coast. From Khabarovsk, they flew in much smaller jets to Vladivostok. They drove through the city to the jetty and took a 45-minute ferry ride to their final destination, a secluded island called Russki Ostrov - their home for the next several months.

. . .

The squadron in-charge, a Russian officer called Commodore Navichenko, was a tall, handsome, and well-built man. He could easily pass off as a film star. He took his job very seriously-he ensured all the team's needs got met, and all rules got understood.

The Indian officer-in-charge of the Indian Naval detachment, Cdr. MB Kunte greeted the exhausted squadron warmly with a hot Indian meal on their arrival. After eating, they got

JUNGEE

assigned their living spaces. Commodore BN Thapar, the appointed Commander of the 25th Missile Boat Squadron, flew in from NHQ, along with his team, which included:

Cdr. VL Koppikar, Chief Staff Officer
Cdr. AK Ghosh, Squadron Engineering Officer
Cdr. S Sikand, Squadron Electrical Officer
Lt. Cdr. Kwatra, Deputy Squadron Engineering Officer
Lt. Cdr. RB Suri (Bunny), Squadron Missile and Gunnery Officer
Lt. AK Verma, Deputy Squadron Electrical Officer
Sub. Lt. Nath, SD-Control of L
Sub. Lt. Sood, SD-Radar of L

The two Division Commanders i.e., Babroo and Amrit, reported to Thapar. Their teams of officers and sailors got divided into eight groups, each of which would be part of one of the eight missile boats acquired from Russia.

The Div-K251 fleet was:
INS Nashak, Cdr. BB Yadav as Commanding Officer (CO) and Div-K251
INS Nirbhik, Lt. Sudhir Issacs - CO
INS Nipat, Lt. Bahadur Kavina - CO
INS Nirghat, Lt. Inderjit Sharma - CO

The Div-K252 fleet was:
INS Vijeta, Cdr. A.R. Parti as CO and Div-K252
INS Vidyut, Lt. B. B. Singh - CO
INS Vinash, Lt. Vijay Jerath - CO
INS Veer, Lt. O. P. Mehta - CO
Lt. Cdr. Ajit Wasu - CO (Additional)

The ferry to Vladivostok was a mile away, and the Training Block was about 2 miles away from the accommodation - North Block for sailors and South Block for officers.

Inder peeped into a classroom on the ground floor of South

393

PRIYA SHARMA SHAIKH

Block. It looked simple and functional. The first floor housed the Div-Ks and senior officers, and the dining hall, while the second floor housed the rest of the project officers, including Inder.

Bahadur and he got allotted a spacious room, a single bed, a desk, a chair, and a chest of drawers. The bathrooms and lavatories at the end of a corridor of rooms that faced each other.

Inder unpacked and settled his things with practiced neatness and sat at his desk overlooking the serenely blue sky above the fairyland-like landscape outside, to write to Rekha.

"It's going to be tough being away from home for so long, huh?" smiled Bahadur walking in on Inder's thoughts.

"Yes, but time will fly once the course starts," said Inder.

"How did your wife take it?"

"I was just thinking of her. She will miss having me around, but she is a tough one, and she will do fine. As for me, I carry a little bit of my world with me wherever I go – this shrine on my desk and a photograph of Rekha and my daughters."

"They are beautiful. What are those?" said Bahadur, pointing to the Lion and the Cow pieces next to the photograph.

"Those are my childhood toys. There is a load of memories around them, from the times I lived in Pakistan before partition. There was a Peacock too, but he seems to have gone missing in transit."

"Wow! Do you remember the partition and your life there?"

"In vivid detail. Living in Tandlianwala, which is now in Pakistan, was the best time of my childhood. Partition took our home and friends. We never really recovered from the wounds of those times. On a lighter note, that is why some course mates call me Pathan," said Inder rolling his eyes.

"Oh yes, I remember hearing of that," laughed Bahadur. "Farida was a bundle of tears. It was so difficult to leave Karl and her. I'm going to miss them, and it's only the second day. God help me!" said Bahadur, looking at a framed photograph of his wife and son.

Inder smiled at Bahadur's expression of warmth for his family and started penning his letter to Rekha. Just as he finished, Jerry stormed into the room.

"Are you guys up for basketball with Bunny and a few of us?"

"Sure," said Bahadur and Inder, together. They looked at each other, smiled, and gave each other a high five and followed Jerry to the play courts below.

. . .

A daily routine soon set in for Inder and Bahadur. Rising early, making their beds, working out, basketball, tea while scanning through the Russian newspaper and the Times of India (a few days late), and finally, bath. While Inder prayed at his shrine, Bahadur, the devout Parsi, murmured prayers on his side of the room dressed in his *sadra kasti*. He was a dedicated practitioner of the Zoroastrian principles of Humata (Good Thoughts), Hukhta (Good Words), and Hvarshta (Good Deeds). Like Inder, Bahadur was neat and clean, pleasant natured, and above all, gave Inder his privacy.

The Russian they learnt in India proved grossly inadequate. The instructor, a Russian woman, was a stern taskmaster. She spoke to them only in Russian, even though she understood and spoke English. Inder and the Maharashtrian and Bengali crew members picked up the language sooner as its grammar rules were similar to their mother-tongues.

The learning apart, the squadron found ways to enjoy their new home away from home. Bunny's room became the hub

PRIYA SHARMA SHAIKH

for evening chatter and games. At the on-campus club, the dance-shy Inder clapped while the rest of the team gyrated to Hindi film songs. After a few drinks, the dancing reached another hysteria level with the enthusiastic dancers who believed they were Shammi Kapoor. Inder sang one song request after another, making them get emotional and miss their families all the more. They also played football, basketball, and hockey, and when the weather permitted, they took hikes in the jungles of Russki Ostrov.

They also visited Vladivostok every other week, a well-planned hilly city with wide roads winding up and down and brown and grey 3-4 storeyed buildings. The city center teemed with people going about their business on foot or in trams and a rare few in cars. Inder enjoyed interacting with the storekeepers and felt good conversing with them in Russian. Inder mostly window shopped, buying only essentials – *I will take home a neat kitty*. On one visit, he watched a French film called Angelique, dubbed in Russian, the storyline being around a girl and her adventurous escapades. That evening Inder wrote to Rekha - *I hope our daughters too will be as courageous as Angelique.*

Within a month of their arrival, autumn had set in. The weather changed, and the trees began to drop their cover of green. The winds became chillier, and clothing layers piled up for the squadron.

The language training lasted three months, after which they got examined uniquely. Each of them picked a chit of paper from a bowl. In each chit was written a topic. They got some time to think about it. They then had to speak on it in Russian in front of the class for a few minutes. They were graded on a scale of 1-5 by a panel of teachers and a squadron member. As per Indian standards, below three was a failure. Inder was intrigued to know that nobody got graded below two in Russia as a student's effort was respected.

JUNGEE

Inder cleared with flying colours with a score of 5. The team was declared proficient enough in Russian to take on the technical study of missile boats.

...

It was the start of November, and snow had come down in full measure, covering everything with a blanket of white. Inder rushed about his morning routine to get to a meeting called by Navichenko. They had already been divided into various classes to commence their technical training. Inder was in the Commanding Officer's Class, comprising Babroo, Amrit, BB, Jerry, Inder, Omi, Ike, Bahadur Ajit, and Koppikar and Bunny from NHQ. Navichenko had a calm face as he reviewed the group sitting in front of him.

"Winter is just starting, and with time it will get tougher and make you wonder how we Russians survive. And yet, our land has its beauty that I hope you, too, will discover. A few words of caution – it is best to stay warm when you step out, as negligence of adequate cover can make you fall very sick. The temperatures will eventually dip to -40 degrees centigrade. And in the winter, if you touch your ear lobes or nose carelessly, you could break them, and you won't even realise the pain because they will be frozen. Also, be careful not to touch any metals with your bare skin to avoid frostbite. Your training will go on even as the toughest weather conditions will set upon us, so get mentally prepared for tough times ahead." Navichenko had an officious smile on his face, and he nodded as if assuring himself that all was good.

Like the rest of the squadron, Inder tried to adjust to the plummeting temperature, wondering how one could admire an endlessly white landscape. The lake froze with up to eight feet of ice below its surface. He walked on the frozen waters and was amazed at the sight of some local enthusiasts diving into the cold water that they accessed by drilling a hole into

PRIYA SHARMA SHAIKH

the thick ice, while others patiently angled for fish! The ferry to Vladivostok had to get chained to a tug that cut through the ice to take them across the river.

In the city, Inder found kids and adults alike covered head to toe with fur revealing only their pink faces, skiing up and down pathways and hills. Navichenko got the unit some skis too. When Inder got his turn, he fell face forward, but after trying a few times, he figured the technique and was eventually one of the few that could ski with ease. He also enjoyed biting into ice cream.

As Navichenko had said, it was a challenging terrain, and it sure took some time getting used to, but Inder could well appreciate the beauty of Russian winter.

. . .

Life without Inder was difficult for Rekha. Her days got spent like clockwork, managing home, work, the children, and Sarla. The routine eased the pain of separation. Anyone leaving for Moscow would collect letters from the families – and Rekha's letter always got accompanied by Priya and Mala's drawings and the most recent photographs of them.

There was not a single day that she did not receive a letter from Inder, telling her about his day, and that he missed them. One day, along with the letter, came a slim package, which was a small record. Rekha took the kids to a friend's place to play it on their record player. The disc rotated as Rekha, and the children listened keenly. Suddenly, Inder's voice came through.

"Kaun hai jo sapnon mein aayaa, kaun hai jo dil mein samaayaa, lo jhukk gaya aasmaan bhi, ishq mera rang laaya. O Priya a a a a, O Priya a a a a ... Hello Rekha, this is your Jungee here. How are my three angels? Priya, Mala, and you? Winter has set in, and it is getting colder with each passing day. The training is great and very intensive. I miss you all a lot."

Priya was delighted, while Mala sulked.

"Why didn't he sing for me? I'm *katti* with him," she whimpered into Rekha's lap.

Rekha got home and wrote Inder a letter stating Mala's anger with him, that she was amused to see her break into a tantrum, as she usually never complained.

In one letter, Inder sent photographs of himself.

"Who is this uncle Mama?" said Priya looking puzzled, at the photograph of a man in a fur jacket and cap.

"It is your Papa. Don't you recognise him, darling?"

"This is our Papa," she pointed to a photograph of a younger Inder.

"Darling, this is your Papa. He is in woollen clothes as it is freezing where he has gone to study, darling. It will take some time before he returns."

"Will he come home for my birthday?" asked Mala, looking up from her toys.

"I don't know about that, my Malkin, but I promise we will have a party for both your birthdays."

"Will we call all my friends?

"Yes, all your friends from class and the building. We will cut a cake and play games, Mama will stitch new party frocks for you and buy you new shoes too," gushed Rekha.

The girls shrieked with excitement and hugged Rekha.

She realised that they were forgetting Inder. From that day on, every weekend, she dressed up in Inder's clothes, pretending to be him and made them play a game called 'Finding Jungee Darling,' wherein she would hide, and their job was to snoop around the house and find her. Each time they found her, they rejoiced and sang a self-created rhyme.

Jungee Darling, come along,
You've been away, for far too long,
Its time to come home and sing a song!

Jungee Darling, come and stay,
Enough of study; its time to play,
With your angels, be happy and gay.

They sang in a chorus loudly, marching in a small parade around the house, saluting to the much amused Sarla and Anandi.

One morning Rekha woke up the girls excitedly. "Mala, Priya, get up quickly, Papa has sent a big parcel for you."

The girls rushed into the living room, rubbing the sleep from their eyes. The package was bigger than them, and it was wrapped tightly with brown paper and strings. They helped Rekha unravel the packaging, and when the covers were off, they all broke into gasps. Inside the box lay two beautiful sleeping dolls. Priya bent down to pick up a doll and cried out in amazement as the doll's lashes opened, revealing beautiful marine blue eyes. Mala hurriedly grabbed her doll too. The dolls were almost as tall as them with blonde hair tied into neat plaits. Their clothes were changeable, and their limbs moved. The girls were mesmerised and beside themselves with joy. The dolls became their inseparable companions, and the anchor - "Our Papa sent them for us."

. . .

Their study continued, as promised by Navichenko. They began learning about the missile construct, its assembly, and its stripping in minute detail. The Tactical Instructor taught them about the ideal firing range of the missile. "15-18 miles

JUNGEE

from the target is the ideal range," he said with aplomb, "It will give the enemy less time to pick you up for a counter strike." He also prepared them for how to get into swift action at wartime. After this, they studied the radars and the navigation equipment.

Inder was intrigued to learn that each of the eight tiny missile boats, made of Duraluminum, weighed a total of 250 tonnes. The boat had a lower than usual upper deck, which was barely six feet above sea level.

Her mast was her most unique characteristic that stood at the height of 30 feet above sea level, on the top of which was mounted the surface specific detection, tracking, and acquisition radar called the Rangout.

Each boat was built to sail at high speed with three modified aircraft engines capable of producing 4000 horsepower, and a water-based cooling mechanism. She could endure a 10-hour sortie and do 25 knots on a full tank, but at 70% fuel, she could sail at her highest speed of 35 knots! Most of the boat's equipment had got miniaturised to reduce weight to attain full speed when required. A water tank of 5 tons got provisioned to allow for the Indian team's daily hygiene needs.

Each boat had four P-15 missiles, which had a combination of lethal chemicals that would explode when they made contact. Ignition would cause the gas release from the missile's rear to propel it forward with full force. A booster rocket with an explosive cryogenic solid fuel would give the missile the initial altitude and propulsion before it propelled at a higher speed towards the target. The missile's in-built navigation system then focused on its target, until its homing head made contact to vanquish it.

...

By the end of January 1970, the temperatures dipped to -40 degrees centigrade. One overcast morning, the team of COs was on board one of the missile boats to watch a live demonstration of fitting the equipment on board. By the time they got done, a bone-chilling blizzard was roaring outside. They were informed to stay put on board as their transport bus had frozen. After waiting for a while, anxiety started surging, and the Squadron Commander decided they would walk back to base.

Darling Rekha,

I hope Priya, Mala, Mummy, and you are well. How is your job? Today the whole squadron walked in a shower of thick ice-like snow for a kilometer to the base. The snowflakes were as sharp as needles and would have cut us had we not been careful. It was nothing short of a nightmare, but it all ended well, and we reached the base safely!

I am happy to share that our technical course training has finally come to an end, and we got administered another examination. I scored 5+, which is very good. We are entering the last leg of our training, and it will soon be time to see you again. This place has enriched me with a vast amount of knowledge, some fantastic experiences, and I have built friendships for a lifetime with Bunny, Bahadur, and BB.

My love to all of you - Jungee

...

By May 1970, the squadron completed the classroom study and was ready to undergo the practical training at sea. They had by now learnt how to sail the boat, prepare the missile, load and unload it, and firing it. Like other commanding officers, Inder would have the opportunity to sail his ship with his crew to get a complete hands-on experience and ensure that his crew understood its workings.

His core team included his ExO, Sub. Lt. ADS Lazaro, nicknamed Tony. He was witty, amiable, and excellent at his job.

Lt. SC Dua, the engineering officer with a strong Punjabi accent, was in-charge of the engines and diesel generators. Sub. Lt. KM Rao, a tall man with drooping shoulders, was the Missile and Gunnery Officer.

Inder went through the brief to understand the expected deliverables. He then held a meeting with his team about his understanding of the brief and answered each of their questions. The meeting got each of them to have the same understanding, and they sailed with confidence. Inder felt a sense of power managing the controls of the missile boat. He and his crew experienced all kinds of situations as a part of the practical training for several days - regular sorties, emergency ones, faults in the engine, steering gear breakdowns, missile attacks under challenging situations, fuel leaks, failed radars, etc.

Once the practical exercises got completed, each team got tested for every possible situation at sea by a Russian Rear Admiral and his team. They were tough to please and expected nothing short of the best possible performance. Inder's team came through with flying colours, as did the rest of the squadron's teams. The Rear Admiral was happy, and he cleared all of them for the final missile-firing training, where each of the two divisions would fire a P-15 missile. The two Div-Ks collected their respective divisional teams on their respective ships.

Babroo and his team, including Inder, were on INS Nashak, and Parti and his team on INS Vijeta. A target got set for both the boats. Everyone got on full alert!

Assembled in the bridge along with Babroo, Inder looked on keenly for the process to unfold. He felt an adrenalin rush as the target got detected and aligned with the radar. Just before the firing, the ship dramatically shut down all her air passages and covered the bridge's glass panes with thick steel blinds;

PRIYA SHARMA SHAIKH

to avoid damage to the glass and crew from the blast's intense glare. Babroo pressed the button to fire the P-15 missile. It pushed through its moorings, making the boat heave back with force, shaking up her crew, and within seconds it was on its towards the target. Sweat collected on Inder's brow as he and the rest of the crew stood stunned on seeing the fumes and flames that emerged in the distance after the impact. The target got decimated within minutes! As Inder joined in the loud cheering on the bridge, he knew they had got equipped with a weapon that could prove lethal to any enemy that crossed their paths. With the missile launch test behind them, all the boxes for their training got checked. It was time for the squadron to go home.

...

It was a humid Sunday morning at the end of July 1970, when Inder reached Navy Nagar. His gaze went up to the balcony of his home as the taxi approached their street. Nobody was in sight. He looked around as he waited to collect the change. The roads were wet from a recent shower, and the air had the heady smells of wet mud.

I have missed this smell so much! He took a deep breath and could not stop smiling. Not much had changed in the 11 months he was away. The weeds around the play area looked overgrown. The Gulmohar tree was taller. Its orange blossoms swayed playfully, while several wafted in the breeze and sprinkled the ground with colour.

He thanked the cabbie, picked up his bag and holdall, and walked towards the entrance quickly. The lift didn't come down soon enough for the eager Inder. So, he took the stairs, lunging over them two at a time, all the way to the fourth floor. He was sweating and breathing heavily when he pressed the doorbell. He smiled as he heard the scamper of tiny footsteps and the shrieks of a squabble to open the door. The door finally opened a crack. *It's my Ladli!* Inder beamed, as tears clouded his eyes. Priya looked up at him, puzzled.

She looks beautiful, and oh my God, so much taller. Her hair was oiled and scraggly, touching her shoulders. She had a missing tooth. And behind her pulling the door wide open, appeared the beady-eyed Mala, with oily hair tied into two loosened pigtails.

"Hello, my darlings," said Inder softly, grinning at them. He stood there holding on to the beauty of the moment with emotion filling his heart, as his daughters stood there gaping at him.

"Who is it, Priya?"

My Rekha!

"Mama, one Uncle, has come," said Mala doing a comical strut and going back inside.

"Priya! Don't you recognise me?" Inder smiled and sat down.

"No," she said, grinning and shaking her head, fidgeting with the gap in her teeth.

"I am your Papa, my darling," said Inder stretching his arms to her.

She pulled back, putting her hands behind her back, unsure of how to react to the stranger who stood before her. Just then, Rekha leaped forward past Mala and Priya, running straight into his arms, crying out aloud. "Jungee, you are home!"

"I'm back, darling," he said, hugging her back and leading the way into the living room.

"Namaste, Mummy," he said, bending to touch Sarla's feet.

"Live long, my son. It has been a long time of separation for you all as a family. May you achieve great heights and happi-

PRIYA SHARMA SHAIKH

ness in your life," she said, blessing his head and gushing over him with tears of joy, seeing her daughter's family reunited after so long.

Priya twiddled her fingers, and Mala climbed onto the sofa, balancing precariously on its arm with a silly grin. They watched the outburst of emotions from a distance.

"Oye, my Rana Sanga, and Ladli come to Papa. They have grown so much!"

"Girls, this is Jungee Darling. He sent you the dolls. Come and hug Papa," urged Rekha.

They walked up to him shyly, and he took them into his arms, embracing them together. His heart swelled with love as he looked at his family.

"They look beautiful, and so do you," said Inder, looking at his wife fondly, just as Sarla discreetly herded the girls into the other room.

. . .

Saturday, the 12th of September 1970, was a flurry of activity at the Sharma household. Priya had just turned five on the 2nd of the month, and Mala was to turn four on the 15th. And as promised to them, Rekha had planned a party. Lists got made of all their friends, and hand-made invitations got sent out. Fifteen kids confirmed, and that meant provisioning for a minimum of 30 people as mothers were likely to accompany their children.

Rekha stitched beautiful white and pink lace frocks for the girls and bought them matching hairbands, white lace stockings, and white patent leather shoes. Closer to the event, Rekha and Inder visited Crawford Market and came back with bags full of paper caps, rollout whistles, paper plates, glasses, and goodies to stuff in the return gift baskets - sweets, balloons, a whistle, and a clickety-clack. On the day of the birthday, Inder decorated the house with festoons while Rekha baked and cooked all day long with Anandi.

The photographer arrived, and Inder switched on the music. Guests started arriving at 5 pm, armed with gifts. Priya soaked in the attention, while Mala kept a close eye on the count of gifts.

Oh, who is that looking at me with perky blue eyes? It was the Peacock poking his head from the balcony, flashing his beautiful feathers. Inder smiled and felt a childlike joy as he joined the children in the games.

When the cake lit with candles was brought in by Rekha, looking gorgeous in a beautiful self-tailored chudidaar-kurta, Inder couldn't help evince at the magic she managed to unfold with her love.

I wish I could be a child once again. He sighed and joined in to clap his hands as the candles got blown out, and everyone sang HAPPY BIRTHDAY. He had never experienced a party like this in his growing years. It was a perfect Kodak moment, and the photographer clicked, preserving the memories forever.

...

In January 1971, camouflaged on merchant ships, stripped-down versions of the missile boats, arrived in Calcutta, the only port with a heavy-duty crane capacity of 200 tonnes. The unloading and reassembly of each boat got supervised by Russian technical officers that had accompanied the boats.

The first boat to be commissioned was of INS Vinash on the 20th of January 1971, with Jerry taking charge as her CO. The next in the queue was Inder. He took charge of INS Nirghat on the 27th of January 1971, along with his crew. The engines of both the boats were given trials in the Hoogly river before sailing out to a large ship in the deep sea. From here, they got towed to Bombay as the Navy wanted to conserve engine hours.

At Bombay, they got greeted by the Commander in Chief Western Naval Command. Although it was a moment of achievement and pride for the Navy and the squadron, all aspects of the boats' arrival and details remained classified. Even access to and knowledge about the ships' leadership, sorties, and commissioning were limited to the squadron and NHQ. By May 1971, all eight missile boats got docked at Bombay harbour.

Each day, Inder's team practiced the loading, unloading, and preparing the missiles and checking the efficiency of all the components involved in firing a missile. Everything got calibrated, and when they felt ready, they got scheduled to do a practice firing on a target, to check and prove the efficiency of the system and the team.

It was a nervous moment for Inder's team on board Nirghat – He assured them that although it was an expensive missile, their training was behind them, and they knew what to do. When they fired the missile, it left its mooring and shot forward with great speed into the horizon, making a direct hit!

The same exercise got done by the other missile boats too. All the teams of the squadron were ready for action.

Inder congratulated his team on a job well done. As he spoke, he saw the Lion walk slowly behind them up to the stern, roaring into the sea.

– – –

CHAPTER 16: TO FIGHT OR NOT TO FIGHT, THAT IS THE QUESTION

December 1971: India Pakistan War

About 2400 kilometres east of Bombay, late in the night, Buchki's eyes blinked open. She lifted the mosquito net and crept out of her four-poster teak bed, making as soft movements as possible. Her mother, Suparna, who was sleeping with her for the night, was facing away and fast asleep. Her snores were louder lately, and they had a strange watery sound to them. Something about them felt comfortable. They talked to her; about her mother's possible thoughts and opinions that went unsaid.

Buchki's father, Professor Subir Das, was an intellectual with an open mind and a man of few words; but words that asserted people to do what he wanted to do. The community respected hugely for all the work he had done in education. He was the family patriarch. At the same time, her mother was an unusually timid woman whose world revolved around her daughter. Buchki was closest to her mother and turned to her for everything. She would often put her head in her mother's soft lap, and her mother would sing to her and move gentle fingers through Buchki's long tresses, sending her off into a dream world with oh, so much ease.

Buchki paused at the side of her bed, looking at the figure of her mother. She then turned to tiptoe past the sleeping house-help, into the bathroom at the far-left end of the large bedroom. The natural blue night light seeped in through the open wooden slats of the window. She hurriedly stripped out of her nightie and reached out behind the flush tank to pull out a cloth bag. Her taut nipples shone on her full breasts, and her long hair swayed over her shapely buttocks as she moved. She hurriedly dressed in dark slacks and tunic and tied her hair into a tight bun. Once done, she covered her head and face with a scarf. She wore the bag across her body, grabbed a stick hidden behind the door, and peered out of the bathroom. The quietness prevailed.

She walked lithely into the living room with a pair of mojhris and the stick in her hand. Lines of beddings of the guests that had arrived a day prior crowded the room. They, too, were in varied sounds of deep slumber. She moved to the main door and turned the latch slowly. A noise from the bedroom on the top floor stopped her, and she ducked behind the sideboard. She looked intently up at the stairway, waiting to see if anyone appeared. There was no movement. She waited a few more moments, breathed in, and quickly let herself out of the house.

Breathing a sigh of relief, she ran barefoot towards the main gate. The watchman was fast asleep in his chair, wrapped in his tattered shawl, with his head thrown back. She opened the small gate a crack and turned to take a brief look back at her house, and then disappeared into the shadows of the moonlit night.

Her breath quickened as she walked briskly past the darkened homes of Dhanmondi, finding her way with just the moonlight and a lone streetlamp. She reached a small alcove by the lake, hidden within the shrubbery overlooking the water, and sat down to catch her breath. She looked at her wristwatch. He had said, 2 am. She sighed deeply and rested back.

JUNGEE

...

It was a bright, sunny afternoon. Hundreds of students were milling around the university campus for the scheduled annual inter-college debate. The subject of discussion was 'Socialism vs. Capitalism.'

Buchki was the undisputed beauty of Dhaka College. Her deep-set dimples appeared when she smiled, dark, well-arched eyebrows, and a finely chiselled nose, all striking features that complimented her oval-shaped face. Many a boy had fallen victim to the combination of her smoky black kohl eyes and full pink lips. She was tall, slim, and always dressed in pure cotton saris, matching them with a well-fitting short-sleeved blouse, and a bindi and bangles.

It was March 1970 then, and she was in the second year of her bachelor's degree. She wore a pink and grey sari. Her long open hair swished below her waist as she moved. She finished lectures for the day and walked towards the lake behind the college grounds to meet her friends for some puchka.

That was when she saw him for the first time. The first thing she noticed about Razzaq Mir was his panther-like walk as he strolled through the college gate. She saw him and then looked again. Unusually tall for a Bengali man. As he got closer, she could see he had an air of unassumed ease. His frame was broad, and he walked at a what's the need to hurry pace. He was dressed casually, with a scraggly mop of black hair. A neglected stubble surrounded his deep brown lips. *A smoker, perhaps.*

She had looked straight into his intense black eyes as he approached her. In those brief moments, something about how he looked at her, and then looked away, tingled her being. She felt a connection. There seemed an unexplainable sadness and anger in them. He was a competitor in the debate, and he was

PRIYA SHARMA SHAIKH

representing Dhaka City College. She dragged her friends to the assembly hall and pushed her way into the girls' section. The competition was already underway.

He spoke with poignant confidence. "... In the present state, socialism, followed by capitalism in the future, is the only solution for our country." The crowd went berserk, clapping and cheering him. His intensity stayed in her thoughts for days.

. . .

A few months later, on a rainy June morning, she again saw Razzaq's familiar frame in the university hallway. He was filling out a form, as was she. His hair was longer, and it's locks veiled his face. She bit her lower lip and stared hard to catch a proper glimpse. *Long hair! Oh, Ma! I want to know him so much. But what shall I say? Oh, just say something, Buchki. Anything!*

Razzaq pushed his hair off his face to reveal a clean-shaven look that showed his sharp jawline and high cheekbones. Gosh! He looks even more handsome. He looked up, and their eyes met. He held her gaze briefly and then blinked and smiled.

She looked away immediately. Razzaq handed his form to the clerk at the counter and walked towards her. *Oh, my gosh, he is coming here.* She looked up at him. The twinkle in my eyes will give me away.

"Stop staring, or I'll think you're in love with me," he whispered.

She blushed and looked down at her form, pretending to be interested in it. Her body tingled at their bodies' proximity, and she bit her lip. She submitted her admission form and turned to look at Razzaq.

"I never forget a beautiful face. I know I have seen you before," said Razzaq in a deep drawl, "Dhaka College! Some months ago, at the debate. Right?"

She nodded, and he said, "Since you must know my name, lady, may I know yours?"

"Aparna. Aparna Das."

"Ms. Das, it's raining. Will you walk with me?"

"Umm," she said, looking up at him hesitantly, not knowing what to say. She smiled awkwardly and looked towards her white Ambassador parked outside the campus. Her driver Khairoon was not in sight.

"I assume that is a yes unless you have to go," he said, following the trail of her sight to the car. She drew her attention back to Razzaq.

"Let's walk," she said, concealing a smile. She opened her umbrella and gestured him to walk with her. His arm touched her bare skin, and she felt his warmth. She could barely breathe.

"What subjects are you studying, Ms. Das?"

"Literature Honours."

"So, is Shakespeare your muse?

"Tagore is my most favourite. And of course, Shakespeare's writing is so intriguing, but also Twain, Elliot, Dickens, Jane Austen. And Wordsworth's poetry is so soulful. Just so many greats," she smiled.

He stepped out of her umbrella, outstretched his arms to the falling rain, and then looked at her with a steady gaze. The raindrops pelted on his head, flattening his locks and soaking his body. He smiled. His teeth glistened like pearls. She started to speak, but stopped herself as his look held hers. It felt magical. "I have something to share. Would you care to listen?" he said aloud.

She nodded and laughed and shivered with excitement. Razzaq stepped onto a bench, even as the rain came down stronger and recited Daffodils by William Wordsworth aloud.

"I wandered lonely as a cloud
That floats on high o'er vales and hills,
When all at once I saw a crowd,
A host, of golden daffodils;
Beside the lake, beneath the trees,
Fluttering and dancing in the breeze.

Continuous as the stars that shine
And twinkle on the Milky Way,
They stretched in never-ending line
Along the margin of a bay;
Ten thousand saw I at a glance,
Tossing their heads in sprightly dance.

The waves beside them danced; but they
Out-did the sparkling waves in glee;
A poet could not but be so gay,
In such a jocund company.
I gazed—and gazed—but little thought
What wealth the show to me had brought.

For oft, when on my couch I lie
In vacant or in pensive mood,
They flash upon that inward eye
Which is the bliss of solitude;
And then my heart with pleasure fills,
And dances with the daffodils."

Razzaq shivered next to her under the umbrella after his dramatic performance ended and said, "It is my favourite poem. Ms. Das, you and I are going to be friends for life. What say?"

"You are crazy. Do you study literature too?" She gasped at

his boldness.

"Just for two years, and then I chose to major in Political Science. Tea?"

"Yes, please."

They stopped under the makeshift awning of a wayside stall, and he bought two teas and a cigarette, as she closed the umbrella.

So, he is a smoker. She watched as he put the cigarette to his lips and lit it, and then blew smoke into the sky away from her.

"So, that's why you speak with such confidence on the subject of government."

"Yes and no. My studies did contribute in a small way, and Nehru, Gandhi, Stalin, Mao, Lenin, Churchill, and Roosevelt inspire me. I've read most of the works of Wordsworth and Shakespeare and Tagore. But what truly gave me the command is my liberation struggle work with Mujibda."

"Freedom is my birth right, huh?"

"Everyone deserves to be free. As do you m 'lady," he said, taking a deep drag while looking at her steadily with a smile. She looked into his eyes self-consciously and smiled.

"Yes, but it seems impossible. In the end, the West will squelch all our attempts and have their way. Where have we had success yet? Mujibda and so many others have been trying for so many years. Matters and carnages are just getting worse. I have stopped reading the newspaper. It is sickening."

"Some would label that as escapism," he said, blowing smoke rings into the air. "It's time we caught the bull by its horns and got our way of life back. What you have seen or heard is nothing. The worst is yet to come, Ms. Das," he said grimly, as his jaw hardened, and his voice trailed off.

PRIYA SHARMA SHAIKH

"Stop calling me, Ms. Das," she said.

"Okay," he smiled, "Should I call you by your *daak naam* then? What is it anyway?"

"Buchki," she said, looking embarrassed.

"And to be fair, mine is Mamun."

They both smiled self-consciously at each other, feeling warmth as their wet bodies stood together under the roadside shack. They sipped tea, smiled, and watched the rain make patterns along the road. Time stood still for Buchki. It was a chance to say how much she thought of him since the last they had met.

"I have to get going," he said, suddenly making her snap out of her moment of fantasy. He stubbed the cigarette and extended a hand to her. She took it, and he held on firmly longer than usual, with a telling smile in his eyes, "Until next time. Sayonara, m'lady."

Her heart flitted like a butterfly after he left. She watched him recede into the distance until he blurred into the rain. On the way back to Dhanmondi, she rolled her window down to take in the odour of wet earth – it would always remind her of Razzaq.

. . .

Buchki looked at her watch again and then gazed at the starry night. Sushmita had been so wrong about Razzaq being a worthless vagabond from the suburbs. She had argued with me for the first time.

They had been eating puchkas outside the college, while Buchki unremittingly spoke about her new beau. "He is intelligent. He looks good. What a walk! He is so cultured. He is respectful – the perfect gentleman. And his command on pol-

416

itics gives me goosebumps."

"He is a Muslim, Buchki," Sushmita had said.

"So, what! They believe in Allah and have a different way of life. My heart melts when he turns to look at me. Nothing seems to matter more than him at that moment. Is this love, Sushmita?"

"No! It is stupidity. You've met him properly just once, and he is a freedom fighter. All of these things smell like trouble to me. You are mad," Sushmita had yelled, before pushing a puchka into her mouth.

. . .

She thought back to the day in the car after she met with Razzaq in the rain. Looking out of the window, she had chuckled with delight.

Meeting Razzaq was unbelievable. His clean-shaven look is even better! Ma will be impressed. He dresses so smartly too. And oh my God, Daffodils! How unreal was that? Buchki darling, are you falling in love?

She beamed, and her head nodded vehemently to her inner voice. YES! No, silly, it is too soon. But what about the butterflies and the excitement I am feeling? How do I explain that? She threw her head against the car seat, revelling in her thoughts. Her attention was drawn to Khairoon, looking at her curiously in the rear-view mirror.

"You should keep the window shut," he said, with concern in his voice, "There is news of attacks on Hindus again."

She blinked back into her senses, sat up, rolled up the window, and drew the curtain to veil herself from the world.

"Who was that boy?" persisted his intrusion.

"Which boy?" she looked at him nervously.

"The boy in the checked waistcoat that you have been talking to for the past hour."

"Oh, he was telling me about his work in the liberation movement. I told him I don't have an interest in joining political activities," said Buchki casually, making her hair into a tight bun. "Dada, I respect you because I have grown up watching you serve our family, but it is not your place to keep a tab on me. I will have to report to Baba that you were missing from the car for so long," she said, fixing her stare at his eyes in the rear-view mirror.

. . .

Buchki fidgeted with her scarf and looked at her watch again.

Falling in love with Razzaq was the best thing that had happened to her. She had a string of admirers, but he was different. Vivid memories of all their meetings came to her. They had met several times after that impromptu rainy day. In the very nook, where she sat - so much had happened.

. . .

Sitting alongside each other in the alcove one rainy August day, they talked for hours until the daylight merged into the emerging pink and orange-hued evening light.

"Twilight is mystical," gasped Razzaq, as the clouds thundered in the distance.

"It is, but I prefer dawn. It symbolises new beginnings." She hugged her knees tightly and turned her head on her knees to look at him.

He also turned to look at her. Their conversation came to a sudden stop. His eyes smiled at her playfully. She looked ahead, feeling conscious of his stare. He adjusted a lock of her hair so to view her dimpled profile. He took a deep breath and sighed at how beautiful she looked. He then moved his fingers along her cheek and her ear. She kept her gaze on the horizon and smiling at how his touch felt so right, warm. It created a desire in her that she had never felt before and she was unsure of how to react. *What could emerge if he continues to stare at me thus?*

And as if on cue, he reached out and gently turned her face towards him, looking intently at her dark eyes and moving his gaze to her sensual lips. She wanted to say something, about how she was feeling; but before she could speak, he bent his head and touched his mouth to moisten her quivering lips. He paused and bit his lower lip, tasting her, looking at her, to seek permission.

Her eyelids felt heavy, and she clutched his shirt, to lean into him as the clouds overhead crackled with lightning, and a heavy rain burst through.

"Oh, Razzaq," she whispered, moving towards him.

He silenced her feeble protest by kissing her passionately while his hands slipped into her loose hair and along her back, gently moving her body towards his. Her pallu slipped, revealing her cleavage. He gasped and enveloped her in his strong arms, fiercely pressing his lips against hers, biting them with increased urgency. He took in her body's scents and smothered her face and neck with his wet kisses. Buchki submitted to the rhythm of his body and the movements of his hands along her body. And when he pressed his face against her breasts, nibbling and kissing them, she groaned in ecstasy. He emerged breathless, pulling away and then clung on again.

"Oh! Razzaq, stop, please," she said abruptly and moved away, feeling surprised at the amount of passion that sizzled between them in such a short time. She gathered her pallu that was trailing on the grass, and covered her heaving breasts, and tried to catch her breath. He protested, but she nervously straightened her hair and nervously stretched her trembling hand out to see if it was still raining. It was down to a drizzle. She got out in the rain.

"It's raining. I should go Razzaq," she said, turning away from him, her body still tingling with the excitement. "I am going insane, and things are sure to get out of control."

"But they are out of control, Aparna because I can't believe how madly I love you. I can't stop thinking of you. I want you to be mine forever," he protested and roughly turned her around to make her face him. He held her at the waist and pulled her hips towards him, as she clenched his shirt and looked into his eyes.

"I love you too, Razzaq, and I want to be yours forever," she mumbled with emotion.

"Then that is all we need," he said, feeling breathless.

He silenced her with his finger on her lips, looking at her as she threw back her head, letting the rain wet her face without care. He kissed her again and again, making her sigh and call out his name in whispers, again and again. She finally hugged him and buried her face within the hair on his chest, wanting to submit to him entirely at that very moment. She swayed to the sound of his breath, the dripping water and chirping birds, until their breathing settled into a lull. The rain stopped. He sighed and she looked around hurriedly.

"Are you scared of something Aparna?" he asked, holding her chin.

"Yes, I fear for what people may think of our love. We live in a ruthless society."

"We made the society, and we have the power to change it."

"But do we have the power? Can you deny we are living

in difficult times? Brothers and friends are up in arms against each other, like we never got independence in 1947."

He sighed and looked away. "It is night. Your parents must worry. I'll walk you home."

"Are you appointing yourself as my guard? I can manage myself."

"This is what I love about you – your confidence to do what you want and the courage to claim what you desire. But there is one truth that I would like to put forth, now that we are talking. I dream of us being together, but I also know that what we desire has no future."

"Don't say that, please. What stops us, Razzaq?"

"My commitment to the liberation movement. I grieve for our nation from the bottom of my heart Aparna. I will sacrifice my very being if need be because we deserve better. It is vital to me, for us, for our country. A better tomorrow is my dream."

"I won't stop you, just as you can't stop my love for you. My waiting for you."

"You don't understand," he said, holding her shoulders and shaking her gently, "I may never return, Aparna. I may die in the struggle," he said.

She put her finger to his lips.

"Hush. Don't speak of death. Whether we marry or not, for me, we are already one. You will always be my treasured love, Razzaq Mir."

. . .

The media screamed news on the Bhola cyclone, which devastated East Pakistan in the first two weeks of November

1970. The water took with it the homes and lives of lakhs of people.

Thousands of students, including Razzaq and Aparna, marched through Dhaka on the 19th of November to protest against the government's slow reaction for aid and relief. Maulana Abdul Khan Bhashani, the peasants' leader, addressed thousands of people at a public gathering, demanding the resignation of Yahya Khan, the President of Pakistan.

Within months the rising political disgruntlement and the cultural xenophobia towards West Pakistan rose. The guerrilla Bengali nationalism came into the fore in many ways. On the 07th of March 1971, Mujibur Rahman of the Awami League stood at the podium at Paltan Maidan to address the multitude that gathered to listen to him. "... This time, the revolution is for freedom. This time, the revolution is for liberation ...," he shouted in Bengali, into the microphone. His voice boomed from the speakers and echoed in the hearts of millions of East Pakistanis who were desperate for change and reached the polity's ears in West Pakistan.

...

Buchki and Razzaq's love and intimacy strengthened with each meeting, and then after some months on the 12th of March 1971, came pain. It was a Sunday morning, and Buchki had just finished eating the puris and mishti doi her mother had prepared. She sat across her Baba. The English news was streaming when they heard a scuffle at the front door. It was Razzaq's father, Mir. He stormed into their living room unannounced, accompanied by two men, and looked straight at Buchki.

"What sort of a daughter have you raised, Subir Da? Do you know that she is a shameful whore? She has spoilt my son's life by having an affair with him for the past several months. Her character is haram and unacceptable in our culture. I am warning you that I will have her picked up if their clandestine activities don't stop immediately."

Subir held up his hand with a collected calm. "Mir sahib, my daughter will be married before the end of next month. Go home in peace," he said unflustered.

Buchki was shocked at the outburst by Mir and her father's response. She sat looking stunned, embarrassed, and scared. That evening Razzaq looked disturbed. There was a showdown in his home too. He had left home for good.

After narrating their own stories, they sat silently, holding each other, looking at the moon's silvery reflection in the water. Silent tears soaked both their cheeks.

"I am leaving, Aparna."

She hugged his warm body, shutting her eyes, taking in his smell as she trembled.

"I am going to war. I have trained hard for this for so many months, Aparna. The revolt is intensifying now, and the West Army is unforgiving. We are amid a ruthless crackdown, and my return is speculative."

"Shh, shh, shh," she said, trying to cover his lips, but this time he held her hand down.

"We have to face the bitter truth, my love. And I want you to promise that you will take care of yourself and not step out of your home. If there is ever a glorious tomorrow, know this, that I will do my best to come back and make you mine. I wish you happiness in life ahead, Aparna. And if you are really to marry another, I will never hold it against you because I know you will do it for your family's respect. And know this...," he stammered and stopped to compose himself. "Wherever you might be in this world when the moon rises into the dark sky every night, I will be thinking of you if I am alive."

He kissed her gently on her lips and then abruptly held her at arm's length.

"I'm sorry if I have hurt you, Aparna. Insha Allah, I will return," he said, looking torn, "Khudahafiz."

"Khudahafiz," she said, as he got up and vanished into the cloak of darkness, leaving her in a pool of tears.

. . .

She stared hard at her wristwatch – 3 am! She heard sounds in the distance coming closer to the alcove, and then they stopped. Perhaps it was an animal. She dared not peek out to see. She waited patiently.

Her father had walked up to her the morning after Mir's disturbing visit. She was nursing her breakfast when he put his hand gently on her head. Her eyes instantly filled with emotion, and she looked up at him with folded hands, "I'm sorry, Baba," her eyes pleaded him to understand what her heart was going through.

"I understand your grief, but nobody beyond these walls will respect your love in these times. You should marry. Will you trust Baba to find you a suitable boy?" he had said in a steady tone.

And she had nodded while her tears flowed incessantly. His words sealed her fate. She was to forget her love and adopt a new mask. Relive her love. Relive life.

. . .

When the small bundle of wedding cards came home, Buchki looked at her groom's name, and her eyes welled up and overflowed. Her name on the card got blotched.

After the Mir escapade, Subir had quickly identified a groom. It was to be a small, only-for-the-core-family affair, in light of the burning unrest.

Aparna Das weds Bikram Das. My wedding is happening. *Oh Ma, can you not help me have the man I love? Every bit of me craves for Razzaq, and all I can do is cry.* She let out a sarcastic laugh.

Her mother stopped knitting and looked at her. *My beautiful child looks distraught, and I can do nothing to help her.*

Bikram, the groom to be, was six years older than Buchki. He was a Professor of Science at the University. She knew him from within their family circles, and although things were hush, family members teased that she had got herself the best catch.

Bikram is a good man, and under other circumstances, I would have celebrated this union. But I cannot love him. Oh, Razzaq, what has become of us? She kept the blotched card with her. Later that day, when Sushmita came over, she put the card discretely into her bag.

"Take this to him, Mita, and tell him I wish to see him one last time. Please."

"See him and do what, Buchki? You cannot be so selfish. Are you willing to ruin your family for your desire? He is doing what he wants to do, and you should do what your Baba wants you to do. It will be best for you. Bikram is a good man. Accept him."

"Bikram is a good man, but I can't marry him. I want to escape with Razzaq to India."

"That is so insane, Buchki! Anyway, the reason I can't help you is that my family is leaving for India. I have come to bid you farewell."

"Oh, no, Mita. You, too, are leaving me," said Buchki with tears in her eyes.

"I have no choice my dear friend. Don't you see the state of the city? Killings and firing are everywhere. That is why I am saying, don't do anything foolish. You might have to pay too heavy a price. Besides, who will be so stupid to take the risk to meet Razzaq now?"

"I will." Buchki got startled and turned around. It was Khairoon.

...

Buchki looked at her hands in the dark. The smell of the dried mehndi was still fresh. It had left a deep brick coloured pattern on her palms. It was finally the day of her wedding, and their country was strife with war. Her wristwatch showed 5 am. There was still no sign of Razzaq. She got a sinking feeling. It will be daybreak soon, and the household will rise to get ready for the big day. Where are you, my Razzaq?

She believed Khairoon – He had told her that he met Razzaq and gave him the card. "He will see you at 2 am tonight at the alcove by the lake. Allah is with you, Buchki," Khairoon had told her in hushed tones. She trusted him. He would not have lied to her.

Razzaq ought to have been here. I just know he will come. I can't leave. Oh, please, Ma, send my love to me, I beg you, Ma.

She heard hurried padded footsteps approaching the alcove, and then an anxious voice called out her name in a loud whisper.

"Aparna!"

She held her breath, quickly covered herself with the scarf, and cautiously crawled out from the shadows.

It was Bikram.

...

The authorities arrested Mujibur for leading the war of independence. The result was colossal unrest, and General Yahya Khan, the President of Pakistan, initiated Operation Searchlight on the 25th of March 1971. Under the wake of this order, atrocities and systematic killing mounted, making the Bengali guerrilla volcano erupt and take on a mammoth-like shape. Several revolutionaries crossed the border to take asylum in India.

On the 26th of March 1971, Chittagong Radio station read out a note written by Mujibur Rahman, which declared Bangladesh free. But the unrest continued. News bulletins everywhere teemed with growing counts of arson, rape, and murder. The world watched in shock the human exodus of Muslims and Hindus from the newly formed Bangladesh.

The refugee camps at Barasat and Taki, some 50 kilometres from Calcutta, India, overflowed with thousands of people. The Indian government and volunteers struggled to manage the unrelenting stream.

. . .

A few months later, on one rainy morning in Bombay, Inder sipped his tea as he poured over the Times of India's headlines. He shook his head and scowled. Rekha looked over his shoulder.

"Gosh! What forlorn expressions! My heart goes out to the children. Nomita just returned from Calcutta. She said that malnourished children and adults are seeping into every possible cranny, huddled together, sleeping, eating and defecating, in the same place."

"Life is precious, and people will do what they have to do to survive."

"But it is all such a mess. Sickness is rife; rotting wounds are

PRIYA SHARMA SHAIKH

drawing pests, medication and sanitation are sparse. It is terrible to see human life treated so poorly, Jungee."

"Thousands arrive every day, darling, so it is bound to be chaotic. The government is doing its best."

"It's unbelievable how their officials harass their very own countrymen and drive them to a fight for freedom. I wonder at the destiny of our motherland - within this century, we have divided twice, and we continue to bleed," said Rekha looking anxious.

Inder looked at her with vacant eyes as his mind clouded with flashes of his childhood nightmare.

Partition. And the unprecedented pain, loss, and hopelessness that came with it. It had all seemed so unfair. And here we are, yet again at crossroads, heartlessly shaking the very being of millions. What is it with our race, us once-upon-a-time Indians, that had the unity and resilience to fight the British empire's might? Why can't peace prevail? Why is our collective wisdom inadequate to find mindful solutions? Why has our plurality become a curse? He got up abruptly.

"Are you okay, Jungee?"

"Yes. I'd like scrambled eggs, please."

...

The wailing grew louder with each day, creating a deafening din that nobody could ignore. India's support of the insurgency-rid Bangladesh caused a further furore in the polity of Pakistan. The Indian armed forces anticipated trouble.

In the last week of November 1971, Inder received a message from the Chief of Naval Staff, Admiral SM Nanda's office, for a meeting with all the missile boats' commanding officers at Lion Gate.

Nanda had met with the Prime Minister, Mrs. Indira Gandhi, a few days before.

"Well, Admiral, if there is war, then there is war," she had said nonchalantly twitching her lips and looked at him through her reading glasses.

The brave lady had conceded to attack Karachi if provoked.

Nanda looked as agile as he did years ago when Inder had served as his coxswain on board Mysore. He smiled stiffly and then looked at the eight commanding officers standing to attention in front of him with sobriety.

"We are going to get tested in the coming weeks. War with Pakistan is imminent. Very soon, you will move to advance bases. If any of you is hesitant to be a part of the oncoming action, I invite you to step back now; and the Navy will find a replacement."

None of the men spoke or moved from their place. The unanimity of readiness was evident. Inder felt a surge of energy and ownership of the power that was bigger than himself. We have trained hard for this. You bet we are ready to face the darkest hour and with bravado at that. Nanda was proud of his formidable team.

"Good luck, boys," he said, taking a few moments to speak to them. When he came to Inder, he shook his hand firmly and smiled.

"Inderjit, I am so proud that you made it to this team. I wish you all the luck!"

"Thank you very much, Sir. It is my honour," smiled Inder.

. . .

Inder was happy to note that the activity of his team was on point. On his orders, they readied themselves to load Nirghat with four missiles. While loading the first missile, the ship suddenly went through a minor rumble due to another boat's approach at a faster than usual pace. The missile's Radom, i.e., the missile's radar's cover, got a small dent. The Technical Position in-charge of the operation viewed the incident as carelessness. He hauled Inder and Babroo to meet Admiral Kohli, who looked visibly upset.

"How did you allow this negligence, IJ?"

"Sir, it was a mishap beyond our control – it was not negligence by my crew," said Inder with absolute composure. Babroo tugged Inder's arm.

"It is damage, dammit," said Kohli. "It is expensive equipment. We are answerable to the Naval treasury for every penny. How are we going to repair the damage at this 11th hour?"

"It is not damage, Sir. It is a mere dent on the cap of the missile's radar. There is no need for any repair, and there will be no charge to the treasury. The missile will fire perfectly."

"How can you be sure, IJ?"

"I'm certain, Sir, because we have checked it after loading it, and I know that it will do its job, as will my men," asserted Inder, feeling in command.

Inder left Kohli's office without turning back. There was no flutter or a moment of doubt in what he had committed. He knew his ship and team well. On his return to Nirghat, Inder weighed anchor and sailed for Okha.

A brave assignment or a suicide mission? The moment to test my mettle is finally here, and my team and I are ready to face the enemy's might.

...

INS Tir, a much bigger ship of World War II vintage, was already stationed at Okha, north of Gujarat. Inder and BB sailed Nirghat and Vidyut and reported to Cdr. Khambatta, the Regional Naval Officer of Kathiawad.

In December, before 6 pm, complete darkness envelopes Okha. The men on board Nirghat dawdled around as the evening set in. Pullovers and jackets helped them escape the stiff nip as did the lounge at the mess.

However, it was action time from the very first night for both Inder and BB as Tir picked up an echo of a suspected target on her radar. They immediately went out to investigate but found nothing. Spurious echoes! The echoes stayed on the radar scan till about 4 am. They returned disgruntled to port early in the morning.

Such sightings went on for a week, and because they couldn't afford to take chances, a subsequent activity of going to action stations followed. But each time, they found no target. It was frustrating, but the forced exercise made them adept navigators of the harbour off the rocky Loshington Shoal.

...

It was the morning of the 03rd of December 1971, and Rekha was having a busy day.

She was in the Staff Room, sorting through the corrected notebooks of her students. Teachers chatted over tea and biscuits, about the speculation of battle with Pakistan.

"Your attention, please!" crackled a loudspeaker in the distance.

Everyone rushed to the window to see naval officials in an open slow-moving jeep. One of them held up a loudspeaker.

"Your attention, please! There will be blackouts from this evening. No light is to leave your home. Please cover your windows with black chart paper or black paint. Keep lights switched off. Pay attention to the sirens. When you hear a long siren, switch off all lights, and stand near your house's pillars or corners or sit under the dining table. Keep children close to you. Trust nobody. Beware of rumours. Your attention, please!"

A cold chill ran down Rekha's spine. Something serious was amiss. Inder had sailed a week before, and there was no news from him ever since. Tears pricked her eyes, remembering the last she saw him. The bell rang. She blinked hard and mumbled a prayer.

"Are you okay, Rekha?" said Rose Gomes, another science teacher, touching her gently.

"Yes, I am fine, thank you, Rose," she said with a forced smile.

She gathered a pile of journals and walked out of the staff room into her class. The students were at the window, discussing the announcement.

"Girls," said Rekha sternly.

They rushed to their seats and chorused, "Good morning Mrs. Sharma."

"Good morning, girls," said Rekha looking at their innocent faces. She smiled and handed the journals to Anju, the class monitor, to distribute. "Open a new page in your journals. Today we will learn about a single-celled organism's tenacity to feed, move, and survive by simply altering its shape at will. It does so by extending and retracting its pseudopods. This unique intelligent animal is called an amoeba."

She drew an amoeba on the board and started to label its parts when the announcement began again. She paused her chalk, and her thoughts went to Inder.

The western support India had sought to resolve matters with Pakistan went unanswered. That means there will be a war, and he is right now in the midst of it. And here I am teaching these girls about how a single-celled organism survives.

"Miss, so are no two amoebae the same?" asked Anju, interrupting her thought.

"Apologies, girls. Yes, you are right, Anju.

She cleared her throat and said, "Each amoeba alters its body shape as it needs to, within the moment. It adapts to take care of itself, as should we, right?"

The school sent the children home early that day. Rekha walked hurriedly with Priya and Mala, who clapped and sang at the top of their voices.

Priya and Mala: "Who stole the cookie from the cookie jar?
Priya: "Mala stole the cookie from the cookie jar."
Mala: "Who me?"
Priya: "Yes, you!"
Mala: "Couldn't be."
Priya: "Then, who?"
Mala: "Priya stole the cookie from the cookie jar!"
Priya: "Who me?"
Mala: "Yes, you!"
Priya: "Couldn't be."
Mala: "Then, who?"
Priya: "Rekha stole the cookie from the cookie jar! Mama, it's your turn."

"Hush girls," said Rekha putting her finger to her lips and leading them into the Church.

Rekha knelt at the altar and closed her eyes. Priya and Mala copied her. "Oh, Mother Mary, have mercy. Please stop the war. Look after my Jungee and his men and his ship and all the

PRIYA SHARMA SHAIKH

people right now in harm's way," she whispered.

"What happened, Mama?" whispered Priya, tugging at Rekha's sari.

"Mama, what happened to Papa?" said Mala.

"I am missing Papa, darling, so I have come to tell God to look after him."

"After this, can we buy peru, Mama?" asked Mala.

"And some imli," added Priya.

"Yes, we will, but first, let us talk to God and ask him to look after our Jungee darling."

They folded their hands and mumbled a quick prayer, as instructed.

. . .

Rekha was anxious. And she was sweating despite the December chill. She and Anandi cut out squares of black chart paper to stick on every window. Priya and Mala were thrilled with the new activity at hand. Priya handed Rekha the squares while Mala held out the tub of homemade rice glue. Rekha covered the windowpanes, then stood on tables to do the ventilators. It had turned out to be a lot more work, and she was anxious about Inder ever since she got news of the war that morning. She kept seeing visions of Inder dressed in a white cape, fighting the sea demon once again. This time he was on a small raft, valiantly brandishing a silver sword. She got restless each time she thought of them. She tried hard to brush them away, but they returned again and again. She started murmuring the Gayatri mantra as she pasted the black squares.

"Om bhur bhava swaha, tatsavitur vareniyam, Bhargo devasya dhimahii, diyoyonah prachodayat"

"What are you saying, Mama?" asked Priya, looking up at her, puzzled.

"Om bhur bhava swaha, tatsavitur vareniyam, Bhargo devasya dhimahii, diyoyonah prachodayat"

"Mama!" called out Mala, tugging at Rekha's feet.

"Om bhur bhava swaha, tatsavitra vare niyam, Bhargo devasya dhimahii, diyoyonah prachodyat"

The doorbell rang. It was Sarla, back from visiting her sister in Khar.

"Mummy, I'm so glad you are back. I was worried," said Rekha hugging Sarla.

"I had so much traffic because of the mela at Mahim," said Sarla looking harrowed.

"Let us go for the mela," bounced up Priya.

"Oh no, we can't, darling. It is a popular event in Bombay, Mummy. We could have gone too, had the impending war not been upon us," said Rekha, looking distressed.

"What is war, Mama?"

Rekha paused to look at Priya. "It is a real fight between two countries, darling. Anandi, get me some orange squash, please."

"I also want squash," perked Mala and Priya.

With all the windows blackened, the house got shrouded in darkness. A lone candle on the side table created an oddly sombre environment. Rekha sat down to drink her juice. She moved her hand gently along the settee. She and Inder had made it by lining up four of his wooden trunk. They had Inder's name imprinted on them in white capital letters. She had placed a thick cotton stuffed mattress and fitted a frilled ochre yellow cover on it and a set of bolsters and cushions. Priya and Mala, sensing she was not happy that evening, climbed onto her lap and hugged her. Their warmth soothed her heart. Sarla touched Rekha gently, "What is bothering you, my child?"

"I'm worried about Inderjit, Mummy. All this precaution means the war is going to happen, or it is already happening."

"Mama, is Papa going to die?"

"No! What made you say that, Priya?"

"A girlie in school said, Mama. Arti. She said people who go to war, die."

"Why do you play with her? She is so much older to you," said Rekha looking cross.

"Mama, she comes to play with us in the recess. She said that many papas have gone to fight with Pakatan, and they will all die. Is it true, Mama?" asked Priya.

"No, darling. Papa has gone for work, and he will be back home soon." She noticed both of them holding small medicine bottles in their hands. "And what are these bottles?" said Rekha, wiping her brow with a napkin.

"It is sugar water, Mama," giggled Priya.

"Is it for your dolls?" said Rekha trying to smile.

"No, it is for the Pakatans. We are going to add poison to them," whispered Mala. "When they come here, they will be thirsty. We will smile and give them these bottles to drink. They will think it is juice and they will drink it. And then they will die. It is our secret. Don't tell anyone."

Rekha looked at her daughters' innocent faces in the candlelight's dancing shadows and hugged them as tears rolled down her cheeks. Anandi rushed to her side, as Ganpat picked up the girls, who started crying, seeing their mother in tears.

...

Inder ate his dinner early. He paced the deck with his hands shoved into his jacket pockets, looking up occasionally at the starlit sky. The moon shone in all her glory, making the waters shimmer in her light. She looked just as spectacular as the previous night when she was a complete circle. Simply stunning. Most of the ship's company were at the mess for drinks and dinner. Nirghat bobbed adjoining Vidyut, to the rhythm of the waves.

Despite the familiar sounds, there seemed to be an unsettling quiet. Inder could hear his breath moving in and out of his body. A sudden chill ran down his spine. He purposefully breathed a few times deeply, calming himself and bringing his focus back to what he needed to do. Slowly he grew comfortable with the silence. He touched his chest pocket to feel the envelope.

The day is finally here. He had grown to love his team. They were unquestioning of his command and unflinching in their duty. *How will my team take the news?*

Inder's thoughts followed him as he stepped into the dimly lit bridge. Tony and Dua were mid-conversation.

"Good evening Sir," said Tony and Dua with polite smiles.

"Evening," said Inder tersely.

The boys exchanged glances. Something was amiss. Inder turned to look at the door as he heard quick steps approaching. It was Rao, the master of the missiles!

"Good evening Sir," he said. His usual imposing stance mellowed, and his smile faded as he entered. He, too, sensed

Inder's sombreness.

"Dua, what is the status of the fuel?"

Dua said the fuelling was underway. Inder looked at his core team with a steady gaze and slowly took out the envelope from his pocket, and handed it to Tony.

"It is to be opened at sea when I tell you. Until then, it is your responsibility to maintain absolute silence about it," instructed Inder firmly. "Get the charts ready and ensure all supplies are adequate. I will be back," he said and left the bridge.

"Aye Sir," said Tony, who saw the security classification and knew they were the action orders. He looked at the others and then after Inder's receding figure with a gleam in his eyes.

. . .

Inder had no indication of things to come, early in the evening, when BB and he went for a walk on the beach.

"The evenings get chilly here," said BB rubbing his hands together.

"Punjab is much harsher. Nothing to beat Russia, of course!"

"Oh, that blizzard could have killed us! What a time that was, huh, IJ?"

"Excellent time!"

All of a sudden, there was a blackout, and they had rushed to meet Khambatta.

"Pakistan has attacked various air bases in North India. India has declared all forces to go to war on the 03rd of December 1971, which is today," said Khambatta stiffly. He handed them a sealed envelope each, marked TOP SECRET and said, "Your orders for OPERATION TRIDENT. You should be proud to be part of independent India's first naval operation, and the first-ever attack on the fortress of the enemy's strength, Karachi,"

"This envelope spells death or glory for your men and you. It is strictly to be opened at a given time, which you will know once you are at sea. May God bless your ship's company and you."

Inder and BB had thanked him and pocketed their respective envelopes. Inder's heart was awash with all that needed to get done.

War with Pakistan is finally upon us. The fate of the several thousand members of the Navy will change, both of India and that of the enemy. Men who have left behind their families to fight a war on behalf of their countries. Wonder what destiny holds in store for us all?

. . .

A loud siren rang out. Rekha gathered her wits and instinctively blew out the candle. She made the children sit with Anandi under the dining table, while she stood clinging onto Sarla in a corner nearby.

After the siren stopped, they all went to the balcony. Suddenly, a burst of shots got fired in the dark sky, shards of fast-moving lights flashed past them in a continuous stream. Ack-ack-ack! The anti-aircraft guns.

The houses in the vicinity broke into screams. Rekha, Priya, Mala, and Sarla hugged each other and cried, shaking with fear as Anandi and Ganpat looked on in despair. Nobody ate dinner that night. The girls clung to Rekha until they fell asleep. Anandi helped Rekha lay them down in bed and offered to bring her some dinner.

"I'm not hungry, Anandi. You go to sleep, thank you."

"You must not be weak like this, Rekha. You have to eat to

stay healthy so that you can think on your feet at a time like this," said Sarla, concerned.

"I can't help it, Mummy. I just can't eat. War is terrible. I wish it would just stop. How can people kill each other in the name of patriotism or righteousness? Talking with love to one another can sort problems. How will the killing of young soldiers on the front solve the issues of a nation?"

"Along with Jungee, so many more of our friends are at war too. People we love and know for so many years. How can we allow their lives and thousands of our soldiers and even the enemy's soldiers to be in harm's way? How can we be okay with that? All of them are to be sacrificed based on a decision taken by both our governments. So many must be in the firing line right now, as we sit here comfortably in our homes eating dinner."

She shook her head in dismay. "I fantasized about warriors, but now after being a wife and a mother, I realise the futility of war. I keep a brave front most of the time and smile and say goodbye when he leaves home. The truth is I can't bear any killing," she snivelled.

"Rekha, I understand your tears. He will come back home safely."

"And what about the enemy's families? What about their wives and children and their old parents? If we celebrate, they will grieve," she said, looking anxious. "We were all one country, one big family at one time, Mummy, and today 24 years later, we are at war with each other. How can anybody not see the pointlessness of this?"

Sarla sighed and hugged her daughter tightly.

"Their administration and officers have done wrong with the people in East Pakistan, which is why they want liberation. Lakhs of people have already died, thanks to the arson and atrocities. Instead of punishing their officers who have caused mayhem, they attack us. And in this process, more people will die!" said Rekha. "I knew something was amiss since Inder didn't come home for so many days. I didn't even say a proper goodbye, Mummy. I was fighting with him."

She got up and paced the room. *Jungee, you are so right; we have so much to celebrate in our marriage. I'm sorry, darling. Come back home soon.*

"Rekha, the speculation of war is finally at rest. I don't know much about all this. All I know is that if Inderjit isn't brave and doesn't do his duty at the front, your innocent children will get attacked, and this comfort you are sitting in right now will get snatched away. Would that be fair? Someone has to be the protector. Thousands of others like Inderjit have chosen to play that part. And as civilians, we should do our bit by abiding with the ground rules and pray that they play their parts well and return home safely," said Sarla, in her gentle voice.

Rekha paused to listen to Sarla, "But mummy, what if something happens..."

"No, buts Rekha. Let us not have negative thoughts. And let us not discuss things over which we have no control. What you can do is care for the girls and yourself and love them during this time so they don't be scared. Tears and fear are not valuable adornments. They are just a dramatic distraction. The girls have slept hungry, and you too haven't eaten. That is not acceptable. It is time to play your part of the true Ardhangini, Rekha. Display your strength, just like Inderjit is doing right now in the battlefield," said Sarla, in a firm tone.

Sarla's simple words of wisdom rang true for Rekha as she walked into the balcony and looked at the night. DhruvTara, the star, twinkled at her. She remembered the story of little Dhruv's trust in God, in the wake of his death. I trust Lord

Shiva to look after my Jungee. With a new resolve, she made her way in the darkness to the fridge. She opened it, took out a bottle of milk, peeled its cover off, and put it straight to her lips to drink. She paused to take a breath and wiped the trail of fluid on her chin. *I am strong, and Jungee will be well.*

. . .

Inder checked his wristwatch. 10 pm. The lights on Nirghat were slowly turning off, even as a few of the ship's company tuned into the news on the radio – Indira Gandhi had declared war with Pakistan. A murmur had been doing rounds on the ship.

"The war is starting. We are going to war!"

"I didn't say goodbye to my family. Yaar, what will happen to our families if we die?"

"Don't think about things that haven't yet happened. Get some sleep."

"Yes, let's sleep - we will need the energy."

In his cabin, Inder yawned loudly, took off his uniform, and hung it neatly on a peg so he could jump back into it later. His reflection in the mirror was grim, but there was a steely look in his eyes. He felt composed within. He felt ready.

He took off his shoes and massaged his feet. They were warm. "Your feet should always be warm, and your forehead cold," Jaikishen would say to him.

He yawned again and lay flat on the narrow bed and shut his eyes. Thoughts of the evening came to him - the order he had received, Nirghat's readiness for action, Rekha, and the girls. His eyes blinked open. He turned to his left and shut his eyes again.

He saw the running footsteps of a child. It is Koogh, wearing a dhoti in Tandlianwala.

He is flying a kite with Bhushan, Bhollu, and Vaid.

They are running carefree through the fields and alleys of Lakkad Mandi.

The Lion, Cow, and Peacock are racing him to the terrace.

He places a note in his treasure box.

He is running midst hordes of people frantically shouting, "Pitaji, Pabbi!"

Daulat Ram is saying, "Seize the opportunity."

He is extending his hand for the postcards from Jaikishen, as the train is leaving.

He is marching on the grounds with the other cadets.

He is doing dips in the quarterdeck with tears in his eyes.

He is in his officer's uniform, carrying Rekha away in his arms.

Rekha laughs and calls him Jungee.

He is sitting behind Rekha as she rides the scooter on Marine Drive.

Gopinathji is at the temple, saying, "Inderjit, you are the commander-in-chief."

He is standing on Sharda's deck, telling the little boy Ravi, "You have to be brave."

He is walking up the red carpet to receive the AVSM from the President of India.

Priya and Mala are cheering him in the audience, "We love you, Papliii."

The bells swing and ring before the glowing deity at Rameshwaram.

He is reciting the Bhagawad Gita with a calm look on his face.

His voice resonates with the mantra *"Karmanye vadhikaraste, Ma phaleshu kadachana, Makarma-phala-hetur bhurmate sangostva akarmani* ... again and again to infinity.

"Sir!" Inder awoke with a start. It was his Forward Gunner. "We have received the execution signal, Sir."

He freshened up and dressed quickly. He stood silent in

PRIYA SHARMA SHAIKH

front of his shrine, while the ship's alarm rang for a full 60 seconds — bells of worship or the call for duty. The noisy clatter of feet indicated his men were heading to their respective stations.

"Good morning Sir," said all the officers and crew as Inder stepped into the bridge.

"Good morning, boys. Hope you all got some rest," said Inder.

"A little Sir, despite the churn in the stomach," said Tony, looking more alert than ever.

The reddish gloom in the bridge felt soothing. This small room is going to double up as the operations room soon. In the dark corner near the radar screen, the communications sailor was completing a final test of the ship's systems by relaying Tony's orders to various stations, checking, and reporting progress.

"The missile checks are complete and ready for action, Sir," reported Rao.

"Good," nodded Inder, looking at the lamps, blinking on the missile control panel. Pressing these buttons will propel the missiles towards destruction!

Inder stepped out of the bridge and walked down the storm corridor to peer into the engine room's hatch. Nothing was audible above the din of the massive generators. The Chief Engineering Repair Artificer, Prakash, gave Inder a thumbs-up and bobbed his head with a smile. The hosepipe connected on board from the jetty indicated that fuelling was still underway. Walking further aft, Inder stopped at the galley to ask for tea and an omelette sandwich. The cook, Chavan, smiled at Inder's calm demeanour. Inder reached the missile control room, which was ringing with singing. They stopped singing and stood up at attention as he entered. The Chief Electrical

Artificer Power, MS Singhal, saluted.

"Good evening, Sir," said Singhal with an embarrassed smile. "All checks on the missiles are complete, Sir, and now we are enjoying."

"Excellent. At ease, boys," said Inder and smiled at the young sailor who was singing. "At the next bada-khana, you should sing for all of us."

"Good idea Sir! He is excellent," said Singhal, as the young sailor blushed. "Except for the chill, all is well," said Singhal with a quick shiver.

"Well, cover-up, Singhal. I need you to have laser focus today," said Inder.

Singhal nodded. "I'll get my sweater right away, Sir," he said, as Inder walked away.

The aft gunner at the quarterdeck saluted stiffly. Inder nodded at him. "At ease, boy."

It was several hours before sunrise, and the breeze was chilly. Inder spent the next few moments in silence, looking at the dark water below. He listened to the lilt in the ripples as they romanced the body of the ship. Buoyancy was at work in the dark of night, keeping Nirghat afloat, even as gravitation worked at pulling her down.

McClain had said, "A boat makes place for herself by displacing water that is heavier than her weight. Hence, she floats despite her weight, while an equally heavy stone will sink." He remembered learning the Archimedes' principle as a sailor. It was confusing at first, but so much knowledge and awareness happened since his early days in the Navy. *The success of our operation will rest heavily on the element of surprise and air cover.*

Inder breathed in deeply and turned to look at the Aft Gunner standing at a respectful distance. He smiled and shifted, gauging Inder's gaze in the dark.

"So, you heard the news on the radio - what do you think will happen today?"

"We will make history, Sir, and I'll have a great story to tell my grandchildren."

Chavan arrived with his breakfast. Inder blew at the tea before sipping it, relishing the warm liquid's nourishment as it entered his body. His thoughts went to Rekha. She knew that she could not probe him about his work, and like any officer's wife, she respected the Navy's need for boundaries. For that matter, any of the crew's families had no idea that their men were standing at the battleground that very minute. And the scale could go this way or that.

What are the chances of me seeing my family again? He worried about Rekha. He had dropped her and the kids off at school before sailing for Okha. Her face looked overcast from the quarrel they had had the night before.

It had all started when he had given his opinion on a woman's role after marriage. Rekha had argued with him, and the discussion had taken an unexpected turn.

"Rekha, every discussion we have can't lead to Pabbi. I have told you to stop living in the past as it can't get undone. We can't change her, and we don't need to be like her."

"Oh, you are incorrigible! You have no guts to tell Mataji that she has wronged me."

"I am tired of this discussion. We've been married for eight years now. We have so much to celebrate. I can't understand what makes you carry this baggage of how Pabbi treated you, for such a long time. Forgive her and move on, darling. It is like spilled milk, and you can't undo it. After my realisation, while talking to you years ago at Chowpatty, I have never looked back at my past. Instead, I have learnt my lesson and just moved on. How would it be if you did that too?" he had said.

But Rekha was furious, and she had got up to leave the room. "Darling, listen to me. Let's talk this through," said Inder holding her hand to stop her.

"We have not met Pabbi for so long. She doesn't even know you are hurting like this. So what is the purpose of holding onto such grudges."

Just then, Priya had come crying out of the bedroom. And Inder had taken her back to sleep. When he got back, Rekha was lying on the bed in tears. He had tried to calm her but to no avail.

"Rekha, it pains my heart to see you like this," he had said softly, holding his head in his hands, feeling drained. "Talk to me, darling. Bottling up will harm you." But she had pushed him away and cried quietly into her pillow.

At the school gate next morning, she had looked at Inder and turned to leave. Inder had caught her arm and said, "Have a good day, darling. Live in the present with your students, with the kids, and mummy. Forget everything else. Okay?"

She had given him a feeble smile, with tears in her eyes, and nodded before walking into the school, behind the kids. "Tata Papa," the kids had said. But Rekha had not turned around. The conversation was over, and yet it wasn't. There was much to be resolved.

He had wanted so much to be with her until she was at peace. But he had driven off with a heavy heart, leaving behind the family he loved, because his duty for his country was calling.

. . .

Inder knew that in loving and respecting Geeta unconditionally, he had paid the price – he had let his beloved Rekha feel let down.

I regret I made you feel unsupported, my darling. I wonder if it is in my destiny to return home and make amends. I will speak to Pabbi about how you feel. And I promise to understand your point of view better and put your mind at peace.

He shut his eyes to soak in his commitment. He breathed deeply and listened to the familiar sounds of the water as silence enveloped him.

Nirghat's engines roared, letting out a cloud of white smoke. It was Inder's cue to return to the bridge. The much larger Petya Class ASW Corvette with anti-aircraft guns and anti-submarine rockets, INS Katchall, with Commander Zaddu as its CO, headed towards the sea. Vidyut powered her engines too, but an unexpected technical challenge precluded her from getting underway.

Dua gave Inder the thumbs up as he passed him. The fuel tanks are full. Inder nodded and looked up, to check that the radar's aerial was rotating as expected. The bridge's glass panes were by now covered with the steel blinds.

"Sir, we are ready to proceed to sea," reported Tony.

"All lines on board," nodded Inder, taking his seat. The crew at Quarterdeck and Fox'l pulled up the lines.

"Slow ahead starboard, slow astern port," said Inder crisply.

"Stop both engines," he said and paused. "Slow astern both engines," he said and paused again. "Stop both engines. Slow ahead both engines. Starboard 15."

It was 3 am on the 04th of December when Nirghat gracefully swung starboard and proceeded at a slow ahead speed of

JUNGEE

10 Knots behind Katchall. What a beauty this boat is.

...

The salty spray of the Arabian Sea's rough waters lashed the ship's port side, moistening Singhal's face as he emerged from the hatch onto the deck. He had decided to take the Captain's advice and dress in a pullover. The wind was chilly, and it blew against his face, made his short crop of hair stand straight. He hurried along the wet deck, wiping his face and body. Emotions were dancing in his heart.

He and the boys had done the preparatory work on the four missiles. It had been a consuming process, but he was sure the checks were thorough. They were ready to follow the orders for action.

He was a handsome young man from North India, having started his career with humble beginnings. He had left his home and family swearing to serve his country. He had joined the Navy as a sailor at 17. Fear was not in his nature, and neither was pride.

He looked fondly at the pullover that was knitted by his new bride. He had called her from the sailor's mess before setting sail from Bombay a few days ago. She had sounded as excited as ever to hear his voice, while he had tried to control his tone and reactions, conscious of his men around him at the mess's reception desk.

He had flirted with her playfully in a monosyllabic code that sounded like gibberish to the clerk on duty. And he had unabashedly blown her soft kisses on the phone. Tickled by his embarrassed romantic overtures, she had laughed out aloud. He adored her unbridled laughter and would do anything to hear it again. He missed her, he had said. And she had instantly responded calling him a liar, saying that if he did miss her, he wouldn't have left her behind. Gibberish had en-

449

PRIYA SHARMA SHAIKH

sued again. He had closed his eyes and reminded her of their last union together. The visions had flashed in front of his eyes, and his cheeks had blushed with embarrassment. And then he had become silent. And following his cue, so had she. They were breathing together in a familiar cadence, soaking in the beauty of their love.

He had opened his eyes to find the clerk glaring at him, whose expression pointedly said he had to stop talking. He had straightened up and turned away from the desk, pulling the wire to a maximum stretch. Knowing that he had to hang up, he had said in a steady tone that he would be back by her side soon. She had protested and he had said he loved her and then he had hung up. He didn't know that she had sat there holding onto the black receiver, with an amused smile as a tear escaped her eye to make a blot on her turquoise dupatta.

He and the rest of the ship's company had waited for this final countdown to action. The Captain was right about them being men with the best mettle. He headed to the storm corridor, manoeuvring his way as crew members rushed past him to get to their action stations, to be with his team next to the missile hangar doors.

. . .

The next morning was the 04th of December 1971. Rekha saw the newspaper in the Staff Room and gasped. The headlines were about soldiers that had lost their life in action. The counting of bodies had already started. Rose and a few other teachers rushed to her side, hugging her as she wept. Mother Helen hugged her warmly. The whole staff room had tear-filled eyes. A few senior girls stood at the doorway, with fear written all over their faces, not knowing what to say.

Mother Helen announced an immediate prayer meeting in the assembly hall. All the teachers and support staff gathered the students, who murmured animatedly about the repeated

450

assembly. Mother Helen stepped onto the raised dais, and the assembly hall hushed into pin-drop silence.

"Our Father and the Son and the holy spirit. Amen. I would like to start by reading something for you all from the Bible." She paused after reciting the prayer. "That was a piece of trust and courage. It is very relevant for all of us today. Thousands of soldiers today fight a war for our country because of their commitment to their motherland. They do so with the trust in their abilities, while they do their best to protect us. Join me in prayer for our dear Mrs. Sharma's husband, Lt. Cdr. Inderjit Sharma, and all our soldiers at war. God will care for them. May peace prevail."

The students murmured AMEN. The school closed early.

...

Meanwhile, Kiltan, another Petya, had escorted two more missile boats, Nipat and Veer, from Bombay, headed by Bahadur and Omi. The officer in tactical command was the Captain of Kiltan, Cdr. Gopal Rao. Babroo, the Squadron Commander or K-25, was on board Nipat. The three commanding officers Bahadur, Omi, and Inder, assembled on board Kiltan, mid-sea, at about 10 am, for the final briefing from K-25.

Babroo stood taller than usual that morning, his well-built torso appearing rock solid above his stocky legs. Apart from being a specialist in torpedo and anti-submarine operations, he was known for his leadership, remarkable intelligence, and brave decision-making. "We have trained hard for this moment. Are you ready, boys?" he said, in his Haryanavi accent to the three commanding officers standing to attention.

"Yes, Sir," boomed the three of them in unison.

"Good. We will enter the prohibited zone during the attack, a 60 nautical miles arc south of Karachi. I will give all orders for the attack and contacts in that area. I will be on board Nipat, and she will be ahead. Nirghat will be on her port quarter and Veer on her starboard quarter. The Petya's astern in a single line, at a distance of 1.5 nautical miles from each other, will complete a trident's formation and ensure there is no possibility to attack them by mistake. We are to maintain absolute secrecy about Operation Trident."

"Aye, Sir."

He then read a signal from the CinC Western Naval Command, "Go with God and give them hell! Operation Trident is the Indian Navy's first such mission, so we will be the first to blaze a path for many to follow. All the best! Let us create history!"

"Aye, Sir."

Inder returned to Nirghat and processed the briefing. The first glorious chapter in the Indian Navy's annals is about to unfold, spelling destruction for her foe, and I am ready to lead the way for my team!

"Half ahead on both engines," said Inder, and proceeded in the trident formation, towards Karachi.

. . .

It was a typical early winter evening at sea, with a fresh breeze coming up. The sun glistened hues of purple, pink, and orange on the horizon as Nirghat glided over the Arabian Sea's calm waters, moving north as a part of the trident formation. Except for some false contacts, their passage had mainly remained uneventful.

As night fell, Inder could barely see the other missile boats from a distance. Strict radio silence was maintained to avoid the enemy to spot them. Communication happened only with semaphores or directional flashlights.

"Tony, I would like to address everyone. Please gather the

boys on the upper deck."

"Aye Sir," said Tony and rang the bell to make the necessary arrangements.

Inder left the bridge in the custody of Tony, to slip on a pullover in his cabin. He stopped at the shrine on his desk. He breathed deeply and listened to his heartbeat. The pace seemed regular, like the slow trot of a graceful horse.

Durga, the warrior Goddess, sat majestically atop the back of her mount, the tiger. Each of her eight hands held a powerful weapon. She looked ready to wage battle against any demons that threatened peace and prosperity. And yet, her expression was calm.

You like a mother does at her child while he shares his woes with her. With unconditional love. It seems inappropriate to pray for the destruction of others. But I will perform my duty to the best of my ability tonight, and I will bring back each member of my ship's company home safely. I leave it to you to justify my cause.

Inder gathered his thoughts as he watched his crew troop onto the deck. Tony soon signalled their readiness, and Inder stepped in front of his men.

"We are on our way to attack the enemy in her harbour. We have with us the most dangerous weapons on this side of the Suez. And tonight, we intend to use them to the best of our ability. The Navy has trained us over the past two years, and each of us has worked very hard to master our craft, for this very moment. We are going to kill many men tonight. In the face of it, that is wrong because the mere killing of another is murder. But we do so with justification and do not doubt that our cause, your cause, is fair." He paused and looked at his team. "We are the liberators of the oppressed, and their eyes are upon us now, as we fight this battle. This operation's success is in our hands, so when we fight tonight, let us fight with that acuity, determination, and courage, accentuated by the might of this ship. I am certain we will succeed because I have before me 30 of the Indian Navy's best men. We are all united as one powerful team that dares to show the enemy our might and return victorious. Are you ready?"

"Aye, Sir!" came a thundering response from the team.

...

The sun had set, and the moon had not yet risen. All the five ships in the squadron had no radio and radar communication; hence it was difficult to know where the other ships were.

The high salinity of the Arabian Sea produced a luminous effect in the wake of the other vessels. With only an occasional flash of a blinker as an indicator, they felt like they were moving in a void. By estimation, seamanship, and sheer good luck, they kept clear of each other. Supper that evening was eaten in near silence.

At 9.40 pm, the junior telegraphist came rattling in with a report from Kiltan. They spotted three targets on the radar, which were heading towards Nirghat at high speed! Orders followed quickly. The whole formation turned abruptly to port and opened up the range and firing arcs. Inder called all hands to action posts, and he began the critical task of missile preparation. However, they soon realised that the echoes were spurious, generated perhaps by a ship positioned south of Karachi. Nirghat resumed the previous course - to set on the last leg of her journey to Karachi.

Inder remained on the bridge with Tony, their eyes glued to the horizon, as they cruised along. And then finally, the moon rose. Around 10.30 pm, Inder lifted radio and radar silence. Reports crackled in, and several targets littered the scan. Tony plotted and shared their updated position on the chart for Inder. One target, about 30 nautical miles south-southwest of Karachi, caught Inder's attention. She was about 20 nautical miles on their port bough, moving at a menacing pace of 24 Knots. "She is a warship," said Inder.

Inder instructed the radio operator to request permission from K-25 to engage the target. Meanwhile, Inder ordered the action alarm to begin preparing the missiles.

In the dim light of the bridge, Tony moved between the chart desk and the radar room. Inder set his eyes on the target's position on the scanner. Over the past two years, he had grown to like and admire Inder a lot. Inder's square frame was sitting up straight as he stared ahead into the night. Tony knew that being in Inder's shoes was not easy. The responsibility of all the decisions and actions he took for Nirghat that night shouldered on him. His decisions would impact the ship, her men, their families, the Navy, and India.

Inder sat calm and composed; his mind focused on nothing but the target as he awaited K-25's response. Just then, Tony's headset beeped, and he instinctively put his hands on the earmuffs to listen carefully.

"Sir, we have permission from K-25 to engage the target," he exclaimed to Inder, holding his breath.

Inder nodded. "Noted. Complete the final checks on the missiles and get ready for launch."

"Aye, Sir," said Tony, and called out the necessary orders.

The crew sprang into action, slamming doors and hatches. The range of the target was now at 18 nautical miles.

"Rajendran, alter the ship's heading to the battle course," said Inder.

Within a few minutes, the ship shut down all her air passages. The operation room's shrouded darkness with just a lone red light gave the room the surreal effect of a disco. Inder and his crew were ready for their dance with destiny.

The range of the target was down to 16 nautical miles. Nirghat altered to a parallel course to allow for the completion of pre-launch checks. The green signal came in from all the teams, one by one.

"Tony, is the pre-launch check complete?"

"Aye, Sir, all done."

Inder once again got Nirghat to approach the battle course. The range of the target was down to 15 nautical miles.

"Standby number 1," ordered Inder, sitting upright.

"Number 1 standby," reported Rao.

"Launch number 1," said Inder in a steady voice, pressing the button to launch the first missile. The red lamp blinked on, indicating readiness in all respect.

Nothing happened.

Nirghat continued to charge towards her target. In the red gloom of the operations room, tension ran high. Cold sweat beaded on the forehead of every man. Everything depended on the missile taking off on time. The ship's company held its breath as a few more moments passed.

Still, nothing happened.

Inder knew Nirghat was already on the auto steer and was closing rapidly towards her target. He clenched his fist, staring wide-eyed at all the indicators, assessing their readings, while the crew waited for further instructions.

He mumbled to himself, "She seems unsteady." His mind raced with possible options, and then he shouted, "Check Bhatti."

Tony charged into the Radar room, and when he stuck his head in, he was shocked at what he saw.

"On it, Sir," Tony shouted back.

Within moments, the ship got aligned with her target, and the booster engine sounded a mighty roar. The entire ship and her men shuddered as the missile left her pads. A blinding light filled the operations room, as a few blast shields broke away due to the enormous pressure.

Inder gathered himself immediately. "Reverse course due south, away from the target," commanded Inder.

As the vessel moved away from the battle course, the men on the bridge stood open-mouthed to watch the missile's effect in the distance.

Aboard Nipat, an officer next to K-25, sighted a stream of fiery light shoot across the sky. "A shooting star, Sir."

"That is not a shooting star. It is IJ in action – the missile from Nirghat is heading towards her target. Indian Navy is making history," said Babroo, punching the air as he watched the movement of the fiery missile across the darkness.

Within seconds, the missile dipped over the horizon, and the entire sky lit up with a blinding flash, like that of the rising sun.

The logbook entry of Nirghat reads: 23.11 hours on the 04th of December 1971, Nirghat shot the first missile in the history of the Indian Navy during the war of India and Pakistan.

Back at the chart desk, Tony said, "Target speed down to 6 Knots, Sir."

Having observed the first missile effect and seeing the target still on the radar, Inder sent another message to K-25, for permission to launch another missile at the same target.

Permission came through instantly, and Inder altered his

course, to attack once again. The enthusiasm for activity started once again, and the ship swung around to the action course.

"Standby 2," said Inder.

"Number 2 standby," reported Rao.

"Launch 2," ordered Inder, and pressed the launch button.

With a roar and blast as loud as the first, ten minutes after the first missile, the second missile set off on her destruction mission.

Inder ordered the hangar doors shut, and equipment switched off. Every man on the ship ran up to the upper deck to follow the missile's flight as it made its way, slicing through the darkness. They saw the striking flash of light in the distance grow, reaching out to the midnight sky, giving it a gold wash.

The missile hit the target's centre, breaking her into two and caving her into the ocean. The target slowly began to disappear on the scanner, and soon, she vanished into the sea's depths.

About 35 miles south south-west of Karachi lies the crypt of the mighty battle destroyer, PNS Khaiber. That night, she went down, taking with her more than 220 men.

Nirghat continued to proceed northward in the direction of Nipat and came within eight nautical miles of her. Inder awaited further instructions from K-25. By then, the ships anchored south of Karachi were visible on his radar scan.

While awaiting further orders, Inder prepared for the launch of the third missile. However, K-25's message came in saying: ANGAR – ANGAR - ANGAR. This codeword meant - action is over, retreat, and act independently. The whole squadron implemented ANGAR. All the five ships turned their radars to the off mode and retreated due south.

Nirghat's constant during the action, Katchall followed her every move. On the return journey, since they were acting independently, Inder did not have any radar contact with the rest of the team or Katchall. Inder suddenly sighted a ship on her starboard side and prepared for missile action once again. They immediately flashed the lights code and asked, "Which ship? Where bound?"

Zadu's team gave the prompt reply, "I am Katchall. I am Katchall."

Inder and Zadu both heaved a sigh of relief as something ugly was averted. Zadu ordered Nirghat to be at a loose station on her beam for the rest of the journey. They sailed southeast with an increased speed of 30 Knots. They appeared to be getting away scot-free when suddenly, they saw a fast-moving air target.

"Sir, aircraft on port side," said Tony.

Inder ordered Nirghat's guns to swing towards her port side. He sent a message to Katchall as well, and she too prepared her fully automatic 76.2 guns for action. The gunners of Nirghat scanned the sky, while Inder watched the target to lock it on the scan. However, after a brief circling, the aircraft swung north and disappeared into the dark sky, leaving both the ships' companies uncertain about what to expect next.

Meanwhile, Nirghat's engines were almost out of fuel. Inder headed for the Saurashtra coast. Veer was already there, and soon after, Nipat arrived too. INS Poshak provided them the requisite refuelling.

Inder learnt that shortly after Nirghat had fired her missiles, Nipat fired at seemingly a cargo vessel carrying ammunition for the Pakistani forces – it too exploded immediately. Nipat had then fired at PNS Shah Jahan and damaged her se-

PRIYA SHARMA SHAIKH

verely. Veer too had fired at PNS Muhafiz, a minesweeper – she too sank. The entire squadron had come through unscathed from a swift and dangerous mission. Once the fleet assembled, the ship's company of each boat came on to their respective decks. Each deck erupted with bugle calling, hooting, cheering, back-slapping, and cap flinging. Operation Trident was a success!

. . .

Shortly after, they set sail for Bombay. Inder sat in his chair to reflect on all that had happened. He looked around at his boys proudly and patted each of their backs as they came by to congratulate him.

Inder called for Bhatti. He was the man in the radar room during the operation-his shaking hands could not keep the target in the centre to lock it, due to which the ship was not getting steady on the firing course during the launch of the first missile. Tony had to jump in to secure the target, and only then had the missile got fired.

Bhatti entered the bridge and stood at attention in front of Inder, with his eyes cast down. He looked nervous.
"Good morning, Sir."

"Bhatti, good job with the execution of the second missile. But what happened to you during the first missile's launch?" Inder asked him in Punjabi.

Bhatti paused and then looked up slowly. "Sir, I had seen the missile's firing in Vladivostok. I saw the damage it had caused to the target. Sir, I couldn't help thinking about the men on board the ship. Their crew was probably full of men like us, following orders from above. I couldn't stop thinking of their families and children, Sir, as they were sure to burn to ashes from our missile's attack or freeze to death in the icy cold water. It just felt unfair that they were to all die."

460

JUNGEE

"What about your family Bhatti? And all our families? What about our ship, and our promise to the Navy and our country's honour? If we had not fired at them last night, they would have certainly fired at us, as they were coming for us. And they would have attacked us, for sure. We cannot afford to have emotions in war – not us, not them, and not any warrior. Our job is to fight with complete presence. We had to attack that ship, and that meant taking the lives of her men too. At that moment, that was what we needed to do, to justify our cause. If we had given them the chance to fire, each of us would have been lying in Davy Jones' locker now. Would that be acceptable to you? And to your family?"

Bhatti looked at Inder and shook his head, "No, Sir."

"Years ago as a young boy in the Navy, I too once thought of what it would be like to attack an enemy vessel and destroy her men. Maybe some of the men would be my classmates, where I lived in Tandlianwala. But last night, I did not hesitate for a moment as I had a single focused aim to fulfil the promise I had made to myself to be responsible for each of you boys and to do my best for my country. At that moment it was just the Operation Trident and me - my focus was my mission and I felt entirely present to what I needed to do. It is good to be good Bhatti but you've got to do what you've got to do and last night we had to pull that trigger – because they had done wrong and we had to play the role of their destroyers. And we did well as a team and achieved success.

"I will always remember this lesson, Sir. Being a part of this operation has been a privilege. Thank you, Sir."

. . .

It was late afternoon of the 06th of December 1971, when Nirghat and the other missile boats came alongside at Ballard Pier, at Bombay, amidst cheers, accolades, and a live Naval band playing the victory tune.

The missile boats' men became heroes overnight. They beamed, pressed against the guard rails, waving their caps in excitement to the assembled officers and crew of various other ships—the realisation of the glory they had achieved for the Indian Navy began to set in for each man on board the three ships. Admiral Kohli was present at the reception, and he too passionately joined in the cheering. He came on board Nirghat and shook Inder's hand and slapped his back.

"Brilliant job, IJ! You have made history for the Indian Navy!" said Kohli shaking Inder's hand joyously, with pride written all over his face.

"Thank you, Sir, I had the best team!" said Inder. "And Sir, the first missile that hit the target was the one I got hauled up for before we went to Okha."

Kohli looked Inder in the eyes and shook his grip even more. "Fantastic, IJ."

Kohli went on board each ship to greet the crew and ended the visit with a photo-op with the Commanding Officers of Nirghat, Nipat, and Veer - Inder, Bahadur, and Omi and their K-25, Babroo.

Inder watched all the celebrations around him and realised what a moment in history it was. The team had exceeded his expectations, and the result was a glorious victory. The Navy's investment in the tiny missile boats and the training of its 300 odd men in the harsh terrain of Vladivostok had paid off. Undoubtedly the cheering and celebration were well deserved as they had returned from a suicidal mission. And Inder soaked in the joy.

The praise will ebb, and there will be other victories to celebrate. But the memory of the moments when we fought fearlessly and with complete presence in the battlegrounds, without a parting word to our families, will remain forever.

The 30 men of INS Nirghat under Inder's command created history together in those moments! And even though the bugles might fade, nobody could take that glorious milestone away from each of them.

...

At about 5 pm on the 18th of December, it was almost sunset. Priya and Mala played close to the window, awaiting Inder's return, peeking out at the driveway, now and then. They played with a toy ship and a tub of water and took turns to sail it around as they sang, "Dip-dip-dip my papa's ship, sailing in the water, Like a cup and saucer. Dip-dip-dip."

Rekha made Inder's favourite trifle pudding and got dressed in a new chudidaar kurta, that she stitched on her Singer Machine, and waited anxiously at the balcony. She had been worried about Inder.

His victorious return home on the 06th of December after Operation Trident was still fresh in her mind. Their hearts had overflowed with emotion when they had met, and he said, "I have understood the value of life, darling."

On the night of his return, Rekha had said, "Jungee, I have been so guilty of parting without resolving our disagreement."

"I didn't know it was wartime, and I felt horrible that God forbid something happened to you, the last thing you would remember is us fighting. I'm never going to leave anything unfinished again. No argument is bigger than my love for you, Jungee."

"I, too, was miserable to have left you in a state of turmoil," he said, hugging Rekha.

"I also had the time to reflect. I realise that Mataji's paradigm is different from mine, and it is not my place to judge her. I chose to marry you, and I commit to working my way around all that comes with that choice."

"That is perfect darling. I commit to speaking with Pabbi on our next trip to Punjab."

And then, on the 10th of December, they had awoken to the news of the sinking of INS Khukri with her Captain, Mahendra Nath Mulla. The news had shaken up the Naval establishment, and endless tears had flowed.

Rekha was still coming to terms with all the destruction in the war when Inder got called to return to the battleground. She feared for him unremittingly, now knowing of the possible danger that lay ahead. And yet she had said goodbye to him with a brave face. Prayer had not left her lips until the announcement on the 16th of December 1971 - the war with Pakistan had ended, and they had conceded defeat in Bangladesh.

. . .

When Buchki entered the shrine of Kali Ma, she reached out to the bells and rang them loudly over the din of Dhaka's people celebrating the defeat of Pakistan at the hands of India. They finally had the freedom to own their identity in Bangladesh. People burst crackers, distributed sweets, and danced in the streets.

She gave the pandit a packet of sweets and some flowers to offer the goddess and folded her hands in prayer. He put a red teeka on her forehead and in the parting of her hair and placed some prasad in her hand. Buchki adjusted her sari to cover her pregnant stomach as she turned and rang the bell again before walking out of the shrine. Her face was ashen even when she saw Bikram, the sworn atheist, smiling at her.

She shuddered as flashes of the unfortunate night that had scarred her for life came to her mind. Khairoon had arrived at Bikram's home in a bloody state in the dead of night.

"Oh, my God! What happened, Khairoon bhai? Who did this to you?"

"The Das family has been barbarically slaughtered, including Buchki's parents. But Buchki is alive – she is waiting for you in the alcove by the lake outside Dhanmondi. Go and get her, son."

"Oh, my God..."

"Give her this card, and she will know I have sent you. Don't let her down, son. She has nobody but you to turn to now. God bless ...," he had said before he had writhed in pain and breathed his last.

And Bikram had come to get her, unsure of what to make of the situation or how to justify his action to his parents. "Aparna!"

"What are you doing here?" Buchki had said as she got out of the alcove.

"I've got this card for you from Khairoon."

"What?" she had gasped.

"I have come to get you. There has been an attack on your family."

She had cried out aloud and run wildly to her home. Bikram had not lied. She saw it all for herself. The attackers had abandoned the strewn pieces of their prey to waste in pools of blood, and she had run like a madwoman screaming from one room to the next looking for someone who might still be alive in the rubble of limbs and heads. They had spared nobody. She had fallen to the floor, screaming and soaking herself in the

PRIYA SHARMA SHAIKH

pool of red. Bikram had picked her up, and she had collapsed in his arms.

When her eyes opened, she was in Bikram's home. The doctor had awkwardly announced that she was pregnant. Bikram said he would marry her, nevertheless. His parents had resisted, saying that she should abort the baby. At that very moment, against their wishes, Bikram had taken a dazed Buchki to court, registered their marriage vows, and filled the parting of her hair with sindoor. "There has been enough killing, and I don't want to carry the sin of one more. We will keep the child, if you will, he or she can have my name. And you never need to give me or anybody else any explanations."

It had been eight months since that fateful day, and the baby was due at any time. Bikram took the puja thali from her hand and put his arm around her. They strolled into the twilight just as the moon rose behind them.

. . .

Rekha's anxious face broke into a smile when Inder rode into their lane, on his scooter. "Mala, Priya, Papa is here," she said and waved to him. Mala and Priya rushed to the balcony. Inder laughed, looking up at his three angels. *Oh, the joy of having their love!* He ran up the stairs to be greeted by them singing 'Jungee, Jungee, Jungee darling' and doing a jig for him, at their doorstep.

"It's good to be home, darling," said Inder as Rekha embraced him, and the girls clung onto his legs.

— — —

JUNGEE

BOOK 3: THE COW

Nandi, the proverbial Cow from Mount Kailasa, walked clip clop clip clop along the Ganga, smiling at the familiar conversations of the downstream water hurtling its way hurriedly. "There, there oh generous one! I understand your hurry - the plains await you eagerly for your abundance and your provision."

It had been a long journey discovering the world as the mount of his lord, Shiva. He loved the play sounds of Ganesha and Kartikeya the most and yearned to spend time being their protector, shielding them from the evil eye. But what made him feel the need to give them protection when Shiva himself looks after their wellbeing?

CHAPTER 17: RADIO CITY HALL, HERE WE COME!

24 May 2019: Celebration of a dream come true

It was a beautiful sunny morning. The Cow grazed blissfully in the open pastures, turning to look up at the Peacock who was perched on a branch of the lone Gulmohar tree, chirping loudly. Through the splatter of orange flora that danced in the gentle breeze, his jewel-toned feather tail glistened, and he curved his neck gracefully to look at the Lion that lay stretched atop a hillock in the distance. The Peacock swept off the branch and soared towards the yawning Lion, squawking as he approached him. He startled the big cat, who lashed out and chased after him. But the Peacock flew above the reach of his sharp claws and flitted through the air.

Jaikishen looked on as Koogh laughed and ran after his avatars. After getting exhausted, he ran back breathless into his father's arms, almost knocking him over.

"There is limitless energy in you when you love what you are doing," said Jaikishen.

"Yes, Pitaji," panted Koogh.

"It's because when you are yourself, you are in sync with the energy of the world and you will rise like the ideal child. Do you enjoy being the fun-loving Peacock?"

"Yes, Pitaji. When I grow up, I will have to become the Lion.

PRIYA SHARMA SHAIKH

But does that mean I can't have fun like the Peacock, when I am older?"

"Great question, my Kooghey. You can have fun all through your life, son. Should I tell you a secret?"

"Yes, please, Pitaji!"

"You can be any of the three avatars at every stage of your life. Do you remember how, as a young boy, you looked after Bhollo and your mother during the partition walk? You were being the Cow then. When you are older, you can be a Peacock and enjoy with your children and grandchildren or your partner and friends. You were the Lion when you were helping Bhollo get through the partition walk by giving her a dream to live for and you can be a Lion even when you become old like me and look for new horizons to occupy your time. What matters is that you remain truly present, and you will instinctively know which avatar is appropriate in that specific moment."

"But can I be more than one avatar at one time?"

"Yes. Nothing stops you if you wish to be more than one. Just be authentic and congruent in every moment of life; because you can fool the world, but you can never fool yourself, my Kooghey," said Jaikishen, hugging his son warmly.

The Peacock suddenly squawked and flew above their heads, startling them and roll over with laughter, as the Cow and the Lion looked on.

. . .

The dream was as vivid as before, and it never failed to leave Inder smiling. The bright green digits of the electronic clock on his bedside read 04.00, 24 May 2019. He looked around the room in the darkness, twiddling his toes and stretching his feet and hands.

He rubbed his face and sat up to let his legs down while still sitting on the bed. He placed his feet into his slip-ons and stretched his arms and yawned. Then holding on to the bed with one hand and bracing one hand on his knee, he lifted himself to a standing position. After decades of training and standing on duty at various ships, his knees had started to feel stiff in the mornings. He adjusted his kurta pyjama while standing in his slip-ons for a few moments for his eyes to get used to the dark in his hotel room. He then moved slowly towards the bathroom to freshen up for the day. After completing his daily Reiki ritual, he switched on the electric kettle to make two cups of tea. He missed having his usual morning concoction of cinnamon, aniseed, turmeric, ginger, lime and a final dash of honey. He picked out two English Breakfast teabags from the hospitality tray and placed them in two mugs.

"Darling, your tea is ready," he said, walking with his cup to the window. He rolled up the blinds to unveil a spectacular Manhattan skyline emerge in the dawn. "What a view!"

He opened the window a crack. The fresh chilly morning breeze filled his lungs, and he took a few deep breaths, looking down from the 17th floor at the toy-like people and cars moving slowly on the street below. A smile lit up his wrinkled face.

Rekha opened her eyes. "What are you smiling at, Jungee?"

"At how beautiful this view of Manhattan is. Pitaji and Pabbi would be so proud."

"Yes, it is going to be a beautiful day for all of us as a family."

...

It had been a chilly morning in the Arabian Sea in 1971, too, when they had regrouped with INS Poshak in Saurashtra after Operation Trident. Sampat, an officer on board Nipat, had enthusiastically painted the word KILLERS on the side of

PRIYA SHARMA SHAIKH

her bridge. Wild cheering and excitement ensued amidst the squadron.

A year after the war, Inder's tenure at Nirghat came to an end. She had given him so much - a great team, victory, and glory. But it was time to move on from the privileged position. At the send-off party the night before his last day, his team made a grand tribute to him and lifted him onto their shoulders, singing "He's a jolly good fellow" at the top of their inebriated voices. It was an emotional moment for them and Inder.

The next morning, he had handed over charge to the next commanding officer and walked off the gangway amidst loud cheers. As is customary, Inder turned around to face Nirghat and salute her and her ship's company. His boys stood in line, saluting him. His chest heaved with pride and as a tingling emotion emerged, he swallowed hard, saluted back stiffly, and walked away. The most important life lesson life and the Navy had taught him was – Be in the present moment without any attachments.

...

Inder got ready to explore a new horizon as the Command Gunnery Officer in Vizag, Eastern Naval Command.

A year later, in January 1973, Rekha, Sarla and Geeta joined Inder for the Presidential Award Ceremony at Rashtrapati Bhavan in Delhi, at which Inder was awarded the gallantry award of *Vir Chakra* for his outstanding display of courage and timely action during the 1971 war.

The ceremony was grand and formal. When the then President of India, Shri V.V. Giri, placed the medal on Inder's chest, Geeta craned her neck to get as clear a view as possible while continually wiping her cheeks. Her tears refused to cease that day.

"Oh, my son," murmured Geeta, as she reached to hold Rekha's hand. "How right he was, about making something more of his life and how wrong I was to want to hold him back. Thank you, Krishna."

"He is what he is because of Pitaji and your blessings, Mataji. We are all so proud of him today," said Rekha and Geeta turned to hug her daughter-in-law.

After the ceremony, Mrs. Indira Gandhi met Inder with Rekha, Sarla, and Geeta at the meet and greet.

"It is so good to see that you have brought your mother and mother-in-law for the ceremony," she had said to him with a smile.

"Thank you, Ma'am."

"You must be so proud," said Mrs. Gandhi, in Hindi to the two mothers.

"Yes," said Geeta and Sarla in unison in Hindi.

"Thank you for the recognition you bestowed on my son," said Geeta with folded hands.

"We are thankful to him for his exemplary service to the nation," said Mrs. Gandhi.

...

A few months after being awarded, Inder got selected to go for a Command Staff Course to Leningrad for over a year. This time he could take his family along.

Priya and Mala, had grown to be eight and seven years old by then. Russia's snow-covered landscape, ice-creams in the bitter cold, sledding and skiing down snowy slopes, learning Russian, and studying in a Russian school were fascinating experiences for them. But nothing could have topped the most valuable gift they received – their baby sister, who was born in

PRIYA SHARMA SHAIKH

Leningrad on 02 October 1973.

"We will name her Anjalika," Inder had said with enthusiasm, holding his daughter in his arms, remembering the adventurous heroine named Angelique, in the French film he had watched in Vladivostok.

When Inder returned to India in early December 1974 with his family, he got posted to NHQ, Delhi. On the 26th of January 1975, he led the Navy contingent at the Republic Day parade in a crisp white ceremonial uniform in a perfectly synchronised marchpast. It was a far improvement, one might say, from the days when he struggled to march as a young sailor with McClain. Priya and Mala screamed out his name as he passed by, pointing his sword in a stiff salute to India's President, Shri Fakhruddin Ali Ahmed, and the guest of honour, Mr. Kenneth Kaunda, President of Zambia.

That evening Inder returned home and announced that he was promoted and his name would now be written as, Commander Inderjit Sharma, AVSM, VrC.

...

Thereafter, Inder served with distinction in various bases within the Navy, always holding leadership positions and receiving excellent commendations. When he got promoted as Commodore, he was posted to Vizag as the Command Operations and Plans Officer, Eastern Naval Command. He left for Vizag as ordained by NHQ and served there for over a year. Priya and Mala were in college by then. Rekha was teaching, and Anjalika was studying at Cathedral & John Connon School. With no accommodation to live in Bombay, the family was separated – Priya and Mala, by then teenagers, lived in a spare room at another officer's house, Rekha and Anjalika stayed in a shared accommodation near the school, and Inder was at Vizag. Inder's heart was not at peace.

"I feel the need to be with all of you now, Rekha. Our daughters will soon fly the nest. This fragmented existence is doing us no good. Much as I love the Navy, I think it is time for me to opt for premature retirement," he had said on the phone one evening.

"Oh, Jungee! You have worked so hard and done so well. You will soon be an Admiral. We will manage somehow, darling," said Rekha.

"CNS, Ram Tahiliani said so too, in a meeting with me today."

"Oh that is lovely."

"But becoming an Admiral is not important for me anymore. My reckoning has already happened in so many ways throughout my career. Who would have thought that a nobody like me from a small place like Tandlianwala, would be presented with some of the most challenging opportunities and receive such high honours."

"An underdog becomes a winner, by sheer perseverance! It was your courage to withstand and keep moving, Jungee. You have fought, not only on the battlefield but in life too. Yours has truly been a warrior's journey - I very rightly named you Jungee."

"It has been quite a journey from fighting odds and feelings of emptiness; to an overflow of experiences and now being in a state of absolute fulfilment. You infused my life with your magical energy too, while you sacrificed your career. I feel blessed. I have achieved enough. My biggest achievement is that I can look back with no regret - The Lion is finally ready to give way to the Cow, putting the children and you ahead of me. It is time."

This was Inder's eighth decision.

. . .

Inder sipped his tea and took out his clothes from the suit-case and put them on a hanger.

"I think I will wear my blue shirt, darling, and this tie."

"Very nice Jungee. I'm wearing my red gown. Oh, I'm so excited."

"I know. I vividly remember talking with Roshni three years ago." Inder smiled mistily.

. . .

Roshni Shaikh came to meet Inder and Rekha straight from work. She hugged them both, warmly. Looking out at the stunning hues of the setting sun on the Versova beach, she sipped on her Coke, ruefully, and absent-mindedly scrolled the feed on her smartphone.

"What happened, darling?" asked Inder.

"Oh nothing! Sorry."

"Something is on your mind. Talk to me, my dear," said Inder with concern.

"I have dreamt of studying abroad for so long, but I am unsure whether I should chase my dream."

"What makes you unsure?"

"Mom is very supportive, but I know it is going to be a financial strain on the family's savings. Papa thinks I should be in India and not waste money on a course. He is right, as it is an expensive proposition. The bank is also being difficult about giving a loan. And then my friends want me to stay, and I know that the Indian economy is growing, and it is a great place to be now, as the world is flocking here. Plus my admission is not going to happen in this fall as the University results have got delayed. Thinking of all this, I feel that since I do have a good job, I should focus on it and forget about wanting to leave."

"Okay that is good. So then, what is the real challenge that is making you sad?"

"That I will not get to test my abilities in the new horizons that I have dreamt of."

And she had teared up.

. . .

The doorbell rang at 4 pm, and Inder rushed to open it.

"Hi, Papa, are Mama and you ready?" said Mala, now a marketing wiz at Silicon Valley, looking dapper with her salt and pepper hair.

"Hi, Mala. We are ready!"

"Hi Nana," said Anika and Arjun, Inder's youngest granddaughter and grandson.

"Hi, my darlings. Where are your parents?" asked Inder, feeling excited.

"They are organising the taxis downstairs," said Arjun.

Rekha and Inderjit trooped along with Mala and the kids into the lift to get to the lobby. Anjalika, Inder's youngest daughter, the most creative of his children, now living in San Diego with her husband Dhaval Sejpal, rushed to meet them.

"Hi, Papa and Mama. You both are looking so good."

"I'm so happy, Dhaval, and you could make it with the kids."

"Of course, Papa. We couldn't miss being here today," said Dhaval, hugging Inder.

. . .

PRIYA SHARMA SHAIKH

Their taxis swerved through the heavy traffic. Everyone seemed to be going to Radio City Music Hall, 1260, 6th Avenue. The GPS map showed red almost all the way.

"I hope we are not late," said Inder, panicking at the slow-moving traffic.

"Don't worry, Papa, our seats are already arranged for," reassured Mala.

Inder thought of how the past two years had flown. Finally, the wait was over. Inder looked at his watch. The ceremony was to start at 5.30 pm, and the time in his wristwatch said 5.25 pm. He muttered under his breath.

"Papa doesn't want to miss anything, darling," said Rekha, knowing Inder's anxiety.

"We won't miss anything, Mama," said Mala, "How far are we, Sir?"

"Another 10 minutes, Ma'am," said the taxi driver.

When Inder and Rekha finally entered the venue, they were both very anxious.

"Hey, Tom! You're looking handsome!" said Raunaq, Inder's second grandchild and first grandson, a handsome young filmmaker and an avid gamer.

"Thank you, my Jerry. Where are Mama and Papa? How much have we missed?"

"They're inside, and you haven't missed anything important, Nana."

"Hey, Pops and Mama and Mala!" said Farrukh Shaikh, aka Raju, their first son-in-law, hugged them. "Come and sit here near the aisle."

"Thank you, Raju. The big day is finally here," said Inder,

478

slapping the back of his son-in-law warmly.

"Yes. I'm feeling very proud and emotional, too," said Far-rukh in his deep baritone, looking at Inder, Rekha and Mala, "Thank you all for your support and blessings, without which this day would not have been possible."

"Please don't say that. Where is Priya?"

"She went out to look for you. There she comes," said Far-rukh, looking at the entrance.

Inder's eyes softened as his firstborn ran up to them with open arms, glowing with happiness. "Hi Mamnii and Paplii," said Priya (yours truly), gushing with excitement.

"Priya, all this is so beautiful, darling. Where is our Roshni?"

"She is somewhere there in that group of students," said Priya, pointing to the right.

"Send her a message that Nana and Nani are here to cele-brate the culmination of her dream to study in New York," said Inder.

"We are proud of her, as much as Raju and you are, as her par-ents," said Rekha with tears in his eyes.

Priya hugged her parents. "Thank you for inspiring me and loving Roshni so much."

"God makes pathways for those who dream, darling," said Inder.

"Ladies and gentlemen, it gives me great pleasure to wel-come you to the convocation ceremony of NYU School of Pro-fessional Studies at Radio City Music Hall. A convocation is a rich, time-honoured tradition, during which we celebrate the accomplishments of our students..." said the announcer.

Inder keenly listened to the speeches and watched each

student come up on stage to shake the Dean's hand and receive their graduation certificate. For each name, the auditorium echoed with cheers of their loved ones.

Finally, the emcee said, "Roshni Shaikh, India," and the Sharmas, Shaikhs, Sejpals, and all of Roshni's friends jumped up from their seats. Inder and Rekha's eyes welled with tears of joy as they watched their first grandchild, Roshni walk onto the stage to receive her certificate. Farrukh and Priya ran down the aisle towards the stage, cheering and waving to their daughter, while Raunaq recorded the moment on his smartphone. She smiled and waved, blowing a kiss at all of them.

At the celebration party that night, the DJ played Bollywood tracks, as snacks and drinks flowed. Roshni cut a cake shaped like a graduation cap. The music grew louder, and the dancing began. Rekha pulled Inder to the centre of the party, and for the first time Inder let himself loose, not feeling awkward about dancing. The song that was playing was *Mika Singh's, Mauja hi Mauja,* from the film *Jab We Met.*

Priya could see happiness on her father's face, that she had never seen before. At the crescendo of the song, he came towards her.

"I am so happy today, beta. *Mauja hi Mauja* should be the theme of life. Make life a celebration by enjoying every moment to its fullest."

...

In an interview in January 2020, with a significant publication writing a story of his victory in 1971, Inder said, "... After Operation Trident, every missile boat painted the word KILLERS on its bridge, and the crew got christened as the Killers Squadron."

"On 4th of December every year, the Navy hosts 'The Killers Night' as a part of the Navy Week celebrations, and Rekha and

JUNGEE

I get invited to the grand event. We never miss it, as we reunite with old friends, and revisit memories of our wonderful times in the Navy," said Inder.

"The 1st of May, 1986 was the last day of my service in the Indian Navy. The adage 'luck favours the brave' is true, because as soon as I moved out of the Navy, I received an assignment with the shipbuilding arm of Mazagon Dock. I served there for nine years as General Manager. After that, I took on a few jobs in the private sector, each related to the high seas."

"Finally, after much insistence of my family, I hung up my boots in 2004 after completing 50 years of work life," reminisced Inder. My daughters are happy in their respective lives. I have the joy of spending my golden years with my beloved wife beside me, in a beautiful building that is fittingly called Anchorage, in the city of my adolescent dreams, now Mumbai, that 66 years ago, drew me away from my family in Phagwara. I wake up every morning to a breath-taking panoramic view of the Arabian Sea."

"Rekha, continues to teach at a street school, tirelessly inspiring underprivileged children and women to lead better lives. Her latest joy is trying recipes she reads off her red iPad."

"As for me, at 84, laughter and games with my grandchildren, some work in the building society, home-cooked food, and a daily fitness regimen is my chosen way of life, which I am not willing to trade for anything in the world. I believe the decisions I took to choose certain paths worked out just fine in the long run."

"My father's lesson to me about presence, when I was a young boy, somehow got engrained in me. And although it took time for me to be completely aware of it and be comfortable with it, I know that whenever I chose to be present and give my best self to a life situation, I have been in alignment of my sadhana or my life purpose. Being presence in every moment has now become my way of being and my life's journey finally feels complete," smiled Inder.

– – –

AUTHOR'S NOTE

This book captures some interesting events / episodes that happened half a century ago and more. It is possible that not all the descriptions are exactly as they happened by chronological or descriptive sequence, some names may have been missed and others included in error - the book merely captures the essence and the spirit of a person's lifetime, and not necessarily the exact details. A lot is learnt from hearsay. Any such omissions or commissions are not deliberate and may kindly be read as such. The effort is not a 'breaking news' of a recent event but of things that happened over a time span of many decades. Kindly bear with the author. Read it as literary fiction if you may but note that the hero of this saga - Commodore (Retd.) Inderjit Sharma, AVSM, VrC, Indian Navy, is real and alive as on date.

I grew up hearing stories about my father, Inderjit Sharma's, grit and glory, but it is only when I turned 50 that I truly listened. I discovered beautiful revelations in the twists and turns of his life that began in pre-partition India. The story Jungee is a quintessential hero's journey. It is a literary fiction novel, based on actual events that are inspiring and sure to change your life, as they did mine.

I put fingers to keyboard in August 2015 - this five-year journey has been pivotal for me and it is my humble attempt at sharing his grand life story with the world. The story telling has been dramatized to make the account of his life read-worthy, so fictional and real characters alike have worked in tandem to provide the reader an engaging experience. This was also done so that as the reader, you too fall in love with

JUNGEE as much as I did since I was a child and take inspiration from his life story, as I have done all my life. I hope you enjoy the storyline and learn from it as much as I have. I have tried my best to do justice to this work and I hope I have been able to capture the essence of the grand life of Inderjit Sharma, in Jungee, the book.

Acknowledgements

I have my father **Inderjit Sharma** to thank, for being my first inspiration by being exemplary in all that he did as a man, a father and husband; my mother **Rekha Sharma** for being a treasure trove of love and my strongest pillar and builder-upper

My sisters **Mala Sharma** and **Anjalika Sharma,** I can't thank enough for their love, support, and friendship - for being the wind beneath my wings, and for trusting me to share their father's story with the world.

My children **Roshni Shaikh** and **Raunaq Shaikh** for their unconditional love for me and being my teachers by choosing to live their lives the way they do. They are the reason, I live and strive to be a better person each day; and my partner **Farrukh Shaikh** for his relentless encouragement and the space I needed to fulfill my dreams and be me, for which I am truly indebted.

My dear uncles in the Navy– **Admiral SK Das, Cdr. Janardhan Deo** and **Cdr. Joginder Singh** for their love for my father and being the constants in our lives.

Mishana Khot for being the first to read, love and give editorial feedback for Jungee.

Pooja (Nicky) Dodd of Dodd & Co for her love and being my copyright consultant.

I want to thank my lovely coaches, **Ujjal Gupta**, for patiently but surely giving my publishing journey direction; **Sudhir Dhar** for instilling a dream in me, that I could publish this year; **Ramya Rajaram** for brainstorming the final touches of the book with me; **Gayatri Krishnamurthy** for making me stop worrying too much and leave some work for the critics and **Mukesh Sharma** for making me set a date to publish the book.

I can't thank **Nicola Gut Jain** enough for his ingenious creative prowess in making all the artwork for the Peacock, Lion and Cow, and **Manasi Gut Jain** for the simple yet masterfully elegant cover design.

Lastly, a special shoutout for my two darlings - **Anjalika**, my sister and **Raunaq**, my son, who time and again over the past five years, have helped me with my manuscript and generously shared their feedback to help make my writing look better. Raunaq in particular for reading my work several times and finally editing it by helping me connect the dots and close all the loose ends of Jungee. Without their support sharing Jungee with the world would not have been possible.

References

My external references to gather facts while writing Jungee have been:
1. Talking to my parents - **Inderjit** and **Rekha**
2. Notes about the war, written by **Lt. Cdr. ADS Lazaro**
3. Books:
   - Transition to Triumph, by **Vice Admiral GM Hiranandani**
   - 25 Missile Boat Squadron, by **Commodore Vijay Jerath**
4. Websites:
http://www.socialismtoday.org/154/bangladesh.html

https://www.wrecksite.eu/wreck.aspx?172659
https://en.wikipedia.org/wiki/Indo-Pakistani_War_of_1971
http://www.indiandefencereview.com/interviews/1971-war-the-first-missile-attack-on-karachi/2/
https://telanganatoday.com/transition-to-triumph

With much love to *all the people,*
Priya Sharma Shaikh
September 2020

Made in the USA
Coppell, TX
29 November 2020